Two books in one special volume

Grace Livingston Hill's

THE GIRL
FROM
MONTANA

A DAILY
RATE

Fleming H. Revell Company
Old Tappan, New Jersey

The Girl from Montana

BOOKS BY GRACE LIVINGSTON HILL IN THIS SERIES

The Man of the Desert
An Unwilling Guest
The Girl From Montana
A Daily Rate
The Story of a Whim
According to the Pattern

GRACE LIVINGSTON HILL

The Girl from Montana

Fleming H. Revell Company
Old Tappan, New Jersey

Library of Congress Cataloging in Publication Data
Hill, Grace Livingston, 1865-1947.
    The girl from Montana.

    I. Title.
PS3515·I486G5   1982   813'.52   81-19274
ISBN 0-8007-1301-X   AACR2

CONTENTS

Introduction

I was still in grade school when letters began arriving from the Far West. All the family gathered around to hear them read. The result of them was this book.

"Westerns" were becoming popular in those days, and someone had suggested that my mother try her hand at them. She had never been west, and had no money for such a trip, so she decided that rather than put on paper her own imaginings about life out there, with the risk of blatant errors, she would advertise for someone who lived there to correspond with her and describe it—the landscapes, the hardships, the delights, the customs, the people. A young woman answered and a friendship developed. Westerners of those days have expressed amazement at the book's accuracy, when they discovered that the author had never been there.

Even though I had read some of the letters (or *because* I had read them), I was fascinated to follow the unfolding of the story. I can remember many a time standing behind my mother's desk chair and reading over her shoulder as the words appeared on the page. She wrote very fast, almost as fast as I could read, and I was breathless to see what would happen next, impatient when a phone call would call her away for a few minutes.

But beyond the excitement of the tale, I soon found myself—like hundreds of other young people who have written in—forming standards and basic patterns for my own life as I considered the experiences of the book characters. I am glad that I did.

RUTH LIVINGSTON HILL

Chapter 1

The Girl, and a Great Peril

The late afternoon sun was streaming in across the cabin floor as the girl stole around the corner and looked cautiously in at the door.

There was a kind of tremulous courage in her face. She had a duty to perform, and she was resolved to do it without delay. She shaded her eyes with her hand from the glare of the sun, set a firm foot upon the threshold, and, with one wild glance around to see whether all was as she had left it, entered her home and stood for a moment shuddering in the middle of the floor.

A long procession of funerals seemed to come out of the past and meet her eye as she looked about upon the signs of the primitive, unhallowed funeral which had just gone out from there a little while before.

The girl closed her eyes, and pressed their hot, dry lids hard with her cold fingers; but the vision was clearer even than with her eyes open.

She could see the tiny baby sister lying there in the middle of the room, so little and white and pitiful; and her handsome, careless father sitting at the head of the rude home-made coffin, sober for the moment; and her tired, disheartened mother, faded before her time, dry-eyed and haggard, beside him. But that was long ago, almost at the beginning of things for the girl.

There had been other funerals, the little brother who had been drowned while playing in a forbidden stream, and the older brother who had gone off in search of gold or his own way, and had crawled back parched with fever to die in his mother's arms. But those, too, seemed long ago to the girl as she stood in the empty cabin and looked fearfully about her. They seemed almost blotted out by the last three

9

that had crowded so close within the year. The father, who even at his worst had a kind word for her and her mother, had been brought home mortally hurt—an encounter with wild cattle, a fall from his horse in a treacherous place—and had never roused to consciousness again.

At all these funerals there had been a solemn service, conducted by a travelling preacher when one happened to be within reach, and, when there was none, by the trembling, determined, untaught lips of the white-faced mother. The mother had always insisted upon it, especially upon a prayer. It had seemed like a charm to help the departed one into some kind of a pitiful heaven.

And when, a few months after the father, the mother had drooped and grown whiter and whiter, till one day she clutched at her heart and lay down gasping, and said: "Good-by, Bess! Mother's good girl! Don't forget!" and was gone from her life of burden and disappointment forever, the girl had prepared the funeral with the assistance of the one brother left. The girl's voice had uttered the prayer, "Our Father," just as her mother had taught her, because there was no one else to do it; and she was afraid to send the wild young brother off after a preacher, lest he should not return in time.

It was six months now since the sad funeral train had wound its way among sage-brush and greasewood; and the body of the mother had been laid to rest beside her husband. For six months the girl had kept the cabin in order, and held as far as possible the wayward brother to his work and home. But within the last few weeks he had more and more left her alone, for a day, and sometimes more, and had come home in a sad condition and with bold, merry companions who made her life a constant terror. And now, but two short days ago, they had brought home his body lying across his own faithful horse, with two shots through his heart. It was a drunken quarrel, they told her; and all were sorry, but no one seemed responsible.

They had been kind in their rough way, those companions of her brother. They had stayed and done all that was necessary, had dug the grave, and stood about their comrade in good-natured grimness, marching in order about him to give the last look; but, when the sister tried to utter the prayer she knew her mother would have spoken, her throat refused to make a sound, and her tongue cleaved to the roof of her mouth. She had taken sudden refuge in the little shed that was her own room, and there had stayed till the rough companions had taken away the still form of the only one left in the family circle.

In silence the funeral procession wound its way to the spot where the others were buried. They respected her tearless grief, these great, passionate, uncontrolled young men. They held in the rude jokes with which they would have taken the awesomeness from the occasion for themselves, and for the most part kept the way silently and gravely, now and then looking back with admiration to the slim girl with the stony face and unblinking eyes who followed them mechanically. They had felt that some one ought to do something; but no one knew exactly what, and so they walked silently.

Only one, the hardest and boldest, the ringleader of the company, ventured back to ask whether there was anything he could do for her, anything she would like to have done; but she answered him coldly with a "No!" that cut him to the quick. It had been a good deal for him to do, this touch of gentleness he had forced himself into. He turned from her with a wicked gleam of intent in his eyes, but she did not see it.

When the crude ceremony was over, the last clod was heaped upon the pitiful mound, and the relentless words, "dust to dust," had been murmured by one more daring than the rest, they turned and looked at the girl, who had all the time stood upon a mound of earth and watched them, as a statue of Misery might look down upon the world. They could not make her out, this silent, marble girl. They hoped now she would change. It was over. They felt an untold relief themselves from the fact that their reckless comrade was no longer lying cold and still among them. They were done with him. They had paid their last tribute, and wished to forget. He must settle his own account with the hereafter now; they had enough in their own lives without the burden of his.

Then there had swept up into the girl's face one gleam of life that made her beautiful for the instant, and she had bowed to them with a slow, almost haughty, inclination of her head, and spread out her hands like one who would like to bless but dared not, and said clearly, "I thank you—all!" There had been just a slight hesitation before the last word "all," as if she were not quite sure, as her eyes rested upon the ringleader with doubt and dislike; then her lips had hardened as if justice must be done, and she had spoken it, "all!" and, turning, sped away to her cabin alone.

They were taken by surprise, those men who feared nothing in the wild and primitive West, and for a moment they watched her go in silence. Then the words that broke upon the air were not all pleasant to hear; and, if the girl could have known, she would have sped far faster, and her cheeks would have burned a brighter red than they did.

But one, the boldest, the ringleader, said nothing. His brows darkened, and the wicked gleam came and sat in his hard eyes with a green light. He drew a little apart from the rest, and walked on more rapidly. When he came to the place where they had left their horses, he took his and went on toward the cabin with a look that did not invite the others to follow. As their voices died away in the distance, and he drew nearer to the cabin, his eyes gleamed with cunning.

The girl in the cabin worked rapidly. One by one she took the boxes on which the crude coffin of her brother had rested, and threw them far out the back door. She straightened the furniture around fiercely, as if by erasing every sign she would force from memory the thought of the scenes that had just passed. She took her brother's coat that hung against the wall, and an old pipe from the mantle, and hid them in the room that was hers. Then she looked about for something else to be done.

A shadow darkened the sunny doorway. Looking up, she saw the man she believed to be her brother's murderer.

"I came back, Bess, to see if I could do anything for you."

The tone was kind; but the girl involuntarily put her hand to her throat, and caught her breath. She would like to speak out and tell him what she thought, but she dared not. She did not even dare let her thought appear in her eyes. The dull, statue-like look came over her face that she had worn at the grave. The man thought it was the stupefaction of grief.

"I told you I didn't want any help," she said, trying to speak in the same tone she had used when she thanked the men.

"Yes, but you're all alone," said the man insinuatingly; she felt a menace in the thought, "and I am sorry for you!"

He came nearer, but her face was cold. Instinctively she glanced to the cupboard door behind which lay her brother's belt with two pistols.

"You're very kind," she forced herself to say; "but I'd rather be alone now." It was hard to speak so when she would have liked to dash on him, and call down curses for the death of her brother; but she looked into his evil face, and a fear of herself worse than death stole into her heart.

He took encouragement from her gentle dignity. Where did she get that manner so imperial, she, born in a mountain cabin and bred on the wilds? How could she speak with an accent so different from those about her? The brother was not so, not so much so; the mother had been plain and quiet. He had not known her father, for he had lately come to this State in hiding from another. He wondered, with his wide knowledge of the world, over her wild, haughty beauty, and gloated over it. He liked to think just what worth was within his easy grasp. A prize for the asking, and here alone, unprotected.

"But it ain't good for you to be alone, you know, and I've come to protect you. Besides, you need cheering up, little girl." He came closer. "I love you, Bess, you know, and I'm going to take care of you now. You're all alone. Poor little girl."

He was so near that she almost felt his breath against her cheek. She faced him desperately, growing white to the lips. Was there nothing on earth or in heaven to save her? Mother! Father! Brother! All gone! Ah! Could she but have known that the quarrel which ended her wild young brother's life had been about her, perhaps pride in him would have salved her grief, and choked her horror.

While she watched the green lights play in the evil eyes above her, she gathered all the strength of her young life into one effort, and schooled herself to be calm. She controlled her involuntary shrinking from the man, only drew herself back gently, as a woman with wider experience and gentler breeding might have done.

"Remember," she said, "that my brother just lay there dead!" and she pointed to the empty centre of the room. The dramatic attitude was almost a condemnation to the guilty man before her. He drew back as if the sheriff had entered the room, and looked instinctively to where the coffin had been but a short time before, then laughed nervously and drew himself together.

The girl caught her breath, and took courage. She had held him for a minute; could she not hold him longer?

"Think!" she said. "He is but just buried. It is not right to talk of such things as love in this room where he had just gone out. You must leave me alone for a little while. I cannot talk and think now. We must respect the dead, you know." She looked appealing at him, acting her part desperately, but well. It was as if she were trying to charm a lion or an insane man.

He stood admiring her. She argued well. He was half-minded to humor her, for somehow when she spoke of the dead he could see the gleam in her brother's eyes just before he shot him. Then there was promise in this wooing. She was no girl to be lightly won, after all. She could hold her own, and perhaps she would be the better for having her way for a little. At any rate, there was more excitement in such game.

She saw that she was gaining, and her breath came freer.

"Go!" she said with a flickering smile. "Go! For—a little while," and then she tried to smile again.

He made a motion to take her in his arms and kiss her; but she drew back suddenly, and spread her hands before her, motioning him back.

"I tell you you must not now. Go! Go! or I will never speak to you again."

He looked into her eyes, and seemed to feel a power that he must obey. Half sullenly he drew back toward the door.

"But, Bess, this ain't the way to treat a fellow," he whined. "I came way back here to take care of you. I tell you I love you, and I'm going to have you. There ain't any other fellow going to run off with you—"

"Stop!" she cried tragically. "Don't you see you're not doing right? My brother is just dead. I must have some time to mourn. It is only decent." She was standing now with her back to the little cupboard behind whose door lay the two pistols. Her hand was behind her on the wooden latch.

"You don't respect my trouble!" she said, catching her breath, and putting her hand to her eyes. "I don't believe you care for me when you don't do what I say."

The man was held at bay. He was almost conquered by her sign of tears. It was a new phase of her to see her melt into weakness so. He was charmed.

"How long must I stay away?" he faltered.

She could scarcely speak, so desperate she felt. O if she dared but say, "Forever," and shout it at him! She was desperate enough to try her chances at shooting him if she but had the pistols, and was sure they were loaded—a desperate chance indeed against the best shot on the Pacific coast, and a desperado at that.

She pressed her hands to her throbbing temples, and tried to think. At last she faltered out,

"Three days!"

He swore beneath his breath, and his brows drew down in heavy frowns that were not good to see. She shuddered at what it would be to be in his power forever. How he would play with her and toss her aside! Or kill her, perhaps, when he was tired of her! Her life on the mountain had made her familiar with evil characters.

He came a step nearer, and she felt she was losing ground.

Straightening up, she said coolly:

"You must go away at once, and not think of coming back at least until to-morrow night. Go!" With wonderful control she smiled at him, one frantic, brilliant smile; and to her great wonder he drew back. At the door he paused, a softened look upon his face.

"Mayn't I kiss you before I go?"

She shuddered involuntarily, but put out her hands in protest again. "Not to-night!" She shook her head, and tried to smile.

He thought he understood her, but turned away half satisfied. Then she heard his step coming back to the door again, and she went to meet him. He must not come in. She had gained in sending him out, if she could but close the door fast. It was in the doorway that she faced him as he stood with one foot ready to enter again. The crafty look was out upon his face plainly now, and in the sunlight she could see it.

"You will be all alone to-night."

"I am not afraid," calmly. "And no one will trouble me. Don't you know what they say about the spirit of a man—" she stopped; she had almost said "a man who has been murdered"—"coming back to his home the first night after he is buried?" It was her last frantic effort.

The man before her trembled, and looked around nervously.

"You better come away to-night with me," he said, edging away from the door.

"See, the sun is going down! You must go now," she said imperiously; and reluctantly the man mounted his restless horse, and rode away down the mountain.

She watched him silhouetted against the blood-red globe of the sun as it sank lower and lower. She could see every outline of his slouch-hat and muscular shoulders as he turned now and then and saw her standing still alone at her cabin door. Why he was going he could not tell; but he went, and he frowned as he rode away, with the wicked gleam still in his eye; for he meant to return.

At last he disappeared; and the girl, turning, looked up, and there rode the white ghost of the moon overhead. She was alone.

Chapter 2

The Flight

A great fear settled down upon the girl as she realized that she was alone and, for a few hours at least, free. It was a miraculous escape. Even now she could hear the echo of the man's last words, and see his hateful smile as he waved his good-by and promised to come back for her to-morrow.

She felt sure he would not wait until the night. It might be he would return even yet. She cast another reassuring look down the darkening road, and strained her ear; but she could no longer hear hoof-beats. Nevertheless, it behooved her to hasten. He had blanched at her suggestion of walking spirits; but, after all, his courage might arise. She shuddered to think of his returning later, in the night. She must fly somewhere at once.

Instantly her dormant senses seemed to become alert. Fully fledged plans flashed through her brain. She went into the cabin, and barred the door. She made every movement swiftly, as if she had not an instant to spare. Who could tell? He might return even before dark. He had been hard to deter, and she did not feel at all secure. It was her one chance of safety to get away speedily, whither it mattered little, only so she was away and hidden.

Her first act inside the cottage was to get the belt from the cupboard and buckle it around her waist. She examined and loaded the pistols. Her throat seemed seized with sudden constriction when she discovered that the barrels had been empty and the weapons would have done her no good even if she could have reached them.

She put into her belt the sharp little knife her brother used to carry, and then began to gather together everything eatable that she could carry with her. There was not much that could be easily carried—some dried beef, a piece of cheese, some corn-meal, a piece of pork, a handful of cheap coffee-berries, and some pieces of hard corn bread. She hesitated over a pan half full of baked beans, and finally added them to the store. They were bulky, but she ought to take them if she could. There was nothing else in the house that seemed advisable to take in the way of edibles. Their stores had been running low, and the trouble of the last day or two had put housekeeping entirely out of her mind. She had not cared to eat, and now it occurred to her that food had not passed her lips that day. With strong self-control she forced herself to eat a few of the dry pieces of corn bread, and to drink some cold coffee that stood in the little coffee-pot. This she did while she worked, wasting not one minute.

There were some old flour-sacks in the house. She put the food into two of them, with the pan of beans on the top, adding a tin cup, and tied them securely together. Then she went into her little shed room, and put on the few extra garments in her wardrobe. They were not many, and that was the easiest way to carry them. Her mother's wedding-ring, sacredly kept in a box since the mother's death, she slipped upon her finger. It seemed the closing act of her life in the cabin, and she paused and bent her head as if to ask the mother's permission that she might wear the ring. It seemed a kind of protection to her in her lonely situation.

There were a few papers and an old letter or two yellow with years, which the mother had always guarded sacredly. One was the certificate of her mother's marriage. The girl did not know what the others were. She had never looked into them closely, but she knew that her mother had counted them precious. These she pinned into the bosom of her calico gown. Then she was ready.

She gave one swift glance of farewell about the cabin where she had spent nearly all of her life that she could remember, gathered up the two flour-sacks and an old coat of her father's that hung on the wall, remembering at the last minute to put into its pocket the few matches and the single candle left in the house, and went out from the cabin, closing the door behind her.

She paused, looking down the road, and listened again; but no sound came to her save a distant howl of a wolf. The moon rode high and clear by this time; and it seemed not so lonely here, with everything bathed in soft silver, as it had in the darkening cabin with its flickering candle.

The girl stole out from the cabin and stealthily across the patch of moonlight into the shadow of the shackly barn where stamped the poor, ill-fed, faithful horse that her brother had ridden to his death upon. All her movements were stealthy as a cat's.

She laid the old coat over the horse's back, swung her brother's saddle into place—she had none of her own, and could ride his, or without any; it made no difference, for she was perfectly at home on horseback—and strapped the girths with trembling fingers that were icy cold with excitement. Across the saddle-bows she hung the two floursacks containing her provisions. Then with added caution she tied some old burlap about each of the horse's feet. She must make no sound and leave no track as she stole forth into the great world.

The horse looked curiously down and whinnied at her, as she tied his feet up clumsily. He did not seem to like his new habiliments, but he suffered anything at her hand.

"Hush!" she murmured softly, laying her cold hands across his nostrils; and he put his muzzle into her palm, and seemed to understand.

She led him out into the clear moonlight then, and paused a second, looking once more down the road that led away in front of the cabin; but no one was coming yet, though her heart beat high as she listened, fancying every falling bough or rolling stone was a horse's hoof-beat.

There were three trails leading away from the cabin, for they could hardly be dignified by the name of road. One led down the mountain toward the west, and was the way they took to the nearest clearing five or six miles beyond and to the supply store some three miles further. One led off to the east, and was less travelled, being the way to the great world; and the third led down behind the cabin, and was desolate and barren under the moon. It led down, back, and away to desolation, where five graves lay stark and ugly at the end. It was the way they had taken that afternoon.

She paused just an instant as if hesitating which way to take. Not the way to the west—ah, any but that! To the east? Yes, surely, that must be the trail she would eventually strike; but she had a duty yet to perform. That prayer was as yet unsaid, and before she was free to seek safety—if safety there were for her in the wide world—she must take her way down the lonely path. She walked, leading the horse, which followed her with muffled tread and arched neck as if he felt he were doing homage to the dead. Slowly, silently, she moved along into the river of moonlight and dreariness; for the moonlight here seemed cold, like the graves it shone upon, and the girl, as she walked with bowed head, almost fancied she saw strange misty forms flit past her in the night.

As they came in sight of the graves, something dark and wild with plumy tail slunk away into the shadows, and seemed a part of the place. The girl stopped a moment to gain courage in full sight of the graves, and the horse snorted, and stopped too, with his ears a-quiver, and a half-fright in his eyes.

She patted his neck and soothed him incoherently, as she buried her face in his mane for a moment, and let the first tears that had dimmed her eyes since the blow had fallen come smarting their way out. Then, leaving the horse to stand curiously watching her, she went down and stood at the head of the new-heaped mound. She tried to kneel, but a shudder passed through her. It was as if she were descending into the place of the dead herself; so she stood up and raised her eyes to the wide white night and the moon riding so high and far away.

"Our Father," she said in a voice that sounded miles away to herself. Was there any Father, and could He hear her? And did He care? "Which art in heaven—" but heaven was so far away and looked so cruelly serene to her in her desolateness and danger! "hallowed be thy name. Thy kingdom come—" whatever that might mean. "Thy will be done in earth, as it is in heaven." It was a long prayer to pray, alone with the pale moon-rain and the graves, and a distant wolf, but it was her mother's wish. Her will being done here over the dead—was that anything like the will of the Father being done in heaven? Her untrained thoughts hovered on the verge of great questions, and then slipped back into her pathetic self and its fear, while her tongue hurried on through the words of the prayer.

Once the horse stirred and breathed a soft protest. He could not understand why they were stopping so long in this desolate place, for nothing apparently. He had looked and looked at the shapeless mound before which the girl was standing; but he saw no sign of his lost master, and his instincts warned him that there were wild animals about. Anyhow, this was no place for a horse and a maid to stop in the night.

A few loose stones rattled from the horse's motion. The girl started, and looked hastily about, listening for a possible pursuer; but everywhere in the white sea of moonlight there was empty, desolate space. On to the "Amen" she finished then, and with one last look at the lonely graves she turned to the horse. Now they might go, for the duty was done, and there was no time to be lost.

Somewhere over toward the east across the untravelled wilderness of white light was the trail that started to the great world from the little cabin she had left. She dared not go back to the cabin to take it, lest she find herself already followed. She did not know the way across this lonely plain, and neither did the horse. In fact, there was no way, for it was all one arid plain so situated that human traveller seldom came near it, so large and so barren that one might wander for hours and gain no goal, so dry that nothing would grow.

With another glance back on the way she had come, the girl mounted the horse and urged him down into the valley. He stepped cautiously into the sandy plain, as if he were going into a river and must try its depth. He did not like the going here, but he plodded on with his burdens. The girl was light; he did not mind her weight; but he felt this place uncanny, and now and then would start on a little spurt of haste, to get into a better way. He liked the high mountain trails, where he could step firmly and hear the twigs crackle under his feet, not this muffled, velvet way where one made so little progress and had to work so hard.

The girl's heart sank as they went on, for the sand seemed deep and drifted in places. She felt she was losing time. The way ahead looked endless, as if they were but treading sand behind them which only returned in front to be trodden over again. It was to her like the valley of the dead, and she longed to get out of it. A great fear lest the moon should go down and leave her in this low valley alone in the dark took hold upon her. She felt she must get away, up higher. She turned the horse a little more to the right, and he paused, and seemed to survey the new direction and to like it. He stepped up more briskly, with a courage that could come only from an intelligent hope for better things. And at last they were rewarded by finding the sand shallower, and now and then a bit of rock cropping out for a firmer footing.

The young rider dismounted, and untied the burlap from the horse's feet. He seemed to understand, and to thank her as he nosed about her neck. He thought, perhaps, that this mission was over and they were going to strike out for home now.

The ground rose steadily before them now, and at times grew quite steep; but the horse was fresh as yet, and clambered upward with good heart; and the rider was used to rough places, and felt no discomfort from her position. The fear of being followed had succeeded to the fear of being lost, for the time being; and instead of straining her ears on the track behind she was straining her eyes to the wilderness before. The growth of sagebrush was dense now, and trees were ahead.

After that the way seemed steep, and the rider's heart stood still with fear lest she could never get up and over to the trail which she knew must be somewhere in that direction, though she had never been far out on its course herself. That it led straight east into all the great cities she never doubted, and she must find it before she was pursued. That man would be angry, *angry* if he came and found her gone! He was not beyond shooting her for giving him the slip in this way.

The more she thought over it, the more frightened she became, till every bit of rough way, and every barrier that kept her from going forward quickly, seemed terrible to her. A bob-cat shot across the way just ahead, and the green gleam of its eyes as it turned one swift glance at this strange intruder in its chosen haunts made her catch her breath and put her hand on the pistols.

They were climbing a long time—it seemed hours to the girl—when at last they came to a space where a better view of the land was possible. It was high, and sloped away on three sides. To her looking now in the clear night the outline of a mountain ahead of her became distinct, and the lay of the land was not what she had supposed. It brought her a curious sense of being lost. Over there ought to be the familiar way where the cabin stood, but there was no sign of anything she had ever seen before, though she searched eagerly for landmarks. The course she had chosen, and which had seemed the only one, would take her straight up, up over the mountain, a way well-nigh impossible, and terrible even if it were possible.

It was plain she must change her course, but which way should she go? She was completely turned around. After all, what mattered it? One way might be as good as another, so it led not home to the cabin which could never be home again. Why not give the horse his head, and let him pick out a safe path? Was there danger that he might carry her back to the cabin again, after all? Horses did that sometimes. But at least he could guide through this maze of perplexity till some surer place was reached. She gave him a sign, and he moved on, nimbly picking a way for his feet.

They entered a forest growth where weird branches let the pale moon through in splashes and patches, and grim moving figures seemed to chase them from every shadowy tree-trunk. It was a terrible experience to the girl. Sometimes she shut her eyes and held to the saddle, that she might not see and be filled with this frenzy of things, living or dead, following her. Sometimes a real black shadow crept across the path, and slipped into the engulfing darkness of the undergrowth to gleam with yellow-lighted eyes upon the intruders.

But the forest did not last forever, and the moon was not yet gone when they emerged presently upon the rough mountain-side. The girl studied the moon then, and saw by the way it was setting that after all they were going in the right general direction. That gave a little comfort until she made herself believe that in some way she might have made a mistake and gone the wrong way from the graves, and so be coming up to the cabin after all.

It was a terrible night. Every step of the way some new horror was presented to her imagination. Once she had to cross a wild little stream, rocky and uncertain in its bed, with slippery, precipitous banks; and twice in climbing a steep incline she came sharp upon sheer precipices down into a rocky gorge, where the moonlight seemed repelled by dark, bristling evergreen trees growing half-way up the sides. She could hear the rush and clamor of a tumbling mountain stream in the depths below. Once she fancied she heard a distant shot, and the horse pricked up his ears, and went forward excitedly.

But at last the dawn contended with the night, and in the east a faint pink flush crept up. Down in the valley a mist like a white feather rose gently into a white cloud, and obscured everything. She wished she might carry the wall of white with her to shield her. She had longed for the dawn; and now, as it came with sudden light and clear revealing of the things about her, it was almost worse than night, so dreadful were the dangers when clearly seen, so dangerous the chasms, so angry the mountain torrents.

With the dawn came the new terror of being followed. The man would have no fear to come to her in the morning, for murdered men were not supposed to haunt their homes after the sun was up, and murderers were always courageous in the day. He might the sooner come, and find her gone, and perhaps follow; for she felt that he was not one easily to give up an object he coveted, and she had seen in his evil face that which made her fear unspeakably.

As the day grew clearer, she began to study the surroundings. All seemed utter desolation. There was no sign that anyone had ever passed that way before; and yet, just as she had thought that, the horse stopped and snorted, and there in the rocks before them lay a man's hat riddled with shot. Peering fearfully around, the girl saw a sight which made her turn icy cold and begin to tremble; for there, below them, as if he had fallen from his horse and rolled down the incline, lay a man on his face.

For the instant fear held her riveted, with the horse, one figure like a statue, girl and beast; the next, sudden panic took hold upon her. Whether the man were dead or not, she must make haste. It might be he would come to himself and pursue her, though there was that in the rigid attitude of the figure down below that made her sure he had been dead some time. But how had he died? Scarcely by his own hand. Who had killed him? Were there fiends lurking in the fastnesses of the mountain growth above her?

With guarded motion she urged her horse forward, and for miles beyond the horse scrambled breathlessly, the girl holding on with shut eyes, not daring to look ahead for fear of seeing more terrible sights, not daring to look behind for fear of—what she did not know.

At last the way sloped downward, and they reached more level ground, with wide stretches of open plain, dotted here and there with sage-brush and greasewood.

She had been hungry back there before she came upon the dead man; but now the hunger had gone from her, and in its place was only faintness. Still, she dared not stop long to eat. She must make as much time as possible here in this open space, and now she was where she could be seen more easily if any one were in pursuit.

But the horse had decided that it was time for breakfast. He had had one or two drinks of water on the mountain, but there had been no time for him to eat. He was decidedly hungry, and, the plain offered nothing in the shape of breakfast. He halted, lingered, and came to a neighing stop, looking around at his mistress. She roused from her lethargy of trouble, and realized that his wants—if not her own—must be attended to.

She must sacrifice some of her own store of eatables, for by and by they would come to a good grazing-place perhaps, but now there was nothing.

The corn-meal seemed the best for the horse. She had more of it than of anything else. She poured a scanty portion out on a paper, and the beast smacked his lips appreciatively over it, carefully licking every grain from the paper, as the girl guarded it lest his breath should blow any away. He snuffed hungrily at the empty paper, and she gave him a little more meal, while she ate some of the cold beans, and scanned the horizon anxiously. There was nothing but sage-brush in sight ahead of her, and more hills farther on where dim outlines of trees could be seen. If she could but get up higher where she could see farther, and perhaps reach a bench where there would be grass and some shelter.

It was only a brief rest she allowed; and then, hastily packing up her stores, and retaining some dry corn bread and a few beans in her pocket, she mounted and rode on.

The morning grew hot, and the way was long. As the ground rose again, it was stony and overgrown with cactus. A great desolation took possession of the girl. She felt as if she were in an endless flight from an unseen pursuer, who would never give up until he had her.

It was high noon by the glaring sun when she suddenly saw another human being. At first she was not quite sure whether he were human. It was only a distant view of a moving speck; but it was coming toward her, though separated by a wide valley that had stretched already for miles. He was moving along against the sky-line on a high bench on one side of the valley, and she mounting as fast as her weary beast would go to the top of another, hoping to find a grassy stretch and a chance to rest.

But the sight of the moving speck startled her. She watched it breathlessly as they neared each other. Could it be a wild beast? No, it must be a horse and rider. A moment later there came a puff of smoke as from a rifle discharged, followed by the distant echo of the discharge. It was a man, and he was yet a great way off. Should she turn and flee before she was discovered? But where? Should she go back? No, a thousand times, no! Her enemy was there. This could not be the one from whom she fled. He was coming from the opposite direction, but he might be just as bad. Her experience taught her that men were to be shunned. Even fathers and brothers were terribly uncertain, sorrow-bringing creatures.

She could not go back to the place where the dead man lay. She must not go back. And forward she was taking the only course that seemed at all possible through the natural obstructions of the region. She shrank to her saddle, and urged the patient horse on. Perhaps she could reach the bench and get away out of sight before the newcomer saw her.

But the way was longer to the top, and steeper than it had seemed at first, and the horse was tired. Sometimes he stopped of his own accord, and snorted appealingly to her with his head turned inquiringly as if to know how long and how far this strange ride was to continue. Then the man in the distance seemed to ride faster. The valley between them was not so wide here. He was quite distinctly a man now, and his horse was going rapidly. Once it seemed as if he waved his arms; but she turned her head, and urged her horse with sudden fright. They were almost to the top now. She dismounted and clambered alongside of the animal up the steep incline, her breath coming in quick gasps, with the horse's breath hot upon her cheek as they climbed together.

At last! They were at the top! Ten feet more and they would be on a level, where they might disappear from view. She turned to look across the valley, and the man was directly opposite. He must have ridden hard to get there so soon. Oh, horror! He was waving his hands and calling. She could distinctly hear a cry! It chilled her senses, and brought a frantic, unreasoning fear. Somehow she felt he was connected with the one from whom she fled. Some emissary of his sent out to foil her in her attempt for safety, perhaps.

She clutched the bridle wildly, and urged the horse up with one last effort; and just as they reached high ground she heard the wild cry ring clear and distinct, "Hello! Hello!" and then something else. It sounded like "Help!" but she could not tell. Was he trying to deceive her? Pretending he would help her?

She flung herself into the saddle, giving the horse the signal to run; and, as the animal obeyed and broke into his prairie run, she cast one fearful glance behind her. The man was pursuing her at a gallop! He was crossing the valley. There was a stream to cross, but he would cross it. He had determination in every line of his flying figure. His voice was pursuing her, too. It seemed as if the sound reached out and clutched her heart, and tried to draw her back as she fled. And now her pursuers were three: her enemy, the dead man upon the mountain, and the voice.

Chapter 3

The Pursuit

Straight across the prairie she galloped, not daring to stop for an instant, with the voice pursuing her. For hours it seemed to ring in her ears, and even after she was far beyond any possibility of hearing it she could not be sure but there was now and then a faint echo of it ringing yet, "Hello!"—ringing like some strange bird amid the silence of the world.

There were cattle and sheep grazing on the bench, and the horse would fain have stopped to dine with them; but the girl urged him on, seeming to make him understand the danger that might be pursuing them.

It was hours before she dared stop for the much-needed rest. Her brain had grown confused with the fright and weariness. She felt that she could not much longer stay in the saddle. She might fall asleep. The afternoon sun would soon be slipping down behind the mountains. When and where dared she rest? Not in the night, for that would be almost certain death, with wild beasts about.

A little group of greasewood offered a scanty shelter. As if the beast understood her thoughts he stopped with a neigh, and looked around at her. She scanned the surroundings. There were cattle all about. They had looked up curiously from their grazing as the horse flew by, but were now going quietly on about their business. They would serve as a screen if any should be still pursuing her. One horse among the other animals in a landscape would not be so noticeable as one alone against the sky. The greasewood was not far from sloping ground where she might easily flee for hiding if danger approached.

The horse had already begun to crop the tender grass at his feet as if his life depended upon a good meal. The girl took some more beans from the pack she carried, and mechanically ate them, though she felt no appetite, and her dry throat almost refused to swallow. She found her eyes shutting even against her will; and in desperation she folded the old coat into a pillow, and with the horse's bridle fastened in her belt she lay down.

The sun went away; the horse ate his supper; and the girl slept. By and by the horse drowsed off too, and the bleating sheep in the distance, the lowing of the cattle, the sound of night-birds, came now and again from the distance; but still the girl slept on. The moon rose full and round, shining with flickering light through the cottonwoods; and the girl stirred in a dream and thought some one was pursuing her, but slept on again. Then out through the night rang a vivid human voice, "Hello! Hello!" The horse roused from his sleep, and stamped his feet nervously, twitching at his bridle; but the relaxed hand that lay across the leather strap did not quicken, and the girl slept on. The horse listened, and thought he heard a sound good to his ear. He neighed, and neighed again; but the girl slept on.

The first ray of the rising sun at last shot through the gray of dawning, and touched the girl full in the face as it slid under the branches of her sheltering tree. The light brought her acutely to her senses. Before she opened her eyes she seemed to be keenly and painfully aware of much that had gone on during her sleep. With another flash her eyes flew open. Not because she willed it, but rather as if the springs that held the lids shut had unexpectedly been touched and they sprang back because they had to.

She shrank, as her eyes opened, from a new day, and the memory of the old one. Then before her she saw something which kept her motionless, and almost froze the blood in her veins. She could not stir nor breathe, and for a moment even thought was paralyzed. There before her but a few feet away stood a man! Beyond him, a few feet from her own horse, stood his horse. She could not see it without turning her head, and that she dared not do; but she knew it was there, felt it even before she noticed the double stamping and breathing of the animals.

Her keen senses seemed to make the whole surrounding landscape visible to her without the moving of a muscle. She knew to a nicety exactly how her weapons lay, and what movement would bring her hand to the trigger of her pistol; yet she stirred not.

Gradually she grew calm enough to study the man before her. He stood almost with his back turned toward her, his face just half turned so that one cheek and a part of his brow were visible. He was broadshouldered and well built. There was strength in every line of his body. She felt how powerless she would be in his grasp. Her only hope would be in taking him unaware. Yet she moved not one atom.

He wore a brown flannel shirt, open at the throat, brown leather belt and boots; in short, his whole costume was in harmonious shades of brown, and looked new as if it had been worn but a few days. His soft felt sombrero was rolled back from his face, and the young red sun tinged the short brown curls to a ruddy gold. He was looking toward the rising sun. The gleam of it shot across his brace of pistols in his belt, and flashed twin rays into her eyes. Then all at once the man turned and looked at her.

Instantly the girl sprang to her feet, her hands upon her pistol, her eyes meeting with calm, desperate defiance the blue ones that were turned to her. She was braced against a tree, and her senses were measuring the distance between her horse and herself, and deciding whether escape were possible.

"Good morning," said the man politely. "I hope I haven't disturbed your nap."

The girl eyed him solemnly, and said nothing. This was a new kind of man. He was not like the one from whom she had fled, nor like any she had ever seen; but he might be a great deal worse. She had heard that the world was full of wickedness.

"You see," went on the man with an apologetic smile, which lit up his eyes in a wonderfully winning way, "you led me such a desperate race nearly all day yesterday that I was obliged to keep you in sight when I finally caught you."

He looked for an answering smile, but there was none. Instead, the girl's dark eyes grew wide and purple with fear. He was the same one, then, that she had seen in the afternoon, the voice who had cried to her; and he had been pursuing her. He was an enemy, perhaps, sent by the man from whom she fled. She grasped her pistol with trembling fingers, and tried to think what to say or do.

The young man wondered at the formalities of the plains. Were all these Western maidens so reticent?

"Why did you follow me? Who did you think I was?" she asked breathlessly at last.

"Well, I thought you were a man," he said, "at least, you appeared to be a human being, and not a wild animal. I hadn't seen anything but wild animals for six hours, and very few of those; so I followed you."

The girl was silent. She was not reassured. It did not seem to her that her question was directly answered. The young man was playing with her.

"What right had you to follow me?" she demanded fiercely.

"Well, now that you put it in that light, I'm not sure that I had any right at all, unless it may be the claim that every human being has upon all creation."

His arms were folded now across his broad brown flannel chest, and the pistols gleamed in his belt below like fine ornaments. He wore a philosophical expression, and looked at his companion as if she were a new specimen of the human kind, and he was studying her variety, quite impersonally, it is true, but interestingly. There was something in his look that angered the girl.

"What do you want?" She had never heard of the divine claims of all the human family. Her one instinct at present was fear.

An expression that was almost bitter flitted over the young man's face, as of an unpleasant memory forgotten for the instant.

"It really wasn't of much consequence when you think of it," he said with a shrug of his fine shoulders. "I was merely lost, and was wanting to inquire where I was—and possibly the way to somewhere. But I don't know as 'twas worth the trouble."

The girl was puzzled. She had never seen a man like this before. He was not like her wild, reckless brother, nor any of his associates.

"This is Montana," she said, "or was, when I started," she added with sudden thought.

"Yes? Well, it was Montana when I started, too; but it's as likely to be the Desert of Sahara as anything else. I'm sure I've come far enough, and found it barren enough."

"I never heard of that place," said the girl seriously; "is it in Canada?"

"I believe not," said the man with sudden gravity; "at least, not that I know of. When I went to school, it was generally located somewhere in Africa."

"I never went to school," said the girl wistfully; "but—" with a sudden resolve—"I'll go now."

"Do!" said the man. "I'll go with you. Let's start at once; for, now that I think of it, I haven't had anything to eat for over a day, and there might be something in that line near a schoolhouse. Do you know the way?"

"No," said the girl, slowly studying him—she began to feel he was making fun of her; "but I can give you something to eat."

"Thank you!" said the man. "I assure you I shall appreciate anything from hardtack to bisque ice-cream."

"I haven't any of those," said the girl, "but there are plenty of beans left; and, if you will get some wood for a fire, I'll make some coffee."

"Agreed," said the man. "That sounds better than anything I've heard for forty-eight hours."

The girl watched him as he strode away to find wood, and frowned for an instant; but his face was perfectly sober, and she turned to the business of getting breakfast. For a little her fears were allayed. At least, he would do her no immediate harm. Of course she might fly from him now while his back was turned; but then of course he would pursue her again, and she had little chance of getting away. Besides, he was hungry. She could not leave him without something to eat.

"We can't make coffee without water," she said as he came back with a bundle of sticks.

He whistled.

"Could you inform me where to look for water?" he asked.

She looked into his face, and saw how worn and gray he was about his eyes; and a sudden compassion came upon her.

"You'd better eat something first," she said, "and then we'll go and hunt for water. There's sure to be some in the valley. We'll cook some meat."

She took the sticks from him, and made the fire in a businesslike way. He watched her, and wondered at her grace. Who was she, and how had she wandered out into this waste place? Her face was both beautiful and interesting. She would make a fine study if he were not so weary of all human nature, and especially woman. He sighed as he thought again of himself.

The girl caught the sound, and, turning with the quickness of a wild creature, caught the sadness in his face. It seemed to drive away much of her fear and resentment. A half-flicker of a smile came to her as their eyes met. It seemed to recognize a comradeship in sorrow. But her face hardened again almost at once into disapproval as he answered her look.

The man felt a passing disappointment. After a minute, during which the girl had dropped her eyes to her work again, he said: "Now, why did you look at me in that way? Ought I to be helping you in some way? I'm awkward, I know, but I can obey if you'll just tell me how."

The girl seemed puzzled; then she replied almost sullenly:

"There's nothing more to do. It's ready to eat."

She gave him a piece of the meat and the last of the corn bread in the tin cup, and placed the pan of beans beside him; but she did not attempt to eat anything herself.

He took a hungry bite or two, and looked furtively at her.

"I insist upon knowing why you looked—" he paused and eyed her—"why you look at me in that way. I'm not a wolf if I am hungry, and I'm not going to eat you up."

The look of displeasure deepened on the girl's brow. In spite of his hunger the man was compelled to watch her. She seemed to be looking at a flock of birds in the sky. Her hand rested lightly at her belt. The birds were coming towards them, flying almost over their heads.

Suddenly the girl's hand was raised with a quick motion, and something gleamed in the sun across his sight. There was a loud report, and one of the birds fell almost at his feet, dead. It was a sage-hen. Then the girl turned and walked towards him with as haughty a carriage as ever a society belle could boast.

"You were laughing at me," she said quietly.

It had all happened so suddenly that the man had not time to think. Several distinct sensations of surprise passed over his countenance. Then, as the meaning of the girl's act dawned upon him, and the full intention of her rebuke, the color mounted in his nice, tanned face. He set down the tin cup, and balanced the bit of corn bread on the rim, and arose.

"I beg your pardon," he said. "I never will do it again. I couldn't have shot that bird to save my life," and he touched it with the tip of his tan leather boot as if to make sure it was a real bird.

The girl was sitting on the ground, indifferently eating some of the cooked pork. She did not answer. Somehow the young man felt uncomfortable. He sat down, and took up his tin cup, and went at his breakfast again; but his appetite seemed in abeyance.

"I've been trying myself to learn to shoot during the last week," he began soberly. "I haven't been able yet to hit anything but the side of a barn. Say, I'm wondering, suppose I had tried to shoot at those birds just now and had missed, whether you wouldn't have laughed at me—quietly, all to yourself, you know. Are you quite sure?"

The girl looked up at him solemnly, without saying a word for a full minute.

"Was what I said as bad as that?" she asked slowly.

"I'm afraid it was," he answered thoughtfully; "but I was a blamed idiot for laughing at you. A girl that shoots like that may locate the Desert of Sahara in Canada if she likes, and Canada ought to be proud of the honor."

She looked into his face for an instant, and noted his earnestness; and all at once she broke into a clear ripple of laughter. The young man was astonished anew that she had understood him enough to laugh. She must be unusually keen-witted, this lady of the desert.

"If 'twas as bad as that," she said in quite another tone, "you c'n laugh."

They looked at each other then in mutual understanding, and each fell to eating his portion in silence. Suddenly the man spoke.

"I am eating your food that you had prepared for your journey, and I have not even said, 'Thank you' yet, nor asked if you have enough to carry you to a place where there is more. Where are you going?"

The girl did not answer at once; but, when she did, she spoke thoughtfully, as if the words were a newly made vow from an impulse just received.

"I am going to school," she said in her slow way, "to learn to 'sight' the Desert of Sahara."

He looked at her, and his eyes gave her the homage he felt was her due; but he said nothing. Here evidently was an indomitable spirit, but how did she get out into the wilderness? Where did she come from, and why was she alone? He had heard of the freedom of Western women, but surely such girls as this did not frequent so vast a waste of uninhabited territory as his experience led him to believe this was. He sat studying her.

The brow was sweet and thoughtful, with a certain keen inquisitiveness about the eyes. The mouth was firm; yet there were gentle lines of grace about it. In spite of her coarse, dark calico garb, made in no particular fashion except with an eye to covering with the least possible fuss and trouble, she was graceful. Every movement was alert and clean-cut. When she turned to look full in his face, he decided that she had almost beautiful eyes.

She had arisen while he was watching her, and seemed to be looking off with sudden apprehension. He followed her gaze, and saw several dark figures moving against the sky.

"It's a herd of antelope," she said with relief; "but it's time we hit the trail." She turned, and put her things together with incredible swiftness, giving him very little opportunity to help, and mounted her pony without more words.

For an hour he followed her at high speed as she rode full tilt over rough and smooth, casting furtive, anxious glances behind her now and then, which only half included him. She seemed to know that he was there and was following; that was all.

The young man felt rather amused and flattered. He reflected that most women he knew would have ridden by his side, and tried to make him talk. But this girl of the wilderness rode straight ahead as if her life depended upon it. She seemed to have nothing to say to him, and to be anxious neither to impart her own history nor to know his.

Well, that suited his mood. He had come out into the wilderness to think and to forget. Here was ample opportunity. There had been a little too much of it yesterday, when he wandered from the rest of his party who had come out to hunt; and for a time he had felt that he would rather be back in his native city with a good breakfast and all his troubles than to be alone in the vast waste forever. But now there was human company, and a possibility of getting somewhere sometime. He was content.

The lithe, slender figure of the girl ahead seemed one with the horse it rode. He tried to think what this ride would be if another woman he knew were riding on that horse ahead, but there was very small satisfaction in that. In the first place, it was highly improbable, and the young man was of an intensely practical turn of mind. It was impossible to imagine the haughty beauty in a brown calico riding a high-spirited horse of the wilds. There was but one parallel. If she had been there, she would, in her present state of mind, likely be riding imperiously and indifferently ahead instead of by his side where he wanted her. Besides, he came out to the plains to forget her. Why think of her?

The sky was exceedingly bright and wide. Why had he never noticed this wilderness in skies at home? There was another flock of birds. What if he should try to shoot one? Idle talk. He would probably hit anything but the birds. Why had that girl shot that bird, anyway? Was it entirely because she might need it for food? She had picked it up significantly with the other things, and fastened it to her saddle-bow without a word. He was too ignorant to know whether it was an edible bird or not, or she was merely carrying it to remind him of her skill.

And what sort of a girl was she? Perhaps she was escaping from justice. She ran from him yesterday, and apparently stopped only when utterly exhausted. She seemed startled and anxious when the antelopes came into sight. There was no knowing whether her company meant safety, after all. Yet his interest was so thoroughly aroused in her that he was willing to risk it.

Of course he might go more slowly and gradually, let her get ahead, and he slip out of sight. It was not likely he had wandered so many miles away from human habitation but that he would reach one sometime; and, now that he was re-enforced by food, perhaps it would be the part of wisdom to part with this strange maiden. As he thought, he unconsciously slackened his horse's pace. The girl was several yards ahead, and just vanishing behind a clump of sage-brush. She vanished, and he stopped for an instant, and looked about him on the desolation; and a great loneliness settled upon him like a frenzy. He was glad to see the girl riding back toward him with a smile of good fellowship on her face.

"What's the matter?" she called. "Come on! There's water in the valley."

The sound of water was good; and life seemed suddenly good for no reason whatever but that the morning was bright, and the sky was wide, and there was water in the valley. He rode forward, keeping close beside her now, and in a moment there gleamed below in the hot sunshine the shining of a sparkling stream.

"You seem to be running away from someone," he explained. "I thought you wanted to get rid of me, and I would give you a chance."

She looked at him surprised.

"I am running away," she said, "but not from you."

"From whom, then, may I ask? It might be convenient to know, if we are to travel in the same company."

She looked at him keenly.

"Who are you, and where do you belong?"

Chapter 4

The Two Fugitives

"**I**'m not anybody in particular," he answered, "and I'm not just sure where I belong. I live in Pennsylvania, but I didn't seem to belong there exactly, at least not just now, and so I came out here to see if I belonged anywhere else. I concluded yesterday that I didn't. At least, not until I came in sight of you. But I suspect I am running away myself. In fact, that is just what I am doing, running away from a woman!"

He looked at her with his honest hazel eyes, and she liked him. She felt he was telling her the truth, but it seemed to be a truth he was just finding out for himself as he talked.

"Why do you run away from a woman? How could a woman hurt you? Can she shoot?"

He flashed her a look of amusement and pain mingled.

"She uses other weapons," he said. "Her words are darts, and her looks are swords."

"What a queer woman! Does she ride well?"

"Yes, in an automobile!"

"What is that?" She asked the question shyly as if she feared he might laugh again; and he looked down, and perceived that he was talking far above her. In fact, he was talking to himself more than to the girl.

There was a bitter pleasure in speaking of his lost lady to this wild creature who almost seemed of another kind, more like an intelligent bird or flower.

"An automobile is a carriage that moves about without horses," he answered her gravely. "It moves by machinery."

"I should not like it," said the girl decidedly. "Horses are better than machines. I saw a machine once. It was to cut wheat. It made a noise, and did not go fast. It frightened me."

"But automobiles go very fast, faster than any horses. And they do not all make a noise."

The girl looked around apprehensively.

"My horse can go very fast. You do not know how fast. If you see her coming, I will change horses with you. You must ride to the nearest bench and over, and then turn backward on your tracks. She will never find you that way. And I am not afraid of a woman."

The man broke into a hearty laugh, loud and long. He laughed until the tears rolled down his cheeks; and the girl, offended, rode haughtily beside him. Then all in a moment he grew quite grave.

"Excuse me," he said; "I am not laughing at you now, though it looks that way. I am laughing out of the bitterness of my soul at the picture you put before me. Although I am running away from her, the lady will not come out in her automobile to look for me. She does not want me!"

"She does not want you! And yet you ran away from her?"

"That's exactly it," he said. "You see, *I* wanted *her!*"

"Oh!" She gave a sharp, quick gasp of intelligence, and was silent. After a full minute she rode quite close to his horse, and laid her small brown hand on the animal's mane.

"I am sorry," she said simply.

"Thank you," he answered. "I'm sure I don't know why I told you. I never told anyone before."

There was a long silence between them. The man seemed to have forgotten her as he rode with his eyes upon his horse's neck, and his thoughts apparently far away.

At last the girl said softly, as if she were rendering return for the confidence given her, "I ran away from a man."

The man lifted his eyes courteously, questioningly, and waited.

"He is big and dark and handsome. He shoots to kill. He killed my brother. I hate him. He wants me, and I ran away from him. But he is a coward. I frightened him away. He is afraid of dead men that he has killed."

The young man gave his attention now to the extraordinary story which the girl told as if it were a common occurrence.

"But where are your people, your family and friends? Why do they not send the man away?"

"They're all back there in the sand," she said with a sad little flicker of a smile and a gesture that told of tragedy. "I said the prayer over them. Mother always wanted it when we died. There wasn't anybody left but me. I said it, and then I came away. It was cold moonlight, and there were noises. The horse was afraid. But I said it. Do you suppose it will do any good?"

She fastened her eyes upon the young man with her last words as if demanding an answer. The color came up to his cheeks. He felt embarrassed at such a question before her trouble.

"Why, I should think it ought to," he stammered. "Of course it will," he added with more confident comfort.

"Did you ever say the prayer?"

"Why—I—yes, I believe I have," he answered somewhat uncertainly.

"Did it do any good?" She hung upon his words.

"Why, I—believe—yes, I suppose it did. That is, praying is always a good thing. The fact is, it's a long time since I've tried it. But of course it's all right."

A curious topic for conversation between a young man and woman on a ride through the wilderness. The man had never thought about prayer for so many minutes consecutively in the whole of his life; at least, not since the days when his nurse tried to teach him "Now I lay me."

"Why don't you try it about the lady?" asked the girl suddenly.

"Well, the fact is, I never thought of it."

"Don't you believe it will do any good?"

"Well, I suppose it might."

"Then let's try it. Let's get off now, quick, and both say it. Maybe it will help us both. Do you know it all through? Can't you say it?" This last anxiously, as he hesitated and looked doubtful.

The color came into the man's face. Somehow this girl put him in a very bad light. He couldn't shoot; and, if he couldn't pray, what would she think of him?

"Why, I think I could manage to say it with help," he answered uneasily. "But what if that man should suddenly appear on the scene?"

"You don't think the prayer is any good, or you wouldn't say that." She said it sadly, hopelessly.

"O, why certainly," he said, "only I thought there might be some better time to try it; but, if you say so, we'll stop right here." He sprang to the ground, and offered to assist her; but she was beside him before he could get around his horse's head.

Down she dropped, and clasped her hands as a little child might have done, and closed her eyes.

"Our Father," she repeated slowly, precisely, as if every word belonged to a charm and must be repeated just right or it would not work. The man's mumbling words halted after hers. He was reflecting upon the curious tableau they would make to the chance passer-by on the desert if there were any passers-by. It was strange, this aloneness. There was a wideness here that made praying seem more natural than it would have been at home in the open country.

The prayer, by reason of the unaccustomed lips, went slowly; but, when it was finished, the girl sprang to her saddle again with a businesslike expression.

"I feel better," she said with a winning smile. "Don't you? Don't you think He heard?"

"Who heard?"

"Why, 'our Father.' "

"O, certainly! That is, I've always been taught to suppose He did. I haven't much experimental knowledge in this line, but I dare say it'll do some good somewhere. Now do you suppose we could get some of that very sparkling water? I feel exceedingly thirsty."

They spurred their horses, and were soon beside the stream, refreshing themselves.

"Did you ride all night?" asked the girl.

"Pretty much," answered the man. "I stopped once to rest a few minutes; but a sound in the distance stirred me up again, and I was afraid to lose my chance of catching you, lest I should be hopelessly lost. You see, I went out with a party hunting, and I sulked behind. They went off up a steep climb, and I said I'd wander around below till they got back, or perhaps ride back to camp; but, when I tried to find the camp, it wasn't where I had left it."

"Well, you've got to lie down and sleep awhile," said the girl decidedly. "You can't keep going like that. It'll kill you. You lie down, and I'll watch, and get dinner. I'm going to cook that bird."

He demurred, but in the end she had her way; for he was exceedingly weary, and she saw it. So he let her spread the old coat down for him while he gathered some wood for a fire, and then he lay down and watched her simple preparations for the meal. Before he knew it he was asleep.

When he came to himself, there was a curious blending of dream and reality. He thought his lady was coming to him across the rough plains in an automobile, with gray wings like those of the bird the girl had shot, and his prayer as he knelt in the sand was drawing her, while overhead the air was full of a wild, sweet music from strange birds that mocked and called and trilled. But, when the automobile reached him and stopped, the lady withered into a little, old, dried-up creature of ashes; and the girl of the plains was sitting in her place radiant and beautiful.

He opened his eyes, and saw the rude little dinner set, and smelt the delicious odor of the roasted bird. The girl was standing on the other side of the fire, gravely whistling a most extraordinary song, like unto all the birds of the air at once.

She had made a little cake out of the corn-meal, and they feasted royally.

"I caught two fishes in the brook. We'll take them along for supper," she said as they packed the things again for starting. He tried to get her to take a rest also, and let him watch; but she insisted that they must go on, and promised to rest just before dark. "For we must travel hard at night, you know," she added fearfully.

He questioned her more about the man who might be pursuing, and came to understand her fears.

"The scoundrel!" he muttered, looking at the delicate features and clear, lovely profile of the girl. He felt a strong desire to throttle the evil man.

He asked a good many questions about her life, and was filled with wonder over the flower-like girl who seemed to have blossomed in the wilderness with no hand to cultivate her save a lazy, clever, drunken father, and a kind but ignorant mother. How could she have escaped being coarsened amid such surroundings? How was it, with such brothers as she had, that she had come forth as lovely and unhurt as she seemed? He somehow began to feel a great anxiety for her lonely future and a desire to put her in the way of protection. But at present they were still in the wilderness; and he began to be glad that he was here too, and might have the privilege of protecting her now, if there should be need.

As it grew toward evening, they came upon a little grassy spot in a coulee where the horses might rest and eat. Here they stopped, and the girl threw herself under a shelter of trees, with the old coat for a pillow, and rested, while the man paced up and down at a distance, gathering wood for a fire, and watching the horizon. As night came on, the city-bred man longed for shelter. He was by no means a coward where known quantities were concerned, but to face wild animals and drunken brigands in a strange, wild plain with no help near was anything but an enlivening prospect. He could not understand why they had not come upon some human habitation by this time. He had never realized how vast this country was before. When he came westward on the train he did not remember to have traversed such long stretches of country without a sign of civilization, though of course a train went so much faster than a horse that he had no adequate means of judging. Then, besides, they were on no trail now, and had probably gone in a most round-about way to anywhere. In reality they had twice come within five miles of little homesteads, tucked away beside a stream in a fertile spot; but they had not known it. A mile further to the right at one spot would have put them on the trail and made their way easier and shorter, but that they could not know.

The girl did not rest long. She seemed to feel her pursuit more as the darkness crept on, and kept anxiously looking for the moon.

"We must go toward the moon," she said as she watched the bright spot coming in the east.

They ate their supper of fish and corn-bread with the appetite that grows on horseback, and by the time they had started on their way again the moon spread a path of silver before them, and they went forward feeling as if they had known each other a long time. For a while their fears and hopes were blended in one.

Meantime, as the sun sank and the moon rose, a traveller rode up the steep ascent to the little lonely cabin which the girl had left. He was handsome and dark and strong, with a scarlet kerchief knotted at this throat; and he rode slowly, cautiously, looking furtively about and ahead of him. He was doubly armed, and his pistols gleamed in the moonlight, while an ugly knife nestled keenly in a secret sheath.

He was wicked, for the look upon his face was not good to see; and he was a coward, for he started at the flutter of a night-bird hurrying late to its home in a rock by the wayside. The mist rising from the valley in wreaths of silver gauze startled him as he rounded the trail to the cabin, and for an instant he stopped and drew his dagger, thinking the ghost he feared was walking thus early. A draught from the bottle he carried in his pocket steadied his nerves, and he went on, but stopped again in front of the cabin; for there stood another horse, and there in the doorway stood a figure in the darkness! His curses rang through the still air and smote the moonlight. His pistol flashed forth a volley of fire to second him.

In answer to his demand who was there came another torrent of profanity. It was one of the comrades of the day before. He explained that he and two others had come up to pay a visit to the pretty girl. They had had a wager as to who could win her, and they had come to try; but she was not here. The door was fastened. They had forced it. There was no sign of her about. The other two had gone down to the place where her brother was buried to see whether she was there. Women were known to be sentimental. She might be that kind. He had agreed to wait here, but he was getting uneasy. Perhaps, if the other two found her, they might not be fair.

The last comer with a mighty oath explained that the girl belonged to him, and that no one had a right to her. He demanded that the other come with him to the grave, and see what had become of the girl; and then they would all go and drink together—but the girl belonged to him.

They rode to the place of the graves, and met the two others returning; but there was no sign of the girl, and the three taunted the one, saying that the girl had given him the slip. Amid much argument as to whose she was and where she was, they rode on cursing through God's beauty. They passed the bottle continually, that their nerves might be the steadier; and, when they came to the deserted cabin once more, they paused and discussed what to do.

At last it was agreed that they should start on a quest after her, and with oaths, and coarse jests, and drinking, they started down the trail of which the girl had gone in search by her roundabout way.

Chapter 5

A Night Ride

It was a wonderful night that the two spent wading the sea of moonlight together on the plain. The almost unearthly beauty of the scene grew upon them. They had none of the loneliness that had possessed each the night before, and might now discover all the wonders of the way.

Early in the way they came upon a prairie-dogs' village, and the man would have lingered watching with curiosity, had not the girl urged him on. It was the time of night when she had started to run away, and the same apprehension that filled her then came upon her with the evening. She longed to be out of the land which held the man she feared. She would rather bury herself in the earth and smother to death than be caught by him. But, as they rode on, she told her companion much of the habits of the curious little creatures they had seen; and then, as the night settled down upon them, she pointed out the dark, stealing creatures that slipped from their way now and then, or gleamed with a fearsome green eye from some temporary refuge.

At first the cold shivers kept running up and down the young man as he realized that here before him in the sage-brush was a real live animal about which he had read so much, and which he had come out bravely to hunt. He kept his hand upon his revolver, and was constantly on the alert, nervously looking behind lest a troop of coyotes or wolves should be quietly stealing upon him. But, as the girl talked fearlessly of them in much the same way as we talk of a neighbor's fierce dog, he grew gradually calmer, and was able to watch a dark, velvet-footed moving object ahead without starting.

By and by he pointed to the heavens, and talked of the stars. Did she know that constellation? No? Then he explained. Such and such stars were so many miles from the earth. He told their names, and a bit of mythology connected with the name, and then went on to speak of the moon, and the possibility of its once having been inhabited.

The girl listened amazed. She knew certain stars as landmarks, telling east from west and north from south; and she had often watched them one by one coming out, and counted them her friends; but that they were worlds, and that the inhabitants of this earth knew anything whatever about the heavenly bodies, she had never heard. Question after question she plied him with, some of them showing extraordinary intelligence and thought, and others showing deeper ignorance than a little child in our kindergartens would show.

He wondered more and more as their talk went on. He grew deeply interested in unfolding the wonders of the heavens to her; and, as he studied her pure profile in the moonlight with eager, searching, wistful gaze, her beauty impressed him more and more. In the East the man had a friend, an artist. He thought how wonderful a theme for a painting this scene would make. The girl in picturesque hat of soft felt, riding with careless ease and grace; horse, maiden, plain, bathed in a sea of silver.

More and more as she talked the man wondered how this girl reared in the wilds had acquired a speech so free from grammatical errors. She was apparently deeply ignorant, and yet with a very few exceptions she made no serious errors in English. How was it to be accounted for?

He began to ply her with questions about herself, but could not find that she had ever come into contact with people who were educated. She had not even lived in any of the miserable little towns that flourish in the wildest of the West, and not within several hundred miles of a city. Their nearest neighbors in one direction had been forty miles away, she said, and said it as if that were an everyday distance for a neighbor to live.

Mail? They had had a letter once that she could remember, when she was a little girl. It was just a few lines in pencil to say that her mother's father had died. He had been killed in an accident of some sort, working in the city where he lived. Her mother had kept the letter and cried over it till almost all the pencil marks were gone.

No, they had no mail on the mountain where their homestead was.

Yes, her father went there first because he thought he had discovered gold, but it turned out to be a mistake; so, as they had no other place to go to, and no money to go with, they had just stayed there; and her father and brothers had been cow-punchers, but she and her mother had scarcely ever gone away from home. There were the little children to care for; and, when they died, her mother did not care to go, and would not let her go far alone.

O, yes, she had ridden a great deal, sometimes with her brothers, but not often. They went with rough men, and her mother felt afraid to have her go. The men all drank. Her brothers drank. Her father drank too. She stated it as if it were a sad fact common to all mankind, and ended with the statement which was almost, not quite, a question, "I guess you drink too."

"Well," said the young man hesitatingly, "not that way. I take a glass of wine now and then in company, you know——"

"Yes, I know," sighed the girl. "Men are all alike. Mother used to say so. She said men were different from women. They had to drink. She said they all did it. Only she said her father never did; but he was very good, though he had to work hard."

"Indeed," said the young man, his color rising in the moonlight, "indeed, you make a mistake. I don't drink at all, not that way. I'm not like them. I—why, I only—well, the fact is, I don't care a red cent about the stuff anyway; and I don't want you to think I'm like them. If it will do you any good, I'll never touch it again, not a drop."

He said it earnestly. He was trying to vindicate himself. Just why he should care to do so he did not know, only that all at once it was very necessary that he should appear different in the eyes of this girl from the other men she had known.

"Will you really?" she asked, turning to look in his face. "Will you promise that?"

"Why, certainly I will," he said, a trifle embarrassed that she had taken him at his word. "Of course I will. I tell you it's nothing to me. I only took a glass at the club occasionally when the other men were drinking, and sometimes when I went to banquets, class banquets, you know, and dinners——"

Now the girl had never heard of class banquets, but to take a glass occasionally when the other men were drinking was what her brothers did; and so she sighed, and said: "Yes, you may promise, but I know you won't keep it. Father promised too; but, when he got with the other men, it did no good. Men are all alike."

"But I'm not," he insisted stoutly. "I tell you I'm not. I don't drink, and I won't drink. I promise you solemnly here under God's sky that I'll never drink another drop of intoxicating liquor again if I know it as long as I live."

He put out his hand toward her, and she put her own into it with a quick grasp for just an instant.

"Then you're not like other men, after all," she said with a glad ring in her voice. "That must be why I wasn't so very much afraid of you when I woke up and found you standing there."

A distinct sense of pleasure came over him at her words. Why it should make him glad that she had not been afraid of him when she had first seen him in the wilderness he did not know. He forgot all about his own troubles. He forgot the lady in the automobile. Right then and there he dropped her out of his thoughts. He did not know it; but she was forgotten, and he did not think about her any more during that journey. Something had erased her. He had run away from her, and he had succeeded most effectually, more so than he knew.

There in the desert the man took his first temperance pledge, urged thereto by a girl who had never heard of a temperance pledge in her life, had never joined a woman's temperance society, and knew nothing about women's crusades. Her own heart had taught her out of a bitter experience just how to use her God-given influence.

They came to a long stretch of level ground then, smooth and hard; and the horses as with common consent set out to gallop shoulder to shoulder in a wild, exhilarating skim across the plain. Talking was impossible. The man reflected that he was making great strides in experience, first a prayer and then a pledge, all in the wilderness. If anyone had told him he was going into the West for this, he would have laughed him to scorn.

Towards morning they rode more slowly. Their horses were growing jaded. They talked in lower tones as they looked toward the east. It was as if they feared they might waken someone too soon. There is something awesome about the dawning of a new day, and especially when one has been sailing a sea of silver all night. It is like coming back from an unreal world into a sad, real one. Each was almost sorry that the night was over. The new day might hold so much of hardship or relief, so much of trouble or surprise; and this night had been perfect, a jewel cut to set in memory with every facet flashing to the light. They did not like to get back to reality from the converse they had held together. It was an experience for each which would never be forgotten.

Once there came the distant sound of shots and shouts. The two shrank nearer each other, and the man laid his strong hand protectingly on the mane of the girl's horse; but he did not touch her hand. The lady of his thoughts had sometimes let him hold her jewelled hand, and smiled with drooping lashes when he fondled it; and, when she had tired of him, other admirers might claim the same privilege. But this woman of the wilderness—he would not even in his thoughts presume to touch her little brown, firm hand. Somehow she had commanded his honor and respect from the first minute, even before she shot the bird.

Once a bob-cat shot across their path but a few feet in front of them, and later a kit-fox ran growling up with ruffled fur; but the girl's quick shot soon put it to flight, and they passed on through the dawning morning of the first real Sabbath day the girl had ever known.

"It is Sunday morning at home," said the man gravely as he watched the sun lift its rosy head from the mist of mountain and valley outspread before them. "Do you have such an institution out here?"

The girl grew white about the lips. "Awful things happen on Sunday," she said with a shudder.

He felt a great pity rising in his heart for her, and strove to turn her thoughts in other directions. Evidently there was a recent sorrow connected with the Sabbath.

"You are tired," said he, "and the horses are tired. See! We ought to stop and rest. The daylight has come, and nothing can hurt us. Here is a good place, and sheltered. We can fasten the horses behind these bushes, and no one will guess we are here."

She assented, and they dismounted. The man cut an opening into a clump of thick growth with his knife, and there they fastened the weary horses, well hidden from sight if anyone chanced that way. The girl lay down a few feet away in a spot almost entirely surrounded by sage-brush which had reached an unusual height and made a fine hiding-place. Just outside the entrance of this natural chamber the man lay down on a fragrant bed of sage-brush. He had gathered enough for the girl first, and spread out the old coat over it; and she had dropped asleep almost as soon as she lay down. But, although his own bed of sage-brush was tolerably comfortable, even to one accustomed all his life to the finest springs and hair mattress that money could buy, and although the girl had insisted that he must rest too, for he was weary and there was no need to watch, sleep would not come to his eyelids.

He lay there resting and thinking. How strange was the experience through which he was passing! Came ever a wealthy, college-bred, society man into the like before? What did it all mean? His being lost, his wandering for a day, the sight of this girl and his pursuit, the prayer under the open sky, and that night of splendor under the moonlight riding side by side. It was like some marvellous tale.

And this girl! Where was she going? What was to become of her? Out in the world where he came from, were they ever to reach it, she would be nothing. Her station in life was beneath his so far that the only recognition she could have would be one which would degrade her. This solitary journey they were taking, how the world would lift up its hands in horror at it! A girl without a chaperon! She was impossible! And yet it all seemed right and good, and the girl was evidently recognized by the angels; else how had she escaped from degradation thus far?

Ah! How did he know she had? But he smiled at that. No one could look into that pure, sweet face, and doubt that she was as good as she was beautiful. If it was not so, he hoped he would never find it out. She seemed to him a woman yet unspoiled, and he shrank from the thought of what the world might do for her—the world and its cultivation, which would not be for her, because she was friendless and without money or home. The world would have nothing but toil to give her, with a meagre living.

Where was she going, and what was she proposing to do? Must he not try to help her in some way? Did not the fact that she had saved his life demand so much from him? If he had not found her, he must surely have starved before he got out of this wild place. Even yet starvation was not an impossibility; for they had not reached any signs of habitation yet, and there was but one more portion of corn-meal and a little coffee left. They had but two matches now, and there had been no more flights of birds, nor brooks with fishes.

In fact, the man found a great deal to worry about as he lay there, too weary with the unaccustomed exercise and experiences to sleep.

He reflected that the girl had told him very little, after all, about her plans. He must ask her. He wished he knew more of her family. If he were only older and she younger, or if he had the right kind of a woman friend to whom he might take her, or send her! How horrible that that scoundrel was after her! Such men were not men, but beasts, and should be shot down.

Far off in the distance, it might have been in the air or in his imagination, there sometimes floated a sound as of faint voices or shouts; but they came and went, and he listened, and by and by heard no more. The horses breathed heavily behind their sage-brush stable, and the sun rose higher and hotter. At last sleep came, troubled, fitful, but sleep, oblivion. This time there was no lady in an automobile.

It was high noon when he awoke, for the sun had reached around the sage-brush, and was pouring full into his face. He was very uncomfortable, and moreover an uneasy sense of something wrong pervaded his mind. Had he or had he not, heard a strange, low, sibilant, writhing sound just as he came to consciousness? Why did he feel that something, someone, had passed him but a moment before?

He rubbed his eyes open, and fanned himself with his hat. There was not a sound to be heard save a distant hawk in the heavens, and the breathing of the horses. He stepped over, and made sure that they were all right, and then came back. Was the girl still sleeping? Should he call her? But what should he call her? She had no name to him as yet. He could not say, "My dear madam" in the wilderness, nor yet "mademoiselle."

Perhaps it was she who had passed him. Perhaps she was looking about for water, or for fire-wood. He cast his eyes about, but the thick growth of sage-brush everywhere prevented his seeing much. He stepped to the right and then to the left of the little enclosure where she had gone to sleep, but there was no sign of life.

At last the sense of uneasiness grew upon him until he spoke.

"Are you awake yet?" he ventured; but the words somehow stuck in his throat, and would not sound out clearly. He ventured the question again, but it seemed to go no further than the gray-green foliage in front of him. Did he catch an alert movement, the sound of attention, alarm? Had he perhaps frightened her?

His flesh grew creepy, and he was angry with himself that he stood here actually trembling and for no reason. He felt that there was danger in the air. What could it mean? He had never been a believer in premonitions or superstitions of any kind. But the thought came to him that perhaps that evil man had come softly while he slept, and had stolen the girl away. Then all at once a horror seized him, and he made up his mind to end this suspense and venture in to see whether she were safe.

Chapter 6

A Christian Endeavor Meeting in the Wilderness

He stepped boldly around the green barrier, and his first glance told him she was lying there still asleep; but the consciousness of another presence held him from going away. There, coiled on the ground with venomous fangs extended and eyes glittering like slimy jewels, was a rattlesnake, close beside her.

For a second he gazed with a kind of fascinated horror, and his brain refused to act. Then he knew he must do something, and at once. He had read of serpents and travellers' encounters with them, but no memory of what was to be done under such circumstances came. Shoot? He dared not. He would be more likely to kill the girl than the serpent, and in any event would precipitate the calamity. Neither was there any way to awaken the girl and drag her from peril, for the slightest movement upon her part would bring the poisoned fangs upon her.

He cast his eyes about for some weapon, but there was not a stick or a stone in sight. He was a good golf-player; if he had a loaded stick, he could easily take the serpent's head off, he thought; but there was no stick. There was only one hope, he felt, and that would be to attract the creature to himself; and he hardly dared move lest the fascinated gaze should close upon the victim as she lay there sweetly sleeping, unaware of her new peril.

Suddenly he knew what to do. Silently he stepped back out of sight, tore off his coat, and then cautiously approached the snake again, holding the coat up before him. There was an instant's pause when he calculated whether the coat could drop between the snake and the smooth brown arm in front before the terrible fangs would get there; and then the coat dropped, the man bravely holding one end of it as a wall between the serpent and the girl, crying to her in an agony of frenzy to awaken and run.

There was a terrible moment in which he realized that the girl was saved and he himself was in peril of death, while he held to the coat till the girl was on her feet in safety. Then he saw the writhing coil at his feet turn and fasten its eyes of fury upon him. He was conscious of being uncertain whether his fingers could let go the coat, and whether his trembling knees could carry him away before the serpent struck; then it was all over, and he and the girl were standing outside the sage-brush, with the sound of the pistol dying away among the echoes, and the fine ache of his arm where her fingers had grasped him to drag him from danger.

The serpent was dead. She had shot it. She took that as coolly as she had taken the bird in its flight. But she stood looking at him with great eyes of gratitude, and he looked at her amazed that they were both alive, and scarcely understanding all that had happened.

The girl broke the stillness.

"You are what they call a 'tenderfoot,' " she said significantly.

"Yes," he assented humbly, "I guess I am. I couldn't have shot it to save anybody's life."

"You are a tenderfoot, and you couldn't shoot," she continued eulogistically, as if it were necessary to have it all stated plainly, "but you—you are what my brother used to call 'a white man.' You couldn't shoot; but you could risk your life, and hold that coat, and look death in the face. *You* are no tenderfoot."

There was eloquence in her eyes, and in her voice there were tears. She turned away to hide if any were in her eyes. But the man put out his hand on her sure little brown one, and took it firmly in his own, looking down upon her with his own eyes filled with tears of which he was not ashamed.

"And what am I to say to you for saving my life?" he said.

"I? O, that was easy," said the girl, rousing to the commonplace. "I can always shoot. Only you were hard to drag away. You seemed to want to stay there and die with your coat."

"They laughed at me for wearing that coat when we started away. They said a hunter never bothered himself with extra clothing," he mused as they walked away from the terrible spot.

"Do you think it was the prayer?" asked the girl suddenly.

"It may be!" said the man with wondering accent.

Then quietly, thoughtfully, they mounted and rode onward.

Their way, due east, led them around the shoulder of a hill. It was tolerably smooth, but they were obliged to go single file, so there was very little talking done.

It was nearly the middle of the afternoon when all at once a sound reached them from below, a sound so new that it was startling. They stopped their horses, and looked at each other. It was the faint sound of singing wafted on the light breeze, singing that came in whiffs like a perfume, and then died out. Cautiously they guided their horses on around the hill, keeping close together now. It was plain they were approaching some human being or beings. No bird could sing like that. There were indistinct words to the music.

They rounded the hillside, and stopped again side by side. There below them lay the trail for which they had been searching, and just beneath them, nestled against the hill, was a little schoolhouse of logs, weather-boarded, its windows open; and behind it and around it were horses tied, some of them tied, some of them hitched to wagons, but most of them with saddles.

The singing was clear and distinct now. They could hear the words. "O, that will be glory for me, glory for me, glory for me——"

"What is it?" she whispered.

"Why, I suspect it is a Sunday school or something of the kind."

"O! A school! Could we go in?"

"If you like," said the man, enjoying her simplicity. "We can tie our horses here behind the building, and they can rest. There is fresh grass in this sheltered place; see?"

He led her down behind the schoolhouse to a spot where the horses could not be seen from the trail. The girl peered curiously around the corner into the window. There sat two young girls about her own age, and one of them smiled at her. It seemed an invitation. She smiled back, and went on to the doorway reassured. When she entered the room, she found them pointing to a seat near a window, behind a small desk.

There were desks all over the room at regular intervals, and a larger desk up in front. Almost all the people sat at desks.

There was a curious wooden box in front at one side of the big desk, and a girl sat before it pushing down some black and white strips that looked like sticks, and making her feet go, and singing with all her might. The curious box made music, the same music the people were singing. Was it a piano? she wondered. She had heard of pianos. Her father used to talk about them. O, and what was that her mother used to want? A "cab'net-organ." Perhaps this was a cab'net-organ. At any rate, she was entranced with the music.

Up behind the man who sat at the big desk was a large board painted black with some white marks on it. The sunlight glinted across it, and she could not tell what they were; but, when she moved a little, she saw quite clearly it was a large cross with words underneath it—"He will hide me."

It was a strange place. The girl looked around shyly, and felt submerged in the volume of song that rolled around her, from voices untrained, perhaps, but hearts that knew whereof they sang. To her it was heavenly music, if she had the least conception of what such music was like. "Glory," "glory," "glory!" The words seemed to fit the day, and the sunshine, and the deliverance that had come to her so recently. She looked around for her companion and deliverer to enjoy it with him, but he had not come in yet.

The two girls were handing her a book now and pointing to the place. She could read. Her mother had taught her just a little before the other children were born, but not much in the way of literature had ever come in her way. She grasped the book eagerly, hungrily, and looked where the finger pointed. Yes, there were the words. "Glory for me!" "Glory for me!" Did that mean her? Was there glory for her anywhere in the world? She sighed with the joy of the possibility, as the "Glory Song" rolled along, led by the enthusiasm of one who had recently come from a big city where it had been sung in a great revival service. Some kind friend had given some copies of a leaflet containing it and a few other new songs to this little handful of Christians, and they were singing them as if they had been a thousand strong.

The singing ceased and the man at the big desk said, "Let us have the verses."

" 'The eternal God is thy refuge, and underneath are the everlasting arms,' " said a careworn woman in the front seat.

" 'He shall cover thee with his feathers, and under his wings shalt thou trust,' " said a young man next.

" 'In the time of trouble he shall hide me in his pavilion; in the secret of his tabernacle shall he hide me,' " read the girl who had handed the book. The slip of paper she had written it on fluttered to the floor at the feet of the stranger, and the stranger stooped and picked it up, offering it back; but the other girl shook her head, and the stranger kept it, looking wonderingly at the words, trying to puzzle out a meaning.

There were other verses repeated, but just then a sound smote upon the girl's ear which deadened all others. In spite of herself she began to tremble. Even her lips seemed to her to move with the weakness of her fear. She looked up, and the man was just coming toward the door; but her eyes grew dizzy, and a faintness seemed to come over her.

Up the trail on horseback, with shouts and ribald songs, rode four rough men, too drunk to know where they were going. The little schoolhouse seemed to attract their attention as they passed, and just for deviltry they shouted out a volley of oaths and vile talk to the worshippers within. One in particular, the leader, looked straight into the face of the young man as he returned from fastening the horses and was about to enter the schoolhouse, and pretended to point his pistol at him, discharging it immediately into the air. This was the signal for some wild firing as the men rode on past the schoolhouse, leaving a train of curses behind them to haunt the air and struggle with the "Glory Song" in the memories of those who heard.

The girl looked out from her seat beside the window, and saw the evil face of the man from whom she had fled. She thought for a terrible minute, which seemed ages long to her, that she was cornered now. She began to look about on the people there helplessly, and wonder whether they would save her, would help her, in her time of need. Would they be able to fight and prevail against those four terrible men mad with liquor?

Suppose he said she was his—his wife, perhaps, or sister, who had run away. What could they do? Would they believe her? Would the man who had saved her life a few minutes ago believe her? Would anybody help her?

The party passed, and the man came in and sat down beside her quietly enough; but without a word or a look he knew at once who the man was he had just seen. His soul trembled for the girl, and his anger rose hot. He felt that a man like that ought to be wiped off the face of the earth in some way, or placed in solitary confinement the rest of his life.

He looked down at the girl, trembling, brave, white, beside him; and he felt like gathering her in his arms and hiding her himself, such a frail, brave, courageous little soul she seemed. But the calm nerve with which she had shot the serpent was gone now. He saw she was trembling and ready to cry. Then he smiled upon her, a smile the like of which he had never given to a human being before; at least, not since he was a tiny baby and smiled confidingly into his mother's face. Something in that smile was like sunshine to a nervous chill.

The girl felt the comfort of it, though she still trembled. Down her eyes drooped to the paper in her shaking hands. Then gradually, letter by letter, word by word, the verse spoke to her. Not all the meaning she gathered, for "pavilion" and "tabernacle" were unknown words to her, but the hiding she could understand. She had been hidden in her time of trouble. Someone had done it. "He"—the word would fit the man by her side, for he had helped to hide her, and to save her more than once; but just now there came a dim perception that it was some other He, some One greater who had worked this miracle and saved her once more to go on perhaps to better things.

There were many things said in that meeting, good and wise and true. They might have been helpful to the girl if she had understood, but her thoughts had much to do. One grain of truth she had gathered for her future use. There was a "hiding" somewhere in this world, and she had had it in a time of trouble. One moment more out upon the open, and the terrible man might have seen her.

There came a time of prayer in which all heads were bowed, and a voice here and there murmured a few soft little words which she did not comprehend; but at the close they all joined in "the prayer"; and, when she heard the words, "Our Father," she closed her eyes, which had been curiously open and watching, and joined her voice softly with the rest. Somehow it seemed to connect her safety with "our Father," and she felt a stronger faith than ever in her prayer.

The young man listened intently to all he heard. There was something strangely impressive to him in this simple worship out in what to him was a vast wilderness. He felt more of the true spirit of worship than he had ever felt at home sitting in the handsomely upholstered pew beside his mother and sister while the choir-boys chanted the processional and the light filtered through costly windows of many colors over the large and cultivated congregation. There was something about the words of these people that went straight to the heart more than all the intonings of the cultured voices he had ever heard. Truly they meant what they said, and God had been a reality to them in many a time of trouble. That seemed to be the theme of the afternoon, the saving power of the eternal God, made perfect through the need and the trust of His people. He was reminded more than once of the incident of the morning and the miraculous saving of his own and his companion's life.

When the meeting was over, the people gathered in groups and talked with one another. The girl who had handed the book came over and spoke to the strangers, putting out her hand pleasantly. She was the missionary's daughter.

"What is this? School?" asked the stranger eagerly.

"Yes, this is the schoolhouse," said the missionary's daughter; "but this meeting is Christian Endeavor. Do you live near here? Can't you come every time?"

"No, I live a long way off," said the girl sadly. "That is, I did. I don't live anywhere now. I'm going away."

"I wish you lived here. Then you could come to our meeting. Did you have a Christian Endeavor where you lived?"

"No. I never saw one before. It's nice. I like it."

Another girl came up now, and put out her hand in greeting. "You must come again," she said politely.

"I don't know," said the visitor. "I sha'n't be coming back soon."

"Are you going far?"

"As far as I can. I'm going East."

"O," said the inquisitor; and then, seeing the missionary's daughter was talking to someone else, she whispered, nodding toward the man, "Is he your husband?"

The girl looked startled, while a slow color mounted into her cheeks.

"No," said she gravely, thoughtfully. "But—he saved my life a little while ago."

"Oh!" said the other, awestruck. "My! And ain't he handsome? How did he do it?"

But the girl could not talk about it. She shuddered.

"It was a dreadful snake," she said, "and I was—I didn't see it. It was awful! I can't tell you about it."

"My!" said the girl. "How terrible!"

The people were passing out now. The man was talking with the missionary, asking the road to somewhere. The girl suddenly realized that this hour of preciousness was over, and life was to be faced again. Those men, those terrible men! She had recognized the others as having been among her brother's funeral train. Where were they, and why had they gone that way? Were they on her track? Had they any clue to her whereabouts? Would they turn back pretty soon, and catch her when the people were gone home?

It appeared that the nearest town was Malta, sixteen miles away, down in the direction where the party of men had passed. There were only four houses near the schoolhouse, and they were scattered in different directions along the stream in the valley. The two stood still near the door after the congregation had scattered. The girl suddenly shivered. As she looked down the road, she seemed again to see the coarse face of the man she feared, and to hear his loud laughter and oaths. What if he should come back again? "I cannot go that way!" she said, pointing down the trail toward Malta. "I would rather die with wild beasts."

"No!" said the man with decision. "On no account can we go that way. Was that the man you ran away from?"

"Yes." She looked up at him, her eyes filled with wonder over the way in which he had coupled his lot with hers.

"Poor little girl!" he said with deep feeling. "You would be better off with the beasts. Come, let us hurry away from here!"

They turned sharply away from the trail, and followed down behind a family who were almost out of sight around the hill. There would be a chance of getting some provisions, the man thought. The girl thought of nothing except to get away. They rode hard, and soon came within hailing-distance of the people ahead of them, and asked a few questions.

No, there were no houses to the north until you were over the Canadian line, and the trail was hard to follow. Few people went that way. Most went down to Malta. Why didn't they go to Malta? There was a road there, and stores. It was by all means the best way. Yes, there was another house about twenty miles away on this trail. It was a large ranch, and was near to another town that had a railroad. The people seldom came this way, as there were other places more accessible to them. The trail was little used, and might be hard to find in some places; but, if they kept the Cottonwood Creek in sight, and followed on to the end of the valley, and then crossed the bench to the right, they would be in sight of it, and couldn't miss it. It was a good twenty miles beyond their house; but, if the travellers didn't miss the way, they might reach it before dark. Yes, the people could supply a few provisions at their house if the strangers didn't mind taking what was at hand.

The man in the wagon tried his best to find out where the two were going and what they were going for; but the man from the East baffled his curiosity in a most dexterous manner, so that, when the two rode away from the two-roomed log house where the kind-hearted people lived, they left no clue to their identity or mission beyond the fact that they were going quite a journey, and had got a little off their trail and run out of provisions.

They felt comparatively safe from pursuit for a few hours at least, for the men could scarcely return and trace them very soon. They had not stopped to eat anything; but all the milk they could drink had been given to them, and its refreshing strength was racing through their veins. They started upon their long ride with the pleasure of their companionship strong upon them.

"What was it all about?" asked the girl as they settled into a steady gait after a long gallop across a smooth level place.

He looked at her questioningly.

"The school. What did it mean? She said it was a Christian Endeavor. What is that?"

"Why, some sort of a religious meeting, or something of that kind, I suppose," he answered lamely. "Did you enjoy it?"

"Yes," she answered solemnly, "I liked it. I never went to such a thing before. The girl said they had one everywhere all over the world. What do you think she meant?"

"Why, I don't know, I'm sure, unless it's some kind of a society. But it looked to me like a prayer meeting. I've heard about prayer meetings, but I never went to one, though I never supposed they were so interesting. That was a remarkable story that old man told of how he was taken care of that night among the Indians. He evidently believes that prayer helps people."

"Don't you?" she asked quickly.

"O, certainly!" he said, "but there was something so genuine about the way the old man told it that it made you feel it in a new way."

"It is all new to me," said the girl. "But mother used to go to Sunday school and church and prayer meeting. She's often told me about it. She used to sing sometimes. One song was 'Rock of Ages.' Did you ever hear that?

   'Rock of Ages, cleft for me,
   Let me hide myself in Thee.' "

She said it slowly and in a singsong voice, as if she were measuring the words off to imaginary notes. "I thought about that the night I started. I wished I knew where that rock was. Is there a rock anywhere that they call the Rock of Ages?"

The young man was visibly embarrassed. He wanted to laugh, but he would not hurt her in that way again. He was not accustomed to talking religion; yet here by this strange girl's side it seemed perfectly natural that he, who knew so very little experimentally himself about it, should be trying to explain the Rock of Ages to a soul in need. All at once it flashed upon him that it was for just such souls in need as this one that the Rock of Ages came into the world.

"I've heard the song. Yes, I think they sing it in all churches. It's quite common. No, there isn't any place called Rock of Ages. It refers—that is, I believe—why, you see the thing is figurative—that is, a kind of picture of things. It refers to the Deity."

"O! Who is that?" asked the girl.

"Why—God." He tried to say it as if he had been telling her it was Mr. Smith or Mr. Jones, but somehow the sound of the word on his lips thus shocked him. He did not know how to go on. "It just means God will take care of people."

"O!" she said, and this time a light of understanding broke over her face. "But," she added, "I wish I knew what it meant, the meeting, and why they did it. There must be some reason. They wouldn't do it for nothing. And how do you know it's all so? Where did they find it out?"

The man felt he was beyond his depth; so he sought to change the subject. "I wish you would tell me about yourself," he said gently. "I should like to understand you better. We have travelled together for a good many hours now, and we ought to know more about each other."

"What do you want to know?" She asked it gravely. "There isn't much to tell but what I've told you. I've lived on a mountain all my life, and helped mother. The rest all died. The baby first, and my two brothers, and father, and mother, and then John. I said the prayer for John, and ran away."

"Yes, but I want to know about your life. You know I live in the East where everything is different. It's all new to me out here. I want to know, for instance, how you came to talk so well. You don't talk like a girl that never went to school. You speak as if you had read and studied. You make so few mistakes in your English. You speak quite correctly. That is not usual, I believe, when people have lived all their lives away from school, you know. You don't talk like the girls I have met since I came out here."

"Father always made me speak right. He kept at every one of us children when we said a word wrong, and made us say it over again. It made him angry to hear words said wrong. He made mother cry once when she said 'done' when she ought to have said 'did.' Father went to school once, but mother only went a little while. Father knew a great deal, and when he was sober he used to teach us things once in a while. He taught me to read. I can read anything I ever saw."

"Did you have many books and magazines?" he asked innocently.

"We had three books!" she answered proudly, as if that were a great many. "One was a grammar. Father bought it for mother before they were married, and she always kept it wrapped up in paper carefully. She used to get it out for me to read in sometimes; but she was very careful with it, and when she died I put it in her hands. I thought she would like to have it close to her, because it always seemed so much to her. You see father bought it. Then there was an almanac, and a book about stones and earth. A man who was hunting for gold left that. He stopped over night at our house, and asked for something to eat. He hadn't any money to pay for it; so he left that book with us, and said when he found the gold he would come and buy it back again. But he never came back."

"Is that all that you have ever read?" he asked compassionately.

"O, no! We got papers sometimes. Father would come home with a whole paper wrapped around some bundle. Once there was a beautiful story about a girl; but the paper was torn in the middle, and I never knew how it came out."

There was great wistfulness in her voice. It seemed to be one of the regrets of her girlhood that she did not know how that other girl in the story fared. All at once she turned to him.

"Now tell me about your life," she said. "I'm sure you have a great deal to tell."

His face darkened in a way that made her sorry.

"O, well," said he as if it mattered very little about his life, "I had a nice home—have yet, for the matter of that. Father died when I was little, and mother let me do just about as I pleased. I went to school because the other fellows did, and because that was the thing to do. After I grew up I liked it. That is, I liked some studies; so I went to a university."

"What is that?"

"O, just a higher school where you learn grown-up things. Then I travelled. When I came home, I went into society a good deal. But"—and his face darkened again—"I got tired of it all, and thought I would come out here for a while and hunt, and I got lost, and I found you!" He smiled into her face. "Now you know the rest."

Something passed between them in that smile and glance, a flash of the recognition of souls, and a gladness in each other's company, that made the heart warm. They said no more for some time, but rode quietly side by side.

They had come to the end of the valley, and were crossing the bench. The distant ranch could quite distinctly be seen. The silver moon had come up, for they had not been hurrying, and a great beauty pervaded everything. They almost shrank from approaching the buildings and people. They had enjoyed the ride and the companionship. Every step brought them nearer to what they had known all the time was an indistinct future from which they had been joyously shut away for a little time till they might know each other.

Chapter 7

Bad News

They found rest for the night at the ranch house. The place was wide and hospitable. The girl looked about her with wonder on the comfortable arrangements for work. If only her mother had had such a kitchen to work in, and such a pleasant, happy home, she might have been living yet. There was a pleasant-faced, sweet-voiced woman with gray hair whom the men called "mother." She gave the girl a kindly welcome, and made her sit down to a nice warm supper, and, when it was over, led her to a little room where her own bed was, and told her she might sleep with her. The girl lay down in a maze of wonder, but was too weary with the long ride to keep awake and think about it.

They slept, the two travellers, a sound and dreamless sleep, wherein seemed peace and moonlight, and a forgetting of sorrows.

Early the next morning the girl awoke. The woman by her side was already stirring. There was breakfast to get for the men. The woman asked her a few questions about her journey.

"He's your brother, ain't he, dearie?" asked the woman as she was about to leave the room.

"No," said the girl.

"O," said the woman, puzzled, "then you and he's goin' to be married in the town."

"O, no!" said the girl with scarlet cheeks, thinking of the lady in the automobile.

"Not goin' to be married, dearie? Now that's too bad. Ain't he any kind of relation to you? Not an uncle nor cousin nor nothin'?"

"No."

"Then how be's you travellin' lone with him? It don't seem just

69

right. You's a sweet, good girl; an' he's a fine man. But harm's come to more'n one. Where'd you take up with each other? Be he a neighbor? He looks like a man from way off, not hereabouts. You sure he ain't deceivin' you, dearie?"

The girl flashed her eyes in answer.

"Yes, I'm sure. He's a good man. He prays to our Father. No, he's not a neighbor, nor an uncle, nor a cousin. He's just a man that got lost. We were both lost on the prairie in the night; and he's from the East, and got lost from his party of hunters. He had nothing to eat, but I had; so I gave him some. Then he saved my life when a snake almost stung me. He's been good to me."

The woman looked relieved.

"And where you goin', dearie, all 'lone? What your folks thinkin' 'bout to let you go 'lone this way?"

"They're dead," said the girl with great tears in her eyes.

"Dearie me! And you so young! Say, dearie, s'pose you stay here with me. I'm lonesome, an' there's no women near by here. You could help me and be comp'ny. The men would like to have a girl round. There's plenty likely men on this ranch could make a good home for a girl sometime. Stay here with me, dearie."

Had this refuge been offered the girl during her first night in the wilderness, with what joy and thankfulness she would have accepted! Now it suddenly seemed a great impossibility for her to stay. She must go on. She had a pleasant ride before her, and delightful companionship; and she was going to school. The world was wide, and she had entered it. She had no mind to pause thus on the threshold, and never see further than Montana. Moreover, the closing words of the woman did not please her.

"I cannot stay," she said decidedly. "I'm going to school. And I do not want a man. I have just run away from a man, a dreadful one. I am going to school in the East. I have some relations there, and perhaps I can find them."

"You don't say so!" said the woman, looking disappointed. She had taken a great fancy to the sweet young face. "Well, dearie, why not stay here a little while, and write to your folks, and then go on with

someone who is going your way? I don't like to see you go off with that
man. It ain't the proper thing. He knows it himself. I'm afraid he's deceivin' you. I can see by his clo'es he's one of the fine young fellows
that does as they please. He won't think any good of you if you keep
travellin' 'lone with him. It's all well 'nough when you get lost, an' he
was nice to help you out and save you from snakes; but he knows he
ain't no business travellin' 'lone with you, you pretty little creature."

"You must not talk so!" said the girl, rising and flashing her eyes
again. "He's a good man. He's what my brother called 'a white man all
through.' Besides, he's got a lady, a beautiful lady, in the East. She
rides in some kind of a grand carriage that goes of itself, and he thinks
a great deal of her."

The woman looked as if she were but half convinced.

"It may seem all right to you, dearie," she said sadly; "but I'm old,
and I've seen things happen. You'd find his fine lady wouldn't go jan-
tin' round the world 'lone with him unless she's married. I've lived
East, and I know; and what's more, he knows it too. He may mean all
right, but you never can trust folks."

The woman went away to prepare breakfast then, and left the girl
feeling as if the whole world was against her, trying to hold her. She
was glad when the man suggested that they hurry their breakfast and
get away as quickly as possible. She did not smile when the old woman
came out to bid her good-by, and put a detaining hand on the horse's
bridle, saying "You better stay with me, after all, hadn't you, dearie?"

The man looked inquiringly at the two women, and saw like a flash
the suspicion of the older woman, read the trust and haughty anger in
the beautiful younger face, and then smiled down on the old woman
whose kindly hospitality had saved them for a while from the terrors of
the open night, and said:

"Don't you worry about her, auntie. I'm going to take good care of
her, and perhaps she'll write you a letter some day, and tell you where
she is and what she's doing."

Half reassured, the old woman gave him her name and address; and
he wrote them down in a little red notebook.

When they were well started on their way, the man explained that he had hurried because from conversation with the men he had learned that this ranch where they had spent the night was on the direct trail from Malta to another small town. It might be that the pursuers would go further than Malta. Did she think they would go so far? They must have come almost a hundred miles already. Would they not be discouraged?

But the girl looked surprised. A hundred miles on horseback was not far. Her brother often used to ride a hundred miles just to see a fight or have a good time. She felt sure the men would not hesitate to follow a long distance if something else did not turn them aside.

The man's face looked sternly out from under his wide hat. He felt a great responsibility for the girl since he had seen the face of the man who was pursuing her.

Their horses were fresh, and the day was fine. They rode hard as long as the road was smooth, and did little talking. The girl was turning over in her mind the words the woman had spoken to her. But the thing that stuck there and troubled her was, "And he knows it is so."

Was she doing something for which this man by her side would not respect her? Was she overstepping some unwritten law of which she had never heard, and did he know it, and yet encourage her in it?

That she need fear him in the least she would not believe. Had she not watched the look of utmost respect on his face as he stood quietly waiting for her to awake the first morning they had met? Had he not had opportunity again and again to show her dishonor by word or look? Yet he had never been anything but gentle and courteous to her. She did not call things by these names, but she felt the gentleman in him.

Besides, there was the lady. He had told about her at the beginning. He evidently honored the lady. The woman had said that the lady would not ride with him alone. Was it true? Would he not like to have the lady ride alone with him when she was not his relative in any way? Then was there a difference between his thought of the lady and of herself? Of course, there was some; he loved the lady, but he should not think less honorably of her than of any lady in the land.

She sat straight and proudly in her man's saddle, and tried to make him feel that she was worthy of respect. She had tried to show him this when she had shot the bird. Now she recognized that there was a fine something, higher than shooting or prowess of any kind, which would command respect. It was something she felt belonged to her, yet she was not sure she commanded it. What did she lack, and how could she secure it?

He watched her quiet, thoughtful face, and the lady of his former troubled thoughts was as utterly forgotten by him as if she had never existed. He was unconsciously absorbed in the study of eye and lip and brow. His eyes were growing accustomed to the form and feature of this girl beside him, and he took pleasure in watching her.

They stopped for lunch in a coulee under a pretty cluster of cedar-trees a little back from the trail, where they might look over the way they had come and be warned against pursuers. About three o'clock they reached a town. Here the railroad came directly from Malta, but there was but one train a day each way.

The man went to the public stopping-place and asked for a room, and boldly demanded a private place for his "sister" to rest for a while. "She is my little sister," he told himself in excuse for the word. "She is my sister to care for. That is, if she were my sister, this is what I should want some good man to do for her."

He smiled as he went on his way after leaving the girl to rest. The thought of a sister pleased him. The old woman at the ranch had made him careful for the girl who was thus thrown in his company.

He rode down through the rough town to the railway station, but a short distance from the rude stopping-place; and there he made inquiries concerning roads, towns, etc., in the neighboring locality, and sent a telegram to the friends with whom he had been hunting when he got lost. He said he would be at the next town about twenty miles away. He knew that by this time they would be back home and anxious about him, if they were not already sending out searching parties for him. His message read:

"Hit the trail all right. Am taking a trip for my health. Send mail to me at——"

Then after careful inquiry as to directions, and learning that there

was more than one route to the town he had mentioned in his telegram, he went back to his companion. She was ready to go, for the
presence of other people about her made her uneasy. She feared again
there would be objection to their further progress together. Somehow
the old woman's words had grown into a shadow which hovered over
her. She mounted her horse gladly, and they went forward. He told her
what he had just done, and how he expected to get his mail the next
morning when they reached the next town. He explained that there
was a ranch half-way there where they might stop all night.

She was troubled at the thought of another ranch. She knew there
would be more questions, and perhaps other disagreeable words said;
but she held her peace, listening to his plans. Her wonder was great
over the telegram. She knew little or nothing about modern discover-
ies. It was a mystery to her how he could receive word by morning
from a place that it had taken them nearly two days to leave behind,
and how had he sent a message over a wire? Yes, she had heard of telegrams, but had never been quite sure they were true. When he saw that
she was interested, he went on to tell her of other wonderful triumphs
of science, the telephone, the electric light, gas, and the modern system
of waterworks. She listened as if it were all a fairy tale. Sometimes she
looked at him, and wondered whether it could be true, or whether he
were not making fun of her; but his earnest, honest eyes forbade
doubt.

At the ranch they found two women, a mother and her daughter.
The man asked frankly whether they could take care of this young
friend of his overnight, saying that she was going on to the town in the
morning, and was in his care for the journey. This seemed to relieve all
suspicion. The two girls eyed each other, and then smiled.

"I'm Myrtle Baker," said the ranch-owner's daughter. "Come; I'll
take you where you can wash your hands and face, and then we'll have
some supper."

Myrtle Baker was a chatterer by nature. She talked incessantly; and,
though she asked many questions, she did not wait for half of them to
be answered. Besides, the traveller had grown wary. She did not intend
to talk about the relationship between herself and her travelling com-

panion. There was a charm in Myrtle's company which made the girl half regret leaving the next morning, as they did quite early, amid protests from Myrtle and her mother, who enjoyed a visitor in their isolated home.

But the ride that morning was constrained. Each felt in some subtle way that their pleasant companionship was coming to a crisis. Ahead in that town would be letters, communications from the outside world of friends, people who did not know or care what these two had been through together, and who would not hesitate to separate them with a firm hand. Neither put this thought into words, but it was there in their hearts, in the form of a vague fear. They talked very little, but each was feeling how pleasant the journey had been, and dreading what might be before.

They wanted to stay in this Utopia of the plains, forever journeying together, and never reaching any troublesome futures where were laws and opinions by which they must abide.

But the morning grew bright, and the road was not half long enough. Though at the last they walked their horses, they reached the town before the daily train had passed through. They went straight to the station, and found that the train was an hour late; but a telegram had arrived for the man. He took it nervously, his fingers trembling. He felt a premonition that it contained something unpleasant.

The girl sat on her horse by the platform, watching him through the open station door where he was standing as he tore open the envelope. She saw a deathly pallor overspread his face, and a look of anguish as if an arrow had pierced his heart. She felt as if the arrow had gone on into her own heart, and then she sat and waited. It seemed hours before he glanced up, with an old, weary look in his eyes. The message read:

"Your mother seriously ill. Wants you immediately. Will send your baggage on morning train. Have wired you are coming."

It was signed by his cousin with whom he had been taking his hunting-trip, and who was bound by business to go further West within a few days more.

The strong young man was almost bowed under this sudden shock.

His mother was very dear to him. He had left her well and happy. He must go to her at once, of course; but what should he do with the girl who had within the last two days taken so strong a hold upon his—he hesitated, and called it "protection." That word would do in the present emergency.

Then he looked, and saw her own face pale under the tan, and stepped out to the platform to tell her.

Chapter 8

The Parting

She took the news like a Spartan. Her gentle pity was simply expressed, and then she held her peace. He must go. He must leave her. She knew that the train would carry him to his mother's bedside quicker than a horse could go. She felt by the look in his eyes and the set of his mouth that he had already decided that. Of course he must go. And the lady was there too! His mother and the lady! The lady would be sorry by this time, and would love him. Well, it was all right. He had been good to her. He had been a strong, bright angel God had sent to help her out of the wilderness; and now that she was safe the angel must return to his heaven. This was what she thought.

He had gone into the station to inquire about the train. It was an hour late. He had one short hour in which to do a great deal. He had very little money with him. Naturally men do not carry a fortune when they go into the wilderness for a day's shooting. Fortunately he had his railroad return ticket to Philadelphia. That would carry him safely. But the girl. She of course had no money. And where was she going? He realized that he had failed to ask her many important questions. He hurried out, and explained to her.

"The train is an hour late. We must sell our horses, and try to get money enough to take us East. It is the only way. Where do you intend going?"

But the girl stiffened in her seat. She knew it was her opportunity to show that she was worthy of his honor and respect.

"I cannot go with you," she said very quietly.

"But you must," said he impatiently. "Don't you see there is no other way? I must take this train and get to my mother as soon as possible. She may not be living when I reach her if I don't." Something caught in his throat as he uttered the horrible thought that kept coming to his mind.

"I know," said the girl quietly. "You must go, but I must ride on."

"And why? I should like to know. Don't you see that I cannot leave you here alone? Those villains may be upon us at any minute. In fact, it is a good thing for us to board the train and get out of their miserable country as fast as steam can carry us. I am sorry you must part with your horse, for I know you are attached to it; but perhaps we can arrange to sell it to someone who will let us redeem it when we send the money out. You see I have not money enough with me to buy you a ticket. I couldn't get home myself if I hadn't my return ticket with me in my pocket. But surely the sale of both horses will bring enough to pay your way."

"You are very kind, but I must not go." The red lips were firm, and the girl was sitting very erect. She looked as she had done after she had shot the bird.

"But why?"

"I cannot travel alone with you. It is not your custom where you come from. The woman on the ranch told me. She said you knew girls did not do that, and that you did not respect me for going alone with you. She said it was not right, and that you knew it."

He looked at her impatient, angry, half ashamed that she should face him with these words.

"Nonsense!" said he. "This is a case of necessity. You are to be taken care of, and I am the one to do it."

"But it is not the custom among people where you live, is it?"

The clear eyes faced him down, and he had to admit that it was not.

"Then I can't go," she said decidedly.

"But you must. If you don't, I won't go."

"But you must," said the girl, "and I mustn't. If you talk that way, I'll run away from you. I've run away from one man, and I guess I can from another. Besides, you're forgetting the lady."

"What lady?"

"Your lady. The lady who rides in a carriage without horses."

"Hang the lady!" he said inelegantly. "Do you know that the train will be along here in less than an hour, and we have a great deal to do before we can get on board? There's no use stopping to talk about this matter. We haven't time. If you will just trust things to me, I'll attend to them all, and I'll answer your questions when we get safely on the train. Every instant is precious. Those men might come around that corner over there any minute. That's all bosh about respect. I respect you more than any woman I ever met. And it's my business to take care of you."

"No, it's not your business," said the girl bravely, "and I can't let you. I'm nothing to you, you know."

"You're every—that is—why, you surely know you're a great deal to me. Why, you saved my life, you know!"

"Yes, and you saved mine. That was beautiful, but that's all."

"Isn't that enough? What are you made of, anyway, to sit there when there's so much to be done, and those villains on our track, and insist that you won't be saved? Respect you! Why, a lion in the wilderness would have to respect you. You're made of iron and steel and precious stones. You've the courage of a—a—I was going to say a man, but I mean an angel. You're pure as snow, and true as the heavenly blue, and firm as a rock; and, if I had never respected you before, I would have to now. I respect, I honor, I—I—I—pray for you!" he finished fiercely.

He turned his back to hide his emotions.

She lifted her eyes to his when he turned again, and her own were full of tears.

"Thank you!" She said it very simply. "That makes me—very—glad! But I cannot go with you."

"Do you mean that?" he asked her desperately.

"Yes," steadily.

"Then I shall have to stay too."

"But you can't! You must go to your mother. I won't be stayed with. And what would she think? Mothers are—everything!" she finished. "You must go quick and get ready. What can I do to help?"

He gave her a look which she remembered long years afterward.

It seemed to burn and sear its way into her soul. How was it that a stranger had the power to scorch her with anguish this way? And she him?

He turned, still with that desperate, half-frantic look in his face, and accosted two men who stood at the other end of the platform. They were not in particular need of a horse at present; but they were always ready to look at a bargain, and they walked speculatively down the uneven boards of the platform with him to where his horse stood, and inspected it.

The girl watched the whole proceeding with eyes that saw not but into the future. She put in a word about the worth of the saddle once when she saw it was going lower than it should. Three other men gathered about before the bargain was concluded, and the horse and its equipment sold for about half its value.

That done, the man turned toward the girl and motioned to her to lead her horse away to a more quiet place, and set him down to plead steadily against her decision. But the talk and the horse-selling had taken more time than he realized. The girl was more decided than ever in her determination not to go with him. She spoke of the lady again. She spoke of his mother, and mothers in general, and finished by reminding him that God would take care of her, and of him, too.

Then they heard the whistle of the train, and saw it growing from a speck to a large black object across the plain. To the girl the sight of this strange machine, that seemed more like a creature rushing toward her to snatch all beauty and hope and safety from her, sent a thrill of horror. To the man it seemed like a dreaded fate that was tearing him asunder. He had barely time to divest himself of his powder-horn, and a few little things that might be helpful to the girl in her journey, before the train was halting at the station. Then he took from his pocket the money that had been paid him for his horse; and, selecting a five-dollar bill for himself, he wrapped the rest in an envelope bearing his own name and address. The envelope was one addressed by the lady at home. It had contained some gracefully worded refusal of a request. But he did not notice now what envelope he gave her.

"Take this," he said. "It will help a little. Yes, you must! I cannot leave you—I *will* not—unless you do," when he saw that she hesitated and looked doubtful. "I owe you all and more for saving my life. I can never repay you. Take it. You may return it sometime when you get plenty more of your own, if it hurts your pride to keep it. Take it, please. Yes, I have plenty for myself. You will need it, and you must stop at nice places overnight. You will be very careful, won't you? My name is on that envelope. You must write to me and let me know that you are safe."

"Someone is calling you, and that thing is beginning to move again," said the girl, an awesome wonder in her face. "You will be left behind! O, hurry ! Quick! Your mother!"

He half turned toward the train, and then came back.

"You haven't told me your name!" he gasped. "Tell me quick!"

She caught her breath.

"Elizabeth!" she answered, and waved him from her.

The conductor of the train was shouting to him, and two men shoved him toward the platform. He swung himself aboard with the accustomed ease of a man who has travelled; but he stood on the platform, and shouted, "Where are you going?" as the train swung noisily off.

She did not hear him, but waved her hand, and gave him a bright smile that was brimming with unshed tears. It seemed like instant, daring suicide in him to stand on that swaying, clattering house as it moved off irresponsibly down the plane of vision. She watched him till he was out of sight, a mere speck on the horizon of the prairie; and then she turned her horse slowly into the road, and went her way into the world alone.

The man stood on the platform, and watched her as he whirled away—a little brown girl on a little brown horse, so stanch and firm and stubborn and good. Her eyes were dear, and her lips as she smiled; and her hand was beautiful as it waved him good-by. She was dear, dear, dear! Why had he not known it? Why had he left her? Yet how could he stay? His mother was dying perhaps. He must not fail her in what might be her last summons. Life and death were pulling at his heart, tearing him asunder.

The vision of the little brown girl and the little brown horse blurred and faded. He tried to look, but could not see. He brought his eyes to nearer vision to fix their focus for another look, and straight before him whirled a shackly old saloon, rough and tumble, its character apparent from the men who were grouped about its doorway and from the barrels and kegs in profusion outside. From the doorway issued four men, wiping their mouths and shouting hilariously. Four horses stood tied to a fence nearby. They were so instantly passed, and so vaguely seen, that he could not be sure in the least, but those four men reminded him strongly of the four who had passed the schoolhouse on Sunday.

He shuddered, and looked back. The little brown horse and the little brown girl were one with the little brown station so far away, and presently the saloon and men were blotted out in one blur of green and brown and yellow.

He looked to the ground in his despair. He *must* go back. He could not leave her in such peril. She was his to care for by all the rights of manhood and womanhood. She had been put in his way. It was his duty.

But the ground whirled by under his madness, and showed him plainly that to jump off would be instant death. Then the thought of his mother came again, and the girl's words, "I am nothing to you, you know."

The train whirled its way between two mountains and the valley, and the green and brown and yellow blur were gone from sight. He felt as if he had just seen the coffin close over the girl's sweet face, and he had done it.

By and by he crawled into the car, pulled his slouch hat down over his eyes, and settled down in a seat; but all the time he was trying to see over again that old saloon and those four men, and to make out their passing identity. Sometimes the agony of thinking it all over, and trying to make out whether those men had been the pursuers, made him feel frantic; and it seemed as if he must pull the bell-cord, and make the train stop, and get off to walk back. Then the utter hopelessness of ever finding her would come over him, and he would settle back in his seat again and try to sleep. But the least drowsiness would bring a vision of the girl galloping alone over the prairie with the four men in full pursuit behind. "Elizabeth, Elizabeth!" the car-wheels seemed to say.

Elizabeth—that was all he had of her. He did not know the rest of her name, nor where she was going. He did not even know where she had come from, just "Elizabeth" and "Montana." If anything happened to her, he would never know. Oh! why had he left her? Why had he not *made* her go with him? In a case like that a man should assert his authority. But, then, it was true he had none, and she had said she would run away. She would have done it too. O, if it had been anything but sickness and possible death at the other end—and his mother, his own little mother! Nothing else would have kept him from staying to protect Elizabeth.

What a fool he had been! There were questions he might have asked, and plans they might have made, all those beautiful days and those moon-silvered nights. If any other man had done the same, he would have thought him lacking mentally. But here he had maundered on, and never found out the all-important things about her. Yet how did he know then how important they were to be? It had seemed as if they had all the world before them in the brilliant sunlight. How could he know that modern improvements were to seize him in the midst of a prairie waste, and whirl him off from her when he had just begun to know what she was, and to prize her company as a most precious gift dropped down from heaven at his feet?

By degrees he came out of his hysterical frenzy, and returned to a somewhat normal state of mind. He reasoned himself several times into the belief that those men were not in the least like the men he had seen Sunday. He knew that one could not recognize one's own brother at that distance and that rate of passing speed. He tried to think that Elizabeth would be cared for. She had come through many a danger, and was it likely that the God in whom she trusted, who had guarded her so many times in her great peril, would desert her now in her dire need? Would He not raise up help for her somewhere? Perhaps another man as good as he, and as trustworthy as he had tried to be, would find her and help her.

But that thought was not pleasant. He put it away impatiently. It cut him. Why had she talked so much about the lady? The lady! Ah! How was it the lady came no more into his thoughts? The memory of her haughty face no more quickened his heart-beats. Was he fickle that he could lose what he had supposed was a lifelong passion in a few days?

The darkness was creeping on. Where was Elizabeth? Had she found a refuge for the night? Or was she wandering on an unknown trail, hearing voices and oaths through the darkness, and seeing the gleaming of wild eyes low in the bushes ahead? How could he have left her? How could he? He must go back even yet. He must, he must, *he must!*

And so it went on through the long night.

The train stopped at several places to take on water; but there seemed to be no human habitation near, or else his eyes were dim with his trouble. Once, when they stopped longer than the other times, he got up and walked the length of the car and down the steps to the ground. He even stood there, and let the train start jerkily on till his car had passed him, and the steps were just sliding by, and tried to think whether he would not stay, and go back in some way to find her. Then the impossibility of the search, and of his getting back in time to do any good, helped him to spring on board just before it was too late. He walked back to his seat saying to himself, "Fool! Fool!"

It was not till morning that he remembered his baggage and went in search of it. There he found a letter from his cousin, with other letters and telegrams explaining the state of affairs at home. He came back to his seat laden with a large leather grip and a suitcase. He sat down to read his letters, and these took his mind away from his troubled thoughts for a little while. There was a letter from his mother, sweet, graceful, half wistfully offering her sympathy. He saw she guessed the reason why he had left her and gone to this far place. Dear little mother! What would she say if she knew his trouble now? And then would return his heart-frenzy over Elizabeth's peril. O to know that she was protected, hidden!

Fumbling in his pocket, he came upon a slip of paper, the slip the girl had given Elizabeth in the schoolhouse on Sunday afternoon. "For in the time of trouble he shall hide me in his pavilion; in the secret of his tabernacle shall he hide me."

Ah! God had hidden her then. Why not again? And what was that he had said to her himself, when searching for a word to cover his emotion? "I pray for you!" Why could he not pray? She had made him pray in the wilderness. Should he not pray for her who was in peril now? He leaned back in the hot, uncomfortable car-seat, pulling his hat down closer over his eyes, and prayed as he had never prayed before. "Our Father" he stumbled through as far as he could remember, and tried to think how her sweet voice had filled in the places where he had not known it the other time. Then, when he was done, he waited and prayed, "Our Father, care for Elizabeth," and added, "For Jesus' sake. Amen." Thereafter through the rest of his journey, and for days and weeks stretching ahead, he prayed that prayer, and sometimes found in it his only solace from the terrible fear that possessed him lest some harm had come to the girl, whom it seemed to him now he had deserted in cold blood.

Chapter 9

In a Trap

ELIZABETH rode straight out to the east, crossing the town as rapidly as possible, going full gallop where the streets were empty. On the edge of the town she crossed another trail running back the way that they had come; but without swerving she turned out toward the world, and soon passed into a thick growth of trees, around a hill.

Not three minutes elapsed after she had passed the crossing of the trails before the four men rode across from the other direction, and, pausing, called to one another, looking this way and that:

"What d'ye think, Bill? Shall we risk the right hand 'r the left?"

"Take the left hand fer luck," answered Bill. "Let's go over to the ranch and ask. Ef she's been hereabouts, she's likely there. The old woman 'll know. Come on, boys!"

And who shall say that the angel of the Lord did not stand within the crossing of the ways and turn aside the evil men?

Elizabeth did not stop her fierce ride until about noon. The frenzy of her fear of pursuit had come upon her with renewed force. Now that she was alone and desolate she dared not look behind her. She had been strong enough as she smiled her farewell; but, when the train had dwindled into a mere speck in the distance, her eyes were dropping tears thick and fast upon the horse's mane. So in the first heaviness of her loneliness she rode as if pursued by enemies close at hand.

But the horse must rest if she did not, for he was her only dependence now. So she sat her down in the shade of a tree, and tried to eat some dinner. The tears came again as she opened the pack which the man's strong hands had bound together for her. How little she had thought at breakfast-time that she would eat the next meal alone!

It was all well enough to tell him he must go, and say she was nothing to him; but it was different now to face the world without a single friend when one had learned to know how good a friend could be. Almost it would have been better if he had never found her, never saved her from the serpent, never ridden beside her and talked of wonderful new things to her; for now that he was gone the emptiness and loneliness were so much harder to bear; and now she was filled with a longing for things that could not be hers.

It was well he had gone so soon, well she had no longer to grow into the charm of his society; for he belonged to the lady, and was not hers. Thus she ate her dinner with the indifference of sorrow.

Then she took out the envelope, and counted over the money. Forty dollars he had given her. She knew he had kept but five for himself. How wonderful that he should have done all that for her! It seemed a very great wealth in her possession. Well, she would use it as sparingly as possible, and thus be able the sooner to return it all to him. Some she must use, she supposed, to buy food; but she would do with as little as she could. She might sometimes shoot a bird, or catch a fish; or there might be berries fit for food by the way. Nights she must stop by the way at a respectable house. That she had promised. He had told her of awful things that might happen to her if she lay down in the wilderness alone. Her lodging would sometimes cost her something. Yet often they would take her in for nothing. She would be careful of the money.

She studied the name on the envelope. George Trescott Benedict, 2——Walnut Street, Philadelphia, Penn. The letters were large and angular, not easy to read; but she puzzled them out. It did not look like his writing. She had watched him as he wrote the old woman's address in his little red book. He wrote small, round letters, slanting backwards, plain as print, pleasant writing to read. Now the old woman's address would never be of any use, and her wish that Elizabeth should travel alone was fulfilled.

There was a faint perfume from the envelope like wildwood flowers. She breathed it in, and wondered at it. Was it perfume from something he carried in his pocket, some flower his lady had once given him? But this was not a pleasant thought. She put the envelope into

her bosom after studying it again carefully until she knew the words by
heart.

Then she drew forth the papers of her mother's that she had brought
from home, and for the first time read them over.

The first was the marriage certificate. That she had seen before, and
had studied with awe; but the others had been kept in a box that was
never opened by the children. The mother kept them sacredly, always
with the certificate on the top.

The largest paper she could not understand. It was something about
a mine. There were a great many "herebys" and "whereases" and
"agreements" in it. She put it back into the wrapper as of little account, probably something belonging to her father, which her mother
had treasured for old time's sake.

Then came a paper which related to the claim where their little log
home had stood, and upon the extreme edge of which the graves were.
That, too, she laid reverently within its wrapper.

Next came a bit of pasteboard whereon was inscribed, "Mrs. Merrill
Wilton Bailey, Rittenhouse Square, Tuesdays." That she knew was her
grandmother's name, though she had never seen the card before—her
father's mother. She looked at the card in wonder. It was almost like a
distant view of the lady in question. What kind of a place might Rittenhouse Square be, and where was it? There was no telling. It might
be near that wonderful Desert of Sahara that the man had talked
about. She laid it down with a sigh.

There was only one paper left, and that was a letter written in pale
pencil lines. It said:

"My dear Bessie: Your pa died last week. He was killed falling from
a scaffold. He was buried on Monday with five carriages and everything nice. We all got new black dresses, and have enough for a stone.
If it don't cost too much, we'll have an angel on the top. I always
thought an angel pointing to heaven was nice. We wish you was here.
We miss you very much. I hope your husband is good to you. Why
don't you write to us? You haven't wrote since your little girl was born.
I s'pose you call her Bessie like you. If anything ever happens to you,

you can send her to me. I'd kind of like her to fill your place. Your sister has got a baby girl too. She calls her Lizzie. We couldn't somehow have it natural to call her 'Lizabeth, and Nan wanted her called for me. I was always Lizzie, you know. Now you must write soon.

"Your loving mother,

"ELIZABETH BRADY."

There was no date nor address to the letter, but an address had been pencilled on the outside in her mother's cramped school-girl hand. It was dim but still readable, "Mrs. Elizabeth Brady , 18—Flora Street, Philadelphia."

Elizabeth studied the last word, then drew out the envelope again, and looked at that. Yes, the two names were the same. How wonderful! Perhaps she would sometime, sometime, see him again, though of course he belonged to the lady. But perhaps, if she went to school and learned very fast, she might sometime meet him at church—he went to church, she was sure—and then he might smile, and not be ashamed of his friend who had saved his life. Saved his life! Nonsense! She had not done much. He would not feel any such ridiculous indebtedness to her when he got back to home and friends and safety. He had saved her much more than she had saved him.

She put the papers all back in safety, and after having prepared her few belongings for taking up the journey, she knelt down. She would say the prayer before she went on. It might be that would keep the terrible pursuers away.

She said it once, and then with eyes still closed she waited a moment. Might she say it for him, who was gone away from her? Perhaps it would help him, and keep him from falling from that terrible machine he was riding on. Hitherto in her mind prayers had been only for the dead, but now they seemed also to belong to all who were in danger or trouble. She said the prayer over once more, slowly, then paused a moment, and added: "Our Father, hide him from trouble. Hide George Trescott Benedict. And hide me, please, too."

Then she mounted her horse, and went on her way.

It was a long and weary way. It reached over mountains and

through valleys, across winding, turbulent streams and broad rivers that had few bridges. The rivers twice led her further south than she meant to go, in her ignorance. She had always felt that Philadelphia was straight ahead east, as straight as one could go to the heart of the sun.

Night after night she lay down in strange homes, some poorer and more forlorn than others; and day after day she took up her lonely travel again.

Gradually, as the days lengthened, and mountains piled themselves behind her, and rivers stretched like barriers between, she grew less and less to dread her pursuers, and more and more to look forward to the future. It seemed so long a way! Would it never end?

Once she asked a man whether he knew where Philadelphia was. She had been travelling then for weeks, and thought she must be almost there. But he said "Philadelphia? O, Philadelphia is in the East. That's a long way off. I saw a man once who came from there."

She set her firm little chin then, and travelled on. Her clothes were much worn, and her skin was brown as a berry. The horse plodded on with a dejected air. He would have liked to stop at a number of places they passed, and remain for life, what there was left of it; but he obediently walked on over any kind of an old road that came in his way, and solaced himself with whatever kind of a bite the roadside afforded. He was becoming a much-travelled horse. He knew a threshing-machine by sight now, and considered it no more than a prairie bobcat.

At one stopping-place a good woman advised Elizabeth to rest on Sundays. She told her God didn't like people to do the same on His day as on other days, and it would bring her bad luck if she kept up her incessant riding. It was bad for the horse too. So, the night being Saturday, Elizabeth remained with the woman over the Sabbath, and heard read aloud the fourteenth chapter of John. It was a wonderful revelation to her. She did not altogether understand it. In fact, the Bible was an unknown book. She had never known that it was different from other books. She had heard it spoken of by her mother, but only as a book. She did not know it was a book of books.

She carried the beautiful thoughts with her on the way, and pondered them. She wished she might have the book. She remembered the name of it, Bible, the Book of God. Then God had written a book! Some day she would try to find it and read it.

"Let not your heart be troubled"; so much of the message drifted into her lonesome, ignorant soul, and settled down to stay. She said it over nights when she found a shelter in some unpleasant place, or days when the road was rough or a storm came up and she was compelled to seek shelter by the roadside under a haystack or in a friendly but deserted shack. She thought of it the day there was no shelter and she was drenched to the skin. She wondered afterward when the sun came out and dried her nicely whether God had really been speaking the words to her troubled heart, "Let not your heart be troubled."

Every night and every morning she said "Our Father" twice, once for herself and once for the friend who had gone out into the world, it seemed about a hundred years ago.

But one day she came across a railroad track. It made her heart beat wildly. It seemed now that she must be almost there. Railroads were things belonging to the East and civilization. But the way was lonely still for days, and then she crossed more railroads, becoming more and more frequent, and came into the line of towns that stretched along beside the snake-like tracks.

She fell into the habit of staying overnight in a town, and then riding on to the next in the morning; but now her clothes were becoming so dirty and ragged that she felt ashamed to go to nice-looking places lest they should turn her out; so she sought shelter in barns and small, mean houses. But the people in these houses were distressingly dirty, and she found no place to wash.

She had lost track of the weeks or the months when she reached her first great city, the only one she had come near in her uncharted wanderings.

Into the outskirts of Chicago she rode undaunted, her head erect, with the carriage of a queen. She had passed Indians and cowboys in her journeying; why should she mind Chicago? Miles and miles of houses and people. There seemed to be no end to it. Nothing but houses everywhere and hurried-looking people, many of them working hard. Surely this must be Philadelphia.

A large, beautiful building attracted her attention. There were handsome grounds about it, and girls playing some game with a ball and curious webbed implements across a net of cords. Elizabeth drew her horse to the side of the road, and watched a few minutes. One girl was skillful, and hit the ball back every time. Elizabeth almost exclaimed out loud once when a particularly fine ball was played. She rode reluctantly on when the game was finished, and saw over the arched gateway the words, "Janeway School for Girls."

Ah! This was Philadelphia at last, and here was her school. She would go in at once before she went to her grandmother's. It might be better.

She dismounted, and tied the horse to an iron ring in a post by the sidewalk. Then she went slowly, shyly up the steps into the charmed circles of learning. She knew she was shabby, but her long journey would explain that. Would they be kind to her, and let her study?

She stood some time before the door, with a group of laughing girls not far away whispering about her. She smiled at them; but they did not return the salutation, and their actions made her more shy. At last she stepped into the open door, and a maid in cap and apron came forward. "You must not come in here, miss," she said imperiously. "This is a school."

"Yes," said Elizabeth gravely, smiling. "I want to see the teacher."

"She's busy. You can't see her," snapped the maid.

"Then I will wait till she is ready. I've come a great many miles, and I must see her."

The maid retreated at this, and an elegant woman in trailing black silk and gold-rimmed glasses approached threateningly. This was a new kind of beggar, of course, and must be dealt with at once.

"What do you want?" she asked frigidly.

"I've come to school," said Elizabeth confidingly. "I know I don't look very nice, but I've had to come all the way from Montana on horseback. If you could let me go where I can have some water and a thread and needle, I can make myself look better."

The woman eyed the girl incredulously.

"You have come to school!" she said; and her voice was large, and frightened Elizabeth. "You have come all the way from Montana! Impossible! You must be crazy."

"No, ma'am, I'm not crazy," said Elizabeth. "I just want to go to school."

The woman perceived that this might be an interesting case for benevolently inclined people. It was nothing but an annoyance to herself. "My dear girl,"—her tone was bland and disagreeable now—"are you aware that it takes money to come to school?"

"Does it?" said Elizabeth. "No, I didn't know it, but I have some money. I could give you ten dollars right now; and, if that is not enough, I might work some way, and earn more."

The woman laughed disagreeably.

"It is impossible," she said. "The yearly tuition here is five hundred dollars. Besides, we do not take girls of your class. This is a finishing school for young ladies. You will have to inquire further," and the woman swept away to laugh with her colleagues over the queer character, the new kind of tramp, she had just been called to interview. The maid came pertly forward, and said that Elizabeth could not longer stand where she was.

Bewilderment and bitter disappointment in her face, Elizabeth went slowly down to her horse, the great tears welling up into her eyes. As she rode away, she kept turning back to the school grounds wistfully. She did not notice the passers-by, nor know that they were commenting upon her appearance. She made a striking picture in her rough garments, with her wealth of hair, her tanned skin, and tear-filled eyes. An artist noticed it, and watched her down the street, half thinking he would follow and secure her as a model for his next picture.

A woman, gaudily bedecked in soiled finery, her face giving evidence of the frequent use of rouge and powder, watched her, and followed, pondering. At last she called, "My dear, my dear, wait a minute." She had to speak several times before Elizabeth saw that she was talking to her. Then the horse was halted by the sidewalk.

"My dear," said the woman, "you look tired and disappointed.

Don't you want to come home with me for a little while, and rest?"

"Thank you," said Elizabeth, "but I am afraid I must go on. I only stop on Sundays."

"But just come home with me for a little while," coaxed the wheedling tones. "You look so tired, and I've some girls of my own. I know you would enjoy resting and talking with them."

The kindness in her tones touched the weary girl. Her pride had been stung to the quick by the haughty woman in the school. This woman would soothe her with kindness.

"Do you live far from here?" asked Elizabeth.

"Only two or three blocks," said the woman. "You ride along by the sidewalk, and we can talk. Where are you going? You look as if you had come a long distance."

"Yes," said the girl wearily, "from Montana. I am going to school. Is this Philadelphia?"

"This is Chicago," said the woman. "There are finer schools here than in Philadelphia. If you like to come and stay at my house awhile, I will see about getting you into a school."

"Is it hard work to get people into schools?" asked the girl wonderingly. "I thought they would want people to teach."

"No, it's very hard," said the lying woman; "but I think I know a school where I can get you in. Where are your folks? Are they in Montana?"

"They are all dead," said Elizabeth, "and I have come away to school."

"Poor child!" said the woman glibly. "Come right home with me, and I'll take care of you. I know a nice way you can earn your living, and then you can study if you like. But you're quite big to go to school. It seems to me you could have a good time without that. You are a pretty girl; do you know it? You only need pretty clothes to make you a beauty. If you come with me, I will let you earn some beautiful new clothes."

"You are very kind," said the girl gravely. "I do need new clothes; and, if I could earn them, that would be all the better." She did not quite like the woman; yet of course that was foolish.

After a few more turns they stopped in front of a tall brick building with a number of windows. It seemed to be a good deal like other buildings; in fact, as she looked up the street, Elizabeth thought there were miles of them just alike. She tied her horse in front of the door, and went in with the woman. The woman told her to sit down a minute until she called the lady of the house, who would tell her more about the school. There were a number of pretty girls in the room, and they made very free to speak to her. They twitted her about her clothes, and in a way reminded Elizabeth of the girls in the school she had just interviewed.

Suddenly she spoke up to the group. An idea had occurred to her. This was the school, and the woman had not liked to say so until she spoke to the leader about her.

"Is this a school?" she asked shyly.

Her question was met with a shout of derisive laughter.

"School!" cried the boldest, prettiest one. "School for scandal! School for morals!"

There was one, a thin, pale girl with dark circles under her eyes, a sad droop to her mouth, and bright scarlet spots in her cheeks. She came over to Elizabeth, and whispered something to her. Elizabeth started forward, unspeakable horror in her face.

She fled to the door where she had come in, but found it fastened. Then she turned as if she had been brought to bay by a pack of lions.

Chapter 10

Philadelphia at Last

"O<small>PEN</small> this door!" she commanded. "Let me out of here at once." The pale girl started to do so, but the pretty one held her back. "No, Nellie; Madam will be angry with us all if you open that door." Then she turned to Elizabeth, and said:

"Whoever enters that door never goes out again. You are nicely caught, my dear."

There was a sting of bitterness and self-pity in the taunt at the end of the words. Elizabeth felt it, as she seized her pistol from her belt, and pointed it at the astonished group. They were not accustomed to girls with pistols. "Open that door, or I will shoot you all!" she cried.

Then, as she heard someone descending the stairs, she rushed again into the room where she remembered the windows were open. They were guarded by wire screens; but she caught up a chair, and dashed it through one, plunging out into the street in spite of detaining hands that reached for her, hands much hindered by the gleam of the pistol and the fear that it might go off in their midst.

It took but an instant to wrench the bridle from its fastening and mount her horse; then she rode forward through the city at a pace that only millionaires and automobiles are allowed to take. She met and passed her first automobile without a quiver. Her eyes were dilated, her lips set; angry, frightened tears were streaming down her cheeks, and she urged her poor horse forward until a policeman here and there thought it his duty to make a feeble effort to detain her. But nothing impeded her way. She fled through a maze of wagons, carriages, automobiles, and trolley-cars, until she passed the whirl of the great city, and at last was free again and out in the open country.

She came toward evening to a little cottage on the edge of a pretty suburb. The cottage was covered with roses, and the front yard was full of great old-fashioned flowers. On the porch sat a plain little old lady in a rocking-chair, knitting. There was a little gate with a path leading up to the door, and at the side another open gate with a road leading around to the back of the cottage.

Elizabeth saw, and murmuring, "O 'our Father,' please hide me!" she dashed into the driveway, and tore up to the side of the piazza at a full gallop. She jumped from the horse; and, leaving him standing panting with his nose to the fence, and a tempting strip of clover in front of him where he could graze when he should get his breath, she ran up the steps, and flung herself in a miserable little heap at the feet of the astonished old lady.

"O, please, please, won't you let me stay here a few minutes, and tell me what to do? I am so tired, and I have had such a dreadful, awful time!"

"Why, dearie me!" said the old lady. "Of course I will. Poor child; sit right down in this rocking-chair, and have a good cry. I'll get you a glass of water and something to eat, and then you shall tell me all about it."

She brought the water, and a tray with nice broad slices of brown bread and butter, a generous piece of apple pie, some cheese, and a glass pitcher of creamy milk.

Elizabeth drank the water, but before she could eat she told the terrible tale of her last adventure. It seemed awful for her to believe, and she felt she must have help somewhere. She had heard there were bad people in the world. In fact, she had seen men who were bad, and once a woman had passed their ranch whose character was said to be questionable. She wore a hard face, and could drink and swear like the men. But that sin should be in this form, with pretty girls and pleasant, wheedling women for agents, she had never dreamed; and this in the great, civilized East! Almost better would it have been to remain in the desert alone, and risk the pursuit of that awful man, than to come all this way to find the world gone wrong.

The old lady was horrified, too. She had heard more than the girl of licensed evil; but she had read it in the paper as she had read about the evils of the slave-traffic in Africa, and it had never really seemed true to her. Now she lifted up her hands in horror, and looked at the beautiful girl before her with something akin to awe that she had been in one of those dens of iniquity and escaped. Over and over she made the girl tell what was said, and how it looked, and how she pointed her pistol, and how she got out; and then she exclaimed in wonder, and called her escape a miracle.

They were both weary from excitement when the tale was told. Elizabeth ate her lunch; then the old lady showed her where to put the horse, and made her go to bed. It was only a wee little room with a cot-bed white as snow where she put her; but the roses peeped in at the window, and the box covered with an old white curtain contained a large pitcher of fresh water and a bowl and soap and towels. The old lady brought her a clean white nightgown, coarse and mended in many places, but smelling of rose leaves; and in the morning she tapped at the door quite early before the girl was up, and came in with an armful of clothes.

"I had some boarders last summer," she explained, "and, when they went away, they left these things and said I might put them into the home-mission box. But I was sick when they sent it off this winter; and, if you ain't a home mission, then I never saw one. You put 'em on. I guess they'll fit. They may be a mite large, but she was about your size. I guess your clothes are about worn out; so you jest leave 'em here fer the next one, and use these. There's a couple of extra shirt-waists you can put in a bundle for a change. I guess folks won't dare fool with you if you have some clean, nice clothes on."

Elizabeth looked at her gratefully, and wrote her down in the list of saints with the woman who read the fourteenth chapter of John. The old lady had neglected to mention that from her own meagre wardrobe she had supplied some under-garments, which were not included in those the boarders had left.

Bathed and clothed in clean, sweet garments, with a white shirt-waist and a dark-blue serge skirt and coat, Elizabeth looked a different girl. She surveyed herself in the little glass over the box-washstand and wondered. All at once vanity was born within her, and an ambition to be always thus clothed, with a horrible remembrance of the woman of the day before, who had promised to show her how to earn some pretty clothes. It flashed across her mind that pretty clothes might be a snare. Perhaps they had been to those girls she had seen in that house.

With much good advice and kindly blessings from the old lady, Elizabeth fared forth upon her journey once more, sadly wise in the wisdom of the world, and less sweetly credulous than she had been, but better fitted to fight her way.

The story of her journey from Chicago to Philadelphia would fill a volume if it were written, but it might pall upon the reader from the very variety of its experiences. It was made slowly and painfully, with many haltings and much lessening of the scanty store of money that had seemed so much when she received it in the wilderness. The horse went lame, and had to be watched over and petted, and finally, by the advice of a kindly farmer, taken to a veterinary surgeon, who doctored him for a week before he finally said it was safe to let him hobble on again. After that the girl was more careful of the horse. If he should die, what would she do?

One dismal morning, late in November, Elizabeth, wearing the old overcoat to keep her from freezing, rode into Philadelphia.

Armed with instructions from the old lady in Chicago, she rode boldly up to a policeman, and showed him the address of the grandmother to whom she had decided to go first, her mother's mother. He sent her on in the right direction, and in due time with the help of other policemen she reached the right number on Flora Street.

It was a narrow street, banked on either side by small, narrow brick houses of the older type. Here and there gleamed out a scrap of a white marble door-step, but most of the houses were approached by steps of dull stone or of painted wood. There was a dejected and dreary air about the place. The street was swarming with children in various stages of the soiled condition.

Elizabeth timidly knocked at the door after being assured by the interested urchins who surrounded her that Mrs. Brady really lived there, and had not moved away or anything. It did not seem wonderful to the girl, who had lived her life thus far in a mountain shack, to find her grandmother still in the place from which she had written fifteen years before. She did not yet know what a floating population most cities contain.

Mrs. Brady was washing when the knock sounded through the house. She was a broad woman, with a face on which the cares and sorrows of the years had left a not too heavy impress. She still enjoyed life, even though a good part of it was spent at the wash-tub, washing other people's fine clothes. She had some fine ones of her own up-stairs in her clothes-press; and, when she went out, it was in shiny satin, with a bonnet bobbing with jet and a red rose, though of late years, strictly speaking, the bonnet had become a hat again, and Mrs. Brady was in style with the other old ladies.

The perspiration was in little beads on her forehead and trickling down the creases in her well-cushioned neck toward her ample bosom. Her gray hair was neatly combed, and her calico wrapper was open at the throat even on this cold day. She wiped on her apron the soapsuds from her plump arms steaming pink from the hot suds, and went to the door.

She looked with disfavor upon the peculiar person on the door-step attired in a man's overcoat. She was prepared to refuse the demands of the Salvation Army for a nickel for Christmas dinners; or to silence the bananaman, or the fish-man, or the man with shoe-strings and pins and pencils for sale; or to send the photograph-agent on his way; yes, even the man who sold albums for postcards. She had no time to bother with anybody this morning.

But the young person in the rusty overcoat, with the dark-blue serge Eton jacket under it, which might have come from Wanamaker's two years ago, who yet wore a leather belt with gleaming pistols under the Eton jacket, was a new species. Mrs. Brady was taken off her guard; else Elizabeth might have found entrance to her grandmother's home as difficult as she had found entrance to the finishing school of Madame Janeway.

"Are you Mrs. Brady?" asked the girl. She was searching the forbidding face before her for some signs of likeness to her mother, but found none. The cares of Elizabeth Brady's daughter had outweighed those of the mother, or else they sat upon a nature more sensitive.

"I am," said Mrs. Brady, imposingly.

"Grandmother, I am the baby you talked about in that letter," she announced, handing Mrs. Brady the letter she had written nearly eighteen years before.

The woman took the envelope gingerly in the wet thumb and finger that still grasped a bit of the gingham apron. She held it at arm's length, and squinted up her eyes, trying to read it without her glasses. It was some new kind of beggar, of course. She hated to touch these dirty envelopes, and this one looked old and worn. She stepped back to the parlor table where her glasses were lying, and, adjusting them, began to read the letter.

"For the land sakes! Where'd you find this?" she said, looking up suspiciously. "It's against the law to open letters that ain't your own. Didn't me daughter ever get it? I wrote it to her meself. How come you by it?"

"Mother read it to me long ago when I was little," answered the girl, the slow hope fading from her lips as she spoke. Was every one, was even her grandmother, going to be cold and harsh with her? "Our Father, hide me!" her heart murmured, because it had become a habit; and her listening thought caught the answer, "Let not your heart be troubled."

"Well, who are you?" said the uncordial grandmother, still puzzled. "You ain't Bessie, me Bessie. Fer one thing, you're 'bout as young as she was when she went off 'n' got married, against me 'dvice, to that drunken, lazy dude." Her brow was lowering, and she proceeded to finish her letter.

"I am Elizabeth," said the girl with a trembling voice, "the baby you talked about in that letter. But please don't call father that. He wasn't ever bad to us. He was always good to mother, even when he was drunk. If you talk like that about him, I shall have to go away."

"Fer the land sakes! You don't say," said Mrs. Brady, sitting down hard in astonishment on the biscuit upholstery of her best parlor chair. "Now you ain't Bessie's child! Well, I *am clear* beat. And growed up so big! You look strong, but you're kind of thin. What makes your skin so black? Your ma never was dark, ner your pa, neither."

"I've been riding a long way in the wind and sun and rain."

"Fer the land sakes!" as she looked through the window to the street. "Not on a horse?"

"Yes."

"H'm! What was your ma thinkin' about to let you do that?"

"My mother is dead. There was no one left to care what I did. I had to come. There were dreadful people out there, and I was afraid."

"Fer the land sakes!" That seemed the only remark that the capable Mrs. Brady could make. She looked at her new granddaughter in bewilderment, as if a strange sort of creature had suddenly laid claim to relationship.

"Well, I'm right glad to see you " she said stiffly, wiping her hand again on her apron and putting it out formally for a greeting.

Elizabeth accepted her reception gravely, and sat down. She sat down suddenly, as if her strength had given way and a great strain was at an end. As she sat down, she drooped her head back against the wall; and a gray look spread about her lips.

"You're tired," said the grandmother, energetically. "Come far this morning?"

"No," said Elizabeth, weakly, "not many miles; but I hadn't any more bread. I used it all up yesterday, and there wasn't much money left. I thought I could wait till I got here, but I guess I'm hungry."

"Fer the land sakes!" ejaculated Mrs. Brady as she hustled out to the kitchen, and clattered the frying-pan onto the stove, shoving the boiler hastily aside. She came in presently with a steaming cup of tea, and made the girl drink it hot and strong. Then she established her in the big rocking-chair in the kitchen with a plate of appetizing things to eat, and went on with her washing, punctuating every rub with a question.

Elizabeth felt better after her meal, and offered to help, but the grandmother would not hear to her lifting a finger.

"You must rest first," she said. "It beats me how you ever got here. I'd sooner crawl on me hands and knees than ride a great, scary horse."

Elizabeth sprang to her feet.

"The horse!" she said. "Poor fellow! He needs something to eat worse than I did. He hasn't had a bite of grass all this morning. There was nothing but hard roads and pavements. The grass is all brown, anyway, now. I found some cornstalks by the road, and once a man dropped a big bundle of hay out of his load. If it hadn't been for Robin, I'd never have got here; and here I've sat enjoying my breakfast, and Robin out there hungry!"

"Fer the land sakes!" said the grandmother, taking her arms out of the suds and looked troubled. "Poor fellow! What would he like? I haven't got any hay, but there's some mashed potatoes left, and what is there? Why, there's some excelsior the lamp-shade come packed in. You don't suppose he'd think it was hay, do you? No, I guess it wouldn't taste very good."

"Where can I put him, Grandmother?"

"Fer the land sakes! I don't know," said the grandmother, looking around the room in alarm. "We haven't any place fer horses. Perhaps you might get him into the back yard fer a while till we think what to do. There's a stable, but they charge high to board horses. Lizzie knows one of the fellers that works there. Mebbe he'll tell us what to do. Anyway, you lead him round to the alleyway, and we'll see if we can't get him in the little ash-gate. You don't suppose he'd try to get in the house, do you? I shouldn't like him to come in the kitchen when I was getting supper."

"O no!" said Elizabeth. "He's very good. Where is the back yard?"

This arrangement was finally made, and the two women stood in the kitchen door, watching Robin drink a bucketful of water and eat heartily of the various viands that Mrs. Brady set forth for him, with the exception of the excelsior, which he snuffed at in disgust.

"Now, ain't he smart?" said Mrs. Brady, watching fearfully from the door-step, where she might retreat if the animal showed any tendency to step nearer to the kitchen. "But don't you think he's cold? Wouldn't he like a—a—shawl or something?"

The girl drew the old coat from her shoulders, and threw it over him, her grandmother watching her fearless handling of the horse with pride and awe.

"We're used to sharing this together," said the girl simply.

"Nan sews in an up-town dressmaker's place," explained Mrs. Brady by and by, when the wash was hung out in fearsome proximity to the weary horse's heels, and the two had returned to the warm kitchen to clean up and get supper. "Nan's your ma's sister, you know, older'n her by two year; and Lizzie, that's her girl, she's about 's old 's you. She's got a good place in the ten-cent store. Nan's husband died four years ago, and her and me've been livin' together ever since. It'll be nice fer you and Lizzie to be together. She'll make it lively fer you right away. Prob'ly she can get you a place at the same store. She'll be here at half past six to-night. This is her week to get out early."

The aunt came in first. She was a tall, thin woman with faded brown hair and a faint resemblance to Elizabeth's mother. Her shoulders stooped slightly, and her voice was nasal. Her mouth looked as if it was used to holding pins in one corner and gossiping out of the other. She was one of the kind who always gets into a rocking-chair to sew if they can, and rock as they sew. Nevertheless, she was skillful in her way, and commanded good wages. She welcomed the new niece reluctantly, more excited over her remarkable appearance among her relatives after so long a silence than pleased, Elizabeth felt. But after she had satisfied her curiosity she was kind, beginning to talk about Lizzie, and mentally compared this thin, brown girl with rough hair and dowdy clothes to her own stylish daughter. Then Lizzie burst in. They could hear her calling to a young man who had walked home with her, even before she entered the house.

"It's just fierce out, Ma!" she exclaimed. "Grandma, ain't supper ready yet? I never was so hungry in all my life. I could eat a house afire."

She stopped short at sight of Elizabeth. She had been chewing gum—Lizzie was always chewing gum—but her jaws ceased action in sheer astonishment.

"This is your cousin Bessie, come all the way from Montana on horseback, Lizzie. She's your aunt Bessie's child. Her folks is dead now, and she's come to live with us. You must see if you can't get her a place in the ten-cent store 'long with you," said the grandmother.

Lizzie came airily forward, and grasped her cousin's hand in mid-air, giving it a lateral shake that bewildered Elizabeth.

"Pleased to meet you," she chattered glibly, and set her jaws to work again. One could not embarrass Lizzie long. But she kept her eyes on the stranger, and let them wander disapprovingly over her apparel in a pointed way as she took out the long hat-pins from the cumbersome hat she wore and adjusted her ponderous pompadour.

"Lizzie 'll have to help fix you up," said the aunt, noting Lizzie's glance. "You're all out of style. I suppose they get behind times out in Montana. Lizzie, can't you show her how to fix her hair pompadour?"

Lizzie brightened. If there was a prospect of changing things, she was not averse to a cousin of her own age; but she never could take such a dowdy-looking girl into society, not the society of the ten-cent store.

"O, cert!" answered Lizzie affably. "I'll fix you fine. Don't you worry. How'd you get so awful tanned? I s'pose riding. You look like you'd been to the seashore, and lay out on the beach in the sun. But 'tain't the right time o' year quite. It must be great to ride horseback!"

"I'll teach you how if you want to learn," said Elizabeth, endeavoring to show a return of the kindly offer.

"Me? What would I ride? Have to ride a counter, I guess. I guess you won't find much to ride here in the city, 'cept trolley-cars."

"Bessie's got a horse. He's out in the yard now," said the grandmother with pride.

"A horse! All your own? Gee whiz! Won't the girls stare when I tell them? Say, we can borrow a rig at the livery some night, and take a ride. Dan'll go with us, and get the rig for us. Won't that be great?"

Elizabeth smiled. She felt the glow of at last contributing something to the family pleasure. She did not wish her coming to be so entirely a wet blanket as it had seemed at first; for, to tell the truth, she had seen blank dismay on the face of each separate relative as her identity had been made known. Her heart was lonely, and she hungered for some-one who "belonged" and loved her.

Supper was put on the table, and the two girls began to get a little acquainted, chattering over clothes and the arrangement of hair.

"Do you know whether there is anything in Philadelphia called 'Christian Endeavor'?" asked Elizabeth after the supper-table was cleared off.

"O, Chrishun 'deavor! Yes, I used t'b'long," answered Lizzie. She had removed the gum from her mouth while she ate her supper, but now it was busy again between sentences. "Yes, we have one down to our church. It was real interesting, too; but I got mad at one of the members, and quit. She was a stuck-up old maid, anyway. She was al-ways turning round and scowling at us girls if we just whispered the least little bit, or smiled; and one night she was leading the meeting, and Jim Forbes got in a corner behind a post, and made mouths at her behind his book. He looked awful funny. It was something fierce the way she always screwed her face up when she sang, and he looked just like her. We girls, Hetty and Em'line and I, got to laughing, and we just couldn't stop; and didn't that old thing stop the singing after one verse, and look right at us, and say she thought Christian Endeavor members should remember whose house they were in, and that the owner was there, and all that rot. I nearly died, I was so mad. Every-body looked around, and we girls choked, and got up and went out. I haven't been down since. The lookout committee came to see us 'bout it; but I said I wouldn't go back where I'd been insulted, and I've never been inside the doors since. But she's moved away now. I wouldn't mind going back if you want to go."

"Whose house did she mean it was? Was it her house?"

"O, no, it wasn't her house," laughed Lizzie. "It was the church. She meant it was God's house, I s'pose, but she needn't have been so per-nickety. We weren't doing any harm."

"Does God have a house?"

"Why, yes; didn't you know that? Why, you talk like a heathen, Bessie. Didn't you have churches in Montana?"

"Yes, there was a church fifty miles away. I heard about it once, but I never saw it," answered Elizabeth. "But what did the woman mean? Who did she say was there? God? Was God in the church? Did you see Him, and know He was there when you laughed?"

"O, you silly!" giggled Lizzie. "Wouldn't the girls laugh at you, though, if they could hear you talk? Why, of course God was there. He's everywhere, you know," with superior knowledge; "but I didn't see Him. You can't see God."

"Why not?"

"Why, because you can't!" answered her cousin with final logic. "Say, haven't you got any other clothes with you at all? I'd take you down with me in the morning if you was fixed up."

Chapter 11

In Flight Again

WHEN Elizabeth lay down to rest that night, with Lizzie still chattering by her side, she found that there was one source of intense pleasure in anticipation, and that was the prospect of going to God's house to Christian Endeavor. Now perhaps she would be able to find out what it all had meant, and whether it were true that God took care of people and hid them in time of trouble. She felt almost certain in her own little experience that He had cared for her, and she wanted to be quite sure, so that she might grasp this precious truth to her heart and keep it forever. No one could be quite alone in the world if there was a God who cared and loved and hid.

The aunt and the grandmother were up betimes the next morning, looking over some meagre stores of old clothing, and there was found an old dress which it was thought could be furbished over for Elizabeth. They were hard-working people with little money to spare, and everything had to be utilized; but they made a great deal of appearance, and Lizzie was proud as a young peacock. She would not take Elizabeth to the store to face the head man without having her fixed up according to the most approved style.

So the aunt cut and fitted before she went off for the day, and Elizabeth was ordered to sew while she was gone. The grandmother presided at the rattling old sewing-machine, and in two or three days Elizabeth was pronounced to be fixed up enough to do for the present till she could earn some new clothes. With her fine hair snarled into a cushion and puffed out into an enormous pompadour that did not suit her face in the least, and with an old hat and jacket of Lizzie's which did not become her nor fit her exactly, she started out to make her way in the world as a saleswoman. Lizzie had already secured her a place if she suited.

The store was a maze of wonder to the girl from the mountains—so many bright, bewildering things, ribbons and tin pans, glassware and toys, cheap jewelry and candies. She looked about with the dazed eyes of a creature from another world.

But the manager looked upon her with eyes of favor. He saw that her eyes were bright and keen. He was used to judging faces. He saw that she was as yet unspoiled, with a face of refinement far beyond the general run of the girls who applied to him for positions. And he was not beyond a friendly flirtation with a pretty new girl himself; so she was engaged at once, and put on duty at the notion-counter.

The girls flocked around her during the intervals of custom. Lizzie had told of her cousin's long ride, embellished, wherever her knowledge failed, by her extremely wild notions of Western life. She had told how Elizabeth arrived wearing a belt with two pistols, and this gave Elizabeth standing at once among all the people in the store. A girl who could shoot, and who wore pistols in a belt like a real cowboy, had a social distinction all her own.

The novel-reading, theatre-going girls rallied around her to a girl; and the young men in the store were not far behind. Elizabeth was popular from the first. Moreover, as she settled down into the routine of life, and had three meals every day, her cheeks began to round out just a little; and it became apparent that she was unusually beautiful in spite of her dark skin, which whitened gradually under the electric light and high-pressure life of the store.

They went to Christian Endeavor, Elizabeth and her cousin; and Elizabeth felt as if heaven had suddenly dropped down about her. She lived from week to week for that Christian Endeavor.

The store, which had been a surprise and a novelty at first, began to be a trial to her. It wore upon her nerves. The air was bad, and the crowds were great. It was coming on toward Christmas time, and the store was crammed to bursting day after day and night after night, for they kept open evenings now until Christmas. Elizabeth longed for a breath from the mountains, and grew whiter and thinner. Sometimes she felt as if she must break away from it all, and take Robin, and ride into the wilderness again. If it were not for the Christian Endeavor, she would have done so, perhaps.

Robin, poor beast, was well housed and well fed; but he worked for his living as did his mistress. He was a grocer's delivery horse, worked from Monday morning early till Saturday night at ten o'clock, subject to curses and kicks from the grocery boy, expected to stand meekly at the curbstones, snuffing the dusty brick pavements while the boy delivered a box of goods, and while trolleys and beer-wagons and automobiles slammed and rumbled and tooted by him, and then to start on the double-quick to the next stopping-place.

He to be thus under the rod who had trod the plains with a free foot and snuffed the mountain air! It was a great come-down, and his life became a weariness to him. But he earned his mistress a dollar a week besides his board. There would have been some consolation in that to his faithful heart if he only could have known it. Albeit she would have gladly gone without the dollar if Robin could have been free and happy.

One day, one dreadful day, the manager of the ten-cent store came to Elizabeth with a look in his eyes that reminded her of the man in Montana from whom she had fled. He was smiling, and his words were unduly pleasant. He wanted her to go with him to the theatre that evening, and he complimented her on her appearance. He stated that he admired her exceedingly, and wanted to give her pleasure. But somehow Elizabeth had fallen into the habit ever since she left the prairies of comparing all men with George Trescott Benedict; and this man, although he dressed well, and was every bit as handsome, did not compare well. There was a sinister, selfish glitter in his eyes that made Elizabeth think of the serpent on the plain just before she shot it. Therefore Elizabeth declined the invitation.

It happened that there was a missionary meeting at the church that evening. All the Christian endeavorers had been urged to attend. Elizabeth gave this as an excuse; but the manager quickly swept that away, saying she could go to church any night, but she could not go to this particular play with him always. The girl eyed him calmly with much the same attitude with which she might have pointed her pistol at his head, and said gravely,

"But I do not want to go with you."

After that the manager hated her. He always hated girls who resisted him. He hated her, and wanted to do her harm. But he fairly persecuted her to receive his attentions. He was a young fellow, extremely young to be occupying so responsible a position. He undoubtedly had business ability. He showed it in his management of Elizabeth. The girl's life became a torment to her. In proportion as she appeared to be the manager's favorite the other girls became jealous of her. They taunted her with the manager's attentions on every possible occasion. When they found anything wrong, they charged it upon her; and so she was kept constantly going to the manager, which was perhaps just what he wanted.

She grew paler and paler, and more and more desperate. She had run away from one man; she had run away from a woman; but here was a man from whom she could not run away unless she gave up her position. If it had not been for her grandmother, she would have done so at once; but, if she gave up her position, she would be thrown upon her grandmother for support, and that must not be. She understood from the family talk that they were having just as much as they could do already to make both ends meet and keep the all-important god of Fashion satisfied. This god of Fashion had come to seem to Elizabeth an enemy of the living God. It seemed to occupy all people's thoughts, and everything else had to be sacrificed to meet its demands.

She had broached the subject of school one evening soon after she arrived, but was completely squelched by her aunt and cousin.

"You're too old!" sneered Lizzie. "School is for children."

"Lizzie went through grammar school, and we talked about high for her," said the grandmother proudly.

"But I just hated school," grinned Lizzie. "It ain't so nice as it's cracked up to be. Just sit and study all day long. Why, they were always keeping me after school for talking or laughing. I was glad enough when I got through. You may thank your stars you didn't have to go, Bess."

"People who have to earn their bread can't lie around and go to school," remarked Aunt Nan dryly, and Elizabeth said no more.

But later she heard of a night-school, and then she took up the subject once more. Lizzie scoffed at this. She said night-school was only for very poor people, and it was a sort of disgrace to go. But Elizabeth stuck to her point, until one day Lizzie came home with a tale about Temple College. She had heard it was very cheap. You could go for ten cents a night, or something like that. Things that were ten cents appealed to her. She was used to bargain-counters.

She heard it was quite respectable to go there, and they had classes in the evening. You could study gymnastics, and it would make you graceful. She wanted to be graceful. And she heard they had a course in millinery. If it was so, she believed she would go herself, and learn to make the new kind of bows they were having on hats this winter. She could not seem to get the right twist to the ribbon.

Elizabeth wanted to study geography. At least, that was the study Lizzie said would tell her where the Desert of Sahara was. She wanted to know things, all kinds of things; but Lizzie said such things were only for children, and she didn't believe they taught such baby studies in a college. But she would inquire. It was silly of Bessie to want to know, she thought, and she was half ashamed to ask. But she would find out.

It was about this time that Elizabeth's life at the store grew intolerable.

One morning—it was little more than a week before Christmas—Elizabeth had been sent to the cellar to get seven little red tin pails and shovels for a woman who wanted them for Christmas gifts for some Sunday-school class. She had just counted out the requisite number and turned to go up-stairs when she heard someone step near her, and, as she looked up in the dim light, there stood the manager.

"At last I've got you alone, Bessie, my dear!" He said it with suave triumph in his tones. He caught Elizabeth by the wrists, and before she could wrench herself away he had kissed her.

With a scream Elizabeth dropped the seven tin pails and the seven tin shovels, and with one mighty wrench took her hands from his grasp. Instinctively her hand went to her belt, where were now no pistols. If one had been there she certainly would have shot him in her horror and fury. But, as she had no other weapon, she seized a little shovel, and struck him in the face. Then with the frenzy of the desert back upon her she rushed up the stairs, out through the crowded store, and into the street, hatless and coatless in the cold December air. The passers-by made way for her, thinking she had been sent out on some hurried errand.

She had left her pocketbook, with its pitifully few nickels for carfare and lunch, in the cloak-room with her coat and hat. But she did not stop to think of that. She was fleeing again, this time on foot, from a man. She half expected he might pursue her, and make her come back to the hated work in the stifling store with his wicked face moving everywhere above the crowds. But she turned not to look back. On over the slushy pavements, under the leaden sky, with a few busy flakes floating about her.

The day seemed pitiless as the world. Where could she go and what should she do? There seemed no refuge for her in the wide world. Instinctively she felt her grandmother would feel that a calamity had befallen them in losing the patronage of the manager of the ten-cent store. Perhaps Lizzie would get into trouble. What should she do?

She had reached the corner where she and Lizzie usually took the car for home. The car was coming now; but she had no hat nor coat, and no money to pay for a ride. She must walk. She paused not, but fled on in a steady run, for which her years on the mountain had given her breath. Three miles it was to Flora Street, and she scarcely slackened her pace after she had settled into the steady half-run, half-walk. Only at the corner of Flora Street she paused, and allowed herself to glance back once. No, the manager had not pursued her. She was safe. She might go in and tell her grandmother without fearing he would come behind her as soon as her back was turned.

Chapter 12

Elizabeth's Declaration of Independence

Mrs. Brady was at the wash-tub again when her most uncommon and unexpected grandchild burst into the room.

She wiped her hands on her apron, and sat down with her usual exclamation. "Fer the land sakes! What's happened? Bessie, tell me quick. Is anything the matter with Lizzie? Where is she?"

But Elizabeth was on the floor at her feet in tears. She was shaking with sobs, and could scarcely manage to stammer out that Lizzie was all right. Mrs. Brady settled back with a relieved sigh. Lizzie was the first grandchild, and therefore the idol of her heart. If Lizzie was all right, she could afford to be patient and find out by degrees.

"It's that awful man, grandmother!" Elizabeth sobbed out.

"What man? That feller in Montana you run away from?" The grandmother sat up with snapping eyes. She was not afraid of a man, even if he did shoot people. She would call in the police and protect her own flesh and blood. Let him come. Mrs. Brady was ready for him.

"No, no, grandmother, the man-man-manager at the ten-cent store," sobbed the girl; "he kissed me! Oh!" and she shuddered as if the memory was the most terrible thing that ever came to her.

"Fer the land sakes! Is that all?" said the woman with much relief and a degree of satisfaction. "Why, that's nothing. You ought to be proud. Many a girl would go boasting round about that. What are you crying for? He didn't hurt you, did he? Why, Lizzie seems to think he's fine. I tell you Lizzie wouldn't cry if he was to kiss her, I'm sure. She'd just laugh, and ask him fer a holiday. Here, sit up, child, and wash your face, and go back to your work. You've evidently struck the manager on the right side, and you're bound to get a rise in your wages.

Every girl he takes a notion to gets up and does well. Perhaps you'll get money enough to go to school. Goodness knows what you want to go for. I s'pose it's in the blood, though Bess used to say our pa wa'n't any great at study. But, if you've struck the manager the right way, no telling what he might do. He might even want to marry you."

"Grandmother!"

Mrs. Brady was favored with the flashing of the Bailey eyes. She viewed it in astonishment not unmixed with admiration.

"Well, you certainly have got spirit," she ejaculated. "I don't wonder he liked you. I didn't know you was so pretty, Bessie; you look like your mother when she was eighteen; you really do. I never saw the resemblance before. I believe you'll get on all right. Don't you be afraid. I wish you had your chance if you're so anxious to go to school. I shouldn't wonder ef you'd turn out to be something and marry rich. Well, I must be getting back to me tub Land sakes, but you did give me a turn. I thought Lizzie had been run over. I couldn't think what else'd make you run off way here without your coat. Come, get up, child, and go back to your work. It's too bad you don't like to be kissed, but don't let that worry you. You'll have lots worse than that to come up against. When you've lived as long as I have and worked as hard, you'll be pleased to have someone admire you. You better wash your face, and eat a bite of lunch, and hustle back. You needn't be afraid. If he's fond of you, he won't bother about your running away a little. He'll excuse you ef 'tis busy times, and not dock your pay neither."

"Grandmother!" said Elizabeth. "Don't! I can never go back to that awful place and that man. I would rather go back to Montana. I would rather be dead."

"Hoity-toity!" said the easy-going grandmother, sitting down to her task, for she perceived some wholesome discipline was necessary. "You can't talk that way, Bess. You got to go to your work. We ain't got money to keep you in idleness, and land knows where you'd get another place as good's this one. Ef you stay home all day, you might make him awful mad; and then it would be no use goin' back, and you might lose Lizzie her place too."

But, though the grandmother talked and argued and soothed by turns, Elizabeth was firm. She would not go back. She would never go back. She would go to Montana if her grandmother said any more about it.

With a sigh at last Mrs. Brady gave up. She had given up once before nearly twenty years ago. Bessie, her oldest daughter, had a will like that, and tastes far above her station. Mrs. Brady wondered where she got them.

"You're fer all the world like yer ma," she said as she thumped the clothes in the wash-tub. "She was jest that way, when she would marry your pa. She could 'a' had Jim Stokes, the groceryman, er Lodge, the milkman, er her choice of three railroad men, all of 'em doing well, and ready to let her walk over 'em; but she *would have* your pa, the drunken, good-for-nothing, slippery dude. The only thing I'm surprised at was that he ever married her. I never expected it. I s'posed they'd run off, and he'd leave her when he got tired of her; but it seems he stuck to her. It's the only good thing he ever done, and I'm not sure but she'd 'a' been better off ef he hadn't 'a' done that."

"Grandmother!" Elizabeth's face blazed.

"Yes, *gran*'mother!" snapped Mrs. Brady. "It's all true, and you might's well face it. He met her in church. She used to go reg'lar. Some boys used to come and set in the back seat behind the girls, and then go home with them. They was all nice enough boys 'cept him. I never had a bit a use for him. He belonged to the swells and the stuck-ups; and he knowed it, and presumed upon it. He jest thought he could wind Bessie round his finger, and he did. If he said, 'Go,' she went, no matter what I'd do. So, when his ma found it out, she was hoppin' mad. She jest came driving round here to me house, and presumed to talk to me. She said Bessie was a designing snip, and a bad girl, and a whole lot of things. Said she was leading her son astray, and would come to no good end, and a whole lot of stuff; and told me to look after her. It wasn't so. Bess got John Bailey to quit smoking for a whole week at a time, and he said if she'd marry him he'd quit drinking too. His ma couldn't 'a' got him to promise that. She wouldn't even believe he got drunk. I told her a few things about her precious son, but she curled her fine, aristocratic lip up, and said, 'Gentlemen never get drunk.' Humph! Gentlemen! That's all she knowed about it. He got drunk all right, and stayed drunk, too. So after that, when I tried to keep Bess at home, she slipped away one night; said she was going to church; and she did too; went to the minister's study in a strange church, and got married, her and John; and then they up and off West. John, he'd sold his watch and his fine diamond stud his ma had give him; and he borrowed some money from some friends of his father's, and he off with three hundred dollars and Bess; and that's all I ever saw more of me Bessie."

The poor woman sat down in her chair, and wept into her apron regardless for once of the soap-suds that rolled down her red, wet arms.

"Is my grandmother living yet?" asked Elizabeth. She was sorry for this grandmother, but did not know what to say. She was afraid to comfort her lest she take it for yielding.

"Yes, they say she is," said Mrs. Brady, sitting up with a show of interest. She was always ready for a bit of gossip. "Her husband's dead, and her other son's dead, and she's all alone. She lives in a big house on Rittenhouse Square. If she was any 'count, she'd ought to provide for you. I never thought about it. But I don't suppose it would be any use to try. You might ask her. Perhaps she'd help you to go to school You've got a claim on her. She ought to give you her son's share of his father's property, though I've heard she disowned him when he married our Bess. You might fix up in some of Lizzie's best things, and go up there and try. She might give you some money."

"I don't want her money," said Elizabeth stiffly. "I guess there's work somewhere in the world I can do without begging even of grandmothers. But I think I ought to go and see her. She might want to know about father."

Mrs. Brady looked at her granddaughter wonderingly. This was a view of things she had never taken.

"Well," said she resignedly, "go your own gait. I don't know where you'll come up at. All I say is, ef you're going through the world with such high and mighty fine notions, you'll have a hard time. You can't pick out roses and cream and a bed of down every day. You have to put up with life as you find it."

Elizabeth went to her room, the room she shared with Lizzie. She wanted to get away from her grandmother's disapproval. It lay on her heart like lead. Was there no refuge in the world? If grandmothers were not refuges, where should one flee? The old lady in Chicago had understood; why had not Grandmother Brady?

Then came the sweet old words, "Let not your heart be troubled." "In the time of trouble he shall hide me in his pavilion; in the secret of his tabernacle shall he hide me." She knelt down by the bed and said "Our Father." She was beginning to add some words of her own now. She had heard them pray so in Christian Endeavor in the sentence prayers. She wished she knew more about God, and His Book. She had had so little time to ask or think about it. Life seemed all one rush for clothes and position.

At supper-time Lizzie came home much excited. She had been in hot water all the afternoon. The girls had said at lunch-time that the manager was angry with Bessie, and had discharged her. She found her coat and hat, and had brought them home. The pocketbook was missing. There was only fifteen cents in it; but Lizzie was much disturbed, and so was the grandmother. They had a quiet consultation in the kitchen; and, when the aunt came, there was another whispered conversation among the three.

Elizabeth felt disapproval in the air. Aunt Nan came, and sat down beside her, and talked very coldly about expenses and being dependent upon one's relatives, and let her understand thoroughly that she could not sit around and do nothing; but Elizabeth answered by telling her how the manager had been treating her. The aunt then gave her a dose of worldly wisdom, which made the girl shrink into herself. It needed only Lizzie's loud-voiced exhortations to add to her misery and make her feel ready to do anything. Supper was a most unpleasant meal. At last the grandmother spoke up.

"Well, Bessie," she said firmly, "we've decided, all of us, that, if you are going to be stubborn about this, something will have to be done;

and I think the best thing is for you to go to Mrs. Bailey and see what she'll do for you. It's her business, anyway."

Elizabeth's cheeks were very red. She said nothing. She let them go on with the arrangements. Lizzie went and got her best hat, and tried it on Elizabeth to see how she would look, and produced a silk waist from her store of garments, and a spring jacket. It wasn't very warm, it is true; but Lizzie explained that the occasion demanded strenuous measures, and the jacket was undoubtedly stylish, which was the main thing to be considered. One could afford to be cold if one was stylish.

Lizzie was up early the next morning. She had agreed to put Elizabeth in battle-array for her visit to Rittenhouse Square. Elizabeth submitted meekly to her borrowed adornings. Her hair was brushed over her face, and curled on a hot iron, and brushed backward in a perfect mat, and then puffed out in a bigger pompadour than usual. The silk waist was put on with Lizzie's best skirt, and she was adjured not to let that drag. Then the best hat with the cheap pink plumes was set atop the elaborate coiffure; the jacket was put on; and a pair of Lizzie's long silk gloves were struggled into. They were a trifle large when on, but to the hands unaccustomed to gloves they were like being run into a mould.

Elizabeth stood it all until she was pronounced complete. Then she came and stood in front of the cheap little glass, and surveyed herself. There were blisters in the glass that twisted her head into a grotesque shape. The hairpins stuck into her head. Lizzie had tied a spotted veil tight over her nose and eyes. The collar of the silk waist was frayed, and cut her neck. The skirt-band was too tight, and the gloves were torture. Elizabeth turned slowly, and went down-stairs, past the admiring aunt and grandmother, who exclaimed at the girl's beauty, now that she was attired to their mind, and encouraged her by saying they were sure her grandmother would want to do something for so pretty a girl.

Lizzie called out to her not to worry, as she flew for her car. She said she had heard there was a variety show in town where they wanted a girl who could shoot. If she didn't succeed with her grandmother, they would try and get her in at the show. The girls at the store knew a man who had charge of it. They said he liked pretty girls, and they thought would be glad to get her. Indeed, Mary James had promised to speak to him last night, and would let her know to-day about it. It would likely be a job more suited to her cousin's liking.

Elizabeth shuddered. Another man! Would he be like all the rest?— all the rest save one!

She walked a few steps in the direction she had been told to go, and then turned resolutely around, and came back. The watching grandmother felt her heart sink. What was this headstrong girl going to do next? Rebel again?

"What's the matter, Bessie?" she asked, meeting her anxiously at the door. "It's bad luck to turn back when you've started."

"I can't go this way," said the girl excitedly. "It's all a cheat. I'm not like this. It isn't mine, and I'm not going in it. I must have my own clothes and be myself when I go to see her. If she doesn't like me and want me, then I can take Robin and go back." And like another David burdened with Saul's armor she came back to get her little sling and stones.

She tore off the veil, and the sticky gloves from her cold hands, and all the finery of silk waist and belt, and donned her old plain blue coat and skirt in which she had arrived in Philadelphia. They had been frugally brushed and sponged, and made neat for a working dress. Elizabeth felt that they belonged to her. Under the jacket, which fortunately was long enough to hide her waist, she buckled her belt with the two pistols. Then she took the battered old felt hat from the closet, and tried to fasten it on; but the pompadour interfered. Relentlessly she pulled down the work of art that Lizzie had created, and brushed and combed her long, thick hair into subjection again, and put it in its long braid down her back. Her grandmother should see her just as she was. She should know what kind of a girl belonged to her. Then, if she chose to be a real grandmother, well and good.

Mrs. Brady was much disturbed in mind when Elizabeth came down-stairs. She exclaimed in horror, and tried to force the girl to go back, telling her it was a shame and disgrace to go in such garments into the sacred precincts of Rittenhouse Square; but the girl was not to be turned back. She would not even wait till her aunt and Lizzie came home. She would go now, at once.

Mrs. Brady sat down in her rocking-chair in despair for full five minutes after she had watched the reprehensible girl go down the street. She had not been so completely beaten since the day when her own Bessie left the house and went away to a wild West to die in her own time and way. The grandmother shed a few tears. The girl was like her own Bessie, and she could not help loving her, though there was a streak of something else about her that made her seem above them all; and that was hard to bear. It must be the Bailey streak, of course. Mrs. Brady did not admire the Baileys, but she was obliged to reverence them.

If she had watched or followed Elizabeth, she would have been still more horrified. The girl went straight to the corner grocery, and demanded her own horse, handing back to the man the dollar he had paid her last Saturday night, and saying she had need of the horse at once. After some parley, in which she showed her ability to stand her own ground, the boy unhitched the horse from the wagon, and got her own old saddle for her from the stable. Then Elizabeth mounted her horse and rode away to Rittenhouse Square.

Chapter 13

Another Grandmother

Elizabeth's idea in taking the horse along with her was to have all her armor on, as a warrior goes out to meet the foe. If this grandmother proved impossible, why, then so long as she had life and breath and a horse she could flee. The world was wide, and the West was still open to her. She could flee back to the wilderness that gave her breath.

The old horse stopped gravely and disappointedly before the tall, aristocratic house in Rittenhouse Square. He had hoped that city life was now to end, and that he and his dear mistress were to travel back to their beloved prairies. No amount of oats could ever make up to him for his freedom, and the quiet, and the hills. He had a feeling that he should like to go back home and die. He had seen enough of the world.

She fastened the halter to a ring in the sidewalk, which surprised him. The grocer's boy never fastened him. He looked up questioningly at the house, but saw no reason why his mistress should go in there. It was not familiar ground. Koffee and Sons never came up this way.

Elizabeth, as she crossed the sidewalk and mounted the steps before the formidable carved doors, felt that here was the last hope of finding an earthly habitation. If this failed her, then there was the desert, and starvation, and a long, long sleep. But while the echo of the bell still sounded through the high-ceiled hall there came to her the words: "Let not your heart be troubled. . . . In my Father's house are many mansions; if it were not so, I would have told you. I go to prepare a place for you. . . . I will come again and receive you." How sweet that was! Then, even if she died on the desert, there was a home prepared for her. So much she had learned in Christian Endeavor meeting.

123

The stately butler let her in. He eyed her questioningly at first, and said madam was not up yet; but Elizabeth told him she would wait.

"Is she sick?" asked Elizabeth with a strange constriction about her heart.

"O no, she is not up yet, miss," said the kind old butler; "she never gets up before this. You're from Mrs. Sands, I suppose." Poor soul, for once his butler eyes had been mistaken. He thought she was the little errand-girl from Madam Bailey's modiste.

"No, I'm just Elizabeth," said the girl, smiling. She felt that this man, whoever he was, was not against her. He was old, and he had a kind look.

He still thought she meant she was not the modiste, just her errand-girl. Her quaint dress and the long braid down her back made her look like a child.

"I'll tell her you've come. Be seated," said the butler, and gave her a chair in the dim hall just opposite the parlor door, where she had a glimpse of elegance such as she had never dreamed existed. She tried to think how it must be to live in such a room and walk on velvet. The carpet was deep and rich. She did not know it was a rug, nor that it was woven in some poor peasant's home and then was brought here years afterward at a fabulous price. She only knew it was beautiful in its silvery sheen, with gleaming colors through it like jewels in the dew.

On through another open doorway she caught a glimpse of a painting on the wall. It was a man as large as life, sitting in a chair; and the face and attitude were her father's—her father at his best. She was fairly startled. Who was it? Could it be her father? And how had they made this picture of him? He must be changed in those twenty years he had been gone from home.

Then the butler came back, and before he could speak she pointed toward the picture. "Who is it?" she asked.

"That, miss? That's Mr. John, Madam's husband that's dead a good many years now. But I remember him well."

"Could I look at it? He is so much like my father." She walked rapidly over the ancient rug, unheeding its beauties, while the wondering butler followed a trifle anxiously. This was unprecedented. Mrs. Sands's errand-girls usually knew their place.

"Madam said you was to come right up to her room," said the butler pointedly. But Elizabeth stood rooted to the ground, studying the picture. The butler had to repeat his message. She smiled and turned to follow him, and as she did so saw on a side wall the portraits of two boys.

"Who are they?" she pointed swiftly. They were much like her own two brothers.

"Them are Mr. John and Mr. James, Madam's two sons. They's both of them dead now," said the butler. "At least, Mr. James is, I'm sure. He died two years ago. But you better come right up. Madam will be wondering."

She followed the old man up the velvet-shod stairs that gave back no sound from footfall, and pondered as she went. Then that was her father, that boy with the beautiful face and the heavy wavy hair tossed back from his forehead, and the haughty, imperious, don't-care look. And here was where he had lived. Here amid all this luxury.

Like a flash came the quick contrast of the home in which he had died, and a great wave of reverence for her father rolled over her. From such a home and such surroundings it would not have been strange if he had grown weary of the rough life out West, and deserted his wife, who was beneath him in station. True, he had not been of much use to her, and much of the time had been but a burden and anxiety; but he had stayed and loved her—when he was sober. She forgave him his many trying ways, his faultfindings with her mother's many little blunders—no wonder, when he came from this place.

The butler tapped on a door at the head of the stairs, and a maid swung it open.

"Why, you're not the girl Mrs. Sands sent the other day," said a querulous voice from a mass of lace-ruffled pillows on the great bed.

"I am Elizabeth," said the girl, as if that were full explanation.

"Elizabeth? Elizabeth who? I don't see why she sent another girl. Are you sure you will understand the directions? They're very particu-

lar, for I want my frock ready for to-night without fail." The woman
sat up, leaning on one elbow. Her lace nightgown and pale-blue silk
dressing-sack fell away from a round white arm that did not look as if
it belonged to a very old lady. Her gray hair was becomingly arranged,
and she was extremely pretty, with small features. Elizabeth looked
and marvelled. Like a flash came the vision of the other grandmother
at the wash-tub. The contrast was startling.

"I am Elizabeth Bailey," said the girl quietly, as if she would break a
piece of hard news gently. "My father was your son John."

"The idea!" said the new grandmother, and promptly fell back upon
her pillows with her hand upon her heart. "John, John, my little John.
No one has mentioned his name to me for years and years. He never
writes to me." She put up a lace-trimmed handkerchief, and sobbed.

"Father died five years ago," said Elizabeth.

"You wicked girl!" said the maid. "Can't you see that Madam can't
bear such talk? Go right out of the room!" The maid rushed up with
smelling-salts and a glass of water, and Elizabeth in distress came and
stood by the bed.

"I'm sorry I made you feel bad, grandmother," she said when she
saw that the fragile, childish creature on the bed was recovering somewhat.

"What right have you to call me that? Grandmother, indeed! I'm not
so old as that. Besides, how do I know you belong to me? If John is
dead, your mother better look after you. I'm sure I'm not responsible
for you. It's her business. She wheedled John away from his home, and
carried him off to that awful West, and never let him write to me. She
has done it all, and now she may bear the consequences. I suppose she
has sent you here to beg, but she has made a mistake. I shall not have a
thing to do with her or her children."

"Grandmother!" Elizabeth's eyes flashed as they had done to the
other grandmother a few hours before. "You must not talk so. I won't
hear it. I wouldn't let Grandmother Brady talk about my father, and
you can't talk so about mother. She was my mother, and I loved her,
and so did father love her; and she worked hard to keep him and take

care of him when he drank years and years, and didn't have any money to help her. Mother was only eighteen when she married father, and you ought not to blame her. She didn't have a nice home like this. But she was good and dear, and now she is dead. Father and Mother are both dead, and all the other children. A man killed my brother, and then as soon as he was buried he came and wanted me to go with him. He was an awful man, and I was afraid, and took my brother's horse and ran away. I rode all this long way because I was afraid of that man, and I wanted to get to some of my own folks, who would love me, and let me work for them, and let me go to school and learn something. But I wish now I had stayed out there and died. I could have lain down in the sage-brush, and a wild beast would have killed me perhaps, and that would be a great deal better than this; for Grandmother Brady does not understand, and you do not want me; but in my Father's house in heaven there are many mansions, and He went to prepare a place for me; so I guess I will go back to the desert, and perhaps He will send for me. Good-by, Grandmother."

Then before the astonished woman in the bed could recover her senses from this remarkable speech Elizabeth turned and walked majestically from the room. She was slight and not very tall, but in the strength of her pride and purity she looked almost majestic to the awe-struck maid and the bewildered woman.

Down the stairs walked the girl, feeling that all the wide world was against her. She would never again try to get a friend. She had not met a friend except in the desert. One man had been good to her, and she had let him go away; but he belonged to another woman, and she might not let him stay. There was just one thing to be thankful for. She had knowledge of her Father in heaven, and she knew what Christian Endeavor meant. She could take that with her out into the desert, and no one could take it from her. One wish she had, but maybe that was too much to hope for. If she could have had a Bible of her own! She had no money left. Nothing but her mother's wedding-ring, the papers, and the envelope that had contained the money the man had given her when he left. She could not part with them, unless perhaps someone would take the ring and keep it until she could buy it back. But she would wait and hope.

She walked by the old butler with her hand on her pistol. She did not intend to let anyone detain her now. He bowed pleasantly, and opened the door for her, however; and she marched down the steps to her horse. But just as she was about to mount and ride away into the unknown where no grandmother, be she Brady or Bailey, would ever be able to search her out, no matter how hard she tried, the door suddenly opened again, and there was a great commotion. The maid and the old butler both flew out, and laid hands upon her. She dropped the bridle, and seized her pistol, covering them both with its black, forbidding nozzle.

They stopped, trembling, but the butler bravely stood his ground. He did not know why he was to detain this extraordinary young person, but he felt sure something was wrong. Probably she was a thief, and had taken some of Madam's jewels. He could call the police. He opened his mouth to do so when the maid explained.

"Madam wants you to come back. She didn't understand. She wants to see you and ask about her son. You must come, or you will kill her. She has heart-trouble, and you must not excite her."

Elizabeth put the pistol back into its holster, and, picking up the bridle again, fastened it in the ring, saying simply, "I will come back."

"What do you want?" she asked abruptly when she returned to the bedroom.

"Don't you know that's a disrespectful way to speak?" asked the woman querulously. "What did you have to get into a temper for, and go off like that without telling me anything about my son? Sit down, and tell me all about it."

"I'm sorry, Grandmother," said Elizabeth, sitting down. "I thought you didn't want me and I better go."

"Well, the next time wait until I send you. What kind of a thing have you got on, anyway? That's a queer sort of a hat for a girl to wear. Take it off. You look like a rough boy with that on. You make me think of John when he had been out disobeying me."

Elizabeth took off the offending headgear, and revealed her smoothly parted, thick brown hair in its long braid down her back.

"Why, you're rather a pretty girl if you were fixed up," said the old lady, sitting up with interest now. "I can't remember your mother, but I don't think she had fine features like that."

"They said I looked like Father," said Elizabeth.

"Did they? Well, I believe it's true," with satisfaction. "I couldn't bear if you looked like those low-down——"

"Grandmother!" Elizabeth stood up, and flashed her Bailey eyes.

"You needn't 'grandmother' me all the time," said the lady petulantly. "But you look quite handsome when you say it. Take off that ill-fitting coat. It isn't thick enough for winter, anyway. What in the world have you got round your waist? A belt? Why, that's a man's belt! And what have you got on it? Pistols? Horrors! Marie, take them away quick! I shall faint! I never could bear to be in a room with one. My husband used to have one on his closet shelf, and I never went near it, and always locked the room when he was out. You must put them out in the hall. I cannot breathe where pistols are. Now sit down and tell me all about it, how old you are, and how you got here."

Elizabeth surrendered her pistols with hesitation. She felt that she must obey her grandmother, but was not altogether certain whether it was safe for her to be weaponless until she was sure this was friendly ground.

At the demand she began back as far as she could remember, and told the story of her life, pathetically, simply, without a single claim to pity, yet so earnestly and vividly that the grandmother, lying with her eyes closed, forgot herself completely, and let the tears trickle unbidden and unheeded down her well-preserved cheeks.

When Elizabeth came to the graves in the moonlight, she gasped, and sobbed: "O Johnny, Johnny, my little Johnny! Why did you always be such a bad, bad boy?" and when the ride in the desert was described, and the man from whom she fled, the grandmother held her breath, and said, "O, how fearful!" Her interest in the girl was growing, and kept at white heat during the whole of the story.

There was one part of her experience, however, that Elizabeth

passed over lightly, and that was the meeting with George Trescott
Benedict. Instinctively she felt that this experience would not find a
sympathetic listener. She passed it over by merely saying that she had
met a kind gentleman from the East who was lost, and that they had
ridden together for a few miles until they reached a town; and he had
telegraphed to his friends, and gone on his way. She said nothing
about the money he had lent to her, for she shrank from speaking
about him more than was necessary. She felt that her grandmother
might feel as the old woman of the ranch had felt about their travelling
together. She left it to be inferred that she might have had a little
money with her from home. At least, the older woman asked no questions about how she secured provisions for the way.

When Elizabeth came to her Chicago experience, her grandmother
clasped her hands as if a serpent had been mentioned, and said: "How
degrading! You certainly would have been justified in shooting the
whole company. I wonder such places are allowed to exist!" But Marie
sat with large eyes of wonder, and retailed the story over again in the
kitchen afterwards for the benefit of the cook and the butler, so that
Elizabeth became henceforth a heroine among them.

Elizabeth passed on to her Philadelphia experience, and found that
here her grandmother was roused to blazing indignation, but the thing
that roused her was the fact that a Bailey should serve behind a
counter in a ten-cent store. She lifted her hands, and uttered a moan of
real pain, and went on at such a rate that the smelling-salts had to be
brought into requisition again.

When Elizabeth told of her encounter with the manager in the cellar, the grandmother said: "How disgusting! The impertinent creature!
He ought to be sued. I will consult the lawyer about the matter. What
did you say his name was? Marie, write that down. And so, dear, you
did quite right to come to me. I've been looking at you while you
talked, and I believe you'll be a pretty girl if you are fixed up. Marie,
go to the telephone, and call up Blandeaux, and tell him to send up a
hair-dresser at once. I want to see how Miss Elizabeth will look with
her hair done low in one of those new coils. I believe it will be becom-

ing. I shall have tried it long ago myself; only it seems a trifle too youthful for hair that is beginning to turn gray."

Elizabeth watched her grandmother in wonder. Here truly was a new phase of woman. She did not care about great facts, but only about little things. Her life was made up of the great pursuit of fashion, just like Lizzie's. Were people in cities all alike? No, for he, the one man she had met in the wilderness, had not seemed to care. Maybe, though, when he got back to the city he did care. She sighed and turned toward the new grandmother.

"Now I have told you everything, Grandmother. Shall I go away? I wanted to go to school; but I see that it costs a great deal of money, and I don't want to be a burden on any one. I came here, not to ask you to take me in, because I did not want to trouble you; but I thought before I went away I ought to see you once because—because you are my grandmother."

"I've never been a grandmother," said the little woman of the world reflectively, "but I don't know but it would be rather nice. I'd like to make you into a pretty girl, and take you out into society. That would be something new to live for. I'm not very pretty myself any more, but I can see that you will be. Do you wear blue or pink? I used to wear pink myself, but I believe you could wear either when you get your complexion in shape. You've tanned it horribly, but it may come out all right. I think you'll take. You say you want to go to school. Why, certainly, I suppose that will be necessary; living out in that barbarous, uncivilized region, of course you don't know much. You seem to speak correctly, but John always was particular about his speech. He had a tutor when he was little who tripped him up every mistake he made. That was the only thing that tutor was good for; he was a linguist. We found out afterwards he was terribly wild, and drank. He did John more harm than good. Marie, I shall want Elizabeth to have the rooms next mine. Ring for Martha to see that everything is in order. Elizabeth, did you ever have your hands manicured? You have a pretty-shaped hand. I'll have the woman attend to it when she comes to shampoo your hair and put it up. Did you bring any clothes along? Of course not. You couldn't on horseback. I suppose you had your trunk sent by express. No trunk? No express? No railroad? How barbarous! How John must have suffered, poor fellow! He, so used to every luxury! Well, I don't see that it was my fault. I gave him everything he wanted except his wife, and he took her without my leave. Poor fellow, poor fellow!"

Mrs. Bailey in due time sent Elizabeth off to the suite of rooms that she said were to be hers exclusively, and arose to bedeck herself for another day. Elizabeth was a new toy, and she anticipated playing with her. It put new zest into a life that had grown monotonous.

Elizabeth, meanwhile, was surveying her quarters, and wondering what Lizzie would think if she could see her. According to orders, the coachman had taken Robin to the stable, and he was already rolling in all the luxuries of a horse of the aristocracy, and congratulating himself on the good taste of his mistress to select such a stopping-place. For his part he was now satisfied not to move further. This was better than the wilderness any day. Oats like these, and hay such as this, were not to be found on the plains.

Toward evening the grave butler, with many a deprecatory glance at the neighborhood, arrived at the door of Mrs. Brady, and delivered himself of the following message to that astonished lady, backed by her daughter and her granddaughter, with their ears stretched to the utmost to hear every syllable:

"Mrs. Merrill Wilton Bailey sends word that her granddaughter, Miss Elizabeth, has reached her home safely, and will remain with her. Miss Elizabeth will come sometime to see Mrs. Brady, and thank her for her kindness during her stay with her."

The butler bowed, and turned away with relief. His dignity and social standing had not been so taxed by the family demands in years. He was glad he might shake off the dust of Flora Street forever. He felt for the coachman. He would probably have to drive the young lady down here sometime, according to that message.

Mrs. Brady, her daughter, and Lizzie stuck their heads out into the lamplighted street, and watched the dignified butler out of sight. Then

they went in and sat down in three separate stages of relief and astonishment.

"Fer the land sakes!" ejaculated the grandmother. "Well, now, if
that don't beat all!" then after a minute: "The impertinent fellow! And
the impidence of the woman! Thank me fer my kindness to me own
grandchild! I'd thank her to mind her business, but then that's just like
her."

"Her nest is certainly well feathered," said Aunt Nan enviously. "I
only wish Lizzie had such a chance."

Said Lizzie: "It's awful queer, her looking like that, too, in that crazy
rig! Well, I'm glad she's gone, fer she was so awful queer it was jest
fierce. She talked religion a lot to the girls, and then they laughed at
her behind her back; and they kep' a telling me I'd be a missionary
'fore long if she stayed with us. I went to Mr. Wray, the manager, and
told him my cousin was awfully shy, and she sent word she wanted to
be excused fer running away like that. He kind of colored up, and said
'twas all right, and she might come back and have her old place if she
wanted, and he'd say no more about it. I told him I'd tell her. But I
guess her acting up won't do me a bit of harm. The girls say he'll make
up to *me* now. Wish he would. I'd have a fine time. It's me turn to have
me wages raised, anyway. He said if Bess and I would come to-morrow
ready to stay in the evening, he'd take us to a show that beat everything he ever saw in Philadelphia. I mean to make him take me, anyway. I'm just glad she's out of the way. She wasn't like the rest of us."

Said Mrs. Brady: "It's the Bailey in her. But she said she'd come
back and see me, didn't she?" and the grandmother in her meditated
over that fact for several minutes.

Chapter 14

In a New World

Meantime the panorama of Elizabeth's life passed on into more peaceful scenes. By means of the telephone and the maid a lot of new and beautiful garments were provided for her, which fitted perfectly, and which bewildered her not a little until they were explained by Marie. Elizabeth had her meals up-stairs until these things had arrived and she had put them on. The texture of the garments was fine and soft, and they were rich with embroidery and lace. The flannels were as soft as the down in a milkweed pod, and everything was of the best. Elizabeth found herself wishing she might share them with Lizzie,— Lizzie who adored rich and beautiful things, and who had shared her meagre outfit with her. She mentioned this wistfully to her grandmother, and in a fit of childish generosity that lady said: "Certainly, get her what you wish. I'll take you downtown some day, and you can pick out some nice things for them all. I hate to be under obligations."

A dozen ready-made dresses had been sent out before the first afternoon was over, and Elizabeth spent the rest of the day in trying on and walking back and forth in front of her grandmother. At last two or three were selected which it was thought would "do" until the dressmaker could be called in to help, and Elizabeth was clothed and allowed to come down into the life of the household.

It was not a large household. It consisted of the grandmother, her dog, and the servants. Elizabeth fitted into it better than she had feared. It seemed pleasanter to her than the house on Flora Street. There was more room, and more air, and more quiet. With her mountain breeding she could not get her breath in a crowd.

She was presently taken in a luxurious carriage, drawn by two

135

beautiful horses, to a large department store, where she sat by the hour and watched her grandmother choose things for her. Another girl might have gone half wild over the delightful experience of being able to have anything in the shops. Not so Elizabeth. She watched it all apathetically, as if the goods displayed about had been the leaves upon the trees set forth for her admiration. She could wear but one dress at once, and one hat. Why were so many necessary? Her main hope lay in the words her grandmother had spoken about sending her to school.

The third day of her stay in Rittenhouse Square, Elizabeth had reminded her of it, and the grandmother had said half impatiently: "Yes, yes, child; you shall go of course to a finishing school. That will be necessary. But first I must get you fixed up. You have scarcely anything to put on." So Elizabeth subsided.

At last there dawned a beautiful Sabbath when, the wardrobe seemingly complete, Elizabeth was told to array herself for church, as they were going that morning. With great delight and thanksgiving she put on what she was told; and, when she looked into the great French plate mirror after Marie had put on the finishing touches, she was astonished at herself. It was all true, after all. She was a pretty girl.

She looked down at the beautiful gown of finest broadcloth, with the exquisite finish that only the best tailors can put on a garment, and wondered at herself. The very folds of dark-green cloth seemed to bring a grace into her movements. The green velvet hat with its long curling plumes of green and cream-color seemed to be resting lovingly above the beautiful hair that was arranged so naturally and becomingly.

Elizabeth wore her lovely ermine collar and muff without ever knowing they were costly. They all seemed so fitting and quiet and simple, so much less obtrusive than Lizzie's pink silk waist and cheap pink plumes. Elizabeth liked it, and walked to church beside her grandmother with a happy feeling in her heart.

The church was just across the Square. Its tall brown stone spire and arched doorways attracted Elizabeth when she first came to the place. Now she entered with a kind of delight.

It was the first time she had ever been to a Sabbath morning regular service in church. The Christian Endeavor had been as much as Lizzie had been able to stand. She said she had to work too hard during the week to waste so much time on Sunday in church. "The Sabbath was made for man" and "for rest," she had quoted glibly. For the first time in her life since she left Montana Elizabeth felt as if she had a real home and was like other people. She looked around shyly to see whether perchance her friend of the desert might be sitting near, but no familiar face met her gaze. Then she settled back, and gave herself up to delight in the service.

The organ was playing softly, low, tender music. She learned afterward that the music was Handel's "Largo." She did not know that the organ was one of the finest in the city, nor that the organist was one of the most skillful to be had; she knew only that the music seemed to take her soul and lift it up above the earth so that heaven was all around her, and the very clouds seemed singing to her. Then came the processional, with the wonderful voices of the choir-boys sounding far off, and then nearer. It would be impossible for anyone who had been accustomed all his life to these things to know how it affected Elizabeth.

It seemed as though the Lord Himself was leading the girl in a very special way. At scarcely any other church in a fashionable quarter of the great city would Elizabeth have heard preaching so exactly suited to her needs. The minister was one of those rare men who lived with God, and talked with Him daily. He had one peculiarity which marked him from all other preachers, Elizabeth heard afterward. He would turn and talk with God in a gentle, sweet, conversational tone right in the midst of his sermon. It made the Lord seem very real and very near.

If he had not been the great and brilliant preacher of an old established church, and revered by all denominations as well as his own, the minister would have been called eccentric and have been asked to resign, because his religion was so very personal that it became embarrassing to some. However, his rare gifts, and his remarkable consecration and independence in doing what he thought right, had produced a most unusual church for a fashionable neighborhood.

Most of his church-members were in sympathy with him, and a

wonderful work was going forward right in the heart of Sodom, un-
hampered by fashion or form or class distinctions. It is true there were
some who, like Madam Bailey sat calmly in their seats, and let the
minister attend to the preaching end of the service without ever bothering their thoughts as to what he was saying. It was all one to them
whether he prayed three times or once, so the service got done at the
usual hour. But the majority were being led to see that there is such a
thing as a close and intimate walk with God upon this earth.

Into this church came Elizabeth, the sweet heathen, eager to learn
all that could be learned about the things of the soul. She sat beside
her grandmother, and drank in the sermon, and bowed her lovely, rev-
erent head when she became aware that God was in the room and was
being spoken to by His servant. After the last echo of the recessional
had died away, and the bowed hush of the congregation had grown
into a quiet, well-bred commotion of the putting on of wraps and the
low Sabbath greetings, Elizabeth turned to her grandmother.

"Grandmother, may I please go and ask that man some questions?
He said just what I have been longing and longing to know, and I must
ask him more. Nobody else ever told me these things. Who is he? How
does he know it is all true?"

The elder woman watched the eager, flushed face of the girl; and her
heart throbbed with pride that this beautiful young thing belonged to
her. She smiled indulgently.

"The rector, you mean? Why, I'll invite him to dinner if you wish to
talk with him. It's perfectly proper that a young girl should understand
about religion. It has a most refining influence, and the Doctor is a
charming man. I'll invite his wife and daughter too. They move in the
best circles, and I have been meaning to ask them for a long time. You
might like to be confirmed. Some do. It's a very pretty service. I was
confirmed myself when I was about your age. My mother thought it a
good thing for a girl before she went into society. Now, just as you are
a schoolgirl, is the proper time. I'll send for him this week. He'll be
pleased to know you are interested in these things. He has some kind
of a young people's club that meets on Sunday. 'Christian Something'
he calls it; I don't know just what, but he talks a great deal about it,

and wants every young person to join. You might pay the dues, whatever they are, anyway. I suppose it's for charity. It wouldn't be necessary for you to attend the meetings, but it would please the Doctor."

"Is it Christian Endeavor?" asked Elizabeth, with her eyes sparkling.

"Something like that, I believe. Good morning, Mrs. Schuyler. Lovely day, isn't it? for December. No, I haven't been very well. No, I haven't been out for several weeks. Charming service, wasn't it? The Doctor grows more and more brilliant, I think. Mrs. Schuyler, this is my granddaughter, Elizabeth. She has just come from the West to live with me and complete her education. I want her to know your daughter."

Elizabeth passed through the introduction as a necessary interruption to her train of thought. As soon as they were out upon the street again she began.

"Grandmother, was God in that church?"

"Dear me, child! What strange questions you do ask! Why, yes, I suppose He was, in a way. God is everywhere, they say. Elizabeth, you had better wait until you can talk these things over with a person whose business it is. I never understood much about such questions. You look very nice in that shade of green, and your hat is most becoming."

So was the question closed for the time, but not put out of the girl's thoughts.

The Christmas time had come and passed without much notice on the part of Elizabeth, to whom it was an unfamiliar festival. Mrs. Bailey had suggested that she select some gifts for her "relatives on her mother's side," as she always spoke of the Bradys; and Elizabeth had done so with alacrity, showing good sense and good taste in her choice of gifts, as well as deference to the wishes of the one to whom they were to be given. Lizzie, it is true, was a trifle disappointed that her present was not a gold watch or a diamond ring; but on the whole she was pleased.

A new world opened before the feet of Elizabeth. School was filled with wonder and delight. She absorbed knowledge like a sponge in the water, and rushed eagerly from one study to another, showing marvellous aptitude, and bringing to every task the enthusiasm of a pleasure-seeker.

Her growing intimacy with Jesus Christ through the influence of the pastor who knew Him so well caused her joy in life to blossom into loveliness.

The Bible she studied with the zest of a novel-reader, for it was a novel to her; and daily, as she took her rides in the park on Robin, now groomed into self-respecting sleekness, and wearing a saddle of the latest approved style, she marvelled over God's wonderful goodness to her, just a maid of the wilderness.

So passed three beautiful years in peace and quietness. Every month Elizabeth went to see her Grandmother Brady, and to take some charming little gifts; and every summer she and her Grandmother Bailey spent at some of the fashionable watering-places or in the Catskills, the girl always dressed in most exquisite taste, and as sweetly indifferent in her clothes as a bird of the air or a flower of the field.

The first pocket-money she had been given she saved up, and before long had enough to send the forty dollars to the address the man in the wilderness had given her. But with it she sent no word. It was like her to think she had no right.

She went out more and more with her grandmother among the fashionable old families in Philadelphia society, though as yet she was not supposed to be "out," being still in school; but in all her goings she neither saw nor heard of George Trescott Benedict.

Often she looked about upon the beautiful women that came to her grandmother's house, who smiled and talked to her, and wondered which of them might be the lady to whom his heart was bound. She fancied she must be most sweet and lovely in every way, else such as he could not care for her; so she would pick out this one and that one; and then, as some disagreeableness or glaring fault would appear, she would drop that one for another. There were only a few, after all, that she felt were good enough for the man who had become her ideal.

But sometimes in her dreams he would come and talk with her, and smile as he used to do when they rode together; and he would lay his hand on the mane of her horse—there were always the horses in her dreams. She liked to think of it when she rode in the park, and to think how pleasant it would be if he could be riding there beside her, and they might talk of a great many things that had happened since he left her alone. She felt she would like to tell him of how she had found a friend in Jesus Christ. He would be glad to know about it, she was sure. He seemed to be one who was interested in such things, not like other people who were all engaged in the world.

Sometimes she felt afraid something had happened to him. He might have been thrown from that terrible train and killed, perhaps; and no one know anything about it. But as her experience grew wider, and she travelled on the trains herself, of course this fear grew less. She came to understand that the world was wide, and many things might have taken him away from his home.

Perhaps the money she had sent reached him safely, but she had put in no address. It had not seemed right that she should. It would seem to draw his attention to her, and she felt "the lady " would not like that. Perhaps they were married by this time, and had gone far away to some charmed land to live. Perhaps—a great many things. Only this fact remained; he never came any more into the horizon of her life; and therefore she must try to forget him, and be glad that God had given her a friend in him for her time of need. Some day in the eternal home perhaps she would meet him and thank him for his kindness to her, and then they might tell each other all about the journey through the great wilderness of earth after they had parted. The links in Elizabeth's theology had been well supplied by this time, and her belief in the hereafter was strong and simple like a child's.

She had one great longing, however, that he, her friend, who had in a way been the first to help her toward higher things, and to save her from the wilderness, might know Jesus Christ as he had not known Him when they were together. And so in her daily prayer she often talked with her heavenly Father about him, until she came to have an abiding faith that some day, somehow, he would learn the truth about his Christ.

During the third season of Elizabeth's life in Philadelphia her grandmother decided that it was high time to bring out this bud of promise, who was by this time developing into a more beautiful girl than even her fondest hopes had pictured.

So Elizabeth "came out," and Grandmother Brady read her doings and sayings in the society columns with her morning coffee and an air of deep satisfaction. Aunt Nan listened with her nose in the air. She could never understand why Elizabeth should have privileges beyond her Lizzie. It was the Bailey in her, of course, and mother ought not to think well of it. But Grandmother Brady felt that, while Elizabeth's success was doubtless due in large part to the Bailey in her, still, she was a Brady, and the Brady had not hindered her. It was a step upward for the Bradys.

Lizzie listened, and with pride retailed at the ten-cent store the doings of "my cousin, Elizabeth Bailey," and the other girls listened with awe.

And so it came on to be the springtime of the third year that Elizabeth had spent in Philadelphia.

Chapter 15

An Eventful Picnic

It was summer and it was June. There was to be a picnic, and Elizabeth was going.

Grandmother Brady had managed it. It seemed to her that, if Elizabeth could go, her cup of pride would be full to overflowing; so after much argument, pro and con, with her daughter and Lizzie, she set herself down to pen the invitation. Aunt Nan was decidedly against it. She did not wish to have Lizzie outshone. She had been working nights for two weeks on an elaborate organdie, with pink roses all over it, for Lizzie to wear. It had yards and yards of cheap lace and insertion, and a whole bolt of pink ribbons of various widths. The hat was a marvel of impossible roses, just calculated for the worst kind of a wreck if a thunder-shower should come up at a Sunday-school picnic. Lizzie's mother was even thinking of getting her a pink chiffon parasol to carry; but the family treasury was well-nigh depleted, and it was doubtful whether that would be possible. After all that, it did not seem pleasant to have Lizzie put in the shade by a fine-lady cousin in silks and jewels.

But Grandmother Brady had waited long for her triumph. She desired above all things to walk among her friends and introduce her granddaughter, Elizabeth Bailey, and inadvertently remark: "You must have seen me granddaughter's name in the paper often, Mrs. Babcock. She was giving a party in Rittenhouse Square the other day."

Elizabeth would likely be married soon, and perhaps go off somewhere away from Philadelphia—New York or Europe, there was no telling what great fortune might come to her. Now the time was ripe for triumph if ever, and when things are ripe they must be picked. Mrs. Brady proceeded to pick.

She gathered together at great pains pen, paper, and ink. A pencil would be inadequate when the note was going to Rittenhouse Square. She sat down when Nan and Lizzie had left for their day's work, and constructed her sentences with great care.

"Dear Bessie—" Elizabeth had never asked her not to call her that, although she fairly detested the name. But still it had been her mother's name, and was likely dear to her grandmother. It seemed disloyalty to her mother to suggest that she be called "Elizabeth." So Grandmother Brady serenely continued to call her "Bessie" to the end of her days. Elizabeth decided that to care much about such little things, in a world where there were so many great things, would be as bad as to give one's mind entirely over to the pursuit of fashion.

The letter proceeded laboriously:

"Our Sunday school is going to have a picnic out to Willow Grove. It's on Tuesday. We're going in the trolley. I'd be pleased if you would go 'long with us. We will spend the day, and take our dinner and supper along, and wouldn't get home till late; so you could stay overnight here with us, and not go back home till after breakfast. You needn't bring no lunch; fer we've got a lot of things planned, and it ain't worth while. But if you wanted to bring some candy, you might. I ain't got time to make any, and what you buy at our grocery might not be fine enough for you. I want you to go real bad. I've never took my two granddaughters off to anything yet, and your Grandmother Bailey has you to things all the time. I hope you can manage to come. I am going to pay all the expenses. Your old Christian Deaver you used to 'tend is going to be there; so you'll have a good time. Lizzie has a new pink organdie, with roses on her hat; and we're thinking of getting her a pink umbreller if it don't cost too much. The kind with chiffon flounces on it. You'll have a good time, fer there's lots of side-shows out to Willow Grove, and we're going to see everything there is to see. There's going to be some music too. A man with a name that sounds like swearing is going to make it. I don't remember it just now, but you can see it advertised round on the trolley-cars. He comes to Willow Grove every year. Now please let me hear if you will go at once, as I want to know how much cake to make.

"Your loving grandmother,

"ELIZABETH BRADY."

Elizabeth laughed and cried over this note. It pleased her to have her grandmother show kindness to her. She felt that whatever she did for Grandmother Brady was in a sense showing her love to her own mother; so she brushed aside several engagements, much to the annoyance of her Grandmother Bailey, who could not understand why she wanted to go down to Flora Street for two days and a night just in the beginning of warm weather. True, there was not much going on just now between seasons, and Elizabeth could do as she pleased; but she might get a fever in such a crowded neighborhood. It wasn't in the least wise. However, if she must, she must. Grandmother Bailey was on the whole lenient. Elizabeth was too much of a success, and too willing to please her in all things, for her to care to cross her wishes.

So Elizabeth wrote on her fine note-paper bearing the Bailey crest in silver:

"Dear Grandmother: I shall be delighted to go to the picnic with you, and I'll bring a nice box of candy, Huyler's best. I'm sure you'll think it's the best you ever tasted. Don't get Lizzie a parasol; I'm going to bring her one to surprise her. I'll be at the house by eight o'clock.

"Your loving granddaughter,

"ELIZABETH."

Mrs. Brady read this note with satisfaction and handed it over to her daughter to read with a gleam of triumph in her eyes at the supper-table. She knew the gift of the pink parasol would go far toward reconciling Aunt Nan to the addition to their party. Elizabeth never did things by halves, and the parasol would be all that could possibly be desired without straining the family pocketbook any further.

So Elizabeth went to the picnic in a cool white dimity, plainly made, with tiny frills of itself, edged with narrow lace that did not shout to the unknowing multitude, "I am real!" but was content with being so; and with a white Panama hat adorned with only a white silken scarf, but whose texture was possible only at a fabulous price. The shape reminded Elizabeth of the old felt hat belonging to her brother, which she had worn on her long trip across the continent. She had put it on in the hat-store one day; and her grandmother, when she found how exquisite a piece of weaving the hat was, at once purchased it for her. It was stylish to wear those soft hats in all sorts of odd shapes. Madam Bailey thought it would be just the thing for the seashore.

Her hair was worn in a low coil in her neck, making the general appearance and contour of her head much as it had been three years before. She wore no jewelry, save the unobtrusive gold buckle at her belt and the plain gold hatpin which fastened her hat. There was nothing about her which marked her as one of the "four hundred." She did not even wear the gloves, but carried them in her hand, and threw them carelessly upon the table when she arrived in Flora Street. Long, soft white ones, they lay there in their costly elegance beside Lizzie's postcard album that the livery-stable man gave her on her birthday, all the long day while Elizabeth was at Willow Grove, and Lizzie sweltered around under her pink parasol in long white silk gloves.

Grandmother Brady surveyed Elizabeth with decided disapproval. It seemed too bad on this her day of triumph, and after she had given a hint, as it were, about Lizzie's fine clothes, that the girl should be so blind or stubborn or both as to come around in that plain rig. Just a common white dress, and an old hat that might have been worn about a livery-stable. It was mortifying in the extreme. She expected a light silk, and kid gloves, and a beflowered hat. Why, Lizzie looked a great deal finer. Did Mrs. Bailey rig her out this way for spite? she wondered.

But, as it was too late to send Elizabeth back for more fitting garments, the old lady resigned herself to her disappointment. The pink parasol was lovely, and Lizzie was wild over it. Even Aunt Nan seemed mollified. It gave her great satisfaction to look the two girls over. Her own outshone the one from Rittenhouse Square by many counts, so thought the mother; but all day long, as she walked behind them or viewed them from afar, she could not understand why it was that the people who passed them always looked twice at Elizabeth and only once at Lizzie. It seemed, after all, that clothes did not make the girl. It was disappointing.

The box of candy was all that could possibly be desired. It was ample for the needs of them all, including the two youths from the livery-stable who had attached themselves to their party from the early morning. In fact, it was two boxes, one of the most delectable chocolates of all imaginable kinds, and the other of mixed candies and candied fruit. Both boxes bore the magic name "Huyler's" on the covers. Lizzie had often passed Huyler's, taking her noon walk on Chestnut Street, and looked enviously at the girls who walked in and out with white square bundles tied with gold cord as if it were an everyday affair. And now she was actually eating all she pleased of those renowned candies. It was almost like belonging to the great élite.

It was a long day and a pleasant one even to Elizabeth. She had never been to Willow Grove before, and the strange blending of sweet nature and Vanity Fair charmed her. It was a rest after the winter's round of monotonous engagements. Even the loud-voiced awkward youths from the livery-stable did not annoy her extremely. She took them as a part of the whole, and did not pay much attention to them. They were rather shy of her, giving the most of their attention to Lizzie, much to the satisfaction of Aunt Nan.

They mounted the horses in the merry-go-rounds, and tried each one several times. Elizabeth wondered why anybody desired this sort of amusement, and after her first trip would have been glad to sit with her grandmother and watch the others, only that the old lady seemed so much to desire to have her get on with the rest. She would not do anything to spoil the pleasure of the others if she could help it; so she obediently seated herself in a great sea-shell drawn by a soiled plaster nymph, and whirled on till Lizzie declared it was time to go to something else.

They went into the Old Mill, and down into the Mimic Mine, and sailed through the painted Venice, eating candy and chewing gum and shouting. All but Elizabeth. Elizabeth would not chew gum nor talk loud. It was not her way. But she smiled serenely on the rest, and did not let it worry her that someone might recognize the popular Miss Bailey in so ill-bred a crowd. She knew that it was their way, and they could have no other. They were having a good time, and she was a part of it for to-day. They weighed one another on the scales with many jokes and much laughter, and went to see all the moving pictures in the place. They ate their lunch under the trees, and then at last the music began.

They seated themselves on the outskirts of the company, for Lizzie declared that was the only pleasant place to be. She did not want to go "way up front." She had a boy on either side of her, and she kept the seat shaking with laughter. Now and then a weary guard would look distressedly down the line, and motion for less noise; but they giggled on. Elizabeth was glad they were so far back that they might not annoy more people than was necessary.

But the music was good, and she watched the leader with great satisfaction. She noticed that there were many people given up to the pleasure of it. The melody went to her soul, and thrilled through it. She had not had much good music in her life. The last three years, of course, she had been occasionally to the Academy of Music; but, though her grandmother had a box there, she very seldom had time or cared to attend concerts. Sometimes, when Melba, or Caruso, or some world-renowned favorite was there, she would take Elizabeth for an hour, usually slipping out just after the favorite solo with noticeable loftiness, as if the orchestra were the common dust of the earth, and she only condescended to come for the soloist. So Elizabeth had scarcely known the delight of a whole concert of fine orchestral music.

She heard Lizzie talking.

"Yes, that's Walter Damrosh! Ain't that name fierce? Grandma thinks it's kind of wicked to pernounce it that way. They say he's fine, but I must say I liked the band they had last year better. It played a whole lot of lively things, and once they had a rattle-box and a squeaking thing that cried like a baby right out in the music, and everybody just roared laughing. I tell you that was great. I don't care much for this here kind of music myself. Do you?" And Jim and Joe both agreed that they didn't, either. Elizabeth smiled, and kept on enjoying it.

Peanuts were the order of the day, and their assertive crackle broke in upon the finest passages. Elizabeth wished her cousin would take a walk; and by and by she did, politely inviting Elizabeth to go along; but she declined, and they were left to sit through the remainder of the afternoon concert.

After supper they watched the lights come out, Elizabeth thinking about the description of the heavenly city as one after another the buildings blazed out against the darkening blue of the June night. The music was about to begin. Indeed, it could be heard already in the distance, and drew the girl irresistibly. For the first time that day she made a move, and the others followed, half wearied of their dissipations, and not knowing exactly what to do next.

They stood the first half of the concert very well, but at the intermission they wandered out to view the electric fountain with its many-colored fluctuations, and to take a row on the tiny sheet of water. Elizabeth remained sitting where she was, and watched the fountain. Even her grandmother and aunt grew restless, and wanted to walk again. They said they had had enough music, and did not want to hear any more. They could hear it well enough, anyway, from further off. They believed they would have some ice-cream. Didn't Elizabeth want some?

She smiled sweetly. Would Grandmother mind if she sat right there and heard the second part of the concert? She loved music, and this was fine. She didn't feel like eating another thing to-night. So the two ladies, thinking the girl queer that she didn't want ice-cream, went off to enjoy theirs with a clear conscience; and Elizabeth drew a long breath, and sat back with her eyes closed, to rest and breathe in the sweet sounds that were beginning to float out delicately as if to feel whether the atmosphere were right for what was to come after.

It was just at the close of this wonderful music, which the programme said was Mendelssohn's "Spring Song," when Elizabeth looked up to meet the eyes of someone who stood near in the aisle watching her, and there beside her stood the man of the wilderness!

He was looking at her face, drinking in the beauty of the profile and wondering whether he was right. Could it be that this was his little brown friend, the maid of the wilderness? This girl with the lovely, refined face, the intellectual brow, the dainty fineness of manner? She looked like some white angel dropped down into that motley company of Sunday-school picknickers and city pleasure-seekers. The noise and clatter of the place seemed far away from her. She was absorbed utterly in the sweet sounds.

When she looked up and saw him, the smile that flashed out upon her face was like the sunshine upon a day that has hitherto been still and almost sad. The eyes said, "You are come at last!" The curve of the lips said, "I am glad you are here!"

He went to her like one who had been hungry for the sight of her for a long time, and after he had grasped her hand they stood so for a moment while the hum and gentle clatter of talk that always starts between numbers seethed around them and hid the few words they spoke at first.

"O, I have so longed to know if you were safe!" said the man as soon as he could speak.

Then straightway the girl forgot all her three years of training, and her success as a débutante, and became the grave, shy thing she had been to him when he first saw her, looking up with awed delight into the face she had seen in her dreams for so long, and yet might not long for.

The orchestra began again, and they sat in silence listening. But yet their souls seemed to speak to each other through the medium of the music, as if the intervening years were being bridged and brought together in the space of those few waves of melody.

"I have found out," said Elizabeth, looking up shyly with a great light in her eyes. "I have found what it all means. Have you? O, I have wanted so much to know whether you had found out too!"

"Found out what?" he asked half sadly that he did not understand.

"Found out how God hides us. Found what a friend Jesus Christ can be."

"You are just the same," said the man with satisfaction in his eyes.

"You have not been changed nor spoiled. They could not spoil you."

"Have you found out too?" she asked softly. She looked up into his eyes with wistful longing. She wanted this thing so very much. It had been in her prayers for so long.

He could not withdraw his own glance. He did not wish to. He longed to be able to answer what she wished.

"A little, perhaps," he said doubtfully. "Not so much as I would like to. Will you help me?"

"*He* will help you. You will find Him if you search for Him with all your heart," she said earnestly. "It says so in His book."

Then came more music, wistful, searching, tender. Did it speak of the things of heaven to other souls there than those two?

He stooped down, and said in a low tone that somehow seemed to blend with the music like the words that fitted it.

"I will try with all my heart if you will help me."

She smiled her answer, brimming back with deep delight.

Into the final lingering notes of an andante from one of Beethoven's sublime symphonies clashed the loud voice of Lizzie:

"O Bess! Bess! B-es-see! I say, Bessie! Ma says we'll have to go over by the cars now if we want to get a seat. The concert's most out, and there'll be a fierce rush. Come on! And Grandma says, bring your friend along with you if you want." This last with a smirking recognition of the man, who had turned around wonderingly to see who was speaking.

With a quick, searching glance that took in bedraggled organdie, rose hat, and pink parasol, and set them aside for what they were worth, George Benedict observed and classified Lizzie.

"Will you excuse yourself, and let me take you home a little later?" he asked in a low tone. "The crowd will be very great, and I have my automobile here."

She looked at him gratefully, and assented. She had much to tell him. She leaned across the seats, and spoke in a clear tone to her cousin.

"I will come a little later," she said, smiling with her Rittenhouse Square look that always made Lizzie a little afraid of her. "Tell Grandmother I have found an old friend I have not seen for a long time. I will be there almost as soon as you are."

They waited while Lizzie explained, and the grandmother and aunt nodded a reluctant assent. Aunt Nan frowned. Elizabeth might have brought her friend along, and introduced him to Lizzie. Did Elizabeth think Lizzie wasn't good enough to be introduced?

He wrapped her in a great soft rug that was in the automobile, and tucked her in beside him; and she felt as if the long, hard days that had passed since they had met were all forgotten and obliterated in this night of delight. Not all the attentions of all the fine men she had met in society had ever been like his, so gentle, so perfect. She had forgotten the lady as completely as if she had never heard of her. She wanted now to tell her friend about her heavenly Friend.

He let her talk, and watched her glowing, earnest face by the dim light of the sky; for the moon had come out to crown the night with beauty, and the unnatural brilliance of electric blaze, with all the glitter and noise of Willow Grove, died into the dim, sweet night as those two sped onward toward the city. The heart of the man kept singing, singing, singing: "I have found her at last! She is safe!"

"I have prayed for you always," he said in one of the pauses. It was just as they were coming into Flora Street. The urchins were all out on the sidewalk yet, for the night was hot; and they gathered about, and ran hooting after the car as it slowed up at the door. "I am sure He did hide you safely, and I shall thank Him for answering my prayer. And now I am coming to see you. May I come to-morrow?"

There was a great gladness in her eyes. "Yes," she said.

The Bradys had arrived from the corner trolley, and were hovering about the door self-assertively. It was almost apparent to an onlooker that this was a good opportunity for an introduction, but the two young people were entirely oblivious. The man touched his hat gravely, a look of great admiration in his eye, and said, "Good night" like a benediction. Then the girl turned and went into the plain little home and to her belligerent relatives with a light in her eyes and a joy in her steps that had not been there earlier in the day. The dreams that visited her hard pillow that night were heavenly and sweet.

Chapter 16

Alone Again

"Now we're goin' to see ef the paper says anythin' about our Bessie," said Grandmother Brady the next morning, settling her spectacles over her nose comfortably and crossing one fat gingham knee over the other. "I always read the society notes, Bess."

Elizabeth smiled, and her grandmother read down the column:

"Mr. George Trescott Benedict and his mother, Mrs. Vincent Benedict, have arrived home after an extended tour of Europe," read Mrs. Brady. "Mrs. Benedict is much improved in health. It is rumored they will spend the summer at their country seat on Wissahickon Heights."

"My!" interrupted Lizzie with her mouth full of fried potatoes. "That's that fellow that was engaged to that Miss What's-her-Name Loring. Don't you 'member? They had his picture in the papers, and her; and then all at once she threw him over for some dook or something, and this feller went off. I heard about it from Mame. Her sister works in a department-store, and she knows Miss Loring. She says she's an awfully handsome girl, and George Benedict was just gone on her. He had a fearful case. Mame says Miss Loring—what *is* her name?—O, Geraldine—Geraldine Loring bought some lace of her. She heard her say it was for the gown she was going to wear at the horse-show. They had her picture in the paper just after the horse-show, and it was all over lace. I saw it. It cost a whole lot. I forget how many dollars a yard. But there was something the matter with the dook. She didn't marry him, after all. In her picture she was driving four horses. Don't you remember it, Grandma? She sat up tall and high on a seat, holding a whole lot of ribbons and whips and things. She has an elegant figger. I guess mebbe the dook wasn't rich enough. She

153

hasn't been engaged to anybody else, and I shouldn't wonder now but she'd take George Benedict back. He was so awful stuck on her!"

Lizzie rattled on, and the grandmother read more society notes, but Elizabeth heard no more. Her heart had suddenly frozen, and dropped down like lead into her being. She felt as if she never would be able to raise it again. The lady! Surely she had forgotten the lady. But Geraldine Loring! Of all women! Could it be possible? Geraldine Loring was almost—well, fast, at least, as nearly so as one who was really of a fine old family, and still held her own in society, could be. She was beautiful as a picture; but her face, to Elizabeth's mind, was lacking in fine feeling and intellect. A great pity went out from her heart to the man whose fate was in that doll-girl's hands. True, she had heard that Miss Loring's family were unquestionable, and she knew her mother was a most charming woman. Perhaps she had misjudged her, for it could not be otherwise.

The joy had gone out of the morning when Elizabeth went home. She went up to her Grandmother Bailey at once, and after she had read her letters for her, and performed the little services that were her habit, she said:

"Grandmother, I'm expecting a man to call upon me to-day. I thought I had better tell you."

"A man!" said Madam Bailey, alarmed at once. She wanted to look over and portion out the right man when the time came. "What man?"

"Why, a man I met in Montana," said Elizabeth, wondering how much she ought to tell.

"A man you met in Montana! Horrors!" exclaimed the now thoroughly aroused grandmother. "Not that dreadful creature you ran away from?"

"O no!" said Elizabeth, smiling. "Not that man. A man who was very kind to me, and whom I like very much."

So much the worse. Immediate action was necessary.

"Well, Elizabeth," said Madam Bailey in her stiffest tones, "I really do not care to have any of your Montana friends visit you. You will have to excuse yourself. It will lead to embarrassing entanglements. You do not in the least realize your position in society. It is all well enough to please your relatives, although I think you often overdo that. You could just as well send them a present now and then, and please them more than to go yourself. But as for any outsiders, it is impossible. I draw the line there. "

"But Grandmother——"

"Don't interrupt me, Elizabeth; I have something more to say. I had word this morning from the steamship company. They can give us our staterooms on the Deutschland on Saturday, and I have decided to take them. I have telegraphed, and we shall leave here to-day for New York. I have one or two matters of business I wish to attend to in New York. We shall go to the Waldorf for a few days, and you will have more opportunity to see New York than you have yet. It will not be too warm to enjoy going about a little, I fancy; and a number of our friends are going to be at the Waldorf, too. The Craigs sail on Saturday with us. You will have young company on the voyage."

Elizabeth's heart sank lower than she had known it could go, and she grew white to the lips. The observant grandmother decided that she had done well to be so prompt. The man from Montana was by no means to be admitted. She gave orders to that effect, unknown to Elizabeth.

The girl went slowly to her room. All at once it had dawned upon her that she had not given her address to the man the night before, nor told him by so much as a word what were her circumstances. An hour's meditation brought her to the unpleasant decision that perhaps even now in this hard spot God was only hiding her from worse trouble. Mr. George Benedict belonged to Geraldine Loring. He had declared as much when he was in Montana. It would not be well for her to renew the acquaintance. Her heart told her by its great ache that she would be crushed under a friendship that could not be lasting.

Very sadly she sat down to write a note.

"My dear Friend," she wrote on plain paper with no crest. It was like her to choose that. She would not flaunt her good fortune to his face. She was a plain Montana girl to him, and so she would remain.

"My grandmother has been very ill, and is obliged to go away for her health. Unexpectedly I find that we are to go to-day. I supposed it would not be for a week yet. I am so sorry not to see you again, but I send you a little book that has helped me to get acquainted with Jesus Christ. Perhaps it will help you too. It is called 'My Best Friend.' I shall not forget to pray always that you may find Him. He is so precious to me! I must thank you in words, though I never can say it as it should be said, for your very great kindness to me when I was in trouble. God sent you to me, I am sure. Always gratefully your friend,

                                   "ELIZABETH."

That was all, no date, no address. He was not hers, and she would hang out no clues for him to find her, even if he wished. It was better so.

She sent the note and the little book to his address on Walnut Street; and then after writing a note to her Grandmother Brady, saying that she was going away for a long trip with Grandmother Bailey, she gave herself into the hands of the future like a submissive but weary child.

The noon train to New York carried in its drawing-room-car Madam Bailey, her granddaughter, her maid, and her dog, bound for Europe. The society columns so stated; and so read Grandmother Brady a few days afterward. So also read George Benedict, but it meant nothing to him.

When he received the note, his mind was almost as much excited as when he saw the little brown girl and the little brown horse vanishing behind the little brown station on the prairie. He went to the telephone, and reflected that he knew no names. He called up his automobile, and tore up to Flora Street; but in his bewilderment of the night before he had not noticed which block the house was in, nor which number. He thought he knew where to find it, but in broad daylight the houses were all alike for three blocks, and for the life of him he could not remember whether he had turned up to the right or the left when he came to Flora Street. He tried both, but saw no sign of the people he had but casually noticed at Willow Grove.

He could not ask where she lived, for he did not know her name. Nothing but Elizabeth, and they had called her Bessie. He could not go from house to house asking for a girl named Bessie. They would think him a fool, as he was, for not finding out her name, her precious name, at once. How could he let her slip from him again when he had just found her?

At last he hit upon a bright idea. He asked some children along the street whether they knew of any young woman named Bessie or Elizabeth living there, but they all with one accord shook their heads, though one volunteered the information that "Lizzie Smith lives there." It was most distracting and unsatisfying. There was nothing for it but for him to go home and wait in patience for her return. She would come back sometime probably. She had not said so, but she had not said she would not. He had found her once; he might find her again. And he could pray. She had found comfort in that; so would he. He would learn what her secret was. He would get acquainted with her "best Friend." Diligently did he study that little book, and then he went and hunted up the man of God who had written it, and who had been the one to lead Elizabeth into the path of light by his earnest preaching every Sabbath, though this fact he did not know.

The days passed, and the Saturday came. Elizabeth, heavy-hearted, stood on the deck of the Deutschland, and watched her native land disappear from view. So again George Benedict had lost her from sight.

It struck Elizabeth, as she stood straining her eyes to see the last of the shore through tears that would burn to the surface and fall down her white cheeks, that again she was running away from a man, only this time not of her own free will. She was being taken away. But perhaps it was better.

And it never once entered her mind that, if she had told her grandmother who the friend in Montana was, and where he lived in Philadelphia, it would have made all the difference in the world.

From the first of the voyage Grandmother Bailey grew steadily worse, and when they landed on the other side they went from one place to another seeking health. Carlsbad waters did not agree with her, and they went to the south of France to try the climate. At each move the little old lady grew weaker and more querulous. She finally made no further resistance, and gave up to the role of invalid. Then Elizabeth must be in constant attendance. Madam Bailey demanded reading, and no voice was so soothing as Elizabeth's.

Gradually Elizabeth substituted books of her own choice as her grandmother seemed not to mind, and now and then she would read a page of some book that told of the best Friend. At first because it was written by the dear pastor at home it commanded her attention, and finally because some dormant chord in her heart had been touched, she allowed Elizabeth to speak of these things. But it was not until they had been away from home for three months, and she had been growing daily weaker and weaker, that she allowed Elizabeth to read in the Bible.

The girl chose the fourteenth chapter of John, and over and over again, whenever the restless nerves tormented their victim, she would read those words, "Let not your heart be troubled" until the selfish soul, who had lived all her life to please the world and do her own pleasure, came at last to hear the words, and feel that perhaps she did believe in God, and might accept that invitation, "Believe also in me."

One day Elizabeth had been reading a psalm, and thought her grandmother was asleep. She was sitting back with weary heart, thinking what would happen if her grandmother should not get well. The old lady opened her eyes.

"Elizabeth," she said abruptly, just as when she was well, "you've been a good girl. I'm glad you came. I couldn't have died right without you. I never thought much about these things before, but it really is worth while. In my Father's house. He is my Father, Elizabeth."

She went to sleep then, and Elizabeth tiptoed out and left her with the nurse. By and by Marie came crying in, and told her that the Madam was dead.

Elizabeth was used to having people die. She was not shocked; only it seemed lonely again to find herself facing the world, in a foreign land. And when she came to face the arrangements that had to be made, which, after all, money and servants made easy, she found herself dreading her own land. What must she do after her grandmother was laid to rest? She could not live in the great house in Rittenhouse

Square, and neither could she very well go and live in Flora Street. O, well, her Father would hide her. She need not plan; He would plan for her. The mansions on the earth were His too, as well as those in heaven.

And so resting she passed through the weary voyage and the day when the body was laid to rest in the Bailey lot in the cemetery, and she went back to the empty house alone. It was not until after the funeral that she went to see Grandmother Brady. She had not thought it wise or fitting to invite the hostile grandmother to the other one's funeral. She had thought Grandmother Bailey would not like it.

She rode to Flora Street in the carriage. She felt too weary to walk or go in the trolley. She was taking account of stock in the way of friends, thinking over whom she cared to see. One of the first bits of news she had heard on arriving in this country had been that Miss Loring's wedding was to come off in a few days. It seemed to strike her like a thunderbolt, and she was trying to arraign herself for this as she rode along. It was therefore not helpful to her state of mind to have her grandmother remark grimly:

"That feller o' yurs 'n his oughtymobble has been goin' up an' down this street, day in, day out, this whole blessed summer. Ain't been a day he didn't pass, sometimes once, sometimes twicet. I felt sorry fer him sometimes. Ef he hadn't been so high an' mighty stuck up that he couldn't recognize me, I'd 'a' spoke to him. It was plain ez the nose on your face he was lookin' fer you. Don't he know where you live?"

"I don't believe he does," said Elizabeth languidly. "Say, Grandmother, would you care to come up to Rittenhouse Square and live?"

"Me? In Rittenhouse Square? Fer the land sakes, child, no. That's flat. I've lived me days out in me own sp'ere, and I don't intend to change now at me time o' life. Ef you want to do somethin' nice for me, child, now you've got all that money, I'd like real well to live in a house that hed white marble steps. It's been me one aim all me life. There's some round on the next street that don't come high. There'd be plenty room fer us all, an' a nice place fer Lizzie to get married when the time comes. The parlor's real big, and you would send her some roses, couldn't you?"

"All right, Grandmother. You shall have it," said Elizabeth with a relieved sigh, and in a few minutes she went home. Some day pretty soon she must think what to do, but there was no immediate hurry. She was glad that Grandmother Brady did not want to come to Rittenhouse Square. Things would be more congenial without her.

But the house seemed great and empty when she entered, and she was glad to hear the friendly telephone bell ringing. It was the wife of her pastor, asking her to come to them for a quiet dinner.

This was the one home in the great city where she felt like going in her loneliness. There would be no form nor ceremony. Just a friend with them. It was good. The doctor would give her some helpful words. She was glad they had asked her.

Chapter 17

A Final Flight and Pursuit

"Ｇᴇᴏʀɢᴇ," said Mrs. Vincent Benedict, "I want you to do something for me."

"Certainly, Mother, anything I can."

"Well, it's only to go to dinner with me to-night. Our pastor's wife has telephoned me that she wants us very much. She especially emphasized you. She said she absolutely needed you. It was a case of charity, and she would be so grateful to you if you would come. She has a young friend with her who is very sad, and she wants to cheer her up. Now don't frown. I won't bother you again this week. I know you hate dinners and girls. But really, George, this is an unusual case. The girl is just home from Europe, and buried her grandmother yesterday. She hasn't a soul in the world belonging to her that can be with her, and the pastor's wife has asked her over to dinner quietly. Of course she isn't going out. She must be in mourning. And you know you're fond of the doctor."

"Yes, I'm fond of the doctor," said George, frowning discouragedly; "but I'd rather take him alone, and not with a girl flung at me everlastingly. I'm tired of it. I didn't think it of Christian people, though; I thought she was above such things."

"Now, George," said his mother severely, "that's a real insult to the girl, and to our friend too. She hasn't an idea of doing any such thing. It seems this girl is quite unusual, very religious, and our friend thought you would be just the one to cheer her. She apologized several times for presuming to ask you to help her. You really will have to go."

"Well, who is this paragon, anyway? Anyone I know? I s'pose I've got to go."

"Why, she's a Miss Bailey," said the mother, relieved. "Mrs. Wilton Merrill Bailey's granddaughter. Did you ever happen to meet her? I never did."

"Never heard of her," growled George. "Wish I hadn't now."

"George!"

"Well, Mother, go on. I'll be good. What does she do? Dance, and play bridge, and sing?"

"I haven't heard anything that she does," said his mother, laughing.

"Well, of course she's a paragon; they all are, Mother. I'll be ready in half an hour. Let's go and get it done. We can come home early, can't we?"

Mrs. Benedict sighed. If only George would settle down on some suitable girl of good family! But he was so queer and restless. She was afraid for him. Ever since she had taken him away to Europe, when she was so ill, she had been afraid for him. He seemed so moody and absent-minded then and afterwards. Now this Miss Bailey was said to be as beautiful as she was good. If only George would take a notion to her!

Elizabeth was sitting in a great arm-chair by the open fire when he entered the room. He had not expected to find anyone there. He heard voices up-stairs, and supposed Miss Bailey was talking with her hostess. His mother followed the servant to remove her wraps, and he entered the drawing-room alone. She stirred, looked up, and saw him.

"Elizabeth!" he said, and came forward to grasp her hand. "I have found you again. How came you here?"

But she had no opportunity to answer, for the ladies entered almost at once, and there stood the two smiling at each other.

"Why, you have met before!" exclaimed the hostess. "How delighted I am! I knew you two would enjoy meeting. Elizabeth, child, you never told me you knew George."

George Benedict kept looking around for Miss Bailey to enter the room; but to his relief she did not come, and, when they went out to the dining-room, there was no place set for her. She must have preferred to remain at home. He forgot her, and settled down to the joy of having Elizabeth by his side. His mother, opposite, watched his face blossom into the old-time joy as he handed this new girl the olives, and had eyes for no one else.

It was to Elizabeth a blessed evening. They held sweet converse one with another as children of the King. For a little time under the old influence of the restful, helpful talk she forgot "the lady," and all the perplexing questions that had vexed her soul. She knew only that she had entered into an atmosphere of peace and love and joy.

It was not until the evening was over, and the guests were about to leave, that Mrs. Benedict addressed Elizabeth as Miss Bailey. Up to that moment it had not entered her son's mind that Miss Bailey was present at all. He turned with a start, and looked into Elizabeth's eyes; and she smiled back to him as if to acknowledge the name. Could she read his thoughts? he wondered.

It was only a few steps across the Square, and Mrs. Benedict and her son walked to Elizabeth's door with her. He had no opportunity to speak to Elizabeth alone, but he said as he bade her good-night, "I shall see you tomorrow, then, in the morning?"

The inflection was almost a question; but Elizabeth only said, "Good night," and vanished into the house.

"Then you have met her before, George?" asked his mother wonderingly.

"Yes," he answered hurriedly, as if to stop her further question. "Yes, I have met her before. She is very beautiful, Mother."

And because the mother was afraid she might say too much she assented, and held her peace. It was the first time in years that George had called a girl beautiful.

Meantime Elizabeth had gone to her own room and locked the door. She hardly knew what to think, her heart was so happy. Yet beneath it all was the troubled thought of the lady, the haunting lady for whom they had prayed together on the prairie. And as if to add to the thought she found a bit of newspaper lying on the floor beside her dressing-table. Marie must have dropped it as she came in to turn up the lights. It was nothing but the corner torn from a newspaper, and should be consigned to the waste-basket; yet her eye caught the words in large head-lines as she picked it up idly, "Miss Geraldine Loring's Wedding to Be an Elaborate Affair." There was nothing more readable. The paper was torn in a zigzag line just beneath. Yet that was enough. It reminded her of her duty.

Down beside the bed she knelt, and prayed: "O my Father, hide me now; hide me! I am in trouble; hide me!" Over and over she prayed till her heart grew calm and she could think.

Then she sat down quietly, and put the matter before her.

This man whom she loved with her whole soul was to be married in a few days. The world of society would be at the wedding. He was pledged to another, and he was not hers. Yet he was her old friend, and was coming to see her. If he came and looked into her face with those clear eyes of his, he might read in hers that she loved him. How dreadful that would be!

Yes, she must search yet deeper. She had heard the glad ring in his voice when he met her, and said, "Elizabeth!" She had seen his eyes. He was in danger himself. She knew it; she might not hide it from herself. She must help him to be true to the woman to whom he was pledged, whom now he would have to marry.

She must go away from it all. She would run away, now at once. It seemed that she was always running away from someone. She would go back to the mountains where she had started. She was not afraid now of the man from whom she had fled. Culture and education had done their work. Religion had set her upon a rock. She could go back with the protection that her money would put about her, with the companionship of some good, elderly woman, and be safe from harm in that way; but she could not stay here and meet George Benedict in the morning, nor face Geraldine Loring on her wedding-day. It would be all the same the facing whether she were in the wedding-party or not. Her days of mourning for her grandmother would of course protect her from this public facing. It was the thought she could not bear. She must get away from it all forever.

Her lawyers should arrange the business. They would purchase the house that Grandmother Brady desired, and then give her her money to build a church. She would go back, and teach among the lonely wastes of mountain and prairie what Jesus Christ longed to be to the people made in His image. She would go back and place above the graves of her father and mother and brothers stones that should bear the words of life to all who should pass by in that desolate region. And that should be her excuse to the world for going, if she needed any excuse—she had gone to see about placing a monument over her father's grave. But the monument should be a church somewhere where it was most needed. She was resolved upon that.

That was a busy night. Marie was called upon to pack a few things for a hurried journey. The telephone rang, and the sleepy night-operator answered crossly. But Elizabeth found out all she wanted to know about the early Chicago trains, and then lay down to rest.

Early the next morning George Benedict telephoned for some flowers from the florist; and, when they arrived, he pleased himself by taking them to Elizabeth's door.

He did not expect to find her up, but it would be a pleasure to have them reach her by his own hand. They would be sent up to her room, and she would know in her first waking thought that he remembered her. He smiled as he touched the bell and stood waiting.

The old butler opened the door. He looked as if he had not fully finished his night's sleep. He listened mechanically to the message, "For Miss Bailey with Mr. Benedict's good-morning," and then his face took on a deprecatory expression.

"I'm sorry, Mr. Benedict," he said, as if in the matter he were personally to blame; "but she's just gone. Miss Elizabeth's mighty quick in her ways, and last night after she come home she decided to go to Chicago on the early train. She's just gone to the station not ten minutes ago. They was late, and had to hurry. I'm expecting the footman back every minute."

"Gone?" said George Benedict, standing blankly on the door-step and looking down the street as if that should bring her. "Gone? To Chicago, did you say?"

"Yes, sir, she's gone to Chicago. That is, she's going further, but she took the Chicago Limited. She's gone to see about a monument for Madam's son John, Miss 'Lizabuth's father. She said she must go at once, and she went."

"What time does that train leave?" asked the young man. It was a thread of hope. He was stung into a superhuman effort as he had been on the prairie when he had caught the flying vision of the girl and horse, and he had shouted, and she would not stop for him.

"Nine-fifty, sir," said the butler. He wished this excited young man would go after her. She needed someone. His heart had often stirred against fate that this pearl among young mistresses should have no intimate friend or lover now in her loneliness.

"Nine-fifty!" He looked at his watch. No chance! "Broad Street?" he asked sharply.

"Yes, sir."

Would there be a chance if he had his automobile? Possibly, but hardly unless the train was late. There would be a trifle more chance of catching the train at West Philadelphia. O for his automobile! He turned to the butler in despair.

"Telephone her!" he said. "Stop her if you possibly can on board the train, and I will try to get there. I must see her. It is important." He started down the steps, his mind in a whirl of trouble. How should he go? The trolley would be the only available way, and yet the trolley would be useless; it would take too long. Nevertheless, he sped down toward Chestnut Street blindly, and now in his despair his new habit came to him. "O my Father, help me! Help me! Save her for me!"

Up Walnut Street at a breakneck pace came a flaming red automobile, sounding its taunting menace, "Honk-honk! Honk-honk!" but George Benedict stopped not for automobiles. Straight into the jaws of death he rushed, and was saved only by the timely grasp of a policeman, who rolled him over on the ground. The machine came to a halt, and a familiar voice shouted: "Conscience alive, George, is that you? What are you trying to do? Say, but that was a close shave! Where you going in such a hurry, anyway? Hustle in, and I'll take you there."

The young man sprang into the seat, and gasped: "West Philadelphia station, Chicago Limited! Hurry! Train leaves Broad Street station at nine-fifty. Get me there if you can, Billy. I'll be your friend forever."

By this time they were speeding fast. Neither of the two had time to consider which station was the easier to make; and, as the machine was headed toward West Philadelphia, on they went, regardless of laws or vainly shouting policemen.

George Benedict sprang from the car before it had stopped, and nearly fell again. His nerves were not steady from his other fall yet. He tore into the station and out through the passageway past the beckoning hand of the ticket-man who sat in the booth at the staircase, and strode up three steps at a time. The guard shouted: "Hurry! You may get it; she's just starting!" and a friendly hand reached out, and hauled him up on the platform of the last car.

For an instant after he was safely in the car he was too dazed to think. It seemed as if he must keep on blindly rushing through that train all the way to Chicago, or she would get away from him. He sat down in an empty seat for a minute to get his senses. He was actually on the train! It had not gone without him!

Now the next question was, Was she on it herself, or had she in some way slipped from his grasp even yet? The old butler might have caught her by telephone. He doubted it. He knew her stubborn determination, and all at once he began to suspect that she was with intention running away from him, and perhaps had been doing so before! It was an astonishing thought and a grave one, yet, if it were true, what had meant that welcoming smile in her eyes that had been like dear sunshine to his heart?

But there was no time to consider such questions now. He had started on this quest, and he must continue it until he found her. Then she should be made to explain once and for all most fully. He would live through no more torturing agonies of separation without a full understanding of the matter. He got upon his shaking feet, and started to hunt for Elizabeth.

Then all at once he became aware that he was still carrying the box of flowers. Battered and out of shape it was, but he was holding it as if it held the very hope of life for him. He smiled grimly as he tottered shakily down the aisle, grasping his floral offering with determination. This was not exactly the morning call he had planned, nor the way he had expected to present his flowers; but it seemed to be the best he could do. Then, at last, in the very furthest car from the end, in the drawing-room he found her, sitting gray and sorrowful, looking at the fast-flying landscape.

"Elizabeth!" He stood in the open door and called to her; and she started as from a deep sleep, her face blazing into glad sunshine at sight of him. She put her hand to her heart, and smiled.

"I have brought you some flowers," he said grimly. "I am afraid there isn't much left of them now; but, such as they are, they are here. I hope you will accept them."

"Oh!" gasped Elizabeth, reaching out for the poor crushed roses as if they had been a little child in danger. She drew them from the battered box and to her arms with a delicious movement of caressing, as if she would make up to them for all they had come through. He watched her, half pleased, half savagely. Why should all that tenderness be wasted on mere fading flowers?

At last he spoke, interrupting her brooding over his roses.

"You are running away from me!" he charged.

"Well, and what if I am?" She looked at him with a loving defiance in her eye.

"Don't you know I love you?" he asked, sitting down beside her and talking low and almost fiercely. "Don't you know I've been torn away from you, or you from me, twice before now, and that I cannot stand it any more? Say, don't you know it? Answer, please!" The demand was kind, but peremptory.

"I was afraid so," she murmured with drooping eyes, and cheeks from which all color had fled.

"Well, why do you do it? Why did you run away? Don't you care for me? Tell me that. If you can't ever love me, you are excusable; but I must know it all now."

"Yes, I care as much as you," she faltered, "but——"

"But what?" sharply.

"But you are going to be married this week," she said in desperation, raising her miserable eyes to his.

He looked at her in astonishment.

"Am I?" said he. "Well, that's news to me; but it's the best news I've heard in a long time. When does the ceremony come off? I wish it was this morning. Make it this morning, will you? Let's stop this blessed old train and go back to the Doctor. He'll fix it so we can't ever run away from each other again. Elizabeth, look at me!"

But Elizabeth hid her eyes now. They were full of tears.

"But the lady—" she gasped out, struggling with the sobs. She was so weary, and the thought of what he had suggested was so precious.

"What lady? There is no lady but you, Elizabeth, and never has been. Haven't you known that for a long time? I have. That was all a hallucination of my foolish brain. I had to go out on the plains to get rid of it, but I left it there forever. She was nothing to me after I saw you."

"But—but people said—and it was in the paper. I saw it. You cannot desert her now; it would be dishonorable."

"Thunder!" ejaculated the distracted young man. "In the paper! What lady?"

"Why, Miss Loring! Geraldine Loring. I saw that the preparations were all made for her wedding, and I was told she was to marry you."

In sheer relief he began to laugh.

At last he stopped, as the old hurt look spread over her face.

"Excuse me, dear," he said gently, "There was a little acquaintance between Miss Loring and myself. It only amounted to a flirtation on her part, one of many. It was a great distress to my mother, and I went out West, as you know, to get away from her. I knew she would only bring me unhappiness, and she was not willing to give up some of her ways that were impossible. I am glad and thankful that God saved me from her. I believe she is going to marry a distant relative of mine by the name of Benedict, but I thank the kind Father that *I* am not going to marry *her*. There is only one woman in the whole wide world that I am willing to marry, or ever will be; and she is sitting beside me now."

The train was going rapidly now. It would not be long before the conductor would reach them. The man leaned over, and clasped the little gloved hand that lay in the girl's lap; and Elizabeth felt the great joy that had tantalized her for these three years in dreams and visions settle down about her in beautiful reality. She was his now forever. She need never run away again.

The conductor was not long in coming to them, and the matter-of-fact world had to be faced once more. The young man produced his card, and said a few words to the conductor, mentioning the name of his uncle, who, by the way, happened to be a director of the road; and then he explained the situation. It was very necessary that the young lady be recalled at once to her home because of a change in the circumstances. He had caught the train at West Philadelphia by automobile, coming as he was in his morning clothes, without baggage and with little money. Would the conductor be so kind as to put them off that they might return to the city by the shortest possible route?

The conductor glared and scolded, and said people "didn't know their own minds," and "wanted to move the earth." Then he eyed Elizabeth, and she smiled. He let a grim glimmer of what might have been a sour smile years ago peep out for an instant, and—he let them off.

They wandered delightedly about from one trolley to another until they found an automobile garage, and soon were speeding back to Philadelphia.

They waited for no ceremony, those two who had met and loved by the way in the wilderness. They went straight to Mrs. Benedict for her blessing, and then to the minister to arrange for his services; and within the week a quiet wedding-party entered the arched doors of the placid brown church with the lofty spire, and Elizabeth Bailey and George Benedict were united in the sacred bonds of matrimony.

There were present Mrs. Benedict, and one or two intimate friends of the family, besides Grandmother Brady, Aunt Nan, and Lizzie.

Lizzie brought a dozen bread-and-butter plates from the ten-cent store. They were adorned with cupids and roses and much gilt. But Lizzie was disappointed. No display, no pomp and ceremony. Just a simple white dress and white veil. Lizzie did not understand that the veil has been in the Bailey family for generations, and that the dress was an heirloom also. It was worn because Grandmother Bailey had given it to her, and told her she wanted her to wear it on her wedding-day. Sweet and beautiful she looked as she turned to walk down the aisle on her husband's arm, and she smiled at Grandmother Brady in a way that filled the grandmother's heart with pride and triumph. Elizabeth was not ashamed of the Bradys even among her fine friends. But Lizzie grumbled all the way home at the plainness of the ceremony, and the lack of bridesmaids and fuss and feathers.

The social column of the daily papers stated that young Mr. and Mrs. George Benedict were spending their honeymoon in an extended tour of the West, and Grandmother Brady so read it aloud at the breakfast table to the admiring family. Only Lizzie looked discontented:

"She just wore a dark blue tricotine one-piece dress and a little plain dark hat. She ain't got a bit of taste. Oh *Boy!* If I just had her pocket book wouldn't I show the world? But anyhow I'm glad she went in a private car. There was a *little* class to her, though if t'had been mine I'd uv preferred ridin' in the parlor coach an' havin' folks see me and my fine husband. He's some looker, George Benedict is! Everybody turns to watch 'em as they go by, and they sail along and never seem to notice. It's all perfectly throwed away on 'em. Gosh! I'd hate to be such a nut!"

"Now, Lizzie, you know you hadn't oughtta talk like that!" reproved her grandmother, "After her giving you all that money fer your own wedding. A thousand dollars just to spend as you please on your cloes and a blowout, and house linens. Jest because she don't care for gewgaws like you do, you think she's a fool. But she's no fool. She's got a good head on her, and she'll get more in the long run out of life than you will. She's been real loving and kind to us all, and she didn't have any reason to neither. We never did much fer her. And look at how nice and common she's been with us all, not a bit high headed. I declare, Lizzie, I should think you'd be ashamed!"

"Oh, well," said Lizzie shrugging her shoulders indifferently, "She's all right in her way, only 'taint my way. And I'm thankful t'goodness that I had the nerve to speak up when she offered to give me my trousseau. She askt me would I druther hav her buy it for me, or have the money and pick it out m'self, and I spoke up right quick and says, 'Oh, cousin Bessie, I wouldn't *think* of givin' ya all that trouble. I'd take the *money* ef it's all the same t'you,' and she jest smiled and said all right, she expected I knew what I wanted better'n she did. So yes'teddy when I went down to the station to see her off she handed me a bank book. And—Oh, say, I fergot! She said there was a good-bye note inside. I ain't had time to look at it since. I went right to the movies on the dead run to get there 'fore the first show begun, and it's in my coat pocket. Wait 'till I get it. I spose it's some of her old *religion!* She's always preaching at me. It ain't that she says so much as that she's always *meanin'* it underneath everything, that gets my goat! It's sorta like having a piece of God round with you all the time watching you. You kinda hate to be enjoyin' yerself fer fear she won't think yer doin' it accordin' to the Bible."

Lizzie hurtled into the hall and brought back her coat, fumbling in the pocket.

"Yes, here 'tis Ma! Wanta see the figgers? You never had a whole thousand dollars in the bank t'woncet yerself, did ya?"

Mrs. Brady put on her spectacles and reached for the book, while Lizzie's mother got up and came behind her mother's chair to look over at the magic figures. Lizzie stooped for the little white note that had fluttered to her feet as she opened the book, but she had little interest to see what it said. She was more intent upon the new bank book.

It was Grandmother Brady that discovered it:

"Why, Lizzie! It ain't *one* thousand, it's *five* thousand, the book says! You don't 'spose she's made a mistake, do you?"

Lizzie seized the book and gazed, her jaw dropping open in amaze.

"Let me have it!" demanded Lizzie's mother, reaching for the book.

"Where's yer note, Lizzie, mebbe it'll explain," said the excited grandmother.

Lizzie recovered the note which again had fluttered to the floor in the confusion and opening it began to read:

"Dear Lizzie," it read

"I've made it five thousand so you will have some over for furnishing your home, and if you still think you want the little bungalow out on the Pike you will find the deed at my lawyer's, all made out in your name. It's my wedding gift to you, so you can go to work and buy your furniture at once, and not wait till Dan gets a raise. And here's wishing you a great deal of happiness,

"Your loving cousin,

"ELIZABETH."

"There!" said Grandmother Brady sitting back with satisfaction and holding her hands composedly, "Whadd' I tell ya?"

"Mercy!" said Lizzie's mother, "Let me see that note! The idea of her *giving* all that money when she didn't have to!"

But Lizzie's face was a picture of joy. For once she lost her hard little worldly screwed-up expression and was wreathed in smiles of genuine eagerness:

"Oh *Boy!*" she exclaimed delightedly, dancing around the room, "Now we can have a victrola, an' a player-piano, and Dan'll get a Ford, one o' those limousine-kind! Won't I be some swell? What'll the girls at the store think now?"

"H'm! You'd much better get a washing machine and a 'lectric iron!" grumbled Grandmother Brady practically.

"Well, all I got to say about it is, she was an awful fool to trust *you* with so much money," said Lizzie's mother discontentedly, albeit with a pleased pride as she watched her giddy daughter fling on hat and coat to go down and tell Dan.

"I sh'll work in the store fer the rest of the week, jest to 'commodate 'em," she announced putting her head back in the door as she went out, "but not a day longer. I got a lot t'do. Say, won't I be some lady in the five-an'-ten the rest o' the week? Oh *Boy! I'll tell the world!*"

Meantime in their own private car the bride and groom were whirled on their way to the west, but they saw little of the scenery, being engaged in the all-absorbing story of each other's lives since they had parted.

And one bright morning, they stepped down from the train at Malta and gazed about them.

The sun was shining clear and wonderful, and the little brown station stood drearily against the brightness of the day like a picture that has long hung on the wall of one's memory and is suddenly brought out and the dust wiped away.

They purchased a couple of horses, and with camp accoutrements following began their real wedding trip, over the road they had come together when they first met. Elizabeth had to show her husband where she had hidden while the men went by, and he drew her close in his arms and thanked God that she had escaped so miraculously.

It seemed so wonderful to be in the same places again, for nothing out here in the wilderness seemed much to have changed, and yet they two were so changed that the people they met did not seem to recognize them as ever having been that way before.

They dined sumptuously in the same coulee, and recalled little things they had said and done, and Elizabeth now worldly wise, laughed at her own former ignorance as her husband reminded her of some questions she had asked him on that memorable journey. And ever through the beautiful journey he was telling her how wonderful she seemed to him, both then and now.

Not however, till they reached the old ranchhouse, where the woman had tried to persuade her to stay, did they stop for long.

Elizabeth had a tender feeling in her heart for that motherly woman who had sought to protect her, and felt a longing to let her know how safely she had been kept through the long journey and how good the Lord had been to her through the years. Also they both desired to reward these kind people for their hospitality in the time of need. So, in the early evening they rode up just as they did before to the little old log house. But no friendly door flung open wide as they came near, and at first they thought the cabin deserted, till a candle flare suddenly shone forth in the bedroom, and then Benedict dismounted and knocked.

After some waiting the old man came to the door holding a candle high above his head. His face was haggard and worn, and the whole place looked dishevelled. His eyes had a weary look as he peered into the night and it was evident that he had no thought of ever having seen them before:

"I can't do much fer ya, strangers," he said, his voice sounding tired and discouraged. "If it's a woman ye have with ye, ye better ride on to the next ranch. My woman is sick. Very sick. There's nobody here with her but me, and I have all I can tend to. The house ain't kept very tidy. It's six weeks since she took to bed."

Elizabeth had sprung lightly to the ground and was now at the threshold:

"Oh, is she sick? I'm so sorry? Couldn't I do something for her? She was good to me once several years ago!"

The old man peered at her blinkingly, noting her slender beauty, the exquisite eager face, the dress that showed her of another world—and shook his head:

"I guess you made a mistake, lady. I don't remember ever seeing you before—"

"But I remember you," she said eagerly stepping into the room, "Won't you please let me go to her?"

"Why, shore, lady, go right in ef you want to. She's layin' there in the bed. She ain't likely to get out of it again I'm feared. The doctor says nothin' but a 'noperation will ever get her up, and we can't pay fer 'noperations. It's a long ways to the hospital in Chicago where he wants her sent, and M'ria and I, we ain't allowin' to part. It can't be many years—"

But Elizabeth was not waiting to hear. She had slipped into the old bedroom that she remembered now so well and was kneeling beside the bed talking to the white faced woman on the thin pillow:

"Don't you remember me," she asked, "I'm the girl you tried to get to stay with you once. The girl that came here with a man she had met in the wilderness. You told me things that I didn't know, and you were kind and wanted me to stay here with you? Don't you remember me? I'm Elizabeth!"

The woman reached out a bony hand and touched the fair young face that she could see but dimly in the flare of the candle that the old man now brought into the room:

"Why, yes, I remember," the woman said, her voice sounded alive yet in spite of her illness, "Yes, I remember you. You were a dear little girl, and I was so worried about you. I would have kept you for my own—but you wouldn't stay. And he was a nice looking young man, but I was afraid for you—You can't always tell about them—You *mostly* can't—!"

"But he was all right, Mother!" Elizabeth's voice rang joyously through the cabin, "He took care of me and got me safely started toward my people, and now he's my husband. I want you to see him. George come here!"

The old woman half raised herself from the pillow and looked toward the young man in the doorway:

"You don't say! He's your *husband!* Well, now isn't that grand! Well, I certainly am glad! I was that worried—!"

They sat around the bed talking, Elizabeth telling briefly of her own experiences and her wedding trip which they were taking back over the old trail, and the old man and woman speaking of their trouble, the woman's break-down and how the doctor at Malta said there was a chance she could get well if she went to a great doctor in Chicago, but how they had no money unless they sold the ranch and that nobody wanted to buy it.

"Oh, but we have money," laughed Elizabeth joyously, "and it is our turn now to help you. You helped us when we were in trouble. How soon can you start? I'm going to play you are my own father and mother. We can send them both, can't we George?"

It was a long time before they settled themselves to sleep that night because there was so much planning to be done, and then Elizabeth and her husband had to get out their stores and cook a good supper for the two old people who had been living mostly on corn meal mush for several weeks.

And after the others were all asleep the old woman lay praying and thanking God for the two angels who had dropped down to help them in their distress.

The next morning George Benedict with one of the men who looked after their camping outfit went to Malta and got in touch with the Chicago doctor and hospital, and before he came back to the ranch that night everything was arranged for the immediate start of the two old people. He had even planned for an automobile and the Malta doctor to be in attendance in a couple of days to get the invalid to the station.

Meantime Elizabeth had been going over the old woman's wardrobe which was scanty and coarse, and selecting garments from her own baggage that would do for the journey.

The old woman looked glorified as she touched the delicate white garments with their embroidery and ribbons:

"Oh, dear child! Why, I couldn't wear a thing like that on my old worn-out body. Those look like angels' clothes." She put a work-worn finger on the delicate tracery of embroidery and smoothed a pink satin ribbon bow.

But Elizabeth overruled her. It was nothing but a plain little garment she had bought for the trip. If the friend thought it was pretty she was glad, but nothing was too pretty for the woman who had taken her in in her distress and tried to help her and keep her safe.

The invalid was thin with her illness, and it was found that she could easily wear the girl's simple dress of dark blue with a white collar, and little dark hat, and Elizabeth donned a khaki shirt and brown cap and sweater herself and gladly arrayed her old friend in her own bridal travelling gown for her journey. She had not brought a lot of things for her journey because she did not want to be bothered, but she could easily get more when she got to a large city, and what was money for but to clothe the naked and feed the hungry? She rejoiced in her ability to help this woman of the wilderness.

On the third day, garbed in Elizabeth's clothes, her husband fitted out for the east in some of George Benedict's extra things, they started. They carried a bag containing some necessary changes, and some wonderful toilet accessories with silver monograms, enough to puzzle the most snobbish nurse, also there was a luscious silk kimona of Elizabeth's in the bag. The two old people were settled in the Benedict private car, and in due time hitched onto the Chicago express and hurried on their way. Before the younger pair went back to their pilgrimage they sent a series of telegrams arranging for every detail of the journey for the old couple, so that they would be met with cars and nurses and looked after most carefully.

And the thanksgiving and praise of the old people seemed to follow them like music as they rode happily on their way.

They paused at the little old school house where they had attended the Christian Endeavor meeting, and Elizabeth looked half fearfully up the road where her evil pursuers had ridden by, and rode closer to her husband's side. So they passed on the way as nearly as Elizabeth could remember every step back as she had come, telling her husband all the details of the journey.

That night they camped in the little shelter where Benedict had come upon the girl that first time they met, and under the clear stars that seemed so near they knelt together and thanked God for His leading.

They went to the lonely cabin on the mountain, shut up and going to ruin now, and Benedict gazing at the surroundings and then looking at the delicate face of his lovely wife was reminded of a white flower he had once seen growing out of the blackness down in a coal mine, pure and clean without a smirch of soil.

They visited the seven graves in the wilderness, and standing reverently beside the sand-blown mounds she told him much of her early life that she had not told him before, and introduced him to her family, telling a bit about each that would make him see the loveable side of them. And then they planned for seven simple white stones to be set up, bearing words from the book they both loved. Over the care worn mother was to be written "Come unto me all ye that labor and are heavy laden and I will give you rest."

It was on that trip that they planned what came to pass in due time. The little cabin was made over into a simple, pretty home, with vines planted about the garden, and a garage with a sturdy little car; and not far away a church nestled into the side of the hill, built out of the stones that were native, with many sunny windows and a belfry in which bells rang out to the whole region round.

At first it had seemed impractical to put a church out there away from the town, but Elizabeth said that it was centrally located, and high up where it could be seen from the settlements in the valleys, and was moreover on a main trail that was much travelled. She longed to have some such spot in the wilderness that could be a refuge for any who longed for better things.

When they went back they sent out two consecrated missionaries to occupy the new house and use the sturdy little car. They were to ring the bells, preach the gospel and play the organ and piano in the little church.

Over the pulpit there was a beautiful window bearing a picture of Christ, the Good Shepherd, and in clear letters above were the words: "And thou shalt remember all the way which the Lord thy God led thee these forty years in the wilderness, to humble thee, and to prove thee, to know what was in thine heart, whether thou wouldst keep his commandments, or no."

And underneath the picture were the words:

" 'In the time of trouble He shall hide me in His pavilion; in the secret of His tabernacle shall He hide me.' In memory of His hidings,
"George and Elizabeth Benedict."

But in the beautiful home in Philadelphia, in an inner intimate room these words are exquisitely graven on the wall, "Let not your heart be troubled."

GRACE LIVINGSTON HILL

Fleming H. Revell Company
Old Tappan, New Jersey

Library of Congress Cataloging in Publication Data

Hill, Grace Livingston, 1865-1947.
    A daily rate.

    I. Title.
PS3515.I486D3   1982   813'.52   81-19941
ISBN 0-8007-1296-X   AACR2

Introduction

It can be an astonishing experience to sit in a "time machine" and be taken back nearly one hundred years. The difference in manners and customs, clothing, and even speech strike us as though we were visiting a foreign land.

Yet basic principles do not change. People one hundred years ago made mistakes as we do, loved and sorrowed as we do, followed their own sinful, rebellious dispositions as we do today. This is what we realize after reading this book

My mother, when she wrote *A Daily Rate,* had not yet developed her later writing technique; still her characters are real individuals, subject to discouragements, depression, self-interest or religious impulses—wise or not—all of which influenced those around them, as they do today.

Having spent fifty years or so with my mother, I can discern, on looking back, a growth in her own spiritual maturity and depth. But no reader of even her early books can miss the one purpose that governed her life: to introduce others to Jesus Christ in reality.

I am grateful that one of my earliest recollections is a few moments in my crib (!) when I was frightened by some imaginary threat; she lovingly told me of the faithful Shepherd who was always caring and able to protect me. How right she was!

RUTH LIVINGSTON HILL

Chapter 1

T he world would not have looked quite so dreary to her perhaps, if it had not been her birthday. Somehow one persists in expecting something unusual to happen on a birthday, no matter how many times one has had nothing but disappointment.

Not that Celia Murray was really expecting anything, even a letter, on this birthday, though she did stand shivering in the half light of the dim, forlorn front room that served as a parlor for Mrs. Morris' boarding-house, watching for the postman to reach their door. She did it merely because she wished to be near, to get the letter at once,—provided there was a letter,—and not that she really hoped for one.

It was Saturday evening, and the close of a half holiday in the store in which she usually stood all day long as saleswoman. The unusual half day off was on account of some parade in the city. Celia had not spent her afternoon at the parade. Instead, she had been in her small, cold, back bedroom on the third story, attending to various worn garments which needed mending. They had been spread out on the bed in a row, and she had gone steadily down the line putting a few stitches here, a button there, and setting in a patch in another, counting every minute of daylight hoping to finish her work before it faded, for the gas in her room was dim, the burner being old and worn out. She tried to be cheerful over the work. She called it her "dress parade." She knew it was the best way in which to accomplish as much as she wished to do.

And now it was six o'clock, and she had turned down the wretched, flickering light in her room and descended to the parlor to watch for the postman.

He was late to-night, probably on account of the parade. She leaned her forehead against the cold glass and looked out into the misty darkness. Everything was murky and smoky. The passers-by seemed tired and in a hurry. Some had their collars turned up. She wondered where they were all going, and whether there were pleasant homes awaiting them. She let her imagination picture the homes of some. There was a young working man hurrying along with breezy step and swinging dinner pail. He had not been to the parade. His parade was at home awaiting his coming,—a laughing baby, a tidy wife, and the house redolent of fried onions and sausage. She had passed houses often at night where these odors were streaming forth from quickly opened and closed doors. The young man would like it; it would be pleasant to him. And the thought brought no less cheer to the watching girl because to her this supper would not be in the least appetizing.

There passed by a strong old German, a day laborer perhaps. She pictured the table full of noisy children of various ages, and the abundance of sauerkraut and cheese and coffee and other viands set out. Then came a stream of girls, some clerks like herself, and some mill girls. On other evenings they would present a different appearance, but many of them to-night were in holiday attire on account of the half holiday which had been generally given throughout the city. These girls, some of them, had homes of more or less attractiveness, and others, like herself, were domiciled in boarding-houses. She sat down on one of the hard haircloth chairs and looked around that parlor. In the dimness of the turned down gas, it appeared more forlorn than usual. The ingrain carpet had long ago lost any claims to respectability. It had a dragged out, sodden appearance, and in places there were unmistakable holes. These, it is true, had been twisted and turned about so as to come mostly under the tables and sofa, but they were generally visible to the casual observer. The parlor suite of haircloth, by reason of being much sat upon, had lost the spring of youth, and several of the chairs and one end of the sofa looked like fallen cake. There was an asthmatic cabinet organ at the end of the room which had been left by some departing boarder, (under compulsion) in lieu of his board. There were a few worn pieces of music scattered upon it. Celia knew that the piece now open on the top was that choice selection "The Cat Came Back," which was a great favorite with a young railroad brakeman who had a metallic tenor voice and good lungs. He was one of the boarders and considered quite a singer in the house. There was a feeble attempt at the aesthetic in the form of a red, bedraggled chenille portière at the doorway, bordered with large pink cabbage roses. The mantel had a worn plush scarf embroidered in a style quite out of date and ugly in the extreme. On it stood a large glass case of wax flowers, several cheap vases, and a match safe. Over it hung a crayon portrait of the landlady's departed husband, and another of herself adorned the opposite wall, both done in staring crayon work from tin types of ancient date, heavily and cheaply framed. These with a marriage certificate of the clasped-hand-and-orange-wreath order, framed in gilt, made up the adornments of the room.

Celia sighed as she looked about and took it all in once more. It was a dreary place. She had been in it but a week. Would she ever get used to it? She did not curl her lip in scorn as many other girls would have done over that room and its furnishings. Neither did she feel that utter distaste that is akin to hatred. Instead was a kind of pity in her heart for it all, and for the poor lonely creatures who had no other place to call home. Where there is such pity, there is sometimes love not far away. She even rose, went to the doorway and looped the loose, discouraged folds of the chenille curtain in more graceful fashion. Somehow her fingers could not help doing so much toward making that room different.

Then she sighed and went to the window again. She could see the belated postman now across the street. She watched him as he flitted back and forth, ringing this bell and that, and searching in the great leather bag for papers or packages. His breath showed white against the dark greyish-blue of the misty evening air. His grey uniform seemed to be a part of the mist. The yellow glare of the street-lamp touched the gilt buttons and made a bright spot of the letters on his cap as he paused a moment to study an address before coming to their door.

Celia opened the door before he had time to ring and took the letters from his hand. There were not many. The boarders in that house had not many correspondents. She stepped into the parlor once more, and turned up the gas now for a moment to see if there were any for herself. Strange to say, there were two, rather thin and unpromising it is true, but they gave a little touch of the unusual to the dull day. She noticed that one bore a familiar postmark and was in her aunt's handwriting. The other held the city mark and seemed to be from some firm of lawyers. She did not feel much curiosity concerning it. It was probably some circular. It did not look in the least interesting. She pushed them both quickly into her pocket as the front door opened letting in several noisy boarders. She did not wish to read her letters in public. They would keep till after supper. The bell was already ringing. It would not be worth while to go upstairs before she went to the diningroom. Experience taught her that the supper was at its very worst the minute after the bell rang. If one waited one must take the consequences, and "the consequences" were not desirable. The meals in that house were not too tempting at any time. Not that she cared much for her supper, she was too weary, but one must eat to live, and so she went to the dining-room.

Out there the gas was turned to its highest. The coarse tablecloth was none of the cleanest. In fact, it reminded one of former breakfasts and dinners. The thick white dishes bore marks of hard usage. They were nicked and cracked. There were plates of heavy, sour-looking bread at either end of the table. The butter looked mussy and uninviting. The inevitable, scanty supply of prunes stood before the plate of the young German clerk, who was already in his chair helping himself to a liberal dish. The clerk was fond of prunes, and always got to the table before any one else. Some of the others good-naturedly called him selfish, and frequently passed meaning remarks veiled in thin jokes concerning this habit of his; but if he understood he kept the matter to himself, and was apparently not thin-skinned.

There was a stew for dinner that night. Celia dreaded stews since the night of her arrival when she had found a long curly hair on her plate in the gravy. There were such possibilities of utility in a stew. It was brought on in little thick white dishes, doled out in exact portions.

There were great green fat pickles, suggesting copper in their pickling, and there was a plate of cheese and another of crackers. A girl brought each one a small spoonful of canned corn, but it was cold and scarcely cooked at all, and the kernels were large and whole. Celia having tasted it, pushed her dish back and did not touch it again. On the side table was a row of plates each containing a slim, thin piece of pale-crusted pie, its interior being dark and of an undefined character. Celia tried to eat. The dishes were not all clean. Her spoon had a sticky handle and so had her fork. The silver was all worn off the blade of her knife, and she could not help thinking that perhaps it was done by being constantly used to convey food to the mouth of the brakeman with the tenor voice.

One by one the boarders drifted in. It was surprising how quickly they gathered after that bell rang. They knew what they had to depend upon in the way of bread and butter, and it was first come first served. Little Miss Burns sat across the table from Celia. She was thin and nervous and laughed a good deal in an excited way, as if everything were unusually funny, and she were in a constant state of embarrassing apology. There were tired little lines around her eyes, and her mouth still wore a baby droop, though she was well along in years. Celia noticed that she drank only a cup of tea and nibbled a cracker. She did not look well. It was plain the dinner was no more appetizing to her than to the young girl who had so recently come there to board. She ought to have some delicate thin slices of nicely browned toast and a cup of good tea with real cream in it, and a fresh egg poached just right, or a tiny cup of good strong beef bouillon, Celia said to herself. She amused herself by thinking how she would like to slip out in the kitchen and get them for her, only—and she almost smiled at the thought—she would hardly find the necessary articles with which to make all that out in the Morris kitchen.

Next to Miss Burns sat two young girls, clerks in a three-cent store. They carried a good deal of would-be style, and wore many bright rings on their grimy fingers, whose nails were never cleaned nor cut apparently—except by their teeth. These girls were rather pretty in a coarse way, and laughed and talked a good deal in loud tones with the tenor brakeman, whose name was Bob Yates, and with the other young men boarders. These young men were respectively a clerk in a department store, a student in the University, and a young teacher in the public schools. Celia noticed that neither the student nor the school-teacher ate heartily, and that the young dry goods salesman had a hollow cough. How nice it would be if they all could have a good dinner just for once, soup and roast beef, and good bread and vegetables, with a delicious old-fashioned apple dumpling smoking hot, such as her aunt Hannah could make. How she would enjoy giving it to them all. How she would like to eat some of it herself! She sighed as she pushed back her plate with a good half of the stew yet untouched, and felt that it was impossible to eat another mouthful of that. Then she felt ashamed to think she cared so much for mere eating, and tried to talk pleasantly to the little old lady beside her, who occupied a small dismal room on the third floor and seemed to stay in it most of the time. Celia had not yet found out her occupation nor her standing in society, but she noticed that she trembled when she tried to cut her meat, and she was shabbily clothed in rusty black that looked as if it had served its time out several times over.

Mrs. Morris came into the dining-room when the pie was being served. She was large and worried-looking, and wore a soiled calico wrapper without a collar. Her hair had not been combed since morning and some locks had escaped in her neck and on her forehead and added to her generally dejected appearance. She sat down heavily and wearily at the head of the table, and added her spiritless voice to the conversation. She asked them all how they enjoyed the parade and declared it would have been enough parade for her if she could have "set down for a couple of hours." Then she sighed and drank a cup of tea from her saucer, holding the saucer on the palm of her hand.

It all looked hopelessly dreary to Celia. And here she expected to spend the home part of her life for several years at least, or if not here, yet in some place equally destitute of anything which constitutes a home.

Except for her brief conversation with the old lady on her right, and a few words to Miss Burns, she had spoken to no one during the meal, and as soon as she had excused herself from the pie and folded her napkin, she slipped upstairs to her room, for the thought of the two letters in her pocket seemed more inviting than the pie. She turned the gas to its highest though it did screech, that she might see to read her letters, and then she drew them forth. Her aunt Hannah's came first. She tore the envelope. Only one sheet and not much written thereon. Aunt Hannah was well, but very busy, for Nettie's children were all down with whooping cough and the baby had been quite sick, poor little thing, and she had no time to write. Hiram, Nettie's husband, too, had been ill and laid up for a week, so aunt Hannah had been nursing night and day. She enclosed a little bookmark to remember Celia's birthday. She wished she could send her something nice, but times were hard and Celia knew she had no money, so she must take it out in love.

Hiram's sickness and the doctor's bills made things close for Nettie or she would have remembered the birthday, too, perhaps. Aunt Hannah felt that it was hard to have to be a burden on Nettie, now when the children were young and she and Hiram needed every cent he could earn, but what else could she do? She sent her love to her dear girl, however, and wanted her to read the verse on the little ribbon enclosed and perhaps it would do her good. She hoped Celia had a nice comfortable "homey" place to board and would write soon.

That was all. The white ribbon bookmark was of satin and bore these words:

"His allowance was a continual allowance ... a daily rate. 2 Kings xxv. 30," and beneath in small letters:

> "Charge not thyself with the weight of a year,
> Child of the Master, faithful and dear,
> Choose not the cross for the coming week,
> For that is more than he bids thee seek.
> Bend not thine arms for to-morrow's load,
> Thou mayest leave that to thy gracious God,
> Daily, only he says to thee,
> 'Take up thy cross and follow me.'"

Chapter 2

Celia read the words over mechanically. She was not thinking so much of what they said, as she was of what her aunt had written, or rather of what she had not written, and what could be read between the lines, by means of her knowledge of that aunt and her surroundings. In other words Celia Murray was doing exactly what the words on the white ribbon told her not to do. She was charging herself "with the weight of a year." She had picked up the cross of the coming months and was bending under it already.

Her trouble was aunt Hannah. Oh, if she could but do something for her. She knew very well that that little sentence about being a burden on Nettie meant more than aunt Hannah would have her know. She knew that aunt Hannah would never feel herself a burden on her niece Nettie,—for whom she had slaved half her life, and was still slaving, unless something had been said or done to make her feel so; and Celia, who never had liked her cousin-in-law, Hiram, at any time, for more reasons than mere prejudice, knew pretty well who it was that had made good, faithful, untiring aunt Hannah feel that she was a burden.

Celia's eyes flashed, and she caught her hands in each other in a quick convulsive grasp. "Oh, if I could but do something to get aunt Hannah out of that and have her with me!" she exclaimed aloud. "But here am I with six dollars and a half a week; paying out four and a quarter for this miserable hole they call a home; my clothes wearing out just as fast as they can, and a possibility hanging over me that I may not suit and may be discharged at any time. How can I ever get ahead enough to do anything!"

14

She sat there thinking over her life and aunt Hannah's. Her own mother and Nettie's mother had died within a year of each other. They were both aunt Hannah's sisters. Mr. Murray did not long survive his wife, and Celia had gone to live with her cousins who were being mothered by aunt Hannah, then a young, strong, sweet woman. Her uncle, Mr. Harmon, had been a hard working, silent man, who had supplied the wants of his family as well as he could, but that had not always been luxuriously, for he had never been a successful man. The children had grown fast and required many things. There were five of his own and Celia, who had shared with the rest,—though never really getting her share, because of her readiness to give up and the others' readiness to take what she gave up. Somehow the Harmon children had a streak of selfishness in them, and they always seemed willing that aunt Hannah and Celia should take a back seat whenever any one had to do so, which was nearly all the time. Celia never resented this for herself, even in her heart; but for aunt Hannah she often and often did so. That faithful woman spent the best years of her life, doing for her sister's children as if they had been her own, and yet without the honor of being their mother, and feeling that the home was her own. She had never married, she was simply aunt Hannah, an excellent housekeeper, and the best substitute for a mother one could imagine. As the children grew up they brought all their burdens to aunt Hannah to bear, and when there were more than she could conveniently carry, they would broadly hint that it was Celia's place to help her, for Celia was the outsider, the dependent, the moneyless one. It had fallen to her lot to tend the babies till they grew from being tended into boys, and then to follow after and pick up the things they left in disorder in their wake. It was she who altered the girls' dresses to suit the style, and fashioned dainty hats from odds and ends, turning and pressing them over to make them as good as new for some special occasion. And then when it came her turn, it was she who had to stay at home, because she had nothing to wear, and no time to make it over, and nothing left to make over, because she had given it all to the others.

Then had come the day,—not so many weeks ago: Celia remembered it as vividly as though it had happened but yesterday; she had gone over the details so many times they were burned upon her brain. And yet, how long the time really had been and how many changes had come! The boy came up from the office with a scared face to say that something had happened to Mr. Harmon, and then they had brought him home and the family all too soon learned that there was no use in trying to resuscitate him,—all hope had been over before he was taken from the office. Heart failure, they said! And instantly following upon this had come that other phrase, "financial failure," and soon the orphans found they were penniless. This was not so bad for the orphans, for they were fully grown and the girls were both married. The three boys all had good positions and could support themselves. But what of aunt Hannah and Celia? Nettie and Hiram had taken aunt Hannah into their family, ill-disguising the fact that she was asked because of the help she could give in bringing up and caring for the children, but Celia had understood from the first that there was no place for her.

She had been given a good education with the others, that is, a common school course followed by a couple of years in the High School. She had her two hands and her bright wits and nothing else. A neighbor had offered to use her influence with a friend of a friend of a partner in a city store, and the result was her position. She had learned since she came that it was a good one as such things went. She had regular hours for meals and occasional holidays, and her work was not heavy. She felt that she ought to be thankful. She had accepted it, of course, there was nothing else to be done, but she had looked at aunt Hannah with a heavy heart and she knew aunt Hannah felt it as keenly. They had been very close to each other, these two, who had been separated from the others, in a sense, and had burdens to bear. Perhaps their sense of loneliness in the world had made them cling the more to each other. Celia would have liked to be able to say "Aunt Hannah, come with me. I can take care of you now. You have cared for me all my life, now I will give you a home and rest." Ah! if that could have been! Celia drew her breath quickly, and the tears came between the closed lids. She knew if she once allowed the tears full sway, they would not stay till they had swept all before them, and left her in no fit state to appear before those dreadful, inquisitive boarders, or perhaps even to sell ribbons in Dobson and Co.'s on Monday. No, she must not give way. She would read that other letter and take her mind from these things, for certain it was that she could do nothing more now than she had done, except to write aunt Hannah a cheering letter, which she could not do unless she grew cheerful herself.

So she opened the other letter.

It was from Rawley and Brown, a firm of lawyers on Fifth Street, desiring to know if she was Celia Murray, daughter of Henry Dean Murray of so forth and so on, and if she was, would she please either write or call upon them at her earliest possible convenience, producing such evidences of her identity as she possessed.

The girl laughed as she read it over again. "The idea!" she said, talking aloud to herself again as she had grown into the habit of doing since she was alone, just to feel as if she were talking to some one. "If they want to identify me, let them do so. I'm not asking anything of them. If I'm I, prove it! How very funny! What for, I wonder? There can't be a fortune, I know, for father didn't have a cent. I'm sure I've had that drummed into my head enough by Nettie, and even uncle Joseph took pains to tell me that occasionally. Well, it is mysterious."

She got up and began to walk about the room singing to herself the old nursery rhyme:

" 'If it be me, as I suppose it be,
I've a little dog at home and he'll know me;
If it be *I,* he'll wag his little tail,
And if it be *not* I, he'll bark, and he'll wail.' "

"Dear me!" said Celia, "I'm worse off than the poor old woman who fell asleep on the king's highway. I haven't even a little dog at home who'll know me." She sighed and sat down, picking up the white ribbon that had fallen to the floor. Then she read it over again carefully.

"How like aunt Hannah that sounds!" she said to herself, as she read the poem slowly over, 'Child of the Master, faithful and dear.' I can hear aunt Hannah saying that to me. She was always one to hunt out beautiful things and say them to me as if they had been written all for my poor self. If aunt Hannah had ever had time, I believe she would have been a poet. She has it in her. How entirely I have been doing just exactly what this poem says I must not do: choosing my cross for the coming week. Yes, and bending my arm for to-morrow's load. I have been thinking what a dreary Sunday I should have, and wondering how I could endure it all day long in this ugly, cold room. And I won't stay down in that mean parlor and listen to their horrible singing. It wouldn't be right anyway, for they have not the slightest idea of Sabbath keeping. Last Sunday was one hurrah all day long. I wonder what that verse at the top is—'His allowance was a continual allowance.' I declare I don't remember to have ever read it before. But trust aunt Hannah to ferret out the unusual verses. I must look it up. Second Kings: who was it about, anyway? The twenty-fifth chapter. Oh! here it is!" She read:

> " 'And it came to pass in the seven and thirtieth year of the captivity of Jehoiachin king of Judah, in the twelfth month, on the seven and twentieth day of the month, that Evil-merodach king of Babylon in the year that he began to reign did lift up the head of Jehoiachin king of Judah out of prison;
> And he spake kindly to him, and set his throne above the throne of the kings that were with him in Babylon;
> And changed his prison garments: and he did eat bread continually before him all the days of his life.
> And his allowance was a continual allowance given him of the king, a daily rate for every day, all the days of his life.' "

Ceila paused and read the verses over again.

She began to see why her aunt had sent it to her, and more than that why her heavenly Father had sent it to her. It was the same thought that was in the bit of a poem. God was taking care of her. He was a king and he was able to lift her head up out of prison, if this was a prison, and set her even on a throne, and change her prison garments, and more than that give her an allowance of grace to meet all the daily needs of her life. A continual allowance: she need never worry lest it should give out. It was "all the days of her life." And aunt Hannah was his also. He would care for her in the same way. There was nothing to be done but to trust and do what he gave her to do. Perhaps it was unusually hard for her to do that. She had always been so accustomed to looking ahead and bearing burdens for others and planning for them.

She recognized her fault and resolved to think more about it. Meantime, obviously the next duty for her to perform, and one by no means a cross, was for her to write a long cheery letter to aunt Hannah, who she could easily see was homesick for her already, though it was but a week since they had been separated. She gathered together her writing materials, drew her chair a little nearer the poor light, put on her heavy outdoor coat, for the room was chilly, though it was only the latter part of October, and began to write; thinking meanwhile that she could perhaps make a pleasant Sabbath afternoon for herself out of the study of Jehoiachin, who was so much a stranger to her that she had hardly remembered there was such a person spoken of in the Bible.

The letter she wrote was long and cheerful. It abounded in pen pictures of the places and things she had seen, and it contained descriptions in detail of the different boarders. She tried not to tell the disagreeable things, for she knew aunt Hannah would be quick to understand how hard it all was for her to bear, and she would not lay a feather's burden upon those dear hard-worked shoulders. So she detailed merry conversations, and made light of the poor fare, saying she had a very good and a very cheap place they all told her and she guessed they were right.

She also drew upon her imagination and described the dear little home she was going to make for aunt Hannah to come and rest in and spend her later years, and she told her she was going to begin right away to save up for it. She made it all so real that the tears came to her eyes for very longing for it, and one dropped down on the paper and blotted a word. She hastily wiped it out, and then took a fresh page, for aunt Hannah's eyes were keen. She would be quick to know what made that blot She paused a minute with her pen in air ere she closed the letter. Should she, or should she not tell aunt Hannah of that letter from the lawyers? No, she would not until she saw whether it came to anything, and if so, what. It might only worry her aunt. There were worries enough at Hiram's without her putting any more in the way. So she finished her letter, sealed and addressed it, and then ran down to put it in the box.

As she returned from her errand into the misty outdoor world, and closed the door behind her shivering, glad she did not have to go out any more, she met the tall, lanky cook in untidy work dress and unkempt hair. Celia noticed instantly that it was curly hair and black, like the one she found in the stew the night she came. She was passing on upstairs but the cook put out her hand and stopped her.

"Say," she said in familiar tones, "I wish you'd jes' step into Mis' Morris' room and stay a spell. She's ben took dreadful sick this evenin', and I've ben with her off an' on most all the time, an' I've got pies yet to bake fer to-morrow, an' I can't spend no more time up there now. She ought to have some one, an' the rest seems all to be gone out 'cept that ol' lady up there, an' she's gone to bed by this time, I reckon."

Celia could do nothing but consent to go, of course, though the task looked anything but a pleasant one. Mrs. Morris had never struck her pleasantly. She enquired as to the sickness. The woman didn't exactly know what was the matter. No, there had not been any physician sent for. "There wan't no one to go in the first place, and, secondly, doctors is expensive things, take 'em anyway you will, medicine and all. Mrs. Morris can't afford no doctors. She's most killed with debt now."

Celia turned on the stairs, and followed the woman's direction to find Mrs. Morris' room.

Over in her mind came those words she had read a little while ago.

"Daily, only, he says to thee,
    'Take up thy cross and follow me.' "

She smiled, and thought how soon the cross had come to her after she had laid down the wrong one of a week ahead, and tapped softly on Mrs. Morris' door, lifting up her heart in a prayer that she might be shown how to do or say the right thing if action were required of her. Then she heard a strained voice, as of one in pain, call "Come in," and she opened the door.

Chapter 3

Mrs. Morris lay on her unmade bed, still in the soiled wrapper. Her expansive face was drawn in agony and she looked white and sick. She seemed surprised to see Celia, and supposed she had come to prefer a request for another towel, perhaps, or to make some complaint.

"You'll have to ask Maggie," she said without waiting to hear what the girl had to say. "I can't talk now, I'm suffering so. It's just terrible. I never was so sick in my life."

"But I've come to see if I can't help you," explained Celia. "Maggie told me you were sick. Tell me what is the matter. Perhaps I can do something for you. I know about sickness and nursing."

"Oh, such awful pain!" said the woman, writhing in agony, "I suppose it's something I've et. Though I never et a thing, all day long, but a little piece of pie at dinner to-night and me tea. Me nerves is all used up with worrying anyway, and me stomach won't stand anything any more."

Celia asked a few practical questions, and then told her she would return in a minute. She found her way in haste to the kitchen, though she had never before penetrated to that realm of darkness—and dirt. She ordered Maggie peremptorily to bring her a large quantity of very hot water as soon as she could, and send somebody for a doctor. Then she went up to her own room and hastily gathered a bottle or two from her small store of medicines and a piece of an old blanket she had brought from home. She hesitated a moment. She ought to have another flannel. The woman was too sick to find anything, and she had

21

said she did not know where there were any old flannels. It was necessary. She must take up this cross to save that poor woman from her
suffering and perhaps save her life, for she was evidently very sick indeed. She waited no longer, but quickly took out her own clean flannel
petticoat. It was nothing very fine, and was somewhat old, but it was a
sacrifice to think of using any of her personal clothing down there in
that dirty room, and for that woman who did not seem to be scrupu-
lously clean herself. However, there was no help for it, and she hurried
back as fast as she could. She gave the poor woman a little medicine
which she thought might help her, and she knew could do no harm till
the doctor could get there, and then plunging the cherished blanket
into the hot water, she wrung it as dry as she could and quickly applied
it to the seat of pain, covering it with the flannel skirt. She knew there
was nothing like hot applications to relieve severe pain. She saw by the
look of relief that passed over the sick woman's face that the pain had
relaxed to some extent. After a moment, Mrs. Morris said:

"I don't know as you'd a needed to send for a doctor, this might
have helped me without him. I can't bear to think of his bill. Bills'll be
the death of me yet, I'm afraid."

But a spasm of pain stopped her speech, and Celia hastened to repeat the applications.

It was some time before the doctor arrived. The girl had to work fast
and hard. It was evident when he came that he thought the patient a
very sick woman. Mrs. Morris realized this, too. After the doctor was
gone and Celia was left alone with her, she asked her if she supposed
the doctor thought she was going to die.

"Though I ain't got much to live for, the land knows—nor to die for
either for the matter of that."

"Oh you forget!" said Celia, reverently, aghast that one should
speak in that tone of dying, "There is Jesus! Don't you know him?"

The woman looked at her as if she had spoken the name of some
heathen deity, and then turned her head wearily.

"No," she said, "I don't suppose I am a Christian. I never had any
time. When I was a girl there was always plenty of fun, and I never
thought about it, and after I got married there wasn't time. I did tell

the minister I would think about joining church the time of my daughter's funeral, but I never did. I kind of wish I had now. One never is ready to die, I s'pose. But then living isn't easy either, the land knows."

A grey ashen look overspread her face. Celia wondered if perhaps she might not be dying even now. She shuddered. It seemed so terrible for any one to die in that way. She had never been with a very sick person near to death, and she did not know the signs well enough to judge how much danger there might be of it. She felt however that she must say something. The woman must have some thread of hope, if she should be really dying. She came close to her and took her hand tenderly.

"Dear Mrs. Morris! Don't talk that way. Dying isn't hard, I'm sure, if you have Jesus, and he's always near and ready, if you will only take him now. I know he helps one to die, for I can remember my own dear mother, though I was but a little girl. She had a beautiful look on her face, when she bade me goodbye, and told me she was going to be with Jesus, and that I must always be a good girl and get ready to come to her. She looked very happy about it."

Mrs. Morris opened her eyes and gave her a searching look. Then she said in a voice halfway between a groan and a frightened shout:

"Why do you talk like that? You don't think I am dying, do you? Tell me, quick! Did the doctor say I was going to die? Why did he go away if that was so? Send for him quick!"

Then the inexperienced young girl realized that she had made a mistake and been too much in earnest. There was danger that the woman might make herself much worse by such excitement. She must calm her. To talk to her thus would do no good. She must wait until a suitable season.

"No, Mrs. Morris," she said, rising and speaking calmly, "he did not say so, and I do not believe you are going to die. You must not get so excited, or you will make yourself worse. Here, take your medicine now, for it is time. I did not mean you to think I thought you were dying, and I'm sorry I spoke about my mother's death, it was very foolish of me. Please forget it now. I only wanted to tell you how Jesus was standing near ready to be a comfort to you always, whether you lived or died. But now you ought to go to sleep. Would you like me to sing to you? Is the pain a little easier? The doctor said you must lie very quiet. Can I get you anything?"

By degrees she calmed the woman again, and then sat down to watch and give her the medicine. There seemed to be no one whose business it was to relieve Celia. Maggie put her head in the door about midnight to say she was going to bed now and had left a fire, if any more hot water was needed. Celia sat there gradually taking in the fact that she was left to sit up all night with this sick woman, an utter stranger to her. It was scarcely what she would choose as a pleasant task. But she recognized it as the cross the Master had laid upon her with his own hand, and there was a sense of sweetness in performing this duty which she would not have had otherwise. It occurred to her that it was well this was Saturday night instead of some other, for she could ill afford to sit up and lose all her sleep when she had to stand at the counter all the next day. She smiled to herself in the dim light and thought this must be part of the Master's plan to fix it so that she could do this duty and her others also. This was all he asked her to do, just what she had strength for. He gave her the daily allowance of that. But what if she should have to sit up to-morrow night? "Daily, only, he says to thee," and "Thou mayest leave that to thy gracious Lord," came the answering words, for now she knew the little poem by heart. She went upstairs, hastily changed her dress for a loose wrapper, and secured her Bible and one or two articles which she thought might be useful in caring for the sick woman. When she came down again Mrs. Morris seemed to be asleep, and Celia settled herself by the dim light with her Bible. She felt that she needed some help and strength. She had not read long when Mrs. Morris said in a low voice, "Is that the Bible you've got? Read a little piece to me."

Celia hardly knew where to turn for the right words just now, but her Bible opened easily of itself to the twenty-third psalm and she read the words in a low, musical voice, praying the while that they might be sent of the Spirit to reach the sick woman's heart. When she stopped reading Mrs. Morris seemed to be asleep again, and Celia settled herself in the least uncomfortable chair in the room, and began to think.

But she had not long for this occupation, for this was to be a night of action. The terrible pain which for a time had been held by some powerful opiate the doctor had given when he first came in, returned in full force, and the patient soon was writhing in mortal agony once more. Celia was roused from her thoughts. She called Maggie and sent for hot water and the doctor again, and it was not until morning was beginning to stain the sky with crimson that she sat down to breathe and realize that Mrs. Morris was still alive. It seemed almost a miracle that she was, for the doctor had said when he arrived that there was doubt whether he could save her.

Early in the morning Miss Burns came in to relieve her watch, and Celia snatched a little sleep, but she found on awaking that she was needed again. Mrs. Morris had asked for her. She went down to the breakfast table and found, what she had not supposed possible, that the breakfast was so much worse than former breakfasts, since the mistress was sick, that it was hardly possible to eat at all. It seemed that Mrs. Morris had made some difference in things, though Celia had thought the night before that they could not very well be much worse. She had yet to find that there were many grades below even this in boarding-houses.

The Sabbath was not spent in studying Jehoiachin. It was full, but not with attending church services. She did not stay in her cold little room. She would have been glad to have been allowed to flee to that refuge. Instead, she made her headquarters in Mrs. Morris' room and from there she began by degrees to order things about her, for Mrs. Morris seemed to have placed all her dependence upon her. It was she who answered the questions of Maggie about this thing and that, and who kept the entire list of boarders from coming in to talk to Mrs. Morris and commiserate her. She also cleared up the room and gave a touch of something like decent care to the sick woman and her surroundings. Once or twice the patient opened her eyes, looked around, seemed to see the subtle difference, and then closed them again. Celia could not tell whether it pleased her or whether she was indifferent. But it was not in Celia's nature to stay in a room and not make those little changes of picking up a shoe and straightening a quilt and hanging clothing out of sight. She did it as a matter of course.

Occasionally, when she had time to do so, she wondered what aunt Hannah would think if she could see her now, and she smiled to think that this was just what she seemed to have had to do all her life,—give up to help other people. Then she thought perhaps it was the most blessed thing that could happen to her.

Occasionally there would come to her a remembrance of that letter from the lawyers, and she would wonder what it meant, and how she could possibly go to work to find out.

Sunday evening she sat with her landlady for a couple of hours. The pain seemed to be a little easier, though she had spent an intensely trying day. She seemed worried and inclined to talk. Celia tried to soothe her and persuade her to get calm for sleeping, but it was of no use.

"How can I sleep," answered the woman impatiently, "with so many things to fret about? Here am I on me back for the land knows how long, and the doctor wanting me to go to the hospital. How can I go to the hospital? What will become of me house, and me business if I up and off that way? And then when I get well, if I ever do, what's to become of me? Me house would be empty, or me goods sold for grocery debts and other things, and I should starve. I might as well take the chances of dying outright now as that. I know I'd die in the hospital anyway, fretting about things. That Maggie never could carry on things, even if I was only to be gone two days. She never remembers to salt anything. Those two girls from that three-cent store have been complaining about the soup to-day already. They say it was just like dish water. And that German fellow came and told me tonight, with me lying sick here, that he'd have to leave if things didn't improve. He said I ought to get better help! Think of it! How am I going about to get help and me on me back not able to stir? I don't much care if he does leave, he always ate more than all the rest of them put together. But land, if I should get well right away and keep on, I don't see where I'm coming to. There's bills everywhere, milk and meat and groceries and dry goods. I don't know how I'm ever to pay 'em. It'll be just go on and pay a little, and get deeper into debt, and pay a little of that and make more debt, till I come to the end sometime, and I s'pose it might as well be now as any time."

Poor Celia! She had no words ready for such trouble as this. Debt had always been to her an awful thing, a great sin, never to be committed. She never realized that there were people to whom to be in debt seemed the normal way of living from day to day. She tried to think of something comforting to say, for how could a woman get well with such a weight as this on her mind? It would do no good to quote verses of Scripture about taking no thought for the morrow, nor to quote that sweet poem of hers about not bearing next week's crosses. The poor woman would not understand. She had not so lived in the past as to know how to claim the promise of being cared for. She would scarcely understand if Celia tried to tell her that if she would but cast her care now on Jesus he would help her in some way at once. This was what she longed to say, but her experience of the night before led her to fear saying anything which might excite the poor nervous woman.

"How much money do you need to pay all your debts and set you straight again?" she asked, thinking a little opportunity to go over her troubles might quiet her.

"Oh, I don't know," wailed the poor woman. "If I just had a thousand dollars, I'd sell out me business and go somewhere and get out of it. Things seem to be getting worse and worse." She began to cry feebly, and Celia was at her wit's end. Everything she said seemed to make matters worse. Suddenly she began to sing in a low soft voice,

"Jesus, Saviour, pilot me,
Over life's tempestuous sea."

Her voice was sweet and pure, and the woman paused to listen while Celia sang on until she fell asleep.

Chapter 4

Celia discovered that the firm of lawyers who had written her, had their office in a building not many blocks from Dobson and Co.'s store. She felt anxious to find out what they wanted of her, and so the next morning she obtained permission for a few minutes' extra time at the lunch hour and hastened there.

She reached the number at last, and searched the dirty sign board for the names "Rawley and Brown." There it was almost the last one on the list, "Fourth floor, back." She climbed up the four flights of stairs, for the elevator was out of order and arrived panting before the dingy office. When she entered the room, two elderly men sat at desks on which were piled many papers, and each was talking with a client who sat near his desk. They did not cease their talking with these men until Celia had stood for some moments by the door. Then the elder of the two looked over his glasses at her, and she ventured to say she was Miss Murray come in response to their letter. She was given a chair and asked to wait until Mr. Rawley was at leisure, and in the course of a few minutes both the clients had withdrawn, and she was left alone with the two lawyers. Over in the corner behind a screen, she could hear the click of a typewriter and see the top of a frizzy head which she knew must belong to the operator, probably the one who had written the letter to her.

Mr. Rawley at last turned to her and began a list of questions. Celia answered everything she could, wondering when this mystery would be explained. As soon as she had finished telling Mr. Rawley the names of her different living relatives, he cleared his throat and looked at her sharply and yet thoughtfully:

"Miss Murray," said he, as if about to ask something very important, "did you ever hear your father speak of having a great uncle?"

Celia paused to think a moment. She had been but ten years old when her father died. She could remember some conversations between her father and mother about relatives whom she had never seen. She searched her mind.

"I'm not sure about the *'great'* part of it. He might have been a great uncle, but I know there was one father called uncle Abner. He must have died long ago. He was a very old man then. I can remember father saying laughingly to mother one day that he would never see anybody prettier than she was, not if he lived to be as old as uncle Abner."

"A-ahem!" said Mr. Rawley, uncrossing his feet and recrossing them again and putting his two thumbs together as he looked at them seriously under his bushy eyebrows. "Yes. Ah! Well, and did that uncle have any—ah—heirs?"

Celia wanted to laugh. She had already begun to plan how she would make aunt Hannah laugh by a letter she would write describing this interview with the lawyers, but she kept her face straight and answered steadily.

"I do not know."

"Well, I must say, my dear young lady," remarked Mr. Rawley, after a somewhat prolonged pause, "that your evidence is somewhat— that is to say,—inadequate. You could hardly expect us, with so little to go upon—that is to say, without more investigation, you could hardly expect us—"

"You forget, sir," said Celia, really laughing now, "that I have not the slightest idea what all this is about. I expect nothing. I came here to be informed."

The old lawyer gave her another searching look and then seemed to conclude that she was honest.

"Well, young lady, I think I may safely tell you this much. There was property of Mr. Abner Murray's, which naturally descended to his only son. This son had been in India for years. He did not return at his father's death, and in fact his whereabouts was not definitely known, until a very short time ago, when positive information of his death without heirs was received. The property would then revert to Mr.

Abner Murray's next of kin, and his heirs. Mr. Abner Murray had a brother, who is supposedly your father's father. If this should prove to be the case, through his death and your father's, his only heir, you being the only living child of your father, the property would naturally fall to you. Do you follow me closely?"

Celia looked at Mr. Rawley respectfully now and very gravely. The matter had taken on a different aspect. It was a complete surprise. She had not even in her wildest dreams allowed herself to hope for any such thing. Fortunes only fell to girls in books, not to flesh-and-blood, hard working, everyday girls.

She looked at the lawyer in silence a minute and then she smiled gravely and said:

"That would be very nice if it's true. I wish it might be. And now I suppose you are done with me for the present, until you have investigated the truth of my statements."

Mr. Rawley seemed surprised that she took it so coolly and asked no more questions. She rose as if to go. The truth was she had caught a glimpse of the clock and she saw that she had barely time to reach her counter before the limit of her nooning would be over, and she had had no lunch. Her position might be forfeited if she exceeded her time. That was worth to her at present all the mythical fortunes that the future might hold for her. So, without more ado, she hurried away, and not even stopping for a single bite to eat, laid aside her wraps and was in her place behind the counter when the minute hand pointed just one minute after the time allotted her.

It was a very busy afternoon. She had not much time to think. Everybody seemed to want ribbons. "Perhaps I shall be in a position to buy some of these yards myself, instead of measuring them off for other people, some time, if that old Mr. Rawley ever finds out whether *I* am *I*," she thought to herself as she skillfully clipped off two yards of blue satin and three yards of pink taffeta.

"Property!" he had said. What did property mean? Had great uncle Abner left an old house standing somewhere, which would be of no earthly use to anybody unless sold, and bring nothing then? Or perhaps it was some musty old library. She had no faith that there was much money. Such things did not run in their family. It would turn out to be very little. But oh, what if it should be something worth while? What, for instance, if it should be a thousand dollars! What might she not do? Why, a thousand dollars would enable her to do some of the nice things she longed so to do. She could bring aunt Hannah here to the city, and set up a tiny home with her in it somewhere. With that much money to start on, they could surely make their living, she in the store and aunt Hannah at home sewing. It flashed across her mind that that was just the sum Mrs. Morris had wished for. She had said if she only had a thousand dollars she could pay her debts and have enough left to start on and get out of her uncomfortable life.

How nice it would be if she, Celia, could have money enough to say, "I have the thousand dollars, Mrs. Morris, and I will give it to you. You may pay those people and go away to some more quiet, restful life." Then how delightful it would be to take that poor miserable boarding-house and make it over. Make the boarders' lives cheerful and pleasant, give them healthful food and clean, inviting rooms to live in! What a work that would be for a lifetime! If she ever did get rich, she believed she would do just that thing. Hunt up the most wretched boarding-house she could find and take it, boarders and all, and make it over. She believed she could do it with aunt Hannah's help. Aunt Hannah could cook and plan, and she could execute and beautify. The thought pleased her so well that she carried it out into details, during the long walk back to her boarding-house that night. She even went so far as to think out what she would give them for dinner the first night, and how the dining-room should appear—and how their faces would look when they saw it all. What fun it would be! Miss Burns should have something every night that would tempt her appetite, and the poor old lady in the third story should be given the very tenderest cut in the whole steak, so she need not tremble so when she cut it. And there was that poor young school-teacher, he needed rich creamy milk. She had heard him decline the muddy coffee several times and once he asked if he might have a glass of milk, and Maggie had told him they were all out of milk.

She debated whether she would retain her position in the store and decided that she would for a time, because that would give her a chance to carry out some plans without letting the boarders know who was at the bottom of it all. Things should not be changed much at first, except that everything should be made entirely clean and wholesome. Then gradually they would begin to beautify. Perhaps the others would help in it. Perhaps she could lure the young man from the dry goods store into spending an evening at home and helping her. She had a suspicion that he spent his evenings out, and remained late in places which did him no good, to say the least. It would do no harm for her to try to get acquainted with him and help him, even if she never got a fortune to enable her to raise her neighbors into better things. She would begin the reformation of young Mr. Knowles that very evening, if there came an opportunity. With these thoughts and plans in mind she completed her long walk in much shorter time than usual and with a lighter heart. It did her good to have an interest in life beyond the mere duties of the hour.

She found Mrs. Morris in much the same state of depression as on the day before. The doctor had urged again that she go to the hospital for regular course of treatment. She was as determined as ever that she would not, or rather *could* not do it. She wanted Celia to come and sit with her. She had taken a liking to her new boarder, and she did not hesitate to say so, and to declare that the others were an unfeeling set who bothered her and didn't care if she was sick. Celia tried to cheer her up. She gave her a flower which one of the other workers in the store had given her, and told her she would come up after dinner was over. Then she went down to the table, and found Mr. Knowles seated before his plate looking cold and coughing. She wondered if her opportunity would come. His seat was at her left hand. They exchanged some remarks about the weather, and Celia told him he seemed to have a bad cold. He told her that was a chronic state with him, and then coughed again as he tried to laugh. She entered into his mock gaiety, and told him that if his mother were there she would tell him not to go out that evening, in such damp weather and with that cough.

His face grew sober instantly, and he said very earnestly:

"I suppose she would."

"Well, then, I suppose you'll stay in, won't you?" said the girl. "It isn't right not to take care of yourself. The wind is very raw to-night. Your cough will be much worse to-morrow if you go out in it. You ought to stay in for your mother's sake, you know."

It was a bow drawn at a venture. Celia stole a glance at him. He looked up at her quickly, his handsome, gay face sober and almost startled.

"But mother isn't here," he said, his voice husky. "She died a year ago."

"But don't you think mothers care for their sons even after they have gone to heaven? I believe they do. I believe in some way God lets them know when they are doing right. You ought to take care of yourself just the same, even if she is not here, for you know she would tell you to do it, now wouldn't she?"

"Yes, I know she would," he answered, and then, after a minute's pause, he added, "but it is so hard to stay in here. There is no place to sit and nothing to do all the evening. Mother used to have things different."

"It *is* hard," said Celia, sympathizingly, "and this is a dreary place. I've thought so myself ever since I came. I wonder if you and I couldn't make things a little pleasanter for us all, if we tried."

"How? I'm sure I never thought I could do anything in that line. How would you go about it?"

"Well, I'm not just sure," said Celia, thinking rapidly and bringing forth some of her half made plans to select one for this emergency. "But I think we ought to have a good light first. The gas is miserable."

"You're right; it is that," responded Mr. Knowles.

"Didn't I see a big lamp on the parlor table?"

"Yes, I think there is a lamp there, but it smokes like an engine, and it gives a wicked flare of a light that stares at you enough to put your eyes out."

"Well, I wonder if we couldn't do something to cure that lamp of smoking. I'm somewhat a doctor of lamps myself, having served a long apprenticeship at them, and I think if you'll help me I'll try. I have some lovely pink crepe paper upstairs that I got to make a shade for my room, but I'll sacrifice that to the house if you can get me a new wick. What do you say? Shall we try it? I'm sure Mrs. Morris won't object, for it will save gas, besides making things pleasanter for the boarders. I have a book I think you will enjoy, after the lamp is fixed for reading. If you are going to be a good boy and stay at home tonight I'll bring it down."

The young man entered into the scheme enthusiastically. He was a very young man, not more than nineteen, or Celia would not have cared or dared to speak to him in this half-commanding way. But she had been used to boys, and to winning them to do what she wished, and she won her way this time surely. The young man was only too glad to have something to keep him in, and his heart was still very tender toward his lost mother. Celia saw that he would not be hard to influence. She wished she were wise and able to help him. Her soul felt with oppression the need of all these other souls in this house with her, and she wished to be great and mighty to lift them up and help them. How strange it was that the way kept opening up before her for daily helping of others. She seemed to be the only Christian in this house full of people. What a weight of responsibility rested upon her if that was so. How she ought to pray to be guided that she might be wise as a serpent and harmless as a dove; that she might, if possible, bring each one of them to a knowledge of Jesus Christ. And what was *she* to do all this? A mere weak girl, who was discouraged and homesick, and could not get enough money together to keep herself from need, perhaps, nor grace enough to keep her own heart from failing or her feet from falling. What was *she* to think of guiding others? How could she do all this work? She must shrink back from the thought. She could not do it. It was too much. Ah! She might leave all that to her gracious Lord. She had forgotten that. All he wanted her to do was to take the duty of the hour or the minute and do it for him. What matter whether there were results that showed or not so long as he was obeyed? When she slipped up to her room for that pink crepe paper she knelt down and asked that it and the book and the lamp and her little effort for the evening might be blessed. Then she went down to conquer that lamp.

Chapter 5

"For the land sake! Yes," said Mrs. Morris, turning wearily on her pillow, "do what you please with it. I wish it was a good one. I'd like to afford a real good one with a silk shade with lace on it, but I can't. There's lots ought to be done here, but there's no use talking about it. I'm clean discouraged anyway. I wish I could sell out, bag and baggage, and go to the poorhouse."

"Oh, Mrs. Morris, don't talk that way!" said Celia, brightly. "You'll get well pretty soon. Don't think about that now. We'll try to keep things in order till you are able to see to them yourself. And meantime, I believe I can make that lamp work beautifully. I'll come back by and by and report progress. Now eat that porridge. I know it can't hurt you. The doctor told me it would be good for you. I made it myself, and it's just such as aunt Hannah used to make for sick people. There's nothing like twice boiled flour porridge. Is it seasoned right? There's the salt."

Then she flitted downstairs to the lamp.

Young Mr. Knowles was already on hand with the new wick he had purchased at the corner grocery, having carefully taken the measure of the burner.

Celia with experienced hand soon had the lamp burning brightly. Frank Hartley, the University student, had been attracted by the unusual light and declared he would bring his books down to the parlor for a while. It was cold as a barn in his room anyway. He and Harry Knowles stood by watching with admiring eyes, as Celia's fingers, now washed from the oil of the lamp, manipulated the pretty rose-colored paper into a shade, and when it was done, with a gathering string, a smoothing out on the edges and a pucker and twist here and there, and then a band and bow of the crepe paper, it all had looked so simple that they marveled at the beauty of the graceful fall of ruffles, like the petals of some lovely flower.

She put the promised book in Harry Knowles' hand, a paper-covered copy of "In His Steps," and saying she would come down later to see what he thought of the story, she slipped away to Mrs. Morris' room. She must get time to write to aunt Hannah some time to-night about her visit to the lawyers, for aunt Hannah might have some evidence which would serve her in good stead, but this duty to the sick woman came first. She turned her head as she left the room and saw the two young men settling themselves in evident comfort around the bright lamp. The school-teacher, George Osborn, came in the front door just then, and catching the rosy light from the room stepped in, looked around surprised, then hung up his hat and went in to stand a minute before the register to warm his hands. It was a touch of cheer he had not expected. Presently he went upstairs and brought down a pile of reports he must make out, and seated himself with the other two around that light.

Celia upstairs was telling Mrs. Morris about the lamp, how well it burned, and giving a glowing account of the three young men seated around it. Mrs. Morris listened astonished.

"Well, I've told them boys time an' again that they ought to stay at home, but they never would before. It must be some sort of a spell you've worked on them. Of course, that teacher he stays up in his room a lot. But he's trying to support his mother and put his brother through college, and you can't expect much of him. He'll just give himself up entirely to them and that'll be the end of his life. There's always some folks in this world have to be sacrificed to a few others. It's the way things are. I'm one of those meself, though the land knows who's the better for me being sacrificed. It does seem as if I had had to give up every blessed thing I ever tried for in me life. Just set down a while. I feel a little easier this evening and I've been a-doing a powerful lot of worrying all day. I haven't a soul to advise me that knows anything.

You seem to be made out of good stuff, and you've been real good to me, and I just wish you'd tell me what you think I ought to do."

Celia sat down. She wondered what could be coming next. It was strange to have her advice asked this way. Coming out into the world alone to earn one's living places a great many responsibilities upon one sometimes. She felt very incapable of advising. She felt she had not wisdom to settle her own life, let alone another's, and one so much older than herself, that it would seem as if experience ought to have taught her much. But she tried to be sympathetic, and told Mrs. Morris to tell her all about it, and she would do the best she could. In her heart she prayed the Father that she might have the wisdom to answer wisely.

"Well, you see it's this way. I'm just deep down in debt. I told you that before. It's been going on worse and worse every year, and every year I'd hope by the next to make the two ends meet somehow. But they never did. I've cut down and cut down. And then I got left two or three times by boarders going off without paying what they owed after I had trusted them a long time. There was that Mr. Perry now, he left that old rickety organ. It was well enough to have an organ for the boarders, but you see I couldn't afford to have one. If I could have, I'd have bought a new one, you know. Well, things like that have happened time and again. Once a woman who recited pieces for a living came into the house. She had a lot of dirty satin clothes, and afterward she left quite suddenly and I never knew she was gone till a man came for her trunk. Of course I got the trunk for her board. She had been here two months and only paid one week's board, kept putting me off and off. When I had that trunk sold at auction it brought me in just one dollar and sixty-two cents. What do you think of that? And she had the second story front alone too; and *airs,* why she'd have her breakfast sent up every morning about ten o'clock. She made me think she was a great woman. Well, I learned better. But it does seem as though I've had more trouble with folks. There was the time the woman was here with her little girl, and the child took scarlet fever and the Board of Health came in and sent everybody off, and scared them so 'twas a long time before I could get them back. Well, there's been a plenty of other things just like that. You don't wonder, do you, that I'm in debt? The worst of it is it's been getting worse and worse. That Maggie just wastes everything she lays her hands on, and I don't know's I'd better myself any if I tried to get somebody else. There's always changes and new things to buy. Now what would you do? You see it's this way. I've got a sister out west that lives by herself in a little village. She's a widow and she's got enough to live on, and she's written to me to come out and live with her, and she thinks I could get a little sewing now and then, and I could help her in her house. I can't ask her for money, for I haven't got the face to, having asked her once before. Besides, she's not one to give out and out that way, even if she could afford to, which I guess she can't, though she'd be willing and glad to give me a home with her. I'm too proud to borrow what I know I never could pay, and I won't skip out here as some would and leave me debts behind me. I'm honest, whatever else I ain't. Now what would you do? No, I don't own this house; if I did I'd been bankrupt long ago with the repairs it needs, that I couldn't get out of the landlord. But I took it for the rest of the year, and the lease don't run out till April, so you see I'm in for that. It's just the same old story. 'A little more money to buy more land, to plant more corn, to feed more hogs, to get more money, to buy more land, to feed more hogs.' Only, I always had a little less of everything each time. Now Miss Murray, what would you do if it was you?"

"Haven't you anything at all to pay with? No,"—she hesitated for a word and the one she had heard that day came to her—"Haven't you any property of any sort? Nothing you could sell?"

Celia was always practical. She wanted to know where she stood before she gave any advice. Mrs. Morris looked at her a moment in a dazed way, trying to think if there was anything at all.

"No, not a thing except my husband's watch and this old furniture. I suppose I might sell out me business, but nobody would buy it and I'd pity 'em, poor things, if they did."

She talked a long time with the woman, trying to find out about boarding-houses and how they were run. Before she was through she began to have some inkling of the reason why Mrs. Morris had failed in business and was so deeply in debt. She was only a girl, young and without experience, but she felt sure she could have avoided some of the mistakes which had been the cause of Mrs. Morris' trouble. Finally, she said in answer to the twentieth "What would you do if you was me?"

"Mrs. Morris, I don't quite know till I have thought about it. I will think and tell you to-morrow, perhaps, or the next day. It seems to me though, that I would stop right now and not run on and get more deeply in debt. That cannot better matters. I think somebody might buy your things, and—some way might be found for you to pay your debts,—but, in the first place, you must get well, and we'll do the very best we can to get on here till you are well enough to know what you will do. Now may I read to you just a few words? And then you ought to go to sleep. Just you rest your mind about all those things, and I promise you I will try to think of something that will help you."

She turned to the little Bible she had brought in with her and read a few verses in the fourteenth chapter of John "Let not your heart be troubled; ye believe in God, believe also in me."

She was very tired when she reached her room that night. The letter she intended to write to aunt Hannah was still unwritten. The book she had taken from the public library to read was lying on her bureau untouched. She had been bearing the burdens of other people, and the day had been full of excitement and hard work. She threw herself on her bed, so nervously tired that she felt convulsive sobs rising in her throat. What had she done? She had promised to think up some way to help Mrs. Morris. Mrs. Morris was nothing to her, why should she take this upon herself? And yet she knew, as she asked herself these questions, that she had felt all along that God had as truly called her to help that poor woman as ever he had called her to sell ribbons for Dobson and Co., or to help aunt Hannah with the mending. She had not wanted to do it, either. It was very unpleasant work, indeed, in many ways, and had required sacrifices of which she had not dreamed when she began. There was the pretty lampshade she was planning to have. She had given that up for the general good of the house. Now, when she got the lamp she intended to buy at a cheap sale somewhere, she would have to wait till she could afford more paper and a frame for her shade. Well, never mind! She surely was repaid for that act, for those young men had enjoyed it. How much pleasure a little thing can give! How many things there were about that house which might be easily done to make things brighter and pleasanter, and how much she would enjoy doing them,—if aunt Hannah were only here! How nice it would be if she had some money and could buy Mrs. Morris out and help the poor thing to get off to her relatives, and then get to work and make that house cheerful and beautiful and a true home for its present inmates. How aunt Hannah would enjoy that work too! It was just such work as would fulfill that good woman's highest dreams of a beautiful vocation in life.

Suddenly Celia sat bolt upright on the hard little bed, and stared at the opposite wall with a thoughtful, and yet energetic expression on her face.

"What if it should!" she said aloud. "What if there should be some money, say as much as a thousand dollars, and maybe a little over, for an allowance lest we might run behind. Wouldn't that be grand! Oh, you dear old uncle Abner, if it proves true, and if you up in heaven can see, I hope you know how happy you'll make several people. I'll do it, I surely will! And aunt Hannah shall come and run the house and be the housekeeper, and maybe we can get old Molly, for I'm certain we never could do a thing with that Maggie, she's so terribly dirty, and Molly would leave anywhere to be with aunt Hannah! There now, I'm talking just as if I was a 'millionairess' and could spend my millions. I ought not to have thought of this, for it will turn my head. I shall be so disappointed when Mr. Rawley tells me, to-morrow or next day, that I'm not myself, or that the property is some old hen house and a family cat, that I'm afraid I shall not be properly thankful for the cat. I wonder if it isn't just as bad to take up the happy crosses for the coming year as the uncomfortable ones. I wonder how that is. I must think about it. Meanwhile, aunt Hannah must be written to, for Mr. Rawley wanted those marriage certificates she has, and somehow I feel quite happy." She sprang from the bed and jumped around her room in such a lively fashion that Miss Burns who roomed below wondered what was the matter.

Writing to her aunt sobered her down somewhat. She began to think of herself a little.

"Celia Murray, do you know what you are doing?" This was what she heard whispered to her from behind. "You have come to the city to earn your living, and you have come here to board, not to nurse sick landladies, nor to become a guardian angel for stray young men, nor to exercise the virtue of benevolence. You must think of yourself, somewhat. How in the world will you ever be fit for your work if you spend so much time and energy on working for other people and staying up nights? Had you not better seek out another boarding-house? There must be plenty in this city, and probably if you looked about a little you might find one where you would have more conveniences and a better room and board. Leave Mrs. Morris to get along the best way she can. You are not responsible for her. She is a grown woman and ought to know enough to take care of herself. Anyway, she is only suffering the consequences of her foolishness. Better try to-morrow to find another boarding-house."

Yet, even as Celia heard these words spoken in a tempting voice, she knew she would not go. She was not made of that kind of stuff. Besides she was interested. Whatever her cross for the coming week was to be, it would not be one to her to remain here now and help work out God's plans, if she might be permitted so to do.

"And if it might only please my King to lift my head up out of prison and set me up where I might help others in this boarding-house, I would try to make as good a use of my liberty and my allowance as Jehoiachin did. I wonder what he did do with his allowance anyway. And it must have been such a pleasant thing to him to know, to fully understand that his allowance would not fail all the days of his life. I wonder if he got downhearted sometimes, and feared lest Evilmerodach might die and leave him in the lurch, or whether he might turn against him some day. Now with me it is so different. My King is all-powerful. What he has promised, *I know* he will perform. I need never dread his dying, for he is everlasting. I can trust him perfectly to give me an allowance all the days of my life of whatever I need. And yet, daily and hourly I distrust, and fear and tremble, and dread lest I may be left hungry some day. What a strange contradiction, what an ungrateful, untrustful, unworthy child of the King I am."

Then she turned out her light and knelt to pray.

Chapter 6

It is said that Satan trembles when he sees the weakest saint upon his knees. It is probably true that he also hies him away to take counsel with his evil angels to see if they cannot by some means overtake that saint in his resolves and endeavors, and make him tremble, and perhaps fall. It certainly seemed to Celia the next morning as if everything had conspired to make her life hard.

In the first place it was raining. A cold, steady drizzle, that bade fair to continue all day and for several days, if it did not turn into snow. The furnace, none too good at any time, was ill-managed. Mrs. Morris usually regulated it herself, but Maggie made a poor hand at it. She chose this morning to forget to see to it at all until the fire had gone out. There was no time to build it up then, for she had breakfast to get for the boarders who must be off to their work at their appointed hours. Celia dressed quickly, for her room was so cold she was in a shiver. With her blue fingers she tried to turn the pages of her Bible to read a few words while she combed her hair, but finally gave it up she was so cold. She was sleepy, too, for she had lost much sleep of late, and it was hard to get up before it was fairly light and hurry around in the cold. Life looked very hard and dreary to her. She thought of aunt Hannah getting breakfast for Nettie's family, and buttoning the children's clothes between times. Somehow the thought of aunt Hannah weighed heavily upon her this morning. She could not get away from it. It brought a sob in her throat and a pain at her heart. Why did they have to separate? It was cruel that life was so. The tears came to her eyes. She jerked a snarl out and broke two teeth of her comb at the same time. This did not serve to help her temper. She did hate to use a comb with the teeth out and once out there was no putting them back. Neither could she afford a new comb for some time to come. She glanced at her plain little silver watch and saw it was later than she usually rose, and she hurried through her toilet as much as possible, and ran downstairs to the dining-room. The clerk stood at the dining-room door, an expression of belligerence on his face and his attitude one of displeasure. He filled up the door so completely that Celia was obliged to ask him to let her pass before he moved. She was indignant at him for this. She found herself likening him to one of the animals condemned in the Bible. It was unchristian of course, but Celia did not feel in a very sweet spirit this morning. She recalled what Mrs. Morris had said and wished he would leave the house. He looked like a man whom it was impossible to please anyway. But she found the cause of his displeasure was that there was no breakfast forthcoming as yet. Mr. Knowles came down, greeted her pleasantly, looked at the empty table, and the clock, filled his pocket with some crackers on a plate there, and remarked that he guessed he would skip, that it was as much as his place was worth if he did not get to the store on time, and he would have to run all the way to the car to make it now, it was so late. Celia felt indignant that this young man was obliged to go to a hard day's work unfed. But there was nothing to be done now, he must go. It was the hard fate of the wage-earner. He must be on time, if the house fell. She went to the kitchen door and peered in. Maggie was slamming about in a grand rage. The biscuits she was baking were not even beginning to brown yet, as Celia saw by a glimpse into the oven door when Maggie opened it and slammed it shut. There was some greasy-looking hash cooking slowly. It did not look as if it ever would be done at the present rate it was cooking. The stove looked sulky and the ashes were not yet taken up.

"Maggie," she said, "can I help you get something on the table? These people all have to go to work and so do I. If we can't eat in five minutes we'll have to go without."

"Well, then, go without!" said Maggie, rising in a towering passion. "I'm sure it won't hurt you fine folks once in a while. I never hired out to do everything and I ain't responsible. I'll get the breakfast as soon as

I can and not a bit sooner, and you can get out of my kitchen. I don't want you bothering 'round. I get all flustered with so many folks coming after me. Go on out now, and wait till yer breakfast's ready. And tell the rest I won't cook any dinner fer 'em, if a soul comes in this kitchen again."

Celia retreated, indignant and outraged. To be spoken to in such a manner when she was but offering help was an insult. It was a peculiarity of hers that when she felt angry the tears would come to her eyes. They came now. It was exasperating. She went quickly to the window to hide them, and looked out in the dim little brick alley that ran between the houses and watched the rain drop all over the bricks. There was a blank brick wall of the next house opposite her, and a little further toward the front she could see a window and some one standing at it. She turned quickly away again. There was no refuge there. Taking in at a glance the table with its unbrushed crumbs, and the dishes of uncooked hash and underdone biscuits that Maggie was just bringing in, she resolved to follow the example of Mr. Knowles and take some crackers. Then seizing her hat and coat from the hall rack where she had put them, on coming downstairs, she started for the store. It was a long, cold walk and she got very wet, but she did not feel justified in spending the five cents which would have carried her there. In her present mood she had no faith in uncle Abner's fortune. It would probably turn out to be some poor land somewhere which would never be worth a cent. That was the kind of inheritance which usually came to any one in their family, like the lot in a new town out west that was left to aunt Hannah by her eldest brother, where the city authorities compelled property holders to pave the streets and pay large taxes and where there were no purchasers. Such inheritances one was better off without. She felt very bitter in her heart. As she walked along in the rain, she remembered that she had forgotten to kneel by her bedside in prayer before she left her room that morning, it was so cold and late. She knew that must be the reason why she felt so cross and unreasonable, and she tried to pray as she walked along in the rain, but there were many things to distract her thoughts, and she had to watch carefully that she did not run into some one with her umbrella turned down in front of her to keep off the driving rain. She thought of aunt Hannah again, now probably washing the breakfast dishes, or doing some sewing or ironing, and she sighed and felt that earth was wet and cold and dreary. Half-way to the store, she encountered a little newsboy who followed by her side, and begged her to buy a paper. He looked hungry. His feet were out at the toes from his shoes, much too large. Celia had no money to buy a paper and she answered the boy in a decided negative that made him turn hopelessly away. It made her cross to see his need, when she had no power to help him. She realized how cross her voice had been and that vexed her. Then she blindly stepped into a mud puddle and splashed the water over the tops of her shoes. She shivered as she felt the dampness through the thin leather of her boot, and wondered what she would do when the inevitable sore throat, which always with her resulted from getting her feet wet, arrived. And so she hurried on, tugging after her the heavy cross which she had carefully made that morning for herself to carry, out of bits of her own and other people's troubles, and letting it spoil the sweet peace God had sent her, and soil the clean heart he had washed from sin for her. It was too bad. Her guardian angel pitied her that she could so soon forget her high resolves, and her heavenly Father.

Matters were no better when she reached the store. One of the girls who belonged at the ribbon counter with her was sick. Celia had to do her duty and the girl's also. This might not have been so bad if she had been left to herself, but the head of that department, a young woman with a sour expression and disappointed eyes, was also out of temper, and did her ordering in an exceedingly disagreeable manner. She found a great deal of fault and kept demanding of Celia more than she could well accomplish in a given time. Celia had hoped it would not be a busy day on account of the rain, but on the contrary every woman in town seemed to be in need of ribbon and to have hit upon that particular rainy morning in which to shop, thinking doubtless that the others would stay at home and leave the store to her. When the noon hour came Celia was cut down to half time on account of the rush, and obliged to take a few precious minutes of that in putting up some ribbons left carelessly on the counter by another saleswoman who had gone to her luncheon leaving them there. To the young girl new to her work, and fresh from a home where every *necessary* comfort at least had been hers, it was a long, hard day, and she looked forward with no hope of a let-up to the evening that was to follow. She grew crosser as the day began to wane, and she grew hungry, and then faint, and then lost both those feelings and settled down to a violent headache. It was then that a new cause for trouble loomed up before her imagination. What if she should get sick? Who would take care of her and how should she live? Aunt Hannah would have to come, and what an expense that would be!—No, aunt Hannah could not come. There was no money anywhere to pay her fare, or her board when she got there, and she was bound to stay with Nettie and Hiram as long as they were supporting her. She would have to get along without telling aunt Hannah. What would become of her? Oh, why of course, she would have to go to the hospital among strangers and be nursed, and perhaps die, and aunt Hannah never hear and then worry and worry and no one would tell her.

It was just in the midst of these thoughts that there came the clear voice of the floor walker:

"Miss Murray, will you step to the office a moment. There is a message there for you, a special delivery letter I believe."

With her heart throbbing violently at thought of the possibilities contained in a special delivery letter, she walked the length of the long store. Aunt Hannah must be sick and they had sent for her. Surely they would do that if aunt Hannah should be so ill she needed care, for Nettie would never care for her, she was no nurse and hated sick rooms. Besides, to be perfectly honest, Nettie would have enough to do in caring for her home and children. There was no hospital in the little town where Hiram lived, so he would, of course, rather pay her fare and keep her while she did the nursing than to hire some one to care for aunt Hannah. All this reasoning went clearly through her brain, as she walked swiftly in the direction of the office. It seemed as if the writing of her name on the receipt book was one of the longest actions she ever performed, and her hand trembled so when she retired to the little cloak room to read her letter that she could scarcely open the envelope, nor take in at first that the letter bore Rawley and Brown's printed heading. And then she read just a few lines from them asking her to call once more upon them and as soon as possible. She went back to her place among the ribbons feeling almost angry with Rawley and Brown that they had frightened her so, and yet relieved that there was nothing the matter with aunt Hannah.

It was nearly five o'clock, and the crowd of women who were doing rainy day shopping had gone home. The rain was pouring down harder than ever. The store was comparatively empty. Perhaps she might get away for a few moments now; she would ask. Permission was granted her, as she had had only half her noon hour, and she hurried up to the dark little office again.

She found that she was not too late, for Mr. Rawley had not yet gone home, though he had his overcoat on as if about to depart. It appeared that he wished to ask a few more questions to establish certain facts. Celia answered them as best she could, and then as he seemed to be through with her, she asked timidly:

"Would you be so kind as to tell me what this is all about, anyway? You said there was property. If it should turn out to be mine, what would it be? I suppose you do not mind giving me a general idea of that, do you?"

He looked at her almost kindly under his shaggy brows. "Why no, child!" he said. "That's perfectly proper, of course. Why, I haven't the exact figures in my head, but it's several thousands, well invested, and an old farm up in New York state that's well rented. There would be enough to give a pretty good income every year you know, and if you left the investments as they are, it would be a continuous one, for they are not likely to fail or fall through. Then, too, there is a considerable accumulation owing to the doubt about the heir. I hope you'll turn out to be that heir and I have no doubt you will. Good-afternoon." Celia tripped down the dark old staircase as if it were covered with the softest carpet ever made. Several thousands! What wealth! What luxury! She had wished for one single thousand, and her Father had sent her not one, but many. For she began to believe now that the money was hers. All the evidence seemed to point that way. The lawyer seemed to be convinced, and it needed only the coming of a few documents in possession of her uncle Joseph's old lawyer to corroborate what she had told him. She felt pretty sure that it was all true. And here she had been cross and growling all day, and worse than that, she had been carrying crosses not meant for her shoulders, and probably leaving undone the things God had laid out for her to do. What wickedness had been hers. Only last night she had knelt in earnest consecration, and now to-day she had fallen so low as almost to forget that she had a Father whose dear child she was, and who was caring for her. Could she not retrieve some of the lost day? She had but one hour left in the store. She would try what she could do. She smiled on the beggar child who stood looking wistfully in at the pretty things, in the store window as she passed in to her work. When she reached the ribbon counter again, she found the head of the department looking very tired, and complaining of a headache. There were other burdens besides her own she could bear. She might offer to do her work for her and let her rest, and she could bring her a glass of water. It was not her business to put up certain ribbons not in her own case, but she could do it for the other girl who was absent and save the head girl. As she made her fingers fly among the bright silks and satins, she wondered if there were more burdens for her to bear for others when she reached the boarding-house, and whether Mrs. Morris would be better to-night and able to sit up and direct things a little, and then there came to her mind the joyous thought that perhaps she was to have the means soon to make that house permanently better in some ways and help its inmates. How light her heart and her shoulders felt now that she had laid down that heavy self-imposed cross! It was wonderful! Oh, why could she not learn to trust her Master? The verse of a loved hymn came and hummed itself over in her mind.

> "Fearest sometimes that thy Father
>   Hath forgot?
> When the clouds around thee gather,
>   Doubt him not!
> Always hath the daylight broken—
> Always hath he comfort spoken—
>   Better hath he been for years,
>   Than thy fears."

Chapter 7

Miss Hannah Grant sat in her room under the eaves darning little Johnnie's stocking. Her hair was grey and rippled smoothly over her finely shaped head. Her sweet face wore a sad, far-away expression. It had grown habitual with her ever since she had come to live with her niece Nettie. Perhaps a close observer would see that the sadness was a shade deeper this afternoon. Her eyes were deep grey and seemed to go well with her hair. She gave one the impression of being able to see further with them than most people, and there was a luminousness about them that lit up her otherwise plain face, and made it truly beautiful. Her gown was plain and old and grey. She always wore grey dresses. They had been becoming long ago in the days when it mattered whether she wore becoming things, and now that she cared no more about the becomingness, she wore them for sweet association's sake, and for the sake of one long gone who used to admire them when she wore them. She did not seem to know that they still suited her better than any other color, or absence of color, could have done.

The hole was large and ill-shaped, for Johnnie was hard on his stockings, but she darned it patiently back and forth, and seemed to be thinking of something else. Once she laid it down and went to the closet for her little grey worsted shawl to throw around her shoulders, for the room was heated only by a drum from the stove downstairs and she felt chilly. She usually sat in the sitting-room in the afternoon to sew or mend, but there had been a reason for her coming up here to-day. She had settled herself as usual by the west window downstairs to get a good light on her work. She had a large peach basket full of stockings by her side, and her workbasket on the window. The baby, creeping about the floor, had upset the peach basket and scattered its contents around, and Nettie, coming down just then in a new red cashmere shirt waist she had finished the day before, had jerked him unceremoniously away from among the stockings and hastily bundled them all into the basket, shoving it behind aunt Hannah's chair and out of her reach. As she did so, she remarked in a disagreeable tone that she wished aunt Hannah wouldn't bring that old thing into the sitting-room. Couldn't she bring a pair of stockings at a time, and not litter up the whole room? She was expecting Mrs. Morgan and her sister in with their embroidery and crocheting, and she did like to have things look a little nice. Aunt Hannah had meekly disposed of the stocking basket behind her ample apron, and there had been silence in the room for a few minutes. Then young Mrs. Bartlett remarked:

"Aunt Hannah, I think you had better go and change your dress, if you are going to sit there. That old grey thing doesn't look very well. I wish to goodness you had a black silk, or something, like other folks. You always waste your money on grey things when you have to buy anything. It's a dreadfully gloomy color. It makes you look sallow, too, now you're getting older."

Nettie had gone out in the kitchen then for a minute and returned just as aunt Hannah was starting upstairs with the darning basket.

"Aunt Hannah!" she called, "take your shawl and bonnet up with you, won't you? I s'pose you'd just as soon keep them up there, wouldn't you? Hiram says he hates to see the hall rack cluttered up so."

Aunt Hannah put down the basket on the stairs, descended swiftly, gathered her shawl and bonnet and one or two other belongings of hers which were downstairs, in inconspicuous places, and carried them all upstairs. She was not in the habit of leaving her bonnet and shawl on the rack, and had only done so last night when she came in from prayer-meeting, because she had buckwheat cakes to set before going to bed, and when that was done and she started to take them away, Nettie had asked her to carry a lamp and two comfortables up for her, and in doing so the shawl and bonnet had escaped her notice. It was a little thing, and she realized that the hall rack looked better without her shawl and bonnet, but somehow it was one of the many things that gave her the feeling that she had no home. She had put them all meekly away and sat down in her little cold room near the drum to darn. She had done what she was asked to do with one exception. She did not change her dress and go down again. She saw that Nettie would like to have her out of the way for the afternoon, and she did not wish to remain where she was not wanted. She did not sigh as some women would have done. Instead, her eyes took on that far-away look. She was beginning to long so sorely for the open gates of her home above where she need never more feel that desolation of not belonging, and where she would meet loved ones, and above all her Father, face to face. Yet she knew her heavenly Father was with her, even in this home where she was treated as a burden, and she could be content to stay and do his bidding, only sometimes that great longing for the face to face view grew upon her till her heart ached with the desire to go.

In her bureau drawer, safe hid in tissue paper in a white box smelling of rose leaves there were some letters, and an old daguerreotype. The picture was in an old-fashioned leather frame that closed with a little brass hook, and was lined with stamped purple velvet. The face inside was of a young man with sweet, serious eyes, a grave, handsome face, smoothly shaven, heavy, dark hair tossed back from a high white forehead, and the dress of the olden time—a high rolling collar and stock. The letters were from this man to Hannah Grant, written when he was in the theological seminary, and they contained bright glad plans for their future, Hannah's and his. They might not have seemed bright to some women, for they were planning, as soon as he had finished his ministerial training, to go to the Foreign Mission field and work together for the Master they both loved better than anything else. And next to him they had loved each other. How bright her life had seemed to her then as she did her daily duties; sang about them; thought of the future and wrote her happy letters; and thanked the Lord daily that she was to be permitted to do his work in this honorable way. The time had gone by rapidly then, and the years of study had been completed. Hannah's wedding day was set, her simple lovely

wedding gown was finished, and it was grey. He loved grey. It had little touches of soft white about the throat and wrists, just enough to
bring out the coloring of Hannah's delicately cut face. And then,—
suddenly there happened one of those mysteries of the kingdom which
we shall understand by and by, and to which now we can only say "It
is the Lord, let him do what seemeth him best," and trust. The earnest
young missionary was taken up higher, there to receive his reward. His
bride, when she could rally from the shock of the sudden ending of her
life joy, bowed to the will of him to whose keeping she had long ago
given her will and her life, and was enabled to say with tears of triumph that like that man of God of old her beloved had "walked with
God and was not, for God took him."

She had thought even then to go alone, and take the message of
Jesus to those who knew him not, and bear her sorrow more easily by
thinking she could do some of the work which they would have done
together. But God opened another door for her and showed her plainly
that he had called her to a duty at home, and so she took her saddened
heart, her sweet face and her tender ways to her sister's motherless little children and had lived there ever since. Sometimes now, when she
thought how she was not wanted in his home, and yet could not go
anywhere else by force of circumstances, she would take out that pictured face and wonder if James could know how she was being treated
what he would think and feel about it, and think how he would guard
her from the world and shield her if he were only here. And then she
would be glad that he could not know, or that if he could, he was
where he knew it would not any of it be for long, and that she would
soon come home to be with Jesus and with him forevermore, and that
time to him was only a brief space. It was at such times that her eyes
would take on their far-away look.

So she sat and worked and thought that afternoon. In due course of
time the expected visitors arrived. The woman upstairs heard their
voices, and presently they drew nearer to the stove in the sitting-room.
Their talk could be quite distinctly heard now, but Hannah was absorbed in her own thoughts, and she paid no attention as they gossiped
on about this one and that, with "You don't say sos," and "Well, I al-

ways thought as muchs," and "Did-she-say thats," until she heard
Nettie say, "Yes, she will stay with us this winter anyway. No, it isn't
quite as pleasant as to be alone you know, but then what could we do?
She had no home to go to. My husband wanted my cousin to come,
too, though it was more than we really could afford to do to feed and
clothe two more, but she was very ungrateful, and wanted to have her
own way and see the world a little. I expect she'll come back humbly
enough when she's been away a couple of weeks longer, and if she
does I'm sure I don't know what in the world we shall do with her. Oh
yes, aunt Hannah helps me a little here and there, but you can't ask
much of people that are getting on in years. (Aunt Hannah was forty-
nine.) My father always kept her in luxury as she was my mother's
only sister. Yes, people do get spoiled sometimes that way. But, dear
me, all she can do wouldn't make up for the outgo. Yes, she was a sort
of acting housekeeper in our home after mother died, but you know no
one can ever take a mother's place. (Johnnie, shut that door and go
away and stop your coaxing, or I'll take you upstairs and give you a
good spanking. No, you *can't* go down by the pond to play to-day.)
No, I never had so much to do with her as the younger children. I was
the elder daughter, you know."

Aunt Hannah quickly and noiselessly moved away from her position by the drum to the other side of the room. And this from the little
girl she had so carefully mothered, and tended, and tried to train! And
had loved, too, for Hannah Grant loved all that God loved and placed
in her way. Ah, this was hard! And must she go on living here and
knowing that she was not wanted, that she was a burden, and that
lies—yes, actually lies, for there was no use trying to call them by a
softer name—were being told to the people in the village about her?
How could she? She could see just how it would go on from year to
year. Hiram would come in cross at night and either ignore her altogether, or else contradict every word she spoke, and find fault with
anything he knew she had done, in a surly, impersonal way, which he
knew and she knew he meant for her. The children would grow up to
disrespect her, as they were beginning to do already. And her dear
Celia! She was toiling bravely far away from her! There was no pros-

pect of anything better for years to come, perhaps never so long as she lived. She knelt down by her bed, and prayed for a long time. Then she arose quietly and went back to her window, a chastened look upon her face. This was not more than he had helped her to bear before. Indeed, it was not nearly so much. It was what Jesus had himself borne, being despised and rejected of men. She darned on till the room grew dark, and then she sat in the twilight and thought. She could not bring herself to go downstairs yet, not till she must to get supper. She thanked the Lord she had a room to herself where she might take refuge alone and think of him. It was seldom that aunt Hannah had had even this privilege in the daytime since she had come to live with Nettie, there was always so much to be done, and Nettie seemed to expect it to be done quickly.

The company below had departed, but Miss Grant took no heed. She sat and watched the grey sky grow into night. There was no sunset. It had been a grey day. There was not even a point of light to make the sky lovely. It sank into darkness quietly, soberly, unnoticed and unlovely. She thought it was like herself. But then there had been some reason why God had not made a bright sunset to-night, and there surely was some reason why he had wanted her life grey instead of rose-colored. She sighed just a little, and now that the darkness had stolen softly upon her, she let a tear have its way down her cheek.

Downstairs Nettie was growing restless. Hiram came in a little earlier than usual with a sour look and asked how long it would be before supper. Nettie said it would not be long, and wondered why aunt Hannah did not come downstairs. Hiram remarked that if the old woman was getting lazy and taking on fine-lady airs they had better give her a warning, for he couldn't support her for nothing. He threw a letter for her upon the table while Nettie was lighting the lamp. Nettie took it up, glanced at the writing, and then sent Johnnie up with it and told him to tell aunt Hannah his father had come and wanted his supper right away.

"It's from Celia again," she said, in a contemptuous tone. "She wastes more money on postage. I don't think it's right to do that in her position. If she has any extra money she better save it up and help with supporting aunt Hannah. A great fat letter, too. I don't see what she finds to write about. This is the third one this week. It's perfectly absurd!"

But aunt Hannah did not hear what they said, she was not sitting near the drum, and would not again, even if she was cold.

Johnny came down and reported that aunt Hannah had a light in her room and Nettie rattled the stove with all her might, and slammed the dishes around more than was necessary, but still aunt Hannah did not come, and finally Nettie began to get supper herself. She sent Johnnie up again pretty soon to tell aunt Hannah she wished she would come downstairs, that she needed her, and Johnnie came back and said aunt Hannah told him to tell mamma she would be down pretty soon, she could not come just now.

"Well, really!" said Hiram, looking up from his paper, "seems to me she is putting on airs at a great rate. If I were you, Nettie, I would just sit down and wait till she comes. I wouldn't get supper at all. If you haven't the grit to tell her to come down now when you send for her, I'll do it for you."

But Nettie rattled the stove and the dishes and managed to get supper ready pretty soon. She did not quite understand her aunt. This was a new development. Never in all the years she had known her and been cared for by her had aunt Hannah ever refused a request for help. It must be something serious. Was she sick? Nettie had some little heart left in her, and it irritated her to have her husband speak so of her relatives, so she bristled up at him, while she made the coffee.

"You'll not do any such thing, Hiram Bartlett. I guess she has a right to stay in her room once in a while. I'm sure I never knew her to do the like before in the whole of her life. If she was your aunt, you wouldn't speak of her in that way. I think you ought to be a little grateful for the way she took care of you last week when you were so sick, and me with the baby sick, too. If she hadn't been here I should have had my hands more than full. I don't know what I should have done. Johnnie, make that baby stop crying! Lillie, pick that doll up off the floor! I keep walking over something of yours all the time. I s'pose Celia's got into some trouble and aunt Hannah's worried about her. I expected as much. That girl hadn't experience enough of the world to go off to the city alone. Somebody ought to have taken her home to live. If one of the boys had been married she could have gone with them, but the boys are so selfish they never think of other people. If you had any sense of the fitness of things you'd have done it yourself."

They talked on in a wrangling way until supper was ready, but it was not until they had nearly finished the evening meal that the hall door opened and aunt Hannah walked in.

Chapter 8

Aunt Hannah had lighted her lamp a few minutes after the light of the day went out, to get a little comfort from her Bible before going downstairs to face her trials, for it must be confessed that aunt Hannah had not had a cross so heavy to bear in many a year, as it was for her to go downstairs that night and face Hiram and Nettie calmly after the words she had heard her niece speak. She had tried to think of all the comfort in the Bible as she sat in the twilight. She had a great store of the precious words to draw from, for her Bible had ever been her chief delight. She knew just where to turn in her memory for the right help and it came trooping forth.

"Fear thou not; for I am with thee: be not dismayed; for I am thy God: I will strengthen thee; yea, I will help thee; yea, I will uphold thee with the right hand of my righteousness.... When thou passest through the waters, I will be with thee; and through the rivers, they shall not overflow thee: when thou walkest through the fire, thou shalt not be burned.... God is faithful, who will not suffer you to be tempted above that ye are able; but will with the temptation also make a way to escape, that ye may be able to bear it.... Blessed is the man that endureth temptation: for when he is tried, he shall receive the crown of life, which the Lord hath promised to them that love him.... For I reckon that the sufferings of this present time are not worthy to be compared with the glory which shall be revealed in us.... All things work together for good to them that love God.... To be conformed to the image of his Son.... If God be for us, who can be against us? ... Nay in all these things we are more than conquerors through him that loved us."

Then she lighted the lamp to search out another promise, for it seemed to her as if just to look upon the words would somehow help her. It was at that moment Johnnie brought up Celia's letter. She opened it quickly, the anticipation of another trouble arising in her mind, for what might not have happened to Celia so far away in that great city alone, since the last letter she wrote?

It was a thick letter and she read it slowly through, taking no thought of time because the matter it contained absorbed her mind completely, and when Johnnie came up the second time, she had something new to think about which demanded immediate attention and had claims prior to any downstairs. The letter read thus:

"DEAR AUNT HANNAH:

"Do you remember the words on the little bookmark you sent me for my birthday? I know you do, for you have a way of hiding all such words away in that wonderful memory of yours. You know the heading was about an allowance, from the king, a continual allowance. When I read it I knew just what you meant by sending it to me. You wanted to remind me that my King had plenty of extra strength to give me, and that he had promised to furnish me with enough for every day of my life to bear that day's trials. It did help me, for I knew I was trying to bear some of them all by myself, and that I often and often forget that I do not have to take up next year's crosses and worry about them. But I remember, when I first read the words, I couldn't help longing deep down in my heart, that I could have a real earthly allowance of money, just solid hard dirty money, coming in every week, and every month, and every year, and enough to supply all the actual needs so that I might live with you and work for you and have you all to myself. Then I felt indeed that my head would be lifted up out of prison forever—for I read the chapter about Jehoiachin as you meant I should, you dear good auntie—and it helped me too. You see I had been taking up a big heavy cross for the year to come for you. I didn't feel happy about you there at Hiram's, for in spite of me I cannot like Hiram's ways and I don't believe you do. I know for one thing, and a very small thing, that you hate tobacco smoke and have never been used to it, and yet Hiram smokes all over the house whenever he pleases, without even so much as caring whether it is repulsive to you or not. In fact, I am wicked enough to suspect that he might do it the more, just because you don't like it, to show you he is master of his own house. I am so sorry I have to feel that way about my cousin-in-law, but I can't help it. There is this comfort about it, I don't believe Nettie minds, and as she is the one that has to be his wife and go through life with him, it is a relief to think she doesn't. But there! That is all out of the way, and unchristian, and I have been too much blessed to allow myself to say anything unchristian about any one. Only I did want you to understand that I appreciated how hard it was for you to cheerfully accept Nettie's proposal and go to live with her for a few years. I did not say so then because I thought any words would only make it harder to bear, and I know my own dear auntie's old way of always finding a thing easier to bear if she succeeds in making other people think she is perfectly happy. That is just one way, and the only way in which you ever are the least little bit dishonest.

"But I must hurry on with my main theme which has not even been hinted at yet. And I have a great deal to write, and must get it in to-night, for I cannot bear to have you wait a minute longer than is necessary to hear the good news.

"In the first place, you are not to stay at Nettie's another day—that is not unless you prefer to, of course—but you are to pack up every scrap that belongs to you and take the first train to Philadelphia, sending me a telegram (at my expense) to say what train you start on. You must come to the Broad Street station—have your trunks checked there too, and don't leave any of your things behind, for there is plenty of room to put all your things here, and you are not to go back to Nettie's unless you go on a visit of pleasure."

Aunt Hannah glanced up to see if the little room with its old ingrain carpet and cheap furniture was still about her. She was almost breathless with the proposal of the letter. Things seemed to whirl around her. She wanted to get something to steady her before she read on. She saw the black side of the sheet-iron drum and remembered the afternoon, and a glance toward her open Bible showed her the lines "God is faithful . . . will with the temptation also make a way to escape, that ye may be able to bear it." She drew a long breath and closed her eyes for a minute's lifting of her heart to God. He was going to make the way to escape. She did not yet understand how it was to be done, but her faith caught at the fact that it was to be done. Then she went back to the letter.

"You are to give your checks to the porter on the car—and you are to take a sleeper if you come at night, or a parlor car if you choose to come in the daytime. I enclose your ticket."

Aunt Hannah noticed then that a small pink and white paper had fallen from the letter when she opened it, and slipped to the floor. She stooped and picked it up in a dazed way. Good for one trip to Philadelphia it certainly was. This was something tangible and brought her back to everyday life. She really was to go, for here was the ticket. She went on with the letter eagerly now.

"You are to have the porter carry your satchel into the station for you, and I will meet you at the gate and take you home. Yes, HOME, aunt Hannah, yours and mine, do you hear that? It isn't very pretty, nor inviting yet, but it is ours for a while, for as long as we want it, and we shall fix it into a charming home. And now you want to know how it all happened and what it means.

"Well, this morning I was sent for again to come to Rawley and Brown's office on very important business, and as they told me it might keep me some time I asked for the day off at the store. I couldn't have had that, if I had not done double duty for the last week in place of a girl who was sick. Mr. Dobson was very nice and said certainly in such a case he would give me permission. Of course, I suppose I'll lose my pay for that day, but it had to be done, and it doesn't matter now anyway. Well, Mr. Rawley hemmed and hawed a good deal, and finally told me that everything was satisfactorily settled at last and that I had been duly declared by the court to be uncle Abner's heir, without any

question or doubt anywhere, and that he wished to go over the papers
with me and place the property in my hands. There was some red tape
to be gone through with which I needn't stop now to tell you about. It
was all very interesting to me, the number of times I had to sign my
name, and all the witnesses, and I felt just like a girl in a book, but I
haven't time for that. There is better to come. It seems uncle Abner
had a farm where he lived after he got old, and his wife died and his
son went to India, and there was a young farmer and his family who
lived there and took care of him, and they have rented the house ever
since. They still live there. The farm is pretty good, way up in New
York somewhere I think, I didn't pay much attention to it. Then he
owned an interest in a coal mine near Scranton and a few government
bonds, not many of those, but the whole is well invested and brings in
a nice little income every year, sure, and I couldn't help thinking of
Jehoiachin when Mr. Rawley was telling me about it. He said it was so
well invested that it was, as near as anything earthly could be, sure, a
continual 'income as long as I lived' if I kept things in their present
shape, for uncle Abner had been a very careful man and always invested in pretty safe things with what little he had. I didn't tell him I
considered it much instead of little, though. It seems a fortune to me. I
suppose I shall learn better hereafter, but I am going to try to be very
wise with it anyway, with God's help.

"Now you want to know how much it is, I know. Well, it amounts
to about nine hundred dollars a year at the lowest calculation, besides
several years of accumulated interest not invested yet. Isn't that riches?
Why, you've often told me that not many ministers and few missionaries get more than that. Now then, why shouldn't you and I be missionaries? I know it has been your dear desire all your life, and I don't
know of anything that would be grander work. And as we can't go as
foreign missionaries just now, what if we should be home missionaries? Of course, two lone women couldn't take mortar and bricks and
build a church and preach, at least I shouldn't like to try it, though I'm
not at all sure but I could do it. You know we always thought, if we
had the time and the material and the pattern, you and I could do almost anything anybody else could if we tried. Well, I began to think

about a mission for us, and before I had gotten half-way home to write to you it came to me just what I would like to do. Why shouldn't you and I make a real home mission for ourselves right here in the city of Philadelphia, by making a good home for a few people who have none of their own? It seems to me there is as much gospel sometimes in a good sweet loaf of bread such as you can make, as there is in—well— *some* sermons. Don't you think so? Then we could get a hold on the people who ate it, and get them to go to the churches, and try to help them in their everyday lives. Why, some of the young men here would stay at home evenings occasionally, perhaps regularly, if they had a pleasant, warm, light place to stay in. Instead of that they go out to the saloons, perhaps. Anyway, auntie dear, they don't look rested in the morning when they come down to breakfast. And oh, what a breakfast we did have this morning! It seems as though I never can like hash again, though I always used to enjoy ours so much at home when you made it. But hash in Mrs. Morris' boarding-house is a very different dish indeed. When I got home I went straight up to Mrs. Morris's room. She has not gotten entirely well from her severe sickness of a few weeks ago yet, though she goes around and directs things, but she seems to be so worried all the time. You know I told you how many bills she has unpaid and how hard times have been for her. You wouldn't wonder a bit if you could be here and watch the way things go a little while. She was lying on her bed when I went in and looking as if she would like to cry, if she only were young enough and had the energy. She told me right away that she was in trouble again. She was a month behind in her rent, and the agent had been around and said it must be paid in advance after this and he couldn't wait longer than till five o'clock. She only pays twenty-five dollars a month, and with all her boarders you might think she could pay it, but she doesn't, that's all. While she was talking I began to revolve my plans very rapidly. I didn't want to act too rashly, for you know you always tell me that is one of my great faults, but I knew if I did anything it ought to be done very soon. Probably it would have been wiser to have asked Mr. Rawley's advice, and perhaps some of my relatives, but I had an innate suspicion that I would not be allowed to do it at all, if I asked. And why shouldn't I? The money is mine, and I am of age if I am not very experienced. I knew you would like it, at least I felt very sure you would, and if you and God like a thing I don't care what all the rest of the world think. So I asked Mrs. Morris a lot of questions, some I had not asked her before. You see I had a whole two hundred dollars in my pocketbook, Mr. Rawley had given me. He said it was mine, and I might as well take it to begin on. So I took it. I knew I would want to do a lot of things right away, and that the first one would be to get you here at once, and to buy your ticket. I was just aching to spend some money, for it was the first time in my life I ever had much to spend. I asked Mrs. Morris about her butcher's bill, and her grocery bill, and things and I found they were not so very big as she had made me think at first. Then I asked her point blank how she would like to let a woman come in here in her place for three months or so, and take the boarding-house off her hands, paying the bills for the present, and letting her pay them by and by, if she chose, or if not, holding the furniture as collateral. She didn't know what I meant by collateral, but she soon understood, and said she would be only too glad, only she never could find any woman who would be so foolish. She said, too, that she was afraid if she once got away she would never be willing to come back, but just stay and leave the old furniture to make it right with her debts, and she sighed and returned to her trouble and began to cry. Then I couldn't stand it any longer. I told her I thought I knew the right one for her, and I would write to her at once and attend to it all if she was sure she agreed to it. It did not take her long to decide what she would do after she was fully convinced that I meant what I said. She began to pack up her clothes right away and to talk about what she would take with her. She hasn't much worth while, I guess. She will want those horrid crayon portraits of her family and herself, I hope, and a few other ornaments. But when we had gotten to this point, we found it was five o'clock, and the door bell made Mrs. Morris remember the rent agent. Sure enough, he had come, and Maggie came up to call Mrs. Morris. She looked at me blankly as much as to say: 'What shall I do?' She had forgotten all about him. I thought just a minute and then I told her I had some money, enough I thought to pay the agent and satisfy him, and I would go down and see if I could make him behave till we got things settled. Then I went downstairs and put on my most dignified air. He bristled at me and demanded Mrs. Morris.

" 'Mrs. Morris is not well and is lying down,' said I, 'and I have come down in her place. Is there anything I can do for you?'

" 'Well, I've got to see her if she *is* lying down," he said in a loud voice, and he took a couple of steps toward the stairs as if he would go up to her at once. 'She's got to pay her rent. She'll be put out if she don't do it at once. This thing has gone——'

" 'Oh,' I said, 'it isn't in the least necessary for you to get excited, if that is all. I can attend to the rent as well as anything else. Are you the agent?'

" 'Yes, I *am*,' he said, 'and I won't have any more talk either. I want my money.'

"I had my pocketbook in my hand, and I tried to freeze him with a look as I opened it. When he saw me bring out a big roll of bills he almost looked faint, he was so astonished.

" 'How much is it that is back?' I asked.

" 'Two months and a half,' he snarled.

"I began to count out the money, and then I remembered my own experience with Rawley and Brown and thought I would give him a little taste of it. I drew back and said, 'You are sure you are the agent and fully entitled to receive this money? Can you give me any credentials?'

"He was very much taken aback, and got red and embarrassed and at last remembered that Mrs. Morris knew him. Then he grew angry again and demanded to see her. I sent a message up to Mrs. Morris that if she was able we would like to have her come down, and she came. When it was finally all settled and the receipt signed, I told the young man that he might tell the owner that the rent hereafter would be paid in advance and on time, and that there were a few repairs which needed immediate attention and we would like to have him call at his earliest convenience. He went away quite crestfallen, and I began to feel quite like a householder. The only thing that troubles me is Mrs. Morris' extreme gratitude, because, dear auntie, I'm afraid I haven't loved her as much as I ought to for Christ's sake, and I therefore can't take to myself the credit she would give me. It is all very selfish in me.

"Now the matter stands this way. If you possibly can come this week, do so. Mrs. Morris will be ready to leave on your arrival. She will go to her sister out West, and I doubt if she ever returns. I have given her some money to go with. It isn't always you can buy a full fledged boarding-house, boarders and all so cheap. I suppose some one would call it dear, but I am very happy in my purchase. I shall keep my place in the store till you come anyway, for I don't care to have the boarders find out my connection with the business, till they see some of the changes I want to have made for the better. The only servant here is worse than none. She is so dirty and saucy you never could stand her. If you possibly can induce Molly to come with you, bring her. I enclose a New York draft which I think will be all the money you will want to bring here, and pay any little bills till you get here. And now, dear auntie, I do hope and pray you will say yes, and come at once, and not find any 'oughts and ought nots' in the way, as you sometimes do. You see I have gone ahead and burned my bridges behind me, because I felt that you 'ought' whether you think so or not, for I mean to take care of you now myself and you are working too hard there. Here we will keep you in pink cotton and only let you direct. I shall keep good servants, and if I don't always make the two ends meet why I shall have 'a continual allowance' given me of my King to draw upon.

"Your loving, eager
"CELIA."

Chapter 9

There was a calmness and "upliftedness" about Miss Grant's face as she entered the dining-room that the people about that table did not understand, and it rather angered them than otherwise. She walked quietly to her accustomed chair and sat down. Nobody spoke, but she had so far forgotten her afternoon's troubles as to be oblivious of this. Hiram was trying to think of the most sarcastic thing he could say, and so failed to say anything, while Nettie in her various revulsions of feeling did not know how to begin. Aunt Hannah herself opened the conversation in the calmest, most self-contained tone possible, as if the question she asked was one she often asked of her nephew.

"Hiram, can you tell me what time the through Philadelphia trains go?"

Hiram raised his cold, black eyes to her face in astonishment, a moment, and stared at her as much as to say, "What possible concern of yours is that?" and then dropped them to his plate again and went on eating. After a suitable pause he said freezingly, "No." Aunt Hannah tried again.

"Isn't there a time-table in the paper? Could you find out for me?"

"I don't know," said Hiram, this time without looking up. "I suppose if it's there you can find it as well as I can."

"What in the world do you want with the time-table, aunt Hannah?" asked Nettie, peevishly, with an undertone of anxiety in her voice. "There isn't anything the matter with Celia, is there? I presume she has lost her place and is coming back on us. I always supposed that was the way her venture would turn out. She ought to have tried to get a place in the country for housework. It was all she was ever trained to do.

Anybody might know she couldn't get on in the city."

"Nothing is the matter with Celia, Nettie," answered her aunt, "except that she has written me to come to Philadelphia. She has found something there for me to do, and I have decided that it will be best for me to go at once. I shall have to start to-morrow, if possible, because I am being waited for."

"You go to Philadelphia!" exclaimed Nettie dropping her fork. "The perfect idea! Has Celia gone crazy? Why aunt Hannah you couldn't get along in the city. Why, you—you—wouldn't know how to get anywhere. You don't understand. Philadelphia is a large city and you couldn't get across the street alone. And what could you do? You are not going to start in as a clerk in a store at your time of life, I hope. You would break down at once, and then we should have you both to care for, for I fully expect to have something happen to Celia soon, and then we should have you both to care for, and you know aunt Hannah, willing as we are, we are not able to do that." Nettie paused for breath.

Then Hiram turned his little black eyes on her and asked contemptuously, "And who is going to pay your fare on this pleasure excursion you are going to take? You certainly can't expect me to do it. I think I've done all I'm called upon to do. I understood the bargain was that you were to work for your board here."

Hiram had never been so openly insolent before. If he had, Miss Grant would have left long ago, even though she had been obliged to walk the streets in search of work for her living. She turned her clear eyes upon him full, and said quietly with the strength of the grace the Father gave her from her communings with him:

"Yes, Hiram, that was the bargain, and I certainly have worked. I consider that I have fully earned all that I have eaten, and the amount of shelter that has been given me. As for any further assistance, I think I have never yet asked it, and I hope I may never be obliged to do so. Celia has sent me money and a ticket,—and I shall not be obliged to ask any favors of any one."

"Celia sent you money!" Nettie fairly screamed it. "Where in the world did she get money?"

"Yes, where did Celia get money?" asked Hiram, sharply. "It seems to me there's something pretty shady about this business. Miss Celia 'll get into serious trouble which will bring no credit to her family, if she keeps on."

Aunt Hannah rose from her untasted supper, drew herself up to her full height and looked down upon Hiram Bartlett till he seemed to shrink beneath her glance. There comes a time when a strong sweet nature like Hannah Grant's can be roused to such a pitch of righteous indignation that it will tower above other smaller natures and make them cower and cringe in their smallness and meanness. She had reached one of those places in her life. Nettie, as she watched her, thought to herself that aunt Hannah must have been almost handsome once when she was young.

"Hiram," said aunt Hannah, and her voice was quite controlled and steady, "don't you ever dare to breathe such a thought as that again about that pure-souled girl. You know in your inmost soul that what you have said would be impossible. Some time, when you stand before God, you will be ashamed of those words, as you will be ashamed of a good many of your other words and actions." That was all she said to him. She did not lose her temper, nor say anything which she did not feel she ought to say, or which she would have taken back afterward. Then she turned to Nettie and quietly said:

"Celia has had a little estate left her from her father's great uncle Abner. She is now quite independent as regards money, and she wishes to have me with her as soon as possible, and I intend to go to-morrow evening, if I can get ready."

She turned from the room then and went upstairs, but when she got there, instead of going to work at packing, she turned the key in the lock and knelt down by her bed, to pray first for Hiram, and second that God might overrule anything that she had said amiss.

Meantime below stairs there was astonishment and confusion. Celia as a poor shop girl, and Celia with money were two very different people. Even Hiram felt that. He retired behind his paper till a suitable time had elapsed for his wife to talk out her anger, astonishment, and humiliation, and then he began to reflect that it would be a very convenient thing to have the management of Celia's money, even though it was not much, for he was just beginning business for himself and every little helped in the matter of capital.

"It would just serve you right, Hiram Bartlett, if Celia should turn out to be rich," said his wife, angrily. "The way you have treated her and aunt Hannah ought to make you ashamed, but I don't suppose it will. Now what am I to do I should like to know? Three children, and one a fretful baby, and all my housework to do all alone. If you had treated aunt Hannah nicely, she would have stayed anyway. Maybe Celia would have come here to live and taught the children. She is real good at teaching little children anything. I remember she used to be so patient with the boys at home. It would be awfully convenient to have somebody around with money."

In the course of the evening, while aunt Hannah swiftly gathered her possessions in array preparatory to packing, Nettie knocked at her door. She wanted to ask a great many questions, and she wanted to argue with aunt Hannah and show her the inadvisability and impossibility of her thinking of such a thing as going to Philadelphia to live with Celia, when her plain duty was here with Nettie and her family. When she saw she was making no headway, she tried to work on her aunt's strong sense of duty, and finally cried, and told her she never thought she would be left by aunt Hannah in that way, with all those children and no help, that she always knew aunt Hannah cared more for Celia than for any of them, and that it was not fair when they had offered her a home and done everything for her, and she had come there with the understanding that she would stay several years anyway. It wasn't fair to Hiram.

When she had talked this way for some time, her aunt turned to her almost desperately. She did not want to say anything rash. But Nettie must be shown how inconsistent she was.

"Nettie," said she, just as calmly as she had talked to Hiram, "you know that you and Hiram never wanted either me or Celia with you. You know that you consider me in the way, and that I am only good to work. I don't say anything against that, for that may be true, but you know that you grudge me my home here, and that you are giving out to your friends that you are doing a great deal to care for me in my helpless old age, and that I am a burden. You know yourself whether that is quite fair, and whether I have not worked as hard as any woman could for my board and lodging. But that is not to the point. You have a perfect right to think so about me. It may be all true, and I cannot stop you in saying such things to outsiders, but I have a right to say whether I will be taken and disposed of as if I was a piece of goods, and cared for as if I was a baby. I am not quite so infirm yet but that I can earn my living where I shall be more welcome. I thank the Lord that a way has been opened for me to go where I am wanted, but I must honestly tell you, Nettie, that I should have gone just the same if I had not known that you felt so, for I feel that my place is with Celia, if I can be with her. She is alone in the world. You have your husband and your children. She has nobody but me. I bear you no grudge, Nettie, and I think you will be happier with me away." Then she went on packing and Nettie retreated to talk with her husband.

The result was a proposition that they should coax Celia to come home and live with them, and Nettie said a few nice things which she hoped would patch up aunt Hannah's feelings, but aunt Hannah was firm, and would not even delay to write to Celia. She went diligently on with her preparations.

Gradually they settled down to the inevitable, and by the next noon had so far calmed down as to be able to ask some questions about the more definite details. Aunt Hannah had started out on an expedition very early in the morning without telling them where she was going, or without seeming to remember that there was breakfast to be gotten and cleared away. She seemed to be living by faith. She certainly ate nothing that morning. She visited a certain little house in a by-street where lived an old servant, Molly by name, who had declined the most earnest solicitations of Nettie to live with her at exceedingly small pay, and preferred to earn her living by doing fine ironing. She also visited the station, the telegraph office, the bank, and the expressman's office, and then went back to her packing again. Later in the afternoon, she went out again and made a few calls, on the minister's wife and the doctor's wife and a few very dear friends, bidding them a quiet good-bye, for she wished to slip away without making any more talk than was necessary. But it was at the dinner-table that Celia's whole plan was ferreted out by Nettie.

"Celia has bought a boarding-house!" exclaimed Nettie. "What an absurd idea! What does she or you either know about keeping boarders? You'll both let them run right over you. You'll get in debt the very first week. Why, aunt Hannah, you have no right to encourage Celia in such a scheme. She's too young, anyway, to be away off there in a city without a guardian. She ought to be here. Hiram could manage her money and make it double itself in time, and if she really has as much as you say, she has plenty to live quite comfortably without doing anything. You ought to tell her so."

But aunt Hannah did not seem to be intimidated by this. Nettie tried again.

"And then think how plebeian it will be! It was bad enough to work in a store, but a boarding-house keeper, and for one who has money of her own. It is simply unheard-of. I shall be ashamed to death to have Mrs. Morgan know about it. I think I have had trouble enough without having to be ashamed of my family. Celia always did do queer things, anyway. Don't you think it is very impractical, Hiram?"

Nettie asked his opinion as if that would settle the matter for everybody concerned, and he answered in the same manner.

"I certainly do think it is the most wild and impossible scheme I ever heard of, and one which ought not to be permitted. It will be the ruin of Celia's property, and when that is all gone, and you and Celia are in trouble, I suppose I shall be called upon to help you out. Of course I shall do the best I can, but you must remember that I have not very much money to throw away on wild childish schemes." He spoke with the air of a martyr, and aunt Hannah answered him cheerily. She had recovered her spirits since she had sent her telegram.

"You needn't worry, Hiram. I don't believe either Celia or I will ever be in need of your help. But if we are, I don't think we shall trouble you. You know they have a good many charitable institutions in the City of Brotherly Love, and we shall surely be well cared for if the improbable happens." Then aunt Hannah placed her nicely prepared little coals of fire in the hands of her two grand nephews and her grand niece, and went smiling upstairs. The coals were tiny paper parcels each containing a bright five dollar gold piece. She had lain awake last night, worried about the sharp words she had felt obliged to speak, and the sentence Nettie had flung out about her leaving her without help, and she wanted to show that she bore no grudge for what they had said. Celia had sent her the money to spend as she thought best, and aunt Hannah knew her girl well enough to feel she would say this was a good way to spend it. Besides, she felt sure she could run a boarding-house successfully in a financial way, as well as some others, if she had the chance, so she might by and by have more five dollar gold pieces to do with as she chose. She was beginning to be very happy, as she packed and strapped the last trunk, and smoothed her hair and tied on her grey bonnet and grey veil. At the last Hiram and Nettie behaved quite well. Those five dollar gold pieces had gone a long way toward making the bereavement of aunt Hannah's departure felt. Hiram took her satchel down, and Nettie walked beside her carrying her umbrella and wheeling the baby, while Johnnie and Lily trotted on ahead. There was an éclat and importance attached to a sudden and first-class departure such as aunt Hannah's was turning out to be, which could not well be carelessly neglected. They made an interesting procession down the street. More than one neighbor looked out of her window, and a few knew that Miss Hannah was going away. But they had said good-bye, and only turned their heads the other way to wipe away a tear of regret, or sigh perhaps that their good friend was not to be near any more with her cheery face and her words of comfort. When it was observed by one or two that Molly Poppleton had also passed down the street accompanied by an old man wheeling her ancient trunk on a wheelbarrow, and carrying a good-sized bundle, several of the good women came to their gates to look down the street, and wait till Nettie returned to ask what it all meant. And Nettie enjoyed a triumphal march back to her home. "Yes, she's gone, we shall miss her very much." Her nose was red with being rubbed and her eyes had a suspicious redness about them. "No, Celia isn't ill, but she couldn't stand it any longer without aunt Hannah. You know Celia has had a fortune left her? Oh yes, she'll have plenty now. Yes, aunt Hannah has to go and be her chaperon. I suppose she'll quite come out in society now she has money enough to do about as she pleases. Oh yes, she's very generous, she always was. She sent the children each handsome presents in gold. Yes, aunt Hannah has taken old Molly for a maid. She'll be obliged to have a maid there, you know. Funny, isn't it, that a woman who knows how to work should need a maid? I shouldn't like it myself, but then one has to do as other people do."

Then Nettie went home and got supper and washed up her dishes and put her three babies to bed, and sat down wearily and wished for aunt Hannah.

But aunt Hannah sat serenely in the sleeper, waiting for her berth to be made up, and thinking to herself that she also, like Jehoiachin, had had her head lifted up out of prison.

Chapter 10

It was perhaps one of the happiest nights that aunt Hannah ever spent. She lay down in her bed in the sleeper and slept like a little child for a time, for she was as tired as a baby after her day and night of excitement, but in the early dawn she awoke and lay there listening to the regular cadence of the moving train. It was music to her. Her life had for years been a monotonous one, and every detail of the journey was a delight to her. The turning wheels seemed to sing a tune to her, "Now hath mine head been lifted up above mine enemies round about me." She tried to turn that thought out of her mind as soon as she discovered its significance, for she did not like to think that even in her heart had hid a feeling that Hiram and Nettie were her enemies, but somehow the rejoicing stayed anyway.

She began to look forward to the morning and the day that was to follow, the opening of her new life. What would it hold of good or of ill for her? Would there be trials? Yes, but there had been trials before. She would have "his strength to bear them, with his might her feet could be shod. She could find her resting-places in the promises of her God," as she had done before. And it was such delightful work before her, a prospect of making over a home and making it pleasant. Aunt Hannah took rest, too, in the thought of experienced Molly Poppleton now reposing in the berth above her. She was going on a mission at last. How good God had been to her! He had tried her for a little while, but he was bringing her out into a large place. She could see that, even though she could not know the trials that were before her. Of course there were trials, she expected that, earth was full of them; but she did not need to carry them; Christ had borne them all for her long ago. She

75

would trust and he would bring her safely through as he had done before and was doing now. Then her thoughts dwelt in sweet reflection upon her Saviour whom she loved so much, and she communed with him and promised to try to help every person who came within that house that she was to make pleasant for him and his children, and to try to live for him before them every day. And that crowded, rushing car became a holy place, because God met her there and blessed her.

The train reached the Broad Street station at a very early hour. Celia was glad of that, for it gave her plenty of time to meet her aunt and go with her back to the house, without being late at the store. She had not had time to reflect yet as to whether she would give up her position. She was hardly ready to do so. It seemed to her that perhaps she might do more good if she retained it for the present, at least until she found some one else who needed it, and to whom she could give it with profit, both to that person and to her employers who had been very kind to her. Besides, she wished not to appear before the boarders yet as an active agent in the reforms of the house.

At exactly half past five she arrived at the Broad Street station. It was an early hour for her to be out alone, and it was still dark save for the electric lights which glared everywhere as if trying to keep off the day. But the train would come in at five minutes to six, and Celia had been too eager and too happy to sleep longer, so she paced up and down in the ladies' room until the train was almost due, watching the people come and go and wondering about them all as she was wont to do. As the time drew near for the train she went out and stood behind the gates watching the trains moving back and forth. She began to say to herself, "Oh, what if she should not come? What if something has happened to the train? Or what if Nettie and Hiram have persuaded her at the last minute not to come? Or what if she missed the train? But no, she would have telegraphed. 'Charge not thyself,'—dear me! How much I do that. I must stop worrying ahead about everything. Aunt Hannah must have seen that fault in me very glaringly. I never realized how much I do it." And then the train whistled and rolled into the station, and the passengers began to alight, and stream into the gates, looking sleepy and cold. Celia stood there in the dim greyness of the cold, foggy morning and began to tremble with the excitement and joy of watching for aunt Hannah. Suddenly she saw the ample form of Molly Poppleton loom up behind the gilt-buttoned porter and she caught a glimpse of a little grey bonnet just behind and knew that aunt Hannah was come.

She took them home in the street-car, and then escorted them up to her little third story back room. She had risen early and put it in order. Molly looked around in disdain.

"Well, Miss Celia, you don't have things as fine in the city as I expected," she said. "The idea of their putting you up in such a room as this! Why, Miss Celia, it ain't as good as the kitchen chamber at Cloverdale. I always heard a city was a dreadful place to live, but I never thought it was this bad. The wonder to me is anybody that don't have to, stays in 'em. But we'll have it *clean* pretty soon anyway, don't you worry." And she stalked to the window and surveyed the narrow court below, where she surmised she would be obliged to dry her clothes. She sniffed to herself, but Celia could see her practical eye already planning how she would change the position of the ash bucket and the garbage pail. She gave a sigh of relief at the thought of Molly Poppleton's ability, and turned to aunt Hannah, fairly smothering her in kisses. Then she put a hand on each soft, loved cheek, held her off at arm's length and looked into her face.

"Now, you dear, good auntie, tell me just what you think of me? Am I a wild, impractical girl, full of crazy schemes? Tell me right away."

"Well," said aunt Hannah, a queer little twinkle in her eyes, "that's what Hiram thinks."

"Oh, he does, does he? Well, I don't really suppose it will matter much, do you? But I mustn't stop now to talk. I have to be at that store in an hour, and it takes half of that to get there. We must talk business. Do you think you can get along to-day by yourself, with Molly? That is, I mean without my worthy advice and assistance? Of course I'll be home at half-past six, and I'll give in my resignation there if you think best, but I hardly like to do it quite so soon after Mrs. Green was so kind about getting it for me. It doesn't seem quite fair to the firm either to stop now, after they have had all the trouble of teaching me. Mrs.

Morris is to leave on the noon train. She is ready, except that her faith hasn't been quite equal to believing that you were really coming to take her place. She told the boarders this morning that she was going away for her health, and that she had secured a woman to take her place for a while. She guessed they would like it just as well. She wasn't sure when she should return. The clerk promptly gave notice that he should leave, and I am glad of it. Some of the others said that if things didn't go better than they had been doing for a week they would have to follow his example, but I think they will change their minds when they see the difference. I amused myself going to market last evening. I bought a great big roast, one of the finest cuts, and some fine potatoes and apples and yeast and flour. I know Mrs. Morris' flour isn't good, for she can't make anything out of it fit to eat. I also got some spinach and celery and sweet potatoes, canned tomatoes and a few other things. I want to have a regular treat the first night regardless of the cost. You can figure things down afterward, but I thought we'd have enough for once to make up for the days of starvation. That Maggie, down in the kitchen, is a slouch and a bear. She gets in a towering rage whenever you go near her. I have not said anything about her, except to ask what contract Mrs. Morris had with her. I find it is on a day to day basis, so you can do as you please. If you and Molly want her, and can get the right kind of help out of her, keep her. If not, get rid of her and we'll find a second girl who knows how to do things right. Now, shall we go down and see Mrs. Morris? And are you sure you are equal to all this, and not too tired to begin to-day? I suppose Mrs. Morris would wait till you are rested, if you want her to."

But aunt Hannah smiled and said no, she was eager to begin. Then she took off her bonnet and smoothed her grey hair and went down.

Mrs. Morris had on the inevitable old calico wrapper. Celia wondered if she meant to travel in it. Her hair had evidently not been combed that morning, only twisted in a knot. She seemed embarrassed by aunt Hannah in her trim grey traveling dress, and hardly knew on what footing to meet her.

"For the land sake!" she exclaimed, wiping her hands, from custom perhaps, on the side of her wrapper before shaking hands. "So you've come! And you're really willing to undertake it, and think you can succeed? I'm afraid you'll be disappointed. It's a hard life! You look too good for such a life. They're an awful torment, boarders are! Me heart has just been broke time an' again with the troubles I've been through with them. I'll show you all around, and if you feel you can't do it, *yet,* I shouldn't feel you was bound in any way to stick to your bargain. Miss Murray she seemed to be so sure, but I wouldn't want you to be took at no disadvantage. You see I am afraid, if I get away, I shan't want to come back again, and I don't want to go off and feel I left you dissatisfied."

They went down to breakfast soon, and Celia saw her aunt seated before the uninviting meal. She felt sorry for her, and yet she thought she would enjoy the meal with the prospect of the one she would give the boarders later in the day. But she was scarcely prepared for the look of horror that gradually overspread the good woman's face, as she tasted dish after dish and found them alike unpalatable. There was oatmeal that morning. It was thick and lumpy, and only half cooked. Besides the salt had been forgotten. There was pork and greasy fried potatoes, but they were both cold, and unseasoned. The coffee was weak and muddy. Celia swallowed a few bites. She felt that she could go hungry for one day. Then she said a soft good-bye to aunt Hannah, squeezing her hand under her napkin so the boarders would not see and slipped away.

Aunt Hannah finished all she cared to of her meal and went back to Mrs. Morris. Molly Poppleton sat down to her breakfast in indisguised disgust. Nothing but the prospect of the power that was to be hers held her tongue from expressing her mind on the subject of good food decently cooked. She did not even pretend to eat much, and she looked at the slatternly form of Maggie as she lounged in to gather some plates, with animosity in her eye. She spent most of her time in the dining-room counting the fly specks and finger marks on the wall and windows. She made up her mind that she would get time for those windows somehow before dinner, if possible. If not, they should be done before another dawn of light and breakfast anyway.

Meantime Mrs. Morris was showing aunt Hannah the house. This room brought so much a week, and that one only so much, and so on, and at each room she had a tale to tell of its various inmates during the years she had kept a boarding-house. Aunt Hannah listened quietly, mentally making notes of what she would and would not do. She saw, without seeming to do so, the worn furniture, the need of a patch on a carpet, or a turning of furniture to hide it, the need of a wardrobe, or bureau in some cases. She set down in her mind the number of window shades torn, or worn out or lacking, and thought how much some cheap muslin curtains would improve things. She felt like a rich fairy, as she went from room to room seeing its need, and knowing that she could wave a wand and change it all. Sometimes the bareness or the attempt at decoration by the boarder was pitiful. She paused a moment before a picture of a quiet sweet-faced woman, in a dark velvet frame on Harry Knowles' bureau, and wondered who she was, and if the young man whom Mrs. Morris said roomed there was worthy of a mother with such a face as that. Then she went at Mrs. Morris' request with her to her room and sat there during an hour of conversation, in which Mrs. Morris, with many sighs and tears, detailed her entire life and troubles for her benefit. Aunt Hannah's quiet, respectful attention and sympathy led her on until she had unburdened all her heart. Then was the Christian woman's opportunity, and she spoke the word in season to the other woman, that word which cannot fail to bear fruit in due time. Mrs. Morris, with her empty life and joyless spirit, while she received the words with tears and some gratitude, but gave no outward sign that they had more than touched the surface of her life, yet remembered what had been said to her, and as she sat in the train that afternoon, speeding far away from the scene of her disappointments and disheartening, her fare paid by one Christian, her house taken and managed by another whom she saw must be a true saint, pondered all these things in her heart.

Mrs. Morris was gone, and aunt Hannah descended to the kitchen, bidding the impatient Molly Foppleton wait until she called her.

Just before Mrs. Morris' departure, she had informed the sullen-looking Maggie that Miss Grant was the woman who was to take her place. Maggie had responded with a significant look, which did not

promise much for taking the new mistress into her favor. She met Miss
Grant in the middle of the dining-room during her progress to the
kitchen. Her hair was frowsy, her dress soiled and torn, and her arms
akimbo. Altogether she would have furnished a formidable encounter
to a woman who was not used to managing servants and holding the
reins of her household well in her own hands.

"I just came to see what you wanted fer dinner," she announced.
"There's some things come from a new place where we never deal. I
thought I'd let you know."

Aunt Hannah thought a minute. Then she said:

"Yes, Maggie, I'll be out in the kitchen soon to attend to dinner, but
meantime it is only one o'clock and there is time enough to get this
room in order first. I think you would better wash those windows."

Maggie stood aghast.

"And what's the matter with this room, I'd like to know?" she said in
a loud, belligerent tone. "It's just the same as it always is, and what's
good enough fer Mis' Morris ought to be good enough fer you. Indeed
I'll wash no windows to-day. I've got me afternoon's work all planned
out. This room'll be swep' when I sets the table fer dinner, an' that's all
it'll get to-day. And you needn't trouble your self about comin' in the
kitchen. I never likes to have the missus in the kitchen, it flusters me. I
know me business and I 'tend to it, and I likes to have them as I live
with attend to theirs. If you've got any orders, give 'em, and I'll get
dinner on time, you needn't worry about that."

Maggie had backed up against the kitchen door, her arms still
akimbo, and stood as if to defend the fortress of her domain.

Aunt Hannah waited till she had drawn down a crooked shade and
rolled it straight again, pinning the torn edge, before she answered.
Then she turned and calmly faced the irate Maggie.

"I always manage my own kitchen, Maggie," she said, in a quiet
voice, "and I intend to do so still. I want this dining-room put in order
first, before anything else is attended to. Get some cloths and hot water
right away, please."

There was a dignity about aunt Hannah that was new in Maggie's
experience. She had been accustomed to intimidate Mrs. Morris by

such conversation as she had just used, and she supposed she could do the same by her new mistress. She never expected to have it treated with such calm indifference. She was forced to her last resort.

"I can't stay in a house where things are managed that way. No lady goes into the kitchen. I know me business, and I don't like to be interfered with. If you ain't suited with me doing as I think best, I can find plenty of places."

"Oh, certainly, if you prefer," said aunt Hannah, pulling down the other shade and fixing it neatly.

"Well, if I do, I'll go right away, and then what'll you do?" burst out the astonished Maggie. "There's all them boarders got to have their dinner. You can't fool with boarders, you know. They'll all leave you."

"I shall do very well," answered aunt Hannah. "I brought one of my home servants with me, and I can get others very easily. If you choose to stay and do as I say I would like to have those windows washed at once, otherwise you may go."

Poor Maggie! She was crestfallen. This was new treatment. The mistresses she was used to had to cater to the desires of their servants. She did a great deal of work, and she preferred to do it her way. But aunt Hannah was firm. Molly at that moment, too impatient to begin to be able to wait any longer, put her head in at the door and asked if Miss Hannah was ready for her. She eyed the crestfallen Maggie with the superiority of a conqueror. That was enough. Maggie tossed her head and declared she would not do another stroke of work in that house, and demanded back pay. Miss Hannah settled up with her, and she departed, leaving Molly monarch of the kitchen and scornfully surveying her new realm.

Chapter 11

It's just a pigpen! That's what it is!" declared Molly Poppleton, holding up her ample calico skirts and clean gingham apron in a gingerly way. "I don't know where to begin. I didn't suppose a human being *could* be so dirty!" Then she plunged into work. The range got such a cleaning as it had not had in years. The ashes were cleaned out, and the soot removed from all its little doors and traps and openings. Molly was not used to a city range with all its numerous appliances, but she had very keen common sense and she used it. She knew dirt and ashes could not help a fire to burn, so she removed them. While she was about it, she gave it a good washing inside and out, for she found the oven encrusted with burned sugar and juice of some sort, and the top was covered with grease. Then, in the most scientific manner, she started a fire, and before very long it was glowing, and the water in the old tank was steaming hot.

It appeared there really was no time for those dining-room windows that day, after all. With skirts tucked together and sleeves rolled high Molly generously used the hot water and soap in the kitchen. She unceremoniously took the old ragged cloths which must have been Maggie's wiping towels for scrubbing rags, trusting to Miss Hannah's sense of the fitness of things to provide others in some way. The kitchen table and shelves and windows and paint and sink were scrubbed, and even the floor, and then Molly stood back and surveyed the room now pervaded with a damp atmosphere redolent of soap.

"There! I guess it'll do fer over night, and the fust chance I get I'll give it a good cleaning. I never saw the like in my life! How them poor boarders stood it eating out of a dirty hole like this I don't see. Now, what's to do? That sink was a caution! The water and dust was all in a mess underneath and the top was slimy! I wonder what the creature that called herself Maggie thought she was made for."

Meanwhile Miss Hannah had gone to her trunk and arrayed herself in an old grey gingham and a dark apron that enveloped her completely. She had discovered that they must begin at the very foundation before they could hope to do anything toward getting dinner. She investigated Celia's stores and found they were ample for present needs. Celia's training had not been for nothing. She knew by intuition that her aunt and Molly would enquire for soap and yeast and baking powder among the first things. She had thought of the little things that might not be in stock in Mrs. Morris' kitchen and had a supply for the present. The stores in the pantry were not very full. There was a plate with a pile of sour white-looking pancakes, another with some lumpy oatmeal, a few boiled potatoes, a bowl of watery soup and two or three ends of baker's loaves. Miss Hannah applied her nose to one of these and then laid it down again and said, "Bah!"

After looking at the array a few minutes, she gathered them all into a pan and dumped them into the garbage pail. A heavy, lifeless pie on a higher shelf also met the same fate. Then she got the dishpan and some clean hot water and washed a few dishes for her immediate use. Having done this she prepared to set some bread. It was late in the day, but it would not take long, and it could rise while she was doing other things and be baked after the dinner was cooked. Then she could hurry up part of it by making it into pulled rolls so that they could be used for dinner. The bread done she started on a searching expedition for bread cloths and clean rags. She could not work without tools. In one of her trunks was a roll of old rags and linen; with Molly's help she unstrapped the trunk and searched it out. It was a great satisfaction to have that bread covered with a clean cloth and feel that so much of her work was going on right. She decided that the dishes must all be washed. She and Molly both worked at this, Molly washing off the shelves while she wiped the dishes. By that time it was four o'clock.

"It's high time we was seeing about the dinner," said Molly, as she thumped the last pile of plates upon the clean shelf. "What are you going to do for a tablecloth? That one in there ain't fit, an' there ain't a clean one about the drawer anywhere. There's a pile of dirty ones behind the door in the back stairway. I reckon I'll have to wash one. As for napkins I should suppose they didn't use 'em. I can't find any."

Miss Hannah went on another hunt, and discovered more soiled tablecloths and a stack of soiled napkins. There was nothing for it but to wash some. Molly already had the washtub going and was working as if her life depended upon it. Well for Miss Hannah's plans and Celia's hopes that Molly was equal to emergencies, nay delighted in them, and that she was a swift worker. By the time Miss Hannah had the tablecloth and dishes off the table and the dining-room swept and dusted that linen was swinging in a brisk breeze in the back yard and the irons were growing hot on the range.

"Five o'clock and the table not set yet!" commented Molly. She was working on time and the pleasure of the race depended upon her getting done before Miss Celia should arrive, and being able to ring that dinner bell exactly on time. "Well, I reckon we'll get through somehow. You can't turn a pigpen into a parlor in one day, you know. I declare, Miss Hannah, it was a pity to turn that girl loose on the community. We ought to have kept her by main force and taught her how to scrub, before we let her go. The things that wasn't too filthy dirty to be burned or rusted is burned and rusted, and the things that had anything about them to get lost and broken has got that the matter with them. I reckon we'll have a few things to buy 'fore we get fixed out for comfort."

But Molly was working swiftly all the while she talked. She had filled the little salts and peppers, and rubbed up the knives. The careful Celia had not forgotten bath brick nor silver polish, though there was very little that had any pretension to silver to clean. The dishes and table appointments were of the plainest. Many would have said it was impossible to make any difference in that table without spending a lot of money. Miss Hannah did not think so. She knew the subtle difference between order and disorder, and the startling contrast between cleanliness and dirt. Cleanliness was next to godliness and she was practicing that to-day. The godliness she hoped would follow hard after. While she pulled the little cushions of responsive velvety dough for the rolls, she prayed a rich blessing on that first meal in the house under her care. Then she let her mind wander for a moment to the home she had left which had been no more of a home to her than this was yet to its inmates. She wondered how they were getting on, and if the baby was well. The only drawback to the joy of leaving Nettie's had been the baby. Aunt Hannah could not help loving babies, and enjoying the clinging of their soft dimpling arms about her neck and their apple blossom breath upon her cheek. The babies always loved aunt Hannah. It was only after they grew older and began to imitate the grown-up people that they began to be saucy, impertinent, and unloving. Even then, Johnnie and Lily had always come to aunt Hannah with a burn or a bump to be comforted, for somehow her motherly arms knew just how best to gather in the troubled little one and comfort it. But aunt Hannah had no time to think of duties past, and troubles. She gave the last little jerk to the puffy roll and tucked it in the pan to rise for the last time, and then hastened in to set that table. Molly had laid the crisp tablecloth which she had literally forced to dry quickly with her hot irons, on the table and was ironing away for dear life at the napkins. Molly and aunt Hannah had high ideals, brought from comfortable private homes, and they wished this house they had come to take care of to be a home in the best sense of the word. They worked faster now, for the clock was warning them that it was getting late. The roast beef well seared in the most scientific way was roasting away in the oven with a good supply of sweet and Irish potatoes on the grate below, grouped about a huge baked apple dumpling which Molly had hastily concocted, and Molly was straining the spinach and subjecting it to a rubbing through the colander, after which it went back on the stove to keep hot before its butter and last peppering were applied. She looked doubtfully at the water the spinach was cooked in and then with a daring glance at the clock rushed about to carry out another resolution, calling to Miss Hannah:

"You ken put on the soup plates ef your a mine to. I've found I can make a taste of spinach soup with the water and some milk and flour and butter. It'll make things seem nicer I guess for the first night, and don't take a minute. That'll give the rolls time to get a little browner before they're needed, you know." Then she began to sing at the top of her voice:

"Am I a soldier of the cross,—"

Molly Poppleton always sang at the top of her lungs when she had some important work to do or was in an unusual hurry with her work. It made her very happy to have a good deal of work, and hard work at that.

Celia, opening the front door with her latch-key just then, heard the singing and rejoiced. There was the old Molly. She had not become discouraged and gone home, but was at work with heart and voice as in their old kitchen at home. She ran out into the dining-room to see how things were getting on before she went upstairs. But she stopped in the doorway astounded. Even her highest hopes had not realized the change there would be. What made it? Was it the shining tablecloth, or the glistening glasses, or the knives and forks laid straight, or what? A nice square cake of butter was in each butter-plate at the ends of the table. The salts were smoothed off and stamped with the bottom of the salt-cellars. The plates were in a pile at one end of the table instead of being upside down on the napkins at each place. Where were the plates of crackers and gingersnaps which had not failed to appear at every dinner since she had been boarding there? Where was the inevitable dish of prunes? Gone, and in its place a dish of translucent cranberry jelly which Molly had found time somehow to fix. It was all very wonderful. Even the gas had a clean globe on it. Celia wondered that so much had been accomplished in one short afternoon. She heard the door being opened from the outside and hurried into the kitchen, closing the dining-room door behind her first. This must burst upon them all at once when they entered the dining-room.

Aunt Hannah was taking the brown balls from the roll pan and piling them on a plate, when she went into the kitchen, and she greeted her with:

"Celia, go upstairs and wash your hands and then come down and fix the celery. Molly and I haven't a second to do it, and it is time to ring that bell in five minutes. Have the boarders come yet?"

Celia rushed away and was soon back, bearing aunt Hannah's white apron and a brush to smooth her hair that she might not be delayed from coming to dinner on account of her appearance, and at last the dinner was ready and it was time to ring the bell. She put the two glasses of celery on the table, and handing Molly the bell went into the parlor. She did not wish anybody yet to know she had a right in the kitchen. She was just the ribbon girl from Dobson and Co.'s. There were things she wanted to accomplish first which could better be done that way, she thought.

The bell rang and the boarders trooped down. The little old lady from upstairs was first and interrupted the advance of the others, for a moment. She walked into the dining-room followed by Miss Burns. Both stopped blinking in the doorway and staring around, before they slowly walked in a dazed way to their respective places. The two girls from the three-cent store became embarrassed, and stood back awkwardly against the wall staring undisguisedly. The three young men came after, Harry Knowles ahead.

He drew a long whistle, and turning on his heel, started back into the hall again. "Whew! this is great!" he said as he went. "I'm going to wash my hands and comb my hair. I don't fit in there."

Aunt Hannah with her grey hair and placid face and grey dress with its white apron presided well over that table. The dishes might be thick and the tablecloth coarse, but no dinner on any rich man's table was ever cooked or served better, nor more thoroughly enjoyed. After they were seated Miss Burns began with her nervous little giggle:

"Oh really, now, this is simply,—simply—simply *fine,* don't you know. This is quite a change, isn't it, dear?" and she looked across the table at Celia who was passing celery and handing soup plates as aunt Hannah ladled out the pale green tempting soup. Her guests ate of it in wonder. They were not acquainted with pureè of spinach. They wondered how it got colored, and what it was anyway, and the most of them ate every drop in their plates, some of them tilting the plates to accomplish it. The three-cent store girls and the university student asked for more and got it, and then Molly, her sleeves rolled decorously down and a white apron over her dark one, took out the soup and brought in the platter with that great brown perfectly cooked roast, and brought potatoes and spinach and hot plates, while aunt Hannah with experienced hand and keen knife, sharpened by herself, cut great juicy pink slices in generous plenty and filled the plates.

They were a rather silent table that first night. They were embarrassed to a degree by their surroundings which were so familiar and yet so unfamiliar. And then the dinner was absorbing. It absorbed their thoughts and they absorbed it.

When it came time for the dessert they sat back satisfied, and feeling that perhaps it were as well that the inevitable pie, which they always had for dessert, did not come to spoil this ideal repast. But they forgot such feelings when that great pudding was brought in, its crust browned to a nicety on the top, and light as feathers when it was cut, its luscious quarters of amber apples in the bottom, and a dressing of some sweet transparent syrup with just a dash of cinnamon.

"I tell you what!" said Harry Knowles, leaning back in his chair to fold his napkin and talking in an aside to Celia, "that was the best dinner I have tasted since I left home. I feel as if I had been invited out, don't you? I don't know what it means, do you? She certainly can't keep it up. I suppose she's just standing treat for the first night, but I declare, if I could have meals like that, I'm not sure but I might be a different kind of a fellow and amount to something. How's our lamp getting on? I thought of a way to fix the spring in that sofa the other night. I believe I'll stay in and try it to-night."

Aunt Hannah, as they were leaving the table, apologized for not having put the rooms in order that day. She had only been in power, she said, since one o'clock, and there had not been time to do everything. She hoped to have things in better shape very soon if they would all be patient. Then the boarders went into the parlor to whisper with one another about that good dinner, and Celia slipped unseen out to the kitchen to exult and to help.

Chapter 12

Out in the street, not far from that boarding-house, two young men met. "How are you, Horace? Glad to see you, old fellow! You look as thin as a rail. What do they feed you on down in that miserable hole where you hide yourself? I say, Horace, you ought to have either a new boarding-place or a wife."

The other man laughed. "I'm hunting one," he said, "that is, a new boarding-house, not a wife."

"Well, you may find the one while in search of the other, you know. They always used to say, when we were children, that if you lost a thing you never could find it till you lost something else and went to hunting that. Now you haven't exactly lost a wife, you know, because you never had one. So that's just as bad, but maybe you'll find her. However, I fear that any one you'd find in hunting a boarding-house wouldn't be worth her salt. That's my experience. Say, old fellow, why don't you come up our way and live? It isn't much further, and you are a good walker. You could walk to that blessed church of yours, if you still hold to your puritanical ideas about not riding on the trolley on Sunday. Now there's the place Royce boards; that would be first-rate, and I happen to know there's a vacant room there now, second story front, fine sunny room, all conveniences and splendid board."

"But I can't afford second story fronts, Roger; my salary has mostly to be paid by myself yet. You know we are building and the church is just struggling to live. It is all made up of poor people."

"Well, what in the world did you go down there for? You might have had a church in Germantown if you would have taken it, and you also had a chance out in West Philadelphia I heard. Why, you've friends enough to have got you hearings in several big churches down

90

in the heart of the city where they pay big salaries. I'm sure I don't see any virtue in your hiding your light under a bushel. For my part, I think you are as good, if not better, than any preacher I've heard in the city, if you only would consent to let go of a few high and impossible views you have about social equality. However, I suppose that's neither here nor there. You're here and the churches are there, and so it will continue to be, I presume, in spite of all I can say, and there'll be nothing for me but to tend you in your last sickness and pay the funeral expenses, if you go on at this rate. I must see what I can do about getting our church to help that mission of yours, if you persist in your folly."

"I wish you would, Roger, for they need help, and a church in this neighborhood is much more needed than in the quarters you have mentioned, where there is a church of some sort every two blocks almost. But I must go on, for I have a meeting this evening, and I want to go to one more place before I go to church."

They parted, the young man Roger wishing the other would reconsider, and come higher up in town to board, and thus be near his friends. Then Horace Stafford went on his way, and having consulted a list of addresses in his notebook, in a moment more paused at a door and rang a bell and the door was opened by Celia.

Now Celia was very happy over the successful dinner. She had lingered about the halls catching words that the boarders had dropped, and she knew that they were intensely pleased and surprised. When she was happy or excited a clear red color came into her cheeks and a brightness into her deep, grey-blue eyes which made her very beautiful. She was not always beautiful, although she was always pleasant to look at: certain conditions, however, had the power of making this charm bloom into beauty. To-night the color and the shine were there, and she seemed a charming picture to the young man who had spent the afternoon in calling at boarding-houses, and had begun to know just what to expect to see when the door opened. He was agreeably surprised, therefore, as he stepped into the hall and waited while Celia called aunt Hannah, for he had said he wanted to see Mrs. Morris, having been directed there for board. He glanced into the parlor and sighed. It was the same grade of parlor he had grown to expect, a dreary enough place, but he did not know what was the matter with it, and as he should have to spend very little time in it, it did not make great difference. He heard a low cultured voice upstairs saying: "Tell Molly I will send her some in a moment," and then Miss Grant appeared before him.

It is true she did not know much about taking new boarders, but she did the best she could. She told him there was one room left vacant that day, that it was not in order yet, but if he cared to see it, he might come upstairs and do so. He followed her to the room. It happened to be the second story front. It was not large, for economy of space had been exercised to a great degree in the building of that house, but it had a sunny exposure, and the young man knew by an uncomfortable experience in a dark room that that was a great advantage in a room. The bed did not look very soft nor inviting, and the two chairs in the room were rather dilapidated. The bureau was a cheap one with a rheumatic castor, which gave it a reeling appearance. The bed clothing was tumbled in a heap on the bed, as the clerk had left it. Altogether it was not just what one would call luxury. But it was so much better than some the weary man had seen that he ventured to ask timidly, "Could I have some sort of a table to write on?"

Miss Hannah thought a moment and told him that she thought he could. He asked the price and it proved to be not much more than he was now paying. After a little reflection he said he would take it. Afterward, when he had gone downstairs to the parlor to wait for the supper which she had said he might have, in response to his question if it was too late for the evening meal, he wondered why he had done so. What power had been upon him upstairs to make him determine to cast his lot in here? It was not that room, even though it was a second story front, for that was very forlorn in the dim flickering gaslight. It was not the general look of the house, for that certainly was not attractive. And now as he sat in the dimness of the shadow of the front window, and watched some of the boarders at the further end of the room, he felt that same sense of desolation steal over him which he had felt in so many boarding-houses that afternoon. He could not hope to find many congenial spirits here. He sighed. It was hard not to have some pleasant friends about one who could talk of the things one knew and loved, when one came in at night after a hard day's work. But as Miss Hannah came back through the hall and in that quiet sweet voice of hers that made one feel as if a benediction had been pronounced upon one, told him that he could come to the dining-room now, he followed her and knew that it was his landlady who had drawn him to select this as his temporary home. She seated him and poured his coffee, and then excused herself and left him. He looked about him after he was left alone, and had bowed his head a moment, more in supplication that the Lord would give him rest and strength for his work, than in thankfulness for his food, for he had learned that there were kinds of food which were as hard to eat as they were to digest. With pleased surprise he saw the tablecloth was clean and free from crumbs. The plate before him held food as appetizing as any he could remember in pleasanter homes than those he had occupied lately. Of course the potatoes had been heated over and were not so nice as when first served, but the meat was tender and juicy, and he ate it with a relish, for he was weary and had not had anything to really tempt his appetite for six weeks, that being the length of time since he had gone to his friend Roger's, to dinner. Those delicious rolls and that coffee were enough in themselves to satisfy a hungry man, and he began to feel that he had not chosen his home amiss. Then the kitchen door opened, and Celia entered bringing a bounteous plate of apple dumpling covered with plenty of sauce. She put it down beside his place and began to remove the empty dishes, asking him if he would have anything more.

"Thank you," he said, looking up and smiling, "I have had plenty and it has been so good. I have been boarding where they had miserable fare, and I did not know how hungry I was. This meal has tasted like my mother's cooking."

Celia's eyes danced as she said demurely she was very glad. As she went back to the kitchen with the dishes, she could not help thinking what handsome eyes that man had, and how they were lit up by his smile. He was tall and thin with an intellectual face which many persons would have called homely, but of the style which Celia always designated to herself and aunt Hannah as "homely handsome."

The new boarder went out after his meal was finished. He had told his landlady that he would bring his belongings when he returned later in the evening, and she had promised to have his room ready for him.

Celia went upstairs to see if she could do anything. She was bubbling over with delight over the house and its inmates and all she wished to do. No child in a fairy tale ever had such delightful possibilities put into her hands, she thought, as had been given to her.

"Now," said aunt Hannah, "that room must be fixed for that man, for he will come back by and by, and what shall we do with it to make it more habitable? Poor fellow! He must have been hard put to it indeed for shelter to have taken it looking like that, or perhaps he doesn't know any better. But it did look so desolate I couldn't bear to take him to it."

"Yes, he does know better, aunt Hannah," said Celia, laughing. "I know he does. He has a mother—and," she added half ashamed, "he has a smile."

"Well, I'm glad he has that," said Miss Hannah, pulling the bedclothes off in a gingerly way and extracting the sheets and pillow-cases from the mass. "He'll need it to keep cheerful in this room to-night, I think. Celia, I do wish I could get into my grandmother's linen and blanket closet for a little while to-night. I should like to burn this quilt." She held it out by her finger and thumb and examined it carefully.

"Burn it, then," said Celia solemnly. "Haven't we got an allowance? We'll buy another." Then she went to work to try and make that room less dreary.

When the bed was made up with the cleanest things aunt Hannah could find, the wash bowl and pitcher and soap dish immaculate, and two copies of those flaring chromos called "Wide Awake" and "Fast Asleep" framed in varnished coffee berries had been removed from the walls, there was not much more to do. It was too late to do more at the paint than to wipe it off with a damp cloth, and the floor needed only brushing up. Aunt Hannah found a kitchen-table in Mrs. Morris' room which had done duty for a dressing-table. She had Molly carry this upstairs for a writing-table, and sighed that there was no cover for it. Celia meditated a moment, and then went up to her own back-room and took the embroidered denim cover from her trunk which she had made for a Christmas present for aunt Hannah and brought it. It was a little sacrifice but the table needed it. It wasn't too fine for use, and it would cause the bare room to look more habitable.

"There, aunt Hannah," she said, "I made it for you, but you may do what you like with it."

Then aunt Hannah took Celia's face between her hands and kissed her and said, "My dear girl!" and put the pretty cover on the table.

"I don't know as I should have done that," meditated Celia later, "if it hadn't been for that smile and his speaking about his mother."

She looked around the room once more as she was about to leave it. Aunt Hannah had gone down to the kitchen to help Molly prepare for breakfast. Her eyes fell upon the two rickety chairs. She thought of Harry Knowles. A moment's reflection, and she ran down to the parlor and beckoned him to come into the hall.

"Harry," said she (they had already gotten well enough acquainted so that she could call him by his first name; she exercised that prerogative which a girl a little older than a young man likes to use and which the young man seems to be proud to have exercised sometimes. It was a pleasant brotherly and sisterly way to treat one another), "did you know there was a new boarder? I was passing the room just now. It looked awfully dreary before it was fixed up. The worst thing is the chairs. I wonder if you couldn't bring up your hammer and fix them a little. It seems too bad for a new boarder to find things all run down on the first night he comes."

"All right, I'm with you, Miss Murray," said Harry, interested at once. "I know how it feels myself. Besides that good dinner has given me a longing to do something for somebody else."

They went upstairs to the chairs, and as they went Harry said in a confiding tone, "Say, Miss Murray, I believe that Miss Grant is going to be great, don't you? She seems kind of like a woman who knew how, don't you know? Sometimes she makes me think of my mother just a little."

Celia smiled and said she thought so, and they went to work.

It was after the room was all in order, and some delicious cakes set rising in the yellow bowl downstairs for the morning breakfast, set with buckwheat that smelled of the waving fields it came from. The lights were out and everything quiet and Celia, lying awake to think over all that had happened, suddenly became aware that her aunt Hannah was awake also. Upon questioning her she at last ferreted out the reason for her wakefulness.

"Well, you see, Celia, I suppose I'm rather tired to-night, though I don't feel it one bit, I've been so interested in it all. But somehow I've just begun to think that maybe I ought not to have let you undertake this scheme. It is all very nice and benevolent, but what if it shouldn't succeed? If it should run behind and take a good deal of your money and you have to work hard for your living again, I should never get over blaming myself. Then too, I'm a little worried about that new man. I don't know as I ought to have taken him into the house without knowing the first thing about him, and I've always heard a city was an awful place to get taken in. He may be a robber, or some dreadful kind of a man, though to be sure he didn't look it. I must confess that I liked his looks very much, but you know, Celia dear, Satan sometimes appears as an angel of light. I have heard that gamblers are often mistaken for ministers. I know perfectly well that I am 'green,' as the boys used to say, and perhaps I have been deceived. He was very late getting in and he looked pale. It may be he is dissipated, though I cannot really think that."

"Now, auntie dear," laughed Celia, putting her arms about her, "that isn't a bit like you. You must be over-tired or you never would talk like that. Just remember your own words to me 'Charge not thyself with the weight of a year' and 'Bend not thine arm for to-morrow's load. Thou mayst leave that to thy gracious Lord.' Don't you fret one bit. What if he is a gambler or a robber? He can't do us any harm. We've nothing to gamble and nothing to rob. Perhaps we'll do him some good, and anyway I don't believe he's anything but good—he talked to me—that is he said he had a mother and she cooked like that, and then he smiled."

Then they both laughed and Miss Hannah kissed her niece and thanked her for the reminder that she need not bear burdens. After that they fell asleep.

Chapter 13

The minister was very weary when he went up to his new room that night, and he put down his satchel and looked around him hoping the bed would be more inviting than when last he saw it, though he had grown accustomed to sleeping soundly on any bed no matter how hard or uneven. He drew a long sigh of relief. It looked clean anyway. He turned down the covering and smoothed the sheets. They had no appearance of having been slept in before. He drew another sigh. That was one fear off his mind. He noticed next the table with its pretty cover. He was not accustomed to fancy work. He did not know whether this was done by hand or machinery. He only knew that it was a touch of beauty in his dreary room and he felt gladdened by it. He went over to the table and awkwardly felt of the material, passed his hand over the embroidery and smiled. He said to himself he would write to his mother about it and she would be pleased. Then he knelt down beside the table and bowed his head in prayer upon it asking that he might receive and give a blessing in that house where he had come to take up his abode, and that if possible, it might be such a place that he would feel it was right and best that he should remain for a time.

About that same time Harry Knowles stood before the bureau in his room and looked at his mother's picture. His face was grave and sad. He looked into the pictured eyes with a questioning longing as if he would have her with him again that he might ask her advice. He looked into her face till the tears started in his own eyes. He let them drop unheeded on the bureau and on the little velvet frame. She seemed to him to be looking into his life, and asking him what he had done with his time since she left him. At last he turned away his head and said aloud, "Well, I'm glad I didn't go to-night anyway. I s'pose the boys'll give me no end of chaff about backing out, but I've proved to myself that I can stay at home *once* when I say so. I wish mother *was* here. I'd tell her all about it, I believe, and promise her to start over again. I wonder if 'twould be any use! If a fellow only had some one to help him!" and he sighed and went to bed.

It is not quite certain what time Molly Poppleton arose the next morning. Celia told her if she had only gotten up a very little earlier, she might have met herself going to bed. The range unused to such treatment brightened up early too, and was soon baking and boiling away to please the most fastidious cook. The oatmeal had been cooking slowly all night, and was getting ready to be a delicious porridge, such as is found in its perfection only in the land of Scotland. Molly had coaxed the milk by all the arts she knew, till it actually gave forth a thin yellow cream for the oatmeal. True, she scoffed at it and said it wasn't as rich as skim milk in Cloverdale, but then the boarders were not used to Cloverdale milk, and they called this cream. She picked and shredded the codfish to a degree of fineness that would have made the departed Maggie stand in amaze at such a waste of labor, and then with all the skill of long experience, she mixed just the right proportion of potatoes for the most delectable codfish balls, when they should be browned to a crisp, that ever any one tasted.

"Codfish balls are good, and anybody that doesn't like 'em when they are made just right doesn't know, that's all. Besides one can't have beefsteak every day and there's plenty else to eat." So said Molly.

Then she tested the buckwheat cakes to be sure there was exactly the right amount of soda and enough milk to make them brown on both sides, and set the coffee where it would get its finishing-off, and rang the bell. Just one minute ahead of time that bell rang. Molly Poppleton did love to get ahead of time, even if it was but one minute.

"I say," said Harry Knowles, holding a golden-brown fish-ball up on his fork and admiring it, "if that is a fish-ball, then I never saw one before. It is a libel on that pretty thing to call it by that name, or else all the ones I ever tried to eat were very poor imitations." Molly, coming in just then with a generous supply of hot buckwheats heard the remark, and her soul swelled with joy and pride, and thereafter Harry Knowles was her favorite of all the boarders unless it was the minister who grew into her good graces by another way not long after. He had come in just a moment before, and was enjoying his dish of oatmeal and wondering what made the difference between it and all the other oatmeal he had tried to eat in the weeks since he came to Philadelphia to live. Was it possible that he had at last found a place where things were really good to eat, or was he getting a good appetite from working so hard? He resolved, at any rate, to ask the cook, sometime when he was well enough acquainted, if he might take a dish of this to the old Scotch woman who was lying sick in an attic and longing for her dear home across the seas.

That breakfast was a pleasant surprise to more than one of the boarders. The brakeman, coming in a little late from his all-night run, having taken his dinner the night before at the other end of his line, and therefore not being prepared for changes except the mere fact that Mrs. Morris had gone away, and some one else was to supply her place for a while, was dumbfounded. He drew his chair up to the table with his usual familiar assurance, and then looked around in almost embarrassment a moment. He was not quite sure what made him feel so. Was it the pleasant-faced, white-haired woman at the head of the table, who smiled a good-morning to him in a tone which was cordial and yet had a note in it that made him feel she was from another world than his own? Or was it the few flowers in the tiny vase in the centre of the table? Or? But he was unable to detail the rest of the changes, they seemed to him so subtle. He turned his attention to the breakfast which certainly was good. Maggie had improved, evidently.

In short, those boarders went to their day's work well fed and comfortable for the first time in many weeks, and were therefore better workers, and better human beings in every way, because they were not all day troubled by the demands and complaints of nature in consequence of what they had eaten, or what they had not eaten.

Just as Celia was going out of the door, Miss Hannah, who had followed her, put her hand on her arm and drew her into the parlor for a moment.

"Celia, dear," she said, "we must have a talk to-night as soon after dinner as possible, and find out how this house is to be run and decide some questions. You know we cannot go ahead blindly and get into debt as Mrs. Morris did."

"I'll risk you, auntie dear," Celia said, as she kissed her behind the red chenille curtain. "But we'll have our talk, and I'll get home just as early as I can to help, if you need me. Then after dinner we'll have a cozy time and do a lot of figuring. I've done some already. Good-bye. Don't try to reform everything to-day, leave just a little for to-morrow. Do you want me to stop at some employment office and get another servant?"

"No, not yet, dear. There's too much to be done before we introduce any new elements, and besides we don't know yet whether we can afford another servant. We mustn't run behind, you know."

Then they parted with a smile of perfect understanding, and aunt Hannah went to her new duties with enthusiasm. There were a few things she meant to have radically different in some of her guests' sleeping rooms before that day drew to a close, and there was much planning and marketing to do. Molly Poppleton was in her element in the kitchen. Miss Hannah could hear her voice singing above the clatter of pots and pans,

> "What though the spicy breezes
> Blow soft o'er Ceylon's isle;
> Though every prospect pleases,
> And only man is vile;—"

Molly was cleaning out the departed Maggie's kettle closet under the back stairs, and stopped occasionally in her singing to express her mind as to some dirty corner and then went on—

> "In vain with lavish kindness
> The gifts of God are strewn;
> The heathen in his blindness,
> Bows down to wood and stone!"

Aunt Hannah smiled as she went upstairs. She knew that the good-hearted Molly was mingling the theme of her song with her own thoughts about the dirty house and the need of the boarders and that she would work it all out by and by.

> "Shall we whose souls are lighted
> With wisdom from on high,—
> Shall we to men benighted,
> The lamp of life deny?"

went on the singer, and Miss Hannah knew the hard working singer's thought was that she would make a cheerful, clean house and good food, and give the rest of them a chance to try and help save the poor city heathen boarders, for Molly Poppleton looked upon all native city boarders as heathen in the truest sense of the word, and she had taken with joy the few words Miss Hannah had spoken to her about the mission they were going to try to start, the mission of making one bright little clean home spot for a few people who had hitherto been in discomfort.

The dining-room windows were washed that morning, and several other windows, and Molly Poppleton sang a great many of Isaac Watts' hymns through before she prepared lunch for herself and Miss Hannah. She did not remember when she had been so happy. Neither, indeed, did Miss Hannah.

It had been the one great ambition of Hannah Grant's life, since she had lost the love of her youth, and been made to see that hers was not to go on the great mission of salvation to the heathen of other nations, that she should have some spot which she could call her own, where she might exercise her powers of helping people. And now it seemed as though she was to have opportunity. She thanked her heavenly Father every hour, even for the dirt and desolation of the place, because he had given to her the sweet privilege of brightening a place that had hitherto been dark.

It was after dinner. The minister was in his room writing to his mother, before he went out to a meeting at the mission. Down in the parlor the brakeman sat at the organ accompanying himself as he sang in stentorian voice the touching ballad of

"Granny's only left to me her old armchair."

Celia smiled as she ran upstairs where her aunt was waiting for the conference.

"Just listen, auntie dear, did you ever hear the like," she said, putting her head in at the door, and the words of the chorus in decided nasal twang floated up the two flights of stairs:

"How they tittered, how they chaffed,
How my brothers and my sisters laughed,
When they heard the lawyers declare,
Granny's only left to me her old armchair."

"Do you really think, aunt Hannah, that it's any use to try to reach and help people who have that sort of taste in music, even if you try through their taste in buckwheat cakes?"

Celia's face was gay with laughter, but there was an undertone of trouble in it which Miss Hannah detected and understood.

"Dearie, Christ died for him, even if he does seem to be too coarse-grained to understand the little refining influences you are trying to weave around him. Yes, of course it is worth while. You can't expect him to turn into a person with the tastes of a Beethoven. You are not that yourself, remember, and it's all in the scale of life. But I know what you mean, and I do think it's worth while to try. You see if it wasn't, God wouldn't have put him just here for us to try on. You mustn't expect the same result as you would from——"

"From your new boarder, auntie? The gambler with the smile you mean?" Celia was laughing now, for both had seen with the morning light that whatever else their new boarder was, he was a man to be trusted.

"Yes," said aunt Hannah. "You mustn't expect the same results from trying to help this man that you would the other, but you'll find he will have a depth to his nature which you don't suspect, if you look for it. Listen! He is singing something else. It may give you a clue."

Again the voice rang out deeply, pathetically and nasally,

"Lost on the Lady Elgin,
Slumbering to wake no more,
Numbering about three hundred,—
Who failed to reach the shore."

"Oh, auntie, I can't stand another line," said Celia rushing into the room and throwing herself on the bed in a paroxysm of laughter. "To have those awful words in that ludicrous song roared out in that dramatic way is too, *too* funny. And he asked me if I would sing 'Where is my wandering boy to-night?' with him. How *could* I?"

"Now, dear girl," said aunt Hannah sitting down on the bed beside her, "perhaps that is just your chance. Sing 'Where is my wandering boy to-night?' with him some time. You may be able to help him to higher, more refining things in some way, even if he does continue to amuse you with his music. If you want to help all these people, you will have to do as Paul did and be all things to all men, that you may by all means save some."

Celia sobered down at once.

"Yes, I know, aunt Hannah, but somehow I never could be that, unless I was interested in people. It troubles me sometimes, but this black-eyebrowed, smiling, conceited brakeman isn't in the least attractive. Now that boy Harry Knowles is. I feel sorry for him. He misses his mother, and I'm afraid he goes with a wild set. I got him to fix some chairs last night and he seemed interested and stayed at home. But to-night he slipped out just before I came up, and looked the other way when I came down the hall, as if he didn't want me to see him and ask him to stay in, at least I fancy that was the reason, because I've asked him to stay once or twice. It worries me to think he is going wrong, and I feel as if I could pray all night that God would save him. I can't get away from that look in the eyes of his mother's picture. He brought it down to the parlor one night and showed it to me. And he is so young, only just eighteen. Auntie, I want to do so much for the people, do you suppose God will let me do something at least?"

"Dear child," said aunt Hannah as she bent over and kissed her, "I feel sure he will, and he will hear your prayers and help you to work in the right way and to be interested in the uninteresting, too. And now get your pencil and paper and let's go to work."

Celia sprang up and soon they were hard at work.

"What I want to do is this, aunt Hannah," said Celia. "I want to make this as pleasant a home for us all, as it can be made on the money that we all pay in for our board. You and I will pay ours too, you know, that is if it can't be run without that, and then we'll just have things as nice as we can on that. If we need anything extra, why you and I can count that a gift, you know, from our allowance. But to be strictly honest as a boarding-house, and not a charitable institution, we ought to run it on what is paid in, oughtn't we? I would like to prove that a boarding-house can be comfortable as well as cheap. Do you think it can be done?"

"I do," said the elder woman, thoughtfully. "I have done some careful thinking myself, and I think it can. I shall enjoy trying, anyway."

"And auntie, there's another thing; this allowance of mine is half yours you know. I won't have it any other way. You and I have nine hundred dollars a year to live on, besides what is now in the bank in cash, and we can do what we please with it, give it away if we want to. If we can make this house pay our board, then we will have the rest to live on. But if we can't, we'll run the house up to the full extent of what we can afford to put into it, for a few months at least, just to give these poor souls a taste of something like home. I would rather do that than give my money somewhere else, for I think they all need it. Do you think, auntie, we have enough money to start on to hope to make things go nicely at the beginning? Nine hundred dollars a year seems to me a great deal of money, but people say that money doesn't go far in the city."

Celia's brow was clouded as she spoke.

"There goes my girl down into her cellar of despair over a thought," said aunt Hannah, leaning over to smooth the pucker out of her niece's brow. "I wish you would get just a little more trust in your heavenly Father, that he will take care of the work he has put into your hands, and see that it prospers in spite of your worries. Now tell me everything you know about this house and the way it is run."

Chapter 14

Aunt Hannah and Celia had finished the last puzzling question, added up the final row of figures, and were peacefully sleeping in their beds. All the lights in the house were out, when there was heard a loud noise at the street door, as if some one was thrown, or threw himself, several times heavily against it. This was followed by voices talking loud and excitedly, and then in more muffled tones. The door knob was turned and rattled, and a latchkey clicked and half turned in the lock as if handled by clumsy or unacquainted fingers.

The minister heard the noise first, as his room was over the front of the house, and rising he opened his window and tried to speak and quiet the disturbance, but he received only curses for his interference, and he thought he recognized in one of the midnight revelers the form of one of the boarders. Closing his window, he dressed as rapidly as possible, that he might go down if his assistance was needed. By the time he was halfway down the stairs, however, and was just striking a match, the fumbling latchkey at last turned, and the door burst open, literally tumbling into the hall three young men just at Horace Stafford's feet. Miss Grant and Celia, though they slept on the third floor, were near the stair landing and had at last heard the noise. They had slipped on wrappers and slippers and stood at the head of the stairs just above Mr. Stafford, as he struck the light.

"What does this mean?" said aunt Hannah, in as stern a voice as she could muster, with Celia, bewildered and trembling, clinging to her arm and begging her to come back.

But there was too much disturbance below for her to be heard, and she and Celia could but stand and watch.

The new boarder seemed to know what to do in the present emergency. He promptly lighted the gas, turning it up to its full strength, and then extricated the three young men, who seemed to be in a helplessly tangled condition on the floor at his feet. Two of them were promptly withdrawn from the hall by their comrades outside, and the one left stood miserably against the wall and looked about him.

It was hard to recognize in this dirty, rough fellow with bloodshot eyes and white face, the gay, bright young man who always looked so neat, and whom everybody liked and called "Harry."

"Oh, auntie, that is Harry Knowles," said Celia, in horrified tones, and then the young man looked up.

"Hulloa, Celia," he called, in a pitifully bright voice, "is that you? Yes, I'm here all right, only I've been out on a lark and the lark's gone to my head. Come down, and talk to a fellow a while, just fer a change, you know."

Celia shrank back in dismay, as she saw the poor fellow stagger toward the stairs and heard him say, "Can't you get down? Well, I'll come up and get you. Awful shaky stairs, I know, but I'll manage 'em yet, don't you be afraid."

And then a strong hand grasped his arm and a clear, commanding voice said,

"Stand right where you are! Don't stir a step, and don't speak another word to those ladies." Then the minister turned to the frightened women and said in low tones,

"Don't be afraid, go to your rooms and I will take care of him."

Harry had sat stupidly down on the stairs saying meekly,

"All right, cap'n, jes's you say. You're boss, an' I'm sleepy."

Miss Hannah took assurance from the calm face and powerful frame of her new boarder and led Celia away, while the minister carefully and even tenderly helped the young man to his room and took care of him as if he had been his own brother.

Miss Hannah had her hands full with Celia. The young girl had thrown herself on the bed in a violent fit of weeping, and it required all her aunt's persuasive powers to quiet her and try to soothe her to sleep.

Celia had not been accustomed to young men who drank. Her cousins had been steady, whatever else they might not have been. She had never seen a man come home at night drunk, and she had never been spoken to by one.

The familiar tone and the vacant, silly stare with which the young man had looked up at her had given her a shock she could not forget. Whenever she tried to be quiet and sit up and listen to aunt Hannah, she would shudder again at the thought of the scene she had just witnessed. By and by, when she was calmer she wailed out,

"Now we shall have to give up the whole thing, auntie. We can't have people getting drunk," and she shuddered again.

"Now, child! Don't get into your cellar of despair again. It's like some people's cyclone cellars out West, always there ready for you, and you fly down the stairs at sign of the first little cloud that appears in your sky. Can't you remember we have a heavenly Father who is looking out for us? Get a little more trust, dear. No, of course we shall not have to give up, just for one boarder who has gone wrong. We are not obliged to keep him, you know, if he makes a disturbance. But I'd not be the first one to turn him out without another trial. What are we here for but to try to help such as he? Maybe he never was really drunk before. He is young and doesn't look to be bad. He'll be sorry enough for it all to-morrow, I'm sure, or I've mistaken the face of that picture of his mother on his bureau. A boy who has had a mother like that can't go wrong all at once. We'll do what we can for him. You have some work to do for him, dear, and you must try and forget to-night for Christ's sake!"

"Oh, aunt Hannah!" groaned Celia, "how can I ever speak to him again, after his talking that way to me, and calling me by my name, too, as if I was a little girl? The idea of his taking the liberty of speaking that way. Oh, I feel as if I never could try to help anybody again."

"Now, Celia!" said aunt Hannah, speaking rather sharply for her, "you must *not* talk that way. That wasn't Harry Knowles that spoke to you to-night. It was a demon that he had swallowed that had taken entire possession, and put out for a time the light of reason in him. You told me yourself that he has always been respectful, and he's nothing but a boy in years, much younger than you. And Celia, he is very dear to your Saviour."

Aunt Hannah's heart had gone out to the poor motherless boy, and she longed to save him from the awful destruction that she saw yawning in front of the path he was treading. Celia knew her aunt was right, and by degrees she regained her composure, and began to mount up into the first story at least of her faith, and believe that everything was not gone to destruction yet. However, she went to the store the next morning with a heavy heart. She had so great a horror of drunkards and drunkenness, and so strong a belief in the power of appetite, that she felt little or no hope of trying to save any one from the awful end of a drunkard, who had once commenced to tread that downward path. She went about all day, feeling as deep sadness as if she had witnessed the terrible death of some friend.

Miss Hannah had spent a long time in prayer that night, after she heard once more the regular breathing of Celia, and knew she was asleep. She asked God's grace to help her do what was best for this poor homeless boy, and if it might be that he would honor her with bearing the message of salvation to his soul, she would give God all the glory. Her soul longed for the soul of the boy whose feet were astray, and she was filled with a kind of divine compassion for him, such as Jesus would have us feel, such as he felt, for those for whom he died.

The minister, meantime, had put the poor boy to bed. He was docile enough, and almost grateful in a maudlin sort of way, for the help given him, and he sank at once into a deep sleep. Horace Stafford turned the gas low, and established himself by the bedside for some time, until he felt certain that there was nothing else the matter with the slumberer. Then he knelt beside the boy, and asked God's mercy for him and went to his own room.

It was not until far into the afternoon that the sleeper roused. Horace Stafford had found out by judicious questioning, and without revealing his condition to the other boarders (who fortunately had none of them heard the disturbance in the night), where the young man worked. He had then gone himself to the store, and asked for the head of the firm, giving his own card and explaining that the young salesman was ill, and unable to come to work that day. The head of the firm had been very kind. He had recognized the name of the minister as well as that of the mission chapel which he mentioned in introducing himself, thinking the word of a minister might go further toward excusing the absence of the young man, and asked kindly how the work was getting on. He said he had meant to send in a contribution to that work, but had let it slip by without attention, and he handed the minister a crisp ten dollar bill. Then he promised to see that young Knowles' place for the day was supplied, and asked to be notified if the illness should prove serious, and there was anything he could do for him. He said he liked the young man, though of course he knew but little of him, but he feared he had not good health, as he looked frail. When Horace Stafford left the store, he had a better opinion of employers than he had been led to hold from some reading he had been doing lately.

When Harry Knowles awoke that afternoon, he was conscious first of his physical condition. His head ached miserably, and he could not bear to stir. His throat burned as with fire, and all things seemed full of a ghastly horror. He opened his eyes, and the first thing he saw was his mother's picture. It stood on the bureau opposite his bed. Miss Hannah had been softly going about the room that morning, putting things to rights, and putting a touch of home here and there where she could do it in a few minutes. She had wiped the dust from the velvet and polished the glass of the frame with a damp cloth, and the clear sweet eyes of Harry's mother looked straight into his, so full of love and compassion and motherly tenderness, that Harry felt it all and suddenly realized his present condition and what had caused it. He could not bear his mother's tender love. She seemed to be looking through into his very soul. He closed his eyes to shut hers out. As he did so, all his experiences of last night came swiftly and stood before him one by one, and passed before his mother's eyes too. He seemed to know at every instant what she would be feeling about it all. He recalled his resolve to stay in, and how the boys called for him before he had settled down to doing anything, and asked him to just come out for a while; how they had coaxed him away from his resolves, and interested him in their plans for the evening. They had planned an evening at the theatre and a supper afterward, and they made him feel that he was being considered mean not to join in and help with the expenses, since they had taken his coming as a matter of course, and ordered a seat and a plate for him. They joked him unmercifully, and said they believed he had been going to Sunday-school again, and had promised his nice little teacher that he would be good. They called him a "dear little fellow," and said they wouldn't bother him any more, he should have a stick of pink and white candy so he should, and one of them actually bought it and presented it to him. He had knocked it into the street, and declared he had no intention of not joining them and bearing his share of the expense, and then they all seemed glad and turned his mind to enjoyment. "We didn't really believe you were getting to be a sissy boy," they said. His conscience had had no time to reproach him. They had not mentioned going in to any of their favorite haunts for a game— that game which he had begun to fear on account of the way it reduced his always scanty funds. They only seemed bent on having an innocent good time. Oh, they had known well how to get him into the thing. They knew they could touch something that he called his sense of honor, when they said he had left them in a tight place, as they had ordered supper for him, and if he didn't pay for it they would have to do it. And they took him to a play that was *very* funny. He enjoyed fun. There were one or two things toward the end that had brought a warm flush to his cheeks at the time, because he couldn't help thinking how ashamed his mother would be to know he was listening to and laughing at such things. But he wouldn't have had the fellows know that for anything. He had gone to that supper and been as jolly as any of them after it. But he had resolved, when he gave in to them, that he would not drink. That had been the great reason why he had tried to decline. When people offered him drink, he could always hear his mother's voice saying, "Harry dear, mother hopes you will always have courage to say no, if you are ever asked to drink wine or any strong drink." He tried to make it right with his conscience when he turned to go with the boys, by saying that he would not drink a drop.

He knew they would ask him, and it would be uncomfortable to refuse, but he had done it heretofore, and he would do it to-night. After to-night, he would try to gradually drift away from that set. It would not do to break off all of a sudden, but he would try to do it gradually. Of course he could. Had he not stayed at home that evening when Miss Murray fixed the lamp, and then again last night? Both of these times he had promised to go with the boys. He felt strong with the sense of having conquered once before. He did not remember a Bible verse then that his mother used often to quote to him, "Let him that thinketh he standeth take heed lest he fall," he only told himself that he had proved to himself that he was fully able to break off going with those boys whenever he chose, and therefore he had a right to go with them for a little innocent fun just once more.

Ah, but he did not know even now, as he lay here in his bed with shame in his heart, and the tears of repentance overflowing his eyes and trickling between the tightly closed lashes, that Satan had leagued against him last night, and that those boys had vowed to conquer his foolish protests once and for all, and get him gloriously drunk. Once let him break down that silly shame, they said, and he would be a jolly good fellow, for Harry was bright and quick-witted. Why they wanted to do it is not quite certain. Perhaps some of them were fiendish enough to want to drag him down as low as themselves, just for very love of deviltry. Others, perhaps, felt rebuked by his shrinking back at daring things which were proposed, and still others, older in their sin, liked him for his gay words and witty sayings, and were resolved to make of him a thoroughly good bad-fellow whom they could enjoy. Their experience had taught them that when one such once goes astray, he will dare more than some who never had any scruples.

Harry only knew that they had passed some cider first. They declared they had ordered it for his sake as they knew his temperance principles, and they laughed and nudged one another as it was passed and winked, and Harry felt goaded to do almost anything to prove that he was just as good, or as bad, as they were.

Now Harry was not fond of sweet cider. The few times he had tasted it, it had seemed insipid to him. He knew, indeed, that there were some people who went so far as to object to cider drinking. In a general way, he knew that there was a difference between sweet and hard cider, and it would have been well for him that night, if he had been possessed of a few decided opinions on the subject himself. He hesitated and then took some, but his hesitation was noticed and the boys had asked him if he were afraid of that too. He had flushed crimson and declared that he was not, and they had unmercifully passed his glass for more, and watched to see if he drank that. Then something else had been brought on, Harry did not just know what, whether wine or beer or something else. The cider had been by no means sweet and must have gone to his head. When they passed by his chair with the wine glasses, he had caught the whispered words and laughs of his companions over him, and turning quick without a thought for anything than to prove his— what?—cowardice? he ordered the waiter to give him some. A tremendous cheer had arisen from the boys, so loud it almost brought him to his senses. He drank that glass and another, and then he felt a feverish desire to swallow more, and they filled his glass again and again, he not asking or caring what it contained. That was the story. He did not know now, or stop to ask himself how he got here, to what he called home. He supposed it was in the same shameful way that some of the others were taken sometimes, the way that had hitherto been a strong barrier in the way of his joining in their drinking festivities. Whether any one saw or knew, he did not dare to ask. He only knew that he lay here, and that his mother's eyes were over there, and that God always seemed to be near his mother, and that he did not dare to open his eyes again. He heard the soft movement of a woman's dress, and a light step. It seemed like his mother's. He could almost think as he lay here that this was his home once more, and his mother was nursing him from some dreadful illness. Only this bed was so hard. Oh, the shame and horror if this had happened at his dear old home with his mother in it. It would have killed her. He groaned aloud, and then he heard that soft step again and wondered. Was he dead? Was this the— where? the judgment seat—perhaps? For his mother surely was there and God! Oh!—

Chapter 15

Some one stood beside him and put a large cool hand on his aching brow, and a woman's voice, gentle and low, said "Drink this."

Then, although his very being was filled with disgust at the thought of eating or drinking anything, he let himself be raised from the pillow and swallow down the hot steaming coffee that was held for him. Miss Hannah gave his pillows a shake, and he settled back again with his eyes closed. He did not care for the coffee; he wondered that he could have drunk it, and yet he knew by the aroma of it that it was unlike any coffee he had ever drank in that house before, and there gradually crept over him a sense of relief from the drinking of it. It was not that the throbbing in his temples was any less, but perhaps he felt a little better able to bear it. Miss Hannah brought a clean linen cloth and a large soft towel, and washed his hot face and hands, just as his mother used to do when he was sick, and gently smoothed his tumbled hair. He did not look at her. His eyes were closed tight, and he was trying with all his might to force back the hot tears that were surely burning their way out beneath his lashes. The tears came and Miss Hannah saw them. She stooped and kissed him softly on his forehead and said in that gentle pitying voice again, "Poor boy!" and then she slipped away and left him alone.

If Hiram Bartlett had been there he would have said that aunt Hannah was encouraging drunkenness by giving the young man so much attention; that pity was not what such a fellow needed, he ought to be soundly thrashed. He would get an idea that it was a fine thing to come home drunk, if he were petted and taken care of for it. But Hiram Bartlett was not there, and aunt Hannah was glad. She did what she felt in her inmost soul Jesus Christ would have her do, if she could hear his voice telling her.

When she slipped away and left Harry alone, it was to tap lightly on the minister's door and tell him Harry was awake.

It was not the first time that day she had been to the minister's room. She had resolved in the watches of the night that she would discover for herself what sort of a man was the stranger whom she had taken in the first night she came. He seemed to be all right, and he had helped nobly in this emergency. Now, if he only were a Christian, how much help he might be with this young man. She thought she knew a way to discover for herself without asking him, so instead of letting Molly "do his room" the next morning, she attended to that hall herself. She knew, if he were a Christian, she would be likely to find evidence of it somewhere about his room. It therefore gave her much pleasure and some surprise, when she found on entering to make the bed, not only the Bible in full view, but also a number of what appeared to be theological books. She glanced them over. There was a row of old familiar ones, in rusty bindings, "Barnes' Notes" and a few kindred commentaries standing against the wall, on the floor. There was a soap box beside them containing other volumes yet unpacked, not many, but at the top lay two of F. B. Meyer's, and Andrew Murray's "With Christ in the School of Prayer." These were dear favorites and friends of hers, and she began to hope that perhaps she was entertaining a minister. This hope was confirmed a few minutes afterward when the postman came and brought several letters for the Rev. Horace Stafford. She made his bed and set in order that room with a light in her face then, for was she not serving one of his Master's high messengers? When Mr. Stafford came in later, she had a short conference about young Mr. Knowles, and they agreed that he should go to the store, and after the young man awoke he should have a little talk with him.

Harry lay still for some minutes reviewing his miserable existence, and going over the last few months of mistakes and sins. Suddenly it occurred to him that it must be late and he ought to get up and go to his work. With a moan, he turned over and tried to get out of bed, but he was dizzy and sick, and he had to sit still and cover his eyes. He was not yet so used to dissipation that he could rise and go about like any one else the next day, and the dissipation had been deeper than he knew. What mixed or drugged glasses were given him, after he began to drink, he did not remember. Therefore, he could scarcely account for the effect they had had.

Just then there came a knock at his door and Mr. Stafford entered. He had been listening for some sound, and was ready. He wanted to help the boy when he should fully come to his senses and realize his condition, and keep him, perhaps, from rushing out to drink again. Of course, he knew nothing about Harry's past life, but he judged from his appearance and from what little he could learn of his character that this was probably a first experience, or if not the first, that at least he was not yet a hardened sinner.

"Do you feel any better?" asked Mr. Stafford, in a pleasant, every-day tone, such as he would use for any illness of any one.

Harry looked up, his bloodshot eyes and white face making a pitiful picture of wretchedness.

"I feel worse than I ever felt in my life before," he answered, all the bright gaiety with which he was usually bubbling over, gone entirely out of his voice.

"Better lie down again," said the visitor. "You are hardly able to get up yet."

"But I must get up," said Harry in a despairing tone. "What time is it? It must be late. I'll get fired if I'm not on time. They're terribly particular down there."

"Never mind the time. You're not to go to the store to-day," answered the other quietly, in a tone that seemed used to commanding obedience.

"Why not!" asked Harry sharply, looking at Mr. Stafford with sudden apprehension in his eyes. "Have they found out and sent me my walking papers already? What time is it? How long have I been here? Let me up. But it's no use if they've found out. I'm done for. I might as well go to destruction first as last," and he sank back with a groan and turned his face to the wall.

"Listen, my boy," said the young minister bending over him and placing a kindly hand on his shoulder. "Don't say that. You are not going to destruction. We won't let you. And you need not feel like that. You have not been dismissed. Your place is waiting for you when you are able to go back. The firm knows nothing but that you are too ill to be at your work today. It is afternoon, and you have slept all day. You are to lie still now until you are perfectly able to get up, and I am going to take care of you. Is there anything you would like to have?"

Harry turned over and opened his eyes in astonishment.

"How do you know I'm not to be dismissed? Has anyone been there?"

"Yes, I was there this morning and had a good long talk with Mr. Prescott. He seemed very sympathetic and asked me to send him word, if you were not better to-morrow."

Harry closed his eyes and swallowed hard. He was almost overcome by the kindness that had been shown him. Suddenly, he remembered dimly the scene of the night before.

"Say," said he, huskily, "where was I, that is—how, what did I—do? Who was down there last night when I came in? How did I get here?"

"I brought you up here," answered Mr. Stafford, quietly, in a matter-of-fact tone. "Miss Grant was present." He thought it as well that Harry should not know that Celia had been there; it could do no good and would only add to his embarrassment. "You have slept ever since," he finished briefly.

"Were the boarders around? Do they know?"

"No."

There was silence a moment. Harry was trying to recall some faint memory. At last he spoke.

"Didn't I,—Wasn't Miss Murray there too? Did I talk nonsense to her?"

The minister turned about and faced the young man and said truthfully, "Yes, she was there, and you didn't speak very respectfully to her, I must own."

Harry groaned again. "Oh, she's been very kind to me," he moaned. Then after a pause. "But yet they didn't turn me out of the house. If they had turned me out I could have stood it, but I can't stand being treated this way. I haven't been treated kindly since mother died." Then his weakened nerves gave way and he cried, as if he had been a girl.

Horace Stafford let him cry for a few minutes. He thought it might do him good. He had no mind to minimize the offence. It was grave and serious and must be realized.

Presently he began to talk in low, grave tones, and the young man on the bed ceased moaning and showed that he was listening. When he was quieter, Mr. Stafford drew from him as much of the story of the evening before as he could remember. He talked with him long and seriously about life and the true meaning of it, about the wonderful trust that God gave each one, when he put him upon the earth and gave him the responsibility of doing the best he was capable of. He drew him on to speak of his mother and his boyhood life. He did not talk too long. This man who was a fisher of men had been gifted with rare tact. He seemed to know just what to say and when to say it and, what is sometimes much more important, he knew when to keep still. He gave just the right note of warning to the young man before him, but he knew enough of human nature to see at once that here was true repentance, and deep humiliation, and that that lesson did not need to be further impressed this time. What he needed now was kindly sympathy and help to get upon his feet again.

Harry, in a pause, reverted to Celia. What should he do? He never could look her in the face again, and she had been so kind to him.

"Tell her so," said Mr. Stafford, promptly, as if it were the easiest thing in the world to do. "Just beg her pardon as manfully as you can, and then look out that you are never so placed that you will do so again."

The slender frame of the young man on the bed shook involuntarily as he said fiercely, "I should hope not."

There came Miss Grant's light tap at the door, and a dainty tray was handed in. Harry thought to himself that he could not eat, that he never could eat again, but when the tray was placed in front of him, and Mr. Stafford said in his quiet, commanding voice, "Now eat every bit of that," he found that he could.

Miss Grant knew by instinct just what to prepare for the invalid. Not dainties, and jellies and confectionery. Just a small, thin, white china bowl of very strong soup, containing much nutrition in small compass and sending forth an odor most delicious; some thin beautifully toasted slices of bread, a ball of sweet butter and more of that black aromatic coffee. The minister mentally decided that aunt Hannah must be an expert in the culinary art. So many kind women would have brought forth sour bread, muddy coffee and a piece of dyspeptic pudding or pie or cake, or perhaps tried more solid substantial foods where there was no appetite. He noted also the fineness of the napkin with which the tray was covered, the thin transparency of the china bowl, and that the spoon was apparently solid silver, old and thin as if it were an heirloom, but bright and unmistakably of aristocratic origin and pleasant withal to use. He noticed these things because they had been a part of his former existence before he had given his life up to saving souls, and because since he came to live in boarding-houses, he had sometimes missed their absence in a vague, undefined way. He had not known that he cared about these little accessories of a refined life, but he was conscious that he recognized a friendly look in that spoon and bowl and fine linen. He did not know that these things were among the very few bits of home that Miss Grant had brought with her, and that she had carefully hunted them out of a trunk that had not yet been unpacked, because she felt that perhaps these dishes might help in the work of saving that soul.

Nor was she wrong. Harry knew silver when he saw it. This lunch seemed like one his mother would have prepared for him.

"Now, sir," said Mr. Stafford, as he lighted the gas and prepared to be cheerful while the young man ate his supper, "you must forget everything about this for a while, and just eat your supper and enjoy it." He laughed pleasantly, and Harry looked up with a wan smile and thanked him in his heart for lifting the heavy burden for a few minutes. Mr. Stafford could talk, even if Harry just then could not, and he showed that he had no trouble in summoning to his command just the right thing at the right time. He began to tell in detail the story of a young man in whom he was interested, who had a wife and young family dependent upon his efforts, and who was out of work, and unable to find a position. He had spent some time that day trying to find him work, unsuccessfully, and he told his various efforts describing the different employers so well, that once Harry forgot his own troubles and was beguiled into a laugh.

Celia, passing the door just then, heard them laughing and one more little wrinkle crept into her white brow of care. She thought Mr. Stafford must be a queer minister to laugh with a young man who had recently committed so grave an offence against the laws of God and of society. Poor Celia, she had had a hard day, what with doing her own work, and carrying on her heart the thought of Harry Knowles drunk. It was not that she cared more for that boy than she would have done for any other, but it was the shock to her faith in human nature to find one whom she had believed to be at least tolerably good and interesting, suddenly appear in the condition in which he had been. Young people are often prone to look upon their faith in human nature as something akin to their faith in God, something holy and religious, which if broken outrages their belief almost in the kindness of their God. Perhaps this is the reason that sometimes, sweet honest souls have to pass through the fiery trial of believing in, even to loving, some human brother or sister, only to find them utterly false. Such need to learn the lesson of quaint George Herbert, that

> "Even the greatest griefs
> May be reliefs,
> Could he but take them right, and in their ways.
> Happy is he whose heart
> Hath found the art
> To turn his double pains to double praise."

Chapter 16

"It's my opinion," said Molly Poppleton, standing with her arms akimbo and facing Miss Grant as she entered the kitchen one morning shortly after breakfast, "that them three-cent girls need 'tendin' to." She set her lips firmly and then returned to the polishing of her range.

Miss Hannah went on with her work. She was rubbing pumpkin through a colander and reducing it to the velvety texture she always required in her pies. She waited calmly for Molly to go on with her reasons, as she knew she would soon. Molly finished the oven door and stood up again.

"Yes, they need 'tendin' to bad. If you'd just go up to their room once you'd find out. There's a stack of paper novils in their closet knee deep, an' there's pictures round that room of women from the-*ay*-tres, without much clo'es on, that are perfickly scand'lous. Besides, they've got a picture of them two took in a tin type down to Atlantic City with bathing suits on, an' two young fellers along side of 'em without much on but a little underclo'es. They are grinning fit to kill, and look real silly. No decent girls would have a picture took like that, let alone keep it round in sight afterward."

"Well, Molly, you know all girls have not been brought up alike," said Miss Hannah, as she measured out the cinnamon and ginger. "Molly, bring me the big yellow bowl and the molasses jug."

"I should hope not," said Molly, as she put the jug down on the table with a thump, and went back to her range. "Not like them, anyway. You don't know all. They have any amount of little pink and blue tickets lying round droppin' out of pockets and the like, an' I give that one they call Mamie one I picked up in the hall, thinkin' it was something valuable, an' she laughed an' said it was no good, just an old the-*ay*-tre ticket, been used. 'My land!' says I, not being able to keep still. 'If all them round your room is the-*ay*-tre tickets, you must've been an awful lot!' Then she giggled an' got red an' says, 'Yes, most every night now,' an' the other one, the one they call Carrie, she spoke up, and says she, 'Yes, she's got plenty of gentlemen friends, Molly, an' so have I,' an' then they both laughed and went out. Now I s'pose it ain't none of my business, but I must say them girls ought to be back with their mothers. They can't be over fifteen a day, or sixteen anyway. They ought to be in bed every night by nine o'clock. They ain't fit to sit at the same table with Miss Celia with their bangs and their dirty teeth and black finger nails. The fact is I'd like to give 'em both a good bath anyway."

Molly slammed out of the kitchen and Miss Hannah heard her sweeping the dining-room with all her might and main.

She went on measuring her milk and beating her eggs, and fashioning the flaky crust in the pie pans, and thinking. The fact was she had been troubled about those two girls herself. She felt that they needed a great deal of help and so far she had been utterly unable to approach them. They seemed shy and uncomfortable when she came near them, and had grown silent at the table, too, unless the tenor brakeman was present. Then the three carried on a bantering conversation in suppressed tones, with half glances toward the others. Miss Grant wondered what it was that there always seemed to be some people about her whose hearts she could not reach. It was just so with Nettie, she never could make any headway in training that child. As a little girl, she had been sullen and silent when she was remonstrated with by her aunt for any fault, and as a young woman she had been impertinent and cold for days after any attempt on the part of aunt Hannah to change her plans. With Hiram too, aunt Hannah had felt the same repellent influence and she wondered why it was, though she had prayerfully and conscientiously longed to be to these people what God wanted her to be, that she did not seem able to reach their hearts in any way. Now these two girls weighed heavily upon her. She had watched them for days and had determined to make some move pretty soon. She felt sure there was need of help for them, and urgent need, far beyond what Molly had bluntly expressed. And while aunt Hannah weighed and measured and baked and thought, she was making in her mind a plan for the salvation of Mamie Williams and Carrie Simmons.

She had noticed Mamie several times lately when Celia came to the table, and she knew that she watched Celia intently and admired her afar, at least she admired her in so far as outward adornments were concerned. Even during the few weeks since aunt Hannah had come to Philadelphia, she had noticed the gradual change in Mamie's dress, from gay and fussy and frivolous, to a style somewhat more subdued and neat. She had reduced the baggy bunches of frizzy hair that used to project over her forehead and loop far down over her ears, till they were more like Celia's graceful braids with a stray curl slipping out here and there. She still wore her many colored finger rings, but there were other little changes about her that showed she was to a certain extent making Celia a model just now. Aunt Hannah's brow cleared. She thought she knew a way to Mamie's heart and perhaps through hers to Carrie's. Celia had an influence and she could help. But how to bring that about in the wisest way, that was aunt Hannah's puzzle, for Celia was very much disgusted with the actions of the two "three-centers" as she called them. She never noticed them in any way, and her dignified bearing at the table was always meant to be a rebuke to them. Celia did not like those two girls, and while she was willing that their lives should be made more comfortable by their sharing in the good food that aunt Hannah now provided for Mrs. Morris' old boarders, still Celia would not have felt badly to have had them leave that their places might be occupied by more interesting people.

Celia was getting to be a sort of a puzzle anyway. She did not enter into some things as her aunt had supposed she would. Instead she held aloof, and seemed troubled about something. She did not even make friends with the young minister, in whom aunt Hannah saw growing possibilities of a valued friendship for them all. He and she had talked together on the themes of mutual interest, and he had shown that he was a man of culture and education. Aunt Hannah was not a matchmaker, and did not immediately think of every young man in the light of a possible husband for her dear Celia, but she did have ambitions that Celia might have friends who would be helpful in every way to her, both spiritually and mentally, and she felt that such a friendship, though it were nothing more than occasional converse on some literary theme, would be excellent for the young girl whose ambitions and abilities were so far beyond her opportunities. But Celia only smiled, and remained quiet and distant, and told aunt Hannah that the young minister belonged to her, and she must not expect her niece to take him on faith. Nevertheless, she knew that no movement or word of Mr. Stafford's at the table escaped Celia. It was evident that she was measuring him.

Celia had not entered very heartily into the plans made for Harry Knowles. She had done what she was told, it was true, but she had not made plans herself. She seemed to have received a set-back on the night when Harry came home drunk. There had been much to do in the evenings, however, and her aunt had not had time to have a good long talk with her. She felt that it ought to come at once. She put the pies in the oven, closed the oven door carefully, and glancing at the clock went to her own room to kneel as was her custom in perplexity and lay her trouble all at her Master's feet. Then she came back to her work about the house with calm brow and untroubled heart, feeling sure the way would be opened and words given her, if she must speak. She would have made a good model for a study of a saint as she stood beside the moulding board soon after and patted the smooth, light loaves into shape for their last rising, bending her sweet, thoughtful face to her work, her mind busy with the problems of souls, while she worked with her hands to feed their bodies.

It was like a revelation of what God can do in a human soul through sorrow, to look at Hannah Grant and think of her past life with its buried and risen joys.

> "Methinks we do as fretful children do,
> Leaning their faces on the window pane
> To sigh the glass dim with their own breath's stain,
> And shut the sky and landscape from their view.
> And thus, alas! since God, the Maker, drew

A mystic separation 'twixt those twain,
The life beyond us, and our souls in pain,
We miss the prospect which we're called unto
By grief we're fools to use. Be still and strong,
O man, my brother! hold thy sobbing breath,
And keep thy soul's large window pure from wrong,
That so, as life's appointment issueth,
Thy vision may be clear to watch along
The sunset consummation-lights of death."

"Auntie, who is the youth in the parlor so redolent of Hoyt's German cologne and cigarette smoke?" asked Celia, gaily, coming into her aunt's room just after dinner that night. "You opened the door for him, you ought to know. I do hope he is not a new boarder, for I'm morally certain he wouldn't be any help, and I think we have enough heathen to work for at present, don't you? Now don't tell me you called me up to ask my permission to take in that oily-looking youth, aunt Hannah."

Aunt Hannah laughed and then grew grave.

"No, dear, not that," she said, and then she drew the little rocker close beside her own and said "Sit down, dear, I want to talk to you."

"Why, aunt Hannah, what have I been doing that's naughty?" asked Celia, pretending to be scared. "This sounds like old times," but she settled herself comfortably and nestled her head lovingly on her aunt's shoulder.

"Well then, first of all, Celia, why do you act so strangely sometimes, and what is the matter with Mr. Stafford? You and he ought to be friends, and he could help much in the work you planned we should do together. You seem to me to have lost your interest in the house and everything in it, and I do not understand it. There is much that you could do and ought to do at once, and you do not seem to care to go about it."

"Why, aunt Hannah, what has the minister to do with it all? I am afraid you are mistaken in him as a helper. In fact I know you are. I had just come home that night—the night after Harry had been drinking, you know,—and was passing the door, and I heard Mr. Stafford's laugh, and then I heard Harry laugh, too, and I couldn't help hearing that Mr. Stafford was telling a funny story to Harry as I went on up the hall. Now just think of that after what had happened. A pretty minister he is, I think. He ought to have been preaching a sermon."

"Celia! Take care how you judge without knowing. You cannot tell what may have been the pointed moral of the funny story, and you do not know but the Lord could use a laugh just then to help that young man better than anything else, and he doubtless put it into the heart of his servant to know that. I believe that man has rare tact in winning souls. Be very careful, and be very slow ever to criticize the actions of a minister. His office brings him nearer to God than most men."

Celia's cheeks flushed a little. She was slightly annoyed to have her aunt speak in that way, but she respected the elder woman's opinion too much to resent the words or refuse the lesson. After a moment she said:

"Well, aunt Hannah, maybe I have been wrong, I'll try to be good." In her heart Celia had another reason for her dignified coldness toward the minister. She had recognized, after a few days, that he was a man of unusual education and refinement. She immediately began to wonder whether or not he looked down upon her, a saleswoman in a store, a poor girl, who had to earn her own living. She settled it in her mind that he probably did in a certain undefined way, though he probably did not confess such things to himself as that might have conflicted with certain Christian theories he felt himself bound to abide by. She told herself that he should see that she never expected anything in the way of courtesy even from him, and that she was one girl in the world, who was not ready to fling herself forward for companionship with any desirable young man that should chance to be thrown in her neighborhood. She had been still further strengthened in her determination by a little occurrence one evening a few days before this talk with her aunt.

The minister had gone to prayer meeting, having been busily engaged in his room all day, so that aunt Hannah had not been able to finish certain dusting and setting to rights there as thoroughly as she desired. The evening had found her hands full of some kitchen work, and she had requested Celia to slip up there when the halls were quiet, while the occupant of the room was in meeting and finish the dusting. Celia had been glad to help. She had turned the gas up and gone to work in earnest, glancing interestedly at the rows of books over the little table against the wall, and wishing she had opportunity to look them over, but she would not put so much as a hand upon them except to do her necessary work, in the absence of their owner. When she came to the bureau she had to remove some things to wipe the dust off beneath them. A Bible was lying there open before a painted miniature of a most lovely young woman. The pictured face was so beautiful that she could not but look at it again as she carefully wiped the dust from the velvet and gold of its case. The blue eyes and golden hair and the sweet intellectual face stayed in her memory, and from the fact that the miniature stood open before his Bible, she judged it was of some one quite near and dear. Celia did not reason it out in words, but she thought it well that she should maintain a maidenly dignity. However, as her aunt talked, she saw that she had carried this feeling to an absurd extremity. What was it to her what the young man thought, or how many velvet-framed girls he carried in his pocket next his heart? She was in the same house with him and must treat him with Christian courtesy, and she need not necessarily make herself prominent before his eyes either. She would try to do differently. He should henceforth be as one of the other boarders to her.

"What else, auntie?" she asked, after a minute of thought, looking up.

"Harry, next," said her aunt. "You ought to interest him in something occasionally, as you once told me you did in a lamp. He is having a very hard struggle to keep away from those companions who are after him every day now, Mr. Stafford says. He does all he can for him, but you know his meetings occupy so many evenings that he can do very little and he hasn't thought it wise to try to take him to church yet. You know he's nothing but a boy. He wants to be interested in something."

"Yes," said Celia, "I know. I'll try. But, auntie, I can't forget how he looked that night," and she shuddered. "But I'll try to get up something to help and that right away. Now what else? You always save the worst dose till the last, I know you of old. Which is it? Miss Burns or the tenor brakeman? Or—O *auntie,* now it *isn't* those three-centers! Don't tell me to try to do something for them, for I can't," and the girl put up her hands in mock horror.

Miss Grant detailed to her what she knew of them, including an account of Molly's moralizing on the subject, and Celia laughed, and then grew grave.

There came a call to the kitchen for Miss Grant then and she left Celia thinking. When she returned a few minutes later she was greeted with "Aunt Hannah, are those boards still in the cellar? Are they of any use there? Because if they are not I'm going to make a cozy corner in the parlor if you don't object. I've thought of a beautiful way. Harry will help, I'm sure. He sat in the parlor looking glum when I came up. Do you suppose I must get the three-centers to help? Would they come, do you think? And say, by the way, auntie, who did you say that oily youth in the parlor was?"

"His name, he said, was Mr. Clarence Jones and he asked for Miss Simmons. I called her and I think she went out with him, for I don't see either of them about. I don't know whether Mamie Williams is in her room or not. I think it would be a good plan to see. By all means make as many cozy corners as you please, dear, and the boards are of no use to me."

Celia departed to find her helpers, and Miss Hannah locked the door and prayed for them before she went about darning some table-cloths.

Chapter 17

"Now, Harry, where are you going?" said Celia, with dismay in her voice, as she ran down the stairs and saw that young man with his overcoat on and his hat in his hand just opening the front door.

He started and looked guilty as she spoke. In truth, he had been sitting in the parlor for an hour trying to keep himself in the house, and away from an especially alluring evening the boys had held out as bait; and one, too, which seemed, from their account of it, to be perfectly harmless.

He hesitated and stammered out:

"Nowhere, I guess," and then laughed and sat down in the hall chair. "Is there anything I can do for you, Miss Murray? The fact is I don't quite know what to do with myself tonight, for some reason."

Celia's heart filled with pity for the poor lonely fellow and with remorse that she had not sooner attempted to do something to cheer him up.

"Oh, I'm so sorry," she said, earnestly, with a true ring of her voice which he recognized at once, "But if you are lonesome and really have nothing pressing to do, why take off your coat and come and help me carry out a scheme. I'm going to make a cozy corner in the parlor. In fact, I think I'll make two, one in the bay window and one over there by the organ. Will you help? You're such a good carpenter, you know, and this parlor does look so bare and desolate."

"All right, I'm with you," answered the young man, taking off his overcoat with alacrity. "Only tell me what to do. I don't know the first thing about cozy corners, but if you know as much as you did about

128

lamps, I'll be willing to say they'll be a success. Let's have a half-dozen of 'em if you say so. Now what'll I do first?"

"Bring that lamp and come down into the cellar. Wait, I don't know whether you can do it alone, they are pretty heavy and there are a good many. Perhaps Mr. Hartley or Mr. Osborn would help a minute in bringing up the boards. I'll show you what we want first, and then you can pick out the right boards. You see I want a good firm seat here in the bay window to fill the whole place to the edge of the window frames either side, just a foot from the floor, so, and then I want another over here, to reach from here to here, so wide, and the same height from the floor. Here is my tape measure. Now you can pick out your lumber." Celia moved about the dull uninteresting parlor, furnishing it with gesture and imagination, till the young carpenter was quite interested. He called the two young men upstairs, who came willingly and helped for a few minutes showing not a little interest and curiosity in the undertaking. They all lingered with advice and offers to help, and when Celia had seen the carpentry work well started, she ran upstairs and knocked at the door of the two young girls.

"Come in," drawled the voice of some one chewing, and after a moment's hesitation she entered.

Mamie Williams lay across the foot of the bed, the two pillows and a comforter under her head, the gas turned as high as it would go, and a paper covered volume in her hand. She was chewing gum. When she saw that it was Celia who had entered, her tone of indifference changed to one of pleased surprise. She sat up quickly and hid her book beneath the pillows. Then she put her hand up to straighten her hair.

"Why, is it you!" she exclaimed, and Celia knew that her aunt's conjecture that she was admired by this girl was true, from the evident pleasure the visit gave. This unbent Celia still more, and she tried to be winning. When Celia tried she was very winning indeed.

"We are having some fun downstairs fixing up that old barn of a parlor," she explained, still standing by the door, though her hostess had slipped from the bed and cleared a chair from a pile of clothing thrown upon it. "I thought maybe you would like to help. Is your friend here?"

"No, she ain't, she's gone out with a gentleman friend," said Mamie, with a conscious giggle. "It's a wonder you found me in. I'm mostly out when she is. Sit down, can't you? I'm really glad you come up, I was lonesome. The book I had wasn't any account either. What did you say you was doing?"

Celia essayed to explain and succeeded in interesting Mamie to the extent that she hunted out her thimble from a mass of ribbons and collars tumbled into a bureau drawer, and went downstairs to see what was going on, though she confessed she was not much used to doing things like that.

They went to work in good earnest. Celia had some printed burlap, which she had brought home from the store one night to make curtains for an improvised clothespress, in her room. It was cheap and there was plenty of it. The clothespress could wait. Those cozy corners must be finished to-night, at least as far as possible. She gave the tick of the cushions to Mamie to run the seams, while she applied herself to sewing the burlap cover for it. Meanwhile, the hammering and sawing and directing went forward, and by half-past nine when Mr. Stafford opened the front door and came in there were two very solid looking rough wooden shelves a foot from the floor, in the parlor, one occupying the entire bay window space in the front of the room, the other one being at the further end of the room. To the sides of this Harry Knowles was just nailing some more boards to serve as ends, under the supervision of the other two young men, while Celia and Mamie were upon their knees in front of the bay window tacking the dark blue burlap printed in a heraldic design, in a pleated valance. A nearly completed cushion lay beside them on the floor, but not tied as yet. Mr. Stafford, attracted by the unusual noises, entered the room and stood behind them looking at the work a moment. Then, as Celia turned from the valance and attempted to thread a large needle with a cord and then vainly endeavored to pull its short proportions through the thick cushion, which had been stuffed with excelsior and a layer of cotton on the top, he said quietly:

"You need an upholsterer's needle for that, Miss Murray. I think I have one upstairs that we used in fixing up the pulpit chairs at the mission. I'll go and get it."

Celia was pleased that he entered into the work and thanked him. As he turned toward Harry, he said, "Knowles, why don't you put springs in? It would be twice as comfortable."

"Springs!" said Harry jumping up and facing round. "Do you expect us to turn into upholsterers the first night?" and he laughed good-naturedly.

"No, but indeed it isn't a difficult job," explained the minister, "you just have to tie them down firmly. I'll show you if you don't mind running out with me to that little upholsterer's around the corner. I think it's open yet. It was when I came by. The people live over the store and they don't shut up shop early."

"By all means, let us have springs," answered Celia to Harry's look of enquiry, "I didn't look for such luxury as that, but we will take what grandeur we can get." Her cheeks had grown red with excitement, and her eyes were shining. The minister, as he turned to go on his self-appointed errand, was reminded of the first evening he had come to that house. Harry and Mr. Stafford were soon back with several sets of springs and the three young men, with Celia demurely in the background, took a lesson in putting in springs, which they found to be not such a very difficult matter after all. The minister had not forgotten to get some small dark blue cotton upholstery buttons when he was out, and Mamie and Celia soon learned how to use the queer double pointed needle and tie the cushion with the little buttons. Altogether it looked very pretty, and quite like real upholsterer's work when it was finished.

In spite of the proverbial "many hands" and "light work," it was nearly eleven o'clock when the two seats were finished, and a light frame work over the seat in the back end of the parlor erected. Miss Hannah had come down to send them all to bed, but found them in a state of childish enthusiasm to see their work completed. Celia had remembered that she had upstairs two or three pieces of plain and printed denim and some turkey red calico. Mounted on the stepladder beside the canopy frame, she deftly draped the rough wood, being materially assisted by Mr. Stafford who seemed to understand what she wanted to do, and to be able to drape a graceful fold of cloth, if he *was* only a man, and that a minister. He, by way of contribution, brought down a Chinese sword made of coins which the Chinese use as a talisman, for the purpose of frightening away evil spirits, and hung it above the drapery. This roused the others to emulate his example. The university student thought he knew where he could get a couple of Arabic spears to help out that canopy drapery, and Harry Knowles declared he would hunt around and find one of those dull old filigree bull's-eye lanterns that hang by long chains from the centre. Mamie said her contribution should be a couple of sofa pillows, and Celia promised to make some more. Miss Burns, coming in just then looking weary and worn, brightened as she came into the parlor and exclaimed over the new furnishings, "They are simply,—now—simply—*fine*— aren't they, Miss Grant? Indeed they *are!* What *wonderful* taste and *skill* has been exhibited here! I declare it is *simply marvelous! Simply fine!* Indeed—*indeed*—it is!" she giggled wearily. She asked permission to contribute a pillow also.

"Now we need a low bookcase running along that wall and turning that corner," said the minister, as they turned to go to their rooms. "Can't you manage that, Knowles?" and Celia's eyes sparkled over the idea. The minister evidently understood esthetics anyway. The bookcase would be a great addition. She went upstairs so excited over her new work she could hardly sleep. She had almost forgotten her three-cent protégée, till Mamie squeezed her hand over the stair railing and said, "Good-night, Miss Murray, I've enjoyed myself ever so much. And say, would you mind coming into my room a few minutes tomorrow night? I want to ask you some questions very particular."

Celia promised readily enough, though the prospect was not a pleasant one, but she had made up her mind to try to help this girl, so she might as well accept the situation and the opportunity together.

But aunt Hannah sat up that night till nearly one o'clock, and looked over the stair railing till she heard the night key click, and saw the befeathered hat of Carrie Simmons as she came airily in.

"Poor child!" murmured the watcher, as she turned out the hall light and went to bed, "something must be done! Out till one o'clock and with that kind of a young man!"

The next morning she noticed that Carrie had dark rings under her eyes, and was developing thin, sharp lines about her nose and mouth, which did not add beauty to her pert, weak face.

The next evening as Celia started for Mamie Williams' room, Carrie having again departed with the aforementioned youth, aunt Hannah called her. "Celia dear, two things," she said, with her hand on Celia's arm. "Don't forget to pray before you go, and if you get a chance mention soap and water. Don't forget that cleanliness is next to godliness. Perhaps in this case it comes first." Celia laughed and said, "All right, auntie," and went back to her room to take the first advice given.

Reinforced by a turning of her heart to her heavenly Father for guidance, she went to her unpleasant task, her mind more than half full of the new bookcase and some other plans she had for the adornment of the parlor. The minister seemed to have taken Harry Knowles away with him immediately after dinner, so she had no one to help her carry out any parlor schemes just at present, and she could not help being disappointed that she must turn aside to another piece of work.

Mamie was evidently expecting her this time. She had given the room some semblance of a clearing up: that is, she had picked up Carrie's old store dress from the floor where she left it, and tumbled everything that was out of place on the bureau and table into a drawer, for the confusion of some future hour of need.

She seemed to be in earnest, and plunged at once into her subject when she had seated Celia.

"Say, I thought maybe you wouldn't mind telling me how you do it. You see I thought you wasn't any more pretty than I, and you haven't got expensive clo'es, but you manage somehow to look awful stylish and pretty in spite of it. I know it takes a knack, but don't you think I could learn? I've been trying ever since you came here to do my hair the way you do, but I can't make it act right. I thought maybe you wouldn't mind doing it a few times for me, to get me started, and perhaps you could tell me what the difference is between you and me. I know it ain't very polite to ask you things like this, but I thought you was so kind last night asking me to help that I'd just be bold and ask you. You ain't mad, are you?"

Celia ignored the doubtful compliments and tried to smile, albeit her very soul shrank within her. What, handle the coarse greasy hair of that girl who seemed actually dirty to her? How could she? Surely the Lord did not require that sacrifice. Why had she undertaken this task anyway? It was *dreadful*. She half rose from her chair, as she began to foresee the magnitude of the possible proportions of this proposition. What might she not be asked to do? Then she remembered whose she was and whom she served, and sank back again in her chair, putting up a petition for help to her heavenly Father.

> "What is prayer? . . .
> 'Tis the telegraphic cord,
> Holding converse with the Lord;
> 'Tis the key of promise given
> Turning in the lock of heaven."

Chapter 18

"Do you think I'm too homely to fix up?" anxiously asked Mamie, as her visitor did not at once respond.

"Oh no, indeed!" said Celia, laughing, "I was only trying to think how to answer you, and it's so funny for you to want to copy me. I have never tried to be 'pretty' as you call it. I only tried to be clean and neat, and have things look as nice as I could without spending much money. But now that you've asked me, if you really want to know how you could improve your appearance, in my eyes at least, I'll try to tell you a few things. What is it that troubles you most? We'll begin with that."

"Oh my sakes!" giggled Mamie. "There's so many things. Well, my hands and my feet. They're so big, and in the way. My hands are red and rough and bony, and my face is always breaking out in little ugly black pimples, and my hair won't get into any shape I want it to, and my teeth aren't pretty, and then of course my clothes, and I just *wish* I could walk across a room like you," she finished with a sigh.

Celia laughed and began,

"Your hands," she said, "let me see them." She turned up the gas and surveyed them critically a moment, while Mamie waited in breathless anxiety comparing her red, beringed fingers to Celia's small white ones.

"Well, if I were you I would take all those rings off first," said Celia, decidedly. "They look gaudy and out of place, except perhaps on a woman in society, and even then I should prefer to see just one or two at a time, and not a whole jewelry store at once."

Mamie looked disappointed. She drew them off slowly. "I thought they were pretty," she said, the least bit of dismay in her voice. "Don't you like any rings?"

"Not for young girls,—unless they mean something. Have you any that have tender associations?"

"Some," simpered Mamie looking conscious.

Celia ignored or did not understand this answer. "Which one?" she asked. "Did your mother, or father, or brother, or sister give it to you?"

Mamie blushed. "Well, yes, I have got one ma give me, but it isn't any of them. It's a little plain gold thing, looks kind of out of style now. I don't wear it any more."

"I'd wear that one," said the oracle, "and put the others all away. You're too young to have rings given you to wear by strangers. Now about training those hands, I can give you some little exercises that they gave me when I was taking music lessons, which I think help the hands to be graceful. First, if I were you, I would go into the bathroom and give them a good washing in hot soap suds, finishing off with cold water. That will make them more pliable. Have you a nail brush? You ought to have one. There is nothing like it for making the nails look rosy. I suppose you find great trouble in keeping them clean, working all day, don't you? I do. But a nail brush makes the work much easier. I would cut the nails more in this shape if I were you, see?" Celia held out one seashell tipped hand to be inspected.

When the hands were duly scrubbed, Celia gave her a short lesson in Delsarte, an exercise for each joint of the finger and hand. Mamie's eyes sparkled and she proved herself an apt pupil. "Now," said Celia, "practice that, but be sure you never do it where any one can see you. It will have its effect on your movements in time, but never practice in public. Don't think about your hands. That's the best way to do. If they are clean they will take care of themselves, and the more you think about them and think how awkward they are, the more awkward they become. Did you never try making people stop staring at you by looking hard at their feet in the street cars? Well, try it some time. It is very funny. I have been annoyed once or twice by somebody staring at me till I was very uncomfortable. I remembered what I had read somewhere, and looked down at their feet as if I was very much interested in them. They very soon took their eyes from me and began to draw their feet back out of sight and to fidget around and wonder what was the matter with their shoes."

Mamie laughed and looked at her new teacher with admiration. She began to think she had made a mistake in saying Celia was not pretty.

"Now the complexion," began Celia again in a business-like tone. "Your general health will affect that. You ought not to eat much fat or sweets for one thing, and you ought to bathe all over every day and rub your skin till it's all in a glow. That will make a great difference in the complexion. How often do you bathe?"

"Oh my!" gasped Mamie, "I do hate to take a bath. Why, ma used always to scrub us children all around oncet a week, and I s'pose I'd ought to keep that up, but sometimes I do skip a week, it's so dreadful cold in the morning."

"Well, if I were you I would bathe every day, for a while anyway. You don't know what a lot of good it will do you, and after a while you will get to love it. Once a week you ought to have a thorough wash with warm water and plenty of soap, and finish off with a cold dash, and a good hard rub, and then every morning take a sponge off in cool water and a good rubbing. That you will find will make your complexion very different. Then I would give the face some treatment of hot and cold water. Wash it in water just as hot as you can stand it every morning and then in very cold. That will make your cheeks have some color, too, I think. As for your teeth, let me see them. Oh, Mamie, it's too bad to let such nice even teeth get into such a condition. They are hopelessly black, and you can't get them white yourself. Do you brush them every day, after every meal?"

"My land, no!" exclaimed Mamie. "What an awful nuisance that would be! I never had a tooth brush but once, and then Carrie used it to scrub the ink off her fingers when she was going to the theatre."

Celia could scarcely repress the exclamation of disgust that rose to her lips on this announcement, but Mamie was luckily too interested in her own words to hear.

"Don't you think I could ever do anything with my teeth?"

"Why yes, you must go to a dentist at once and have them attended to. They need a good cleaning, and while you are there you ought to have him go over your teeth and put them in first-class order. It doesn't pay to let your teeth go before you are a woman yet. He will tell you how to take care of them. You ought not to eat much candy or to chew gum. That injures the teeth."

"Oh!" said Mamie, in a sort of despair. "You don't have much fun, do you, if you try to do all them things? But I don't mind, for I do want to look pretty, an' I'm willin' for it all, if it'll do any good."

Celia's pulses quickened, for she thought if this girl would do so much for the outward adorning, perhaps she might be able some time to persuade her to do as much for the beautiful inward adorning of a meek and quiet spirit which is in the sight of God of great price.

"Then your hair," went on Celia, "needs to be washed often. I would wash it first with powdered borax in the water. It isn't good to use borax often, for it makes the hair so brittle it breaks, but it will take out the extra oil now, and that is what you need. Then it will need to be thoroughly rinsed, and dried and combed. After that you can do almost anything you want to with it. I'll let you watch me do mine once, and then you will see how it is done. That is the best way to learn. And then about your dress, why that is a long subject. You will need to take a lot of time for that. You'll have to decide things one at a time. One rule I go by, in buying. I never buy a thing that is in the very extreme of fashion, because for one reason it will look queer very soon, and for another it is sure to be poor material, or else it is very expensive. It is always best to get good material. The plainer things are the better, you can be sure, as a general rule. Then you ought to study your complexion and eyes and buy things to become you. You will excuse me, if I mention the necktie you have on. I don't think you ought ever to wear that color. Cerise may be becoming to some people with dark eyes and a very clear complexion, but it ought not to be worn by blue-eyed people with light brown hair. Dark blue would be more becoming to you. Then too, I think a necktie is an unbecoming thing on you anyway. You would look much better in a close, round collar."

Mamie looked down at her cherished silk scarf, to be able to buy which she had gone without new stockings for some time. Her mind was something akin to the maiden's about whom our grandmothers used to tell, who said: "I ken wear my palm-leaf and go bare-footed, but I *must* have a buzzom pin."

Celia's zeal was perhaps on the eve of getting the better of her wisdom. She was growing interested in making over this girl as her aunt was interested in making over Mrs. Morris' boarding-house, and she forgot that there were probably a long line of prejudices to be overcome before the girl would be willing to walk in the way laid out for her, even though she had asked to be directed in that path. It would look thorny to her at first.

"Mamie," she said, seeing the downcast expression on the young girl's face, "don't get discouraged with all these new things. You can't do every one of them right at first, but, do you know, I think it makes a great difference when people try to be and look the best that is in them. You must not think you are a homely looking girl. You are not. You were meant to be a pretty one, and I think you can make yourself look ever so much prettier, I do indeed. Now I wonder if you would be willing to do something just to please me."

"Why of course I would!" said Mamie, readily enough and brightening up at the encouraging words. "What is it? You've been awful kind to me and I sha'n't forget it, Miss Murray," she added.

"Well then, it is this. You see out in Cloverdale, where I used to live, I belonged to a little society of girls. We were each pledged to read one verse of the Bible every day, and to pray every day, and when some of us left the home and the society, we each promised to try and get up another band where we were going, even if we could get but one other person to join it. Now I was wondering if you wouldn't join it to start my new circle? We called ourselves the Bible Band. I believe there are a good many such bands all over the country. We have this little gold badge. Isn't it pretty?" and Celia held out a tiny scarf pen with a pendant gold heart, on which were the letters engraved B. B. "If you will join us, I'll give you this pin of mine, and I can send and get another."

Mamie grew interested as soon as she saw the pin. Jewelry of all sorts was attractive to her. It would be quite delightful to appear in the store with a new pin on, engraved with mysterious letters, and let the girls and the young men there try to guess what they meant. Of course she didn't need to tell them if she didn't want to. She asked again what would be required of her, though Mamie belonged to the class, from which are derived so many untrue members of the Christian Endeavor societies, and, sad to say, also of the church; that class who are eager and willing to join anything, and care very little what obligations they thus take upon themselves; as little as they care when they break these solemn vows. To such, indeed, might apply the many and various arguments against pledge taking, not because pledge taking is bad, but because the pledgers themselves are not made to understand the solemnity of the pledge they take. Mamie cared very little what pledge she took, so long as the performing of it might be done in private and at her own discretion. She did not stop to think long, but accepted the pledge card and donned the pin with pride, thanking Celia.

"Though I ain't much of a hand at prayin', Miss Murray, I never could think of anything to say when I was a little girl, and ma used to make us say our prayers every Saturday night. I guess I could learn a prayer and say the same one every time, if that would do. You write me out one, can't you? 'Course I'll do it to please you, you've been so good to me, and I'm awfully obliged for this pin. It's a beauty, and won't I have fun to-morrow at the store with it? Say, I don't mind telling you why I want all this fixin' up to be pretty, you know. You won't tell Carrie, will you? I wouldn't have her know, for the first you'd see her settin' up to the same thing. Why, you see it's this way. There's a new boss to our store. The head of the firm's going out to Chicago, and he's put this feller, Mr. Adams, Harold Adams his name is, in at the head. He's only just nineteen or twenty, though he made them think he was twenty-one, but he's dreadful smart. His father's been at the head of a three-cent store in Baltimore for a long time, and he kind of growed up in the business. He's handsome, too, and everybody likes him, and the girls will just stand on their heads to please him, and you see he's been payin' me attention for four weeks now, takin' me to theatres, and gettin' me flowers and candy, and all the other girls was hoppin' mad. They've just done everything they could to get him to look at them, but he never did till there come a new girl to the china teacup counter. She has gold hair and I believe she paints her cheeks, and she's awful stylish, and has the littlest mite of a waist, and he's just gone clean crazy over her. He's nice to me yet, but she gets half the flowers now, and I want to get him back. You see, I don't mind telling you I'm in love with him myself, and of course I ain't willin' to just give him up without tryin', so I made up my mind if I could get to be good lookin' an' stylish, maybe I could do something."

Before Celia had time to collect her thoughts, and say something in response to this startling disclosure, there came a hurried knock at the door, and Molly Poppleton's strong voice demanded, "Is Miss Celia there? Miss Hannah, she wants her right away bad. That old lady up-stairs's got a fainting spell. She says to come right away."

Celia dropped everything and ran. She wondered afterward if the heavenly Father arranged that call to her for just that moment on purpose to prevent her saying anything to Mamie, for she felt sure if she had spoken then she would have expressed her mind in what might have proved, for the sake of her influence on the girl, the wrong words.

> "Blind unbelief is sure to err,
> And scan his work in vain;
> God is his own interpreter,
> And he will make it plain."

Chapter 19

Old Mrs. Belden was made comfortable at last. It appeared that she had worked too hard for the last three weeks, sitting up far into the night to finish an order. She was a knitter of fancy hoods, sacques, socks and mittens. Miss Hannah, while she ministered to her, heard a feeble account of the poor soul's life. Her husband and her children were all dead, except one boy who was a sailor, and who, perhaps, might be dead, too, for she had not heard from him for over four years. She resorted to the only thing she knew how to do to earn her living, and it had been pretty hard work sometimes, though, perhaps, no harder than many another woman had to do. She was very thankful for the good food which had come in with the advent of Miss Grant. She murmured her gratitude in an apologetic way for everything that was done for her, and said she did not see why they made so much trouble, they might just as well have let her slip quietly away, if it had been the Lord's will. Her life wasn't worth much anyway, and she was only making a lot of trouble that would all have to be done over again pretty soon, maybe. Miss Hannah and Celia had looked around the room and resolved that there should be more comforts there before another night, and when she was at last ready for sleep, and they felt sure that all she needed to restore her to her usual health was a good rest, they left her, with a promise from Molly Poppleton, whose room was next to Mrs. Belden's, that she would sleep with one ear open and step in occasionally to see that she was all right and give her anything she needed.

Celia sat down on the bed and rested her forehead on the footboard, after she and her aunt had gone to their room for the night.

"Aunt Hannah," she said, "I'm just discouraged. There are so many things to worry about in the world I don't see how I can keep from it."

"Celia! Celia!" said aunt Hannah, laying her hand on the brown head bent on the footboard, "is my little girl questioning the wisdom of God? You sound like a little child, to-night, who thinks his parents cruel that they will not give him fire to play with. Remember that God knows all, and that he does all for good. It may be that old lady needs just the kind of thing she is going through now to fit her for heaven. I do not know whether she is getting ready for heaven or not. Maybe God had to call her to himself by taking all her dear ones first, or maybe she is set to be a help to some one else,—perhaps you. Does my little girl doubt him because she cannot see and understand? Oh, Celia! You will grieve him."

"Well, auntie, I did not mean all that, of course, only I am so tired and disheartened. I meant to try to plan a grill work for the parlor to-night, and I couldn't find Harry at all. I am afraid he has gone out again with those dreadful fellows. What is the use in trying to do anything with setbacks all the time?"

"But your heavenly Father had another plan for you to-night, and the parlor can wait, you know. As for Harry, I think he is safe in his room by this time. He went out with the minister, and while you were up with Mrs. Belden they came in with a lot of boards and screws and a saw and hammer and a pot of varnish, and they went to work in good earnest. The other young men went down and helped, and in the morning I think you will find something new in the parlor. Didn't you smell new varnish? They asked for you before they began, but I told them how you were occupied and said I was sure you would want them to go ahead and not wait for you."

Celia sat up and smiled through her tears.

"Did they really, auntie? How nice! What did they make? A book-case? I am sure it must have been that, for Mr. Stafford spoke of it, and asked me if I did not like the low kind running around the room. I am so glad. And Harry stayed in! I was afraid he was with those awful young men again."

She brushed away the tears and began to take down her hair, when she remembered another discouragement.

"Oh, aunt Hannah," she said, "but you don't know what an utter failure my three-cent enterprise was," and she gave a detailed account of her interview with Mamie Williams.

Miss Grant listened intently, sometimes laughing with Celia, and sometimes looking grave over possibilities of danger for the girl, which perhaps the younger woman hardly understood. When she had finished, Miss Grant's face was very serious.

"Celia, dear, you have made a good beginning. Your first trial was by no means a failure, and I do not believe you half understand in what great need of help that young girl stands. She has revealed volumes in her few frank sentences. Be careful that you keep her confidence, and ask to be guided in what you shall say, that you may be both wise as a serpent and harmless as a dove. That is one of the greatest gifts God gives to his workers, and it needs to be carefully watched and tended daily to keep it fit for work,—that mixture of wisdom and gentleness."

"But, auntie," said Celia, doubtfully, "do you believe I can ever accomplish anything? What is the good of getting such a girl to read a verse every day in the Bible? As likely as not, she will choose one among the minor prophets, which won't mean anything to her, and as for praying, she said she did not know how. What good will it do her to pray, 'Now I lay me down to sleep' for instance, every night, not meaning a word of it, nor scarcely knowing what she is saying?"

"Remember, Celia, it is his work. You have not to do with the end of it, nor are any results in your hand. Don't you know he says, 'Ye have not chosen me, but *I* have chosen *you,* and ordained you, that ye should go and bring forth fruit, and that your fruit should *remain:* that whatsoever ye shall ask of the Father in my name, he may give it you.' After I read that verse I always feel comforted to do the work without seeing the results, knowing that God has planned all that out from the beginning, and all I have to do is to execute the little part of the plan which he has entrusted to my hand. As for saying that such a girl will not get any good out of the Bible, you talk as if you did not believe in the Holy Spirit, Celia. Will he not guide her to the right words that will help her? And do you not remember that the Bible says about itself, that it is written so plainly that 'he who runs may read' and that the way of life is made so plain that the 'wayfaring man, though a fool, need not err therein'? Then even if her heart and her lips do not know how to pray, if she truly tries to kneel and present herself every day before her Maker, don't you believe he can find ways and means to speak to her heart and teach her lips the right phrases? It is a great thing to have a habit of prayer, even though your heart is not always in it, for you at least bring your body to the trysting-place with God, and give him a little chance to call to the inattentive heart. Don't you know how Daniel had a habit three times a day of praying with his face toward Jerusalem?"

"Oh yes, aunt Hannah, I see it all. You always have a Bible verse ready for every one of my doubts and murmurs. I wish I had the Bible all labeled and put away in the cabinets of my brain the way you have, ready to put my hand on the verse I need at the right time," interrupted Celia, laughing, and putting her arms around aunt Hannah's neck to kiss her. "Come now, it's late and you look tired. I'll be good and go to bed without fretting any more, and to-morrow I'll try to think up more ways of helping that feather-headed girl."

Meantime, up in the third story room of the "three-cent" girls, quiet and darkness reigned. Miss Simmons had come in a few moments before, tired and cross. Her mind was wrought up by a play she had just witnessed, and she had been quarreling with her escort about something which she did not deign to explain to her roommate, so they had gone to bed at last without the usual giggling confidences, and Mamie lay there in the darkness thinking over her evening and the advice given her, and wondering what the adorable Mr. Harold Adams would think of the changes in her when she had been fully made over to suit her new guide. Suddenly she sat straight up in bed with a jerk, which threw the clothes off Miss Simmons' shoulders, and exclaimed:

"My land alive! If I didn't forget the very first night," and with that she flung herself out of bed, and striking a match, relit the gas.

"What in the world is the matter with you, Mame?" said Miss Simmons, pulling the bed clothes up angrily. "I was fast asleep and you woke me up! Turn that gas out and come back to bed! Come! We won't be fit to get up in the morning, if you keep rampaging round all night."

But Mamie imperturbably proceeded with what she was doing. She tumbled two great piles of paper-covered books over in the closet, searched among a motley collection of boxes, old hats and odds and ends on the closet shelf, and then began hunting in the bottom of her trunk. It was some minutes before she succeeded in finding what she wanted, and by that time Miss Simmons was asleep. Mamie drew forth from an entanglement of soiled ribbons and worn-out garments a small, fine-print red Bible with an old-fashioned gilt clasp. It was stained on one side and blistered as if a tumbler of water had been left standing wet upon it. Mamie remained seated on the floor beside her trunk while she turned over the leaves rapidly, intent upon keeping the letter of her promise in as short a time as possible, for the furnace fire was low for the night and she was beginning to feel cold. She opened near the beginning of the book and chanced upon a list of long, hard names which she could not pronounce. Perhaps her conscience would have been eased as well by a verse there as anywhere, but it was too much trouble for her unaccustomed mind to pronounce the words to herself, so she opened again at random toward the end, and letting her eye run down the page in search of something attractive and brief, she was caught by this verse:

"And to her was granted that she should be arrayed in fine linen, clean and white: for the fine linen is the righteousness of saints."

"Well now, ain't that funny!'" she said to herself, as she paused to read it over before she turned out the gas again. "That seems kind of like her talk. Dressed in fine linen! It would be kind of nice and pretty, and real stylish, too, if it was tailor-made. I saw a girl on Chestnut street last summer in a tailor-made white linen that was awful pretty. It sort of rustled as if there was silk underneath, and her hair was all gold and fluffy under a big white hat with chiffon on it. She looked real elegant. It would take an awful lot of washing though, to keep her in fine linen 'clean and white.' "

She glanced at the verse again with her hand outstretched to turn out the gas, and read it over once more, and then got into bed. "For the fine linen is the righteousness of the saints!" "Well, it does seem a sort o' saint-like dress, now that's so, and come to think of it, Miss Murray, she's got a sort of a saint face. I knew it was something kind o' strikin', and I couldn't think what, 'cause you wouldn't exactly call her pretty, and yet she ain't the other thing, and some folks—most folks maybe— would like it better than to have her pretty. Maybe it's because she's got the righteousness this talks about. She does look like a saint, that's certain. Anyway, she will when she's as old as Miss Grant. Miss Grant, now, she's a saint sure! And she would look nice in a fine linen dress all white, too. I wish she'd put one on some time, so I could see. How funny it is to have the Bible talk about dress. I supposed the Bible thought clo'es was wicked. I'm sure the Sunday-school teachers always say you mustn't think about 'em. Well, that's a pretty verse anyhow. I wonder who it was that had that fine linen dress granted to her, and if she wore it all the time, that is, clean ones every day, all fresh and crisp! My! I wish 'twas me! Wouldn't I be happy though! I guess this reading's going to be real interesting, maybe. I never thought there could be any verse in it like that. Most things I've read before was about sinning and dying and heaven, and scarey things like that. Anyhow, I've kept my promise. Why, no I haven't, either!" she exclaimed aloud, and suddenly bounced out of bed again, to the detriment of her bed-fellow's temper.

She knelt down beside the bed, and her thoughts paused a brief moment, while she tried to put her mind in praying frame. She tried to think how to pray aright. She wanted to feel the satisfaction of having performed this duty that she had felt in her Bible reading. She must ask for something. She was conscious of a vague wish in her heart that she were good enough and had friends great enough that this that she had read of might be granted to her, to be arrayed in spotless, neat apparel, beautiful, and given by the love of some one who cared for her above others. How to put such a thought into fitting phrase, or even if this were done, whether it would be a proper wish to express in prayer she did not know. At last she whispered, "Oh God—" and paused, and waited and tried to collect some better words, and then murmured again, "Oh God—" and then—"Amen."

When she lay down to rest again, it was with a sense of awe upon her which would not let her sleep for some time. She had been near to the great God, and touched as it were the hem of his garment, with curious perfunctory fingers, like a child who had been dared to do a certain thing, and coming, curious, unthinking, heedless, had touched and suddenly felt the power and greatness and beauty of that which he had touched, and had stolen away ashamed.

Altogether Mamie Williams was not as satisfied with her first effort at prayer as she had been with her Bible reading. But yet in heaven it was recorded, "Behold, she prayeth!"

Chapter 20

The next day was Sunday.

Celia had wakened early, in spite of the fact that she was up late the night before. She lay thinking over the changes that had come into her life, and wondering how things were going to work out. Somehow there seemed a cloud over what she had been trying to do. She had not accomplished much with Harry. She had kept him in the house a few evenings, it is true, and interested him in a few good books, but nothing really to much purpose after all. To be safe from all the temptations that beset his path every day, he needed to be anchored on the Rock of Christ. She did not feel that she knew how to help him in that way, he was such a bright fellow, so ready to laugh. She thought of the minister and the influence he seemed to have over the young man, and felt half indignant at him for not exercising it in a religious way, instead of merely a personal one, and then she realized that she knew nothing at all about what influences he was using, and ought not to judge him. For aught she knew, he had spoken to him many times. How unjust she had been! Then she remembered what her aunt had told her about the improvements made last evening in the parlor, and jumped up to dress and run down to see them. Aunt Hannah had already completed her toilet and gone down to the kitchen to help Molly Poppleton, and to direct the new waitress who had been in the house but three days.

Celia was delighted with the bookcase. Somebody had an artistic eye and constructive ability. The bookcase was exactly the right height, and filled the long bare wall on one side of the room beautifully. It was finished with a neat molding of natural wood, and the

149

whole nicely oiled. There were a few books piled on the floor beside it, waiting till the shelves should be perfectly dry to receive them, evidently contributions to the new case. She stooped to read their titles, and was astonished and pleased to find among them several new books by best authors, which she had been longing to read, but had as yet not seen. They were nearly all in new bindings as if fresh from the bookstore, though one or two had the names written inside in fine, strong handwriting "Horace L. Stafford."

Celia drew back, a slight flush creeping over her face. She was grateful for the books thus loaned or donated. The newcomer was evidently bound to be helpful, and seemed to know how to do it. Now if they could have a few games under the lighted lamp on the table, perhaps some of the young people might be kept in evenings. Would such things reach Mamie Williams and her friend, she wondered? And she sighed and feared that Mamie was too much interested in other things to be reached so simply. She remembered that Mamie had been reading the other night. Perhaps some of these delightful stories would reach her. There were one or two religious books, small and daintily bound, which looked attractive. Celia picked them up and turned the pages, her expressive face kindling with a thought she read here and there. Then she went to the small cozy corner by the organ and sat down. She looked about her at the few changes they had made, and remembered the night when she had looked around on that parlor waiting for the postman. How much difference a few little things had made! She could see other changes that might be made to improve matters, and she resolved to try them as soon as possible. Then she sat down at the organ. She had never tried that whining instrument, since she had been in the house. It had pained her some times to hear it groaning and wheezing under the bold touch of the tenor brakeman as he ground out an accompaniment to some of his solos. Celia did not like a cabinet organ. She longed for a piano, but there was no piano, and here was this organ. What could be made of it? Perhaps it might be tuned and answer for singing occasionally. Certainly, if it was to stay there and be used, it would conduce to her own comfort to have it put in order. She touched the keys softly to see how bad it was, and went on playing chords gently. She was not a finished musician, but she had learned to play a little for the home pleasure, and now instinctively her fingers sought out some of the old favorite tunes.

"Safely through another week,
    God has brought us on our way,
Let us now a blessing seek,
    Waiting in his courts to-day."

Her conscience pricked her, as the words rang themselves over in her mind. She had not been going to church very regularly since she came to the city. She had wandered around from one church to another, feeling forlorn and lonely at all, not going often enough to one place to become noticed as a stranger and welcomed, even if the people had had the disposition to welcome her. Since aunt Hannah had been there, she had made an excuse to stay at home with her if she was not able to go out, and at such times when her aunt could go, she had taken her to the different churches near by in rotation, that she might choose where they should go. The elder lady had not as yet made any choice, nor, indeed, had she expressed her mind concerning the places of worship they had visited. Celia thought of it now, and wished their dear old church from Cloverdale could be transplanted bodily. It was so desolate to go among strangers and not have any place or work in the church home. She sighed and made up her mind that she must go more regularly and perhaps offer to take a class in Sunday-school or something of the sort. Of course it was not right to live this way; but her heart was not in her resolve. She played on, not realizing what tune she had started till she began to hum the words in a low sweet voice:

"The day of rest once more comes round,
    A day to all believers dear;
The silver trumpets seem to sound,
    That call the tribes of Israel near;
        Ye people all,
        Obey the call,
And in Jehovah's courts appear——"

She broke off suddenly and played a few stray chords. She knew that the next verse began:

"Obedient to thy summons, Lord,
We to thy sanctuary come;"

It was strange that all the words were on that subject. She would choose something else. She thought a moment, her fingers lingering on the keys. Then she began to sing:

"Father in thy mysterious presence kneeling,
Fain would our souls feel all thy kindling love;
For we are weak, and need some deep revealing
Of trust, and strength, and calmness from above."

She felt the beauty of the words and the depth of meaning, and sang with her heart, each word as a prayer. Her voice grew fuller and sweeter as she went on.

"Lord! we have wandered forth through doubt and sorrow,
And thou hast made each step an onward one;
And we will ever trust each unknown morrow;
Thou wilt sustain us till its work is done."

She had not heard the step upon the stairs and did not know that some one entered the parlor and sat down on the divan near by, until, as she commenced the third verse, a rich, sweet tenor, full of cultivation and feeling, joined with her in the words:

"Now, Father! now in thy dear presence kneeling,
Our spirits yearn to feel thy kindling love;
Now make us strong; we need thy deep revealing
Of trust, and strength, and calmness from above."

Celia's voice trembled at first, but the stronger one sustained the tune and she kept on, the pink color stealing up her cheeks and to the tips of her ears. If the other singer saw her embarrassment, he did not notice it. When the last note died slowly away and Celia was wondering what she should do and how she should get away from the room, he said quite in a matter-of-fact voice, as if he and she were accustomed to singing together early on Sabbath mornings: "Will you play 'Lead Kindly Light,' please?" And she had played on, glad that she knew it well enough to do so, and they sang together.

"Thank you!" he said simply, when the last verse was finished.

"That has helped me for the work that I have to do to-day. In fact that song always helps me. Do you, sometimes, come to a place where you want to look ahead and see whether things are coming out as you wish? Isn't it blessed to think he leads the way, and makes the gloom for our sakes that we shall not fear for what is to come, while perhaps if we could look and see the blessings—in disguise—sometimes we might turn and flee. You belong to him, do you not, Miss Murray? I thought I could not be mistaken. I want to thank you for this pleasant bit of morning praise. It has been like home."

Celia had raised her eyes in one swift glad glance of recognition of their kindred discipleship, when he asked her if she was a Christian and had answered, low and earnestly, "Yes, I do," feeling in her heart how very wrong she had been in calling this man unspiritual. Her heart longed to reach that high plane of trustful living where he seemed to move. She lifted her eyes again and timidly asked:

"Do you think it is possible for every one to feel that perfect assurance where they cannot see the way? I wish I knew how to trust that way and not worry over things."

"It is hard sometimes, isn't it, to just lay down the burdens at the Father's feet and realize that we need not carry them? But isn't it strange that it is hard?" And he looked at her with that peculiarly bright smile which she had noticed the first night he came to the house. "One would think that we would be only too glad to get rid of the burden and the worry, when he, so strong and willing offers to take it. Perhaps that is one reason why I like that hymn. It seems to help me to remember whose I am and who is my Saviour. I am prone to forget when I think, for instance, of some dear one whom I see fading day by day and know cannot be long upon this earth, that the night ever will be gone.

"'And with the morn, those angel faces smile
Which I have loved long since, and lost awhile!'"

A deep sadness had settled over his face, as he looked up to her and repeated the lines of the hymn they had just sung, and her heart was filled with pity for some sorrow she felt he was bearing. Instinctively she remembered the sweet beautiful face in the velvet case, and while he seemed set apart and sacred in her thought of his sorrow, she let a shade of her old dignity creep back into her voice, which had fallen from it for a few moments. The breakfast bell had sounded, and the boarders were coming downstairs. With one accord the two rose and went toward the dining-room, feeling that they did not care to have the quiet confidences of the few moments they had spent together intruded upon or misunderstood. Celia thanked Mr. Stafford for his words a little stiffly, as one, as a matter of form, might thank any strange minister for a good sermon, and perhaps the young man wondered a little at her seemingly variable moods.

It was after breakfast, and the church bells were sending their various calls to worship through the clear cold air of the city. Celia stood ready dressed for church, waiting for her aunt in the front hall. Miss Grant had been called back by Molly Poppleton, just as they were starting out the door, and Celia tapped her foot impatiently on the hall oilcloth and wished aunt Hannah would hurry. Not that she was anxious to go to church, but she wanted to get the duty done with and come back, for Mr. Stafford had slipped a most inviting little book into her hand, as he passed her in the upper hall after breakfast, saying "Have you read Daniel Quorm? If not, it will interest you, perhaps. It is along the line of our talk this morning, and it has helped me to trust him where I couldn't trace him."

She had read a few pages while aunt Hannah tied her bonnet and put on her gloves, and had already grown deeply interested in the quaint phrases of Daniel in his story of his little maid. She wanted to get back to it. She stilled her conscience when it pricked her for not caring to go to church, by telling it that the book would probably do her more good than a sermon in a strange church, but her conscience was too well trained to let her forget that God had promised to meet her in the church.

Some one was standing in the shadow of the parlor curtains, Celia did not know who. She thought that perhaps it was the brakeman. He had returned the night before, and was off duty for the day. She unfastened the door and breathed in the clear sunny air with delight, then glanced up the stairs to see if aunt Hannah was coming. But just then came Miss Grant's voice, as she leaned over the stair railing, and Celia saw that her gloves were off and her bonnet untied again.

"Celia, don't wait for me. I am not going this morning. I have made up my mind my duty is with Mrs. Belden. She is feeling very despondent. Go on without me. Isn't there some one else you can go with?" she asked, as she saw the look of dismay on Celia's face and heard her exclaim, "Oh auntie!"

Then the figure that had been standing in the shadow of the window curtain in the parlor moved forward and Harry Knowles stepped out.

"Miss Murray would *I* do?" he asked humbly, "or—would you rather not go with me?" There was a hesitancy and shamefacedness about him which was not like his usual manner, and he seemed anxious to have her accept. While Celia hesitated, Miss Grant said:— "Why, yes, Celia, that is very nice. You and Mr. Knowles go together. I am so glad he is going," and then slipped away from the stairs pleased in her heart, both for Celia's sake that she would not be alone, and for the young man that he was willing to go to the house of the Lord!

As Celia turned to go with him, she reflected that she had been wishing he would go to church, or wishing she might say some word to help him, and now he had himself opened the way by inviting her to go. She felt reproached, that she had never invited him before. But Harry seemed uncomfortable, and when he had closed the door, he stopped on the upper step and asked again, "You are sure you are willing to go with me? You aren't afraid or anything?" and Celia looked up in surprise, and saw the earnest, eager, shamed face and said, "Why surely, Harry, I am willing. Why should I be afraid?"

"Well, I thought,—I was afraid you—after that night—you know—" he said, growing red and grinding his heel into the stone on which he stood, "I can't forgive myself, Miss Murray, that's all, and I thought you didn't like me asking you." He looked up bravely through his embarrassment with his sorry, boyish eyes asking forgiveness.

"Harry," said Celia turning her clear, honest gaze full upon him, "I was truly glad, and was only being ashamed myself because *I* had not asked *you* before, for I have been wishing you would go to church, and—I have been praying for you."

She spoke the words low and embarrassedly, for she was not used to talking much about such things to strangers, but the young man's eyes filled with moisture, and he said, "Thank you," in such hearty tones that she knew he meant it. Then he added, "So is the minister, and maybe I'll amount to something, after all."

Celia was surprised to find that she suddenly felt a sense of satisfaction in what he had told her about the minister. She did not understand all her feelings to-day. She must sit down and analyze them when she reached home.

"But where are we to go, Harry?" she asked, pausing on the sidewalk a moment. "Have you any choice? I have not put my letter into any church yet, though I ought to have done so before this."

She tried to remember in her mind which of the churches she had attended would be the most likely to help the young man, but could not remember any of them definitely, and concluded that since she had been in the city she had taken her body to the church and left her soul at home, or wandering in fields of other thoughts than those presented for her deliberation at the sanctuary.

Harry's face grew eager again.

"Well, then, that's nice. Maybe you wouldn't mind going to hear Mr. Stafford, because I've half promised him that I would come there this morning, you see."

"Oh, of course we will," said Celia, wondering why it was she had never thought to go and hear him before, and why it was that the thought of hearing him preach had suddenly become so pleasant.

She wondered again as she listened to his opening prayer. Every word seemed to be prayed for her, and to fit her needs exactly and she pulled herself up sharply when she found that she was actually imagining that he remembered their talk before breakfast, and was praying thus for her. The hymn just before the sermon was wonderful, and again she reprimanded herself severely, for thinking he looked at her while he read that last verse, so perfectly did it appeal to her need. He read it exquisitely and tenderly, and as he reached the last line he looked at her again, and it gave her a strange pleasure to feel those words spoken so to her, even as if the Father himself had sent her an especial message that morning, and by a noble messenger.

> "Take, my soul, thy full salvation!
>   Rise from sin, and fear, and care.
> Joy to find in every station
>   Something still to do or dare.
> Think what Spirit dwells within thee.
>   Think what Father's smiles are thine!
> Think what Saviour died to win thee!
>   Child of heaven, shouldst thou repine?"

Chapter 21

That Sabbath afternoon was one of deep thought and soul searching for Celia. The sermon she had heard, the hymns she had sung, the prayer she had listened to, the book she had partly read, all seemed to bring her the one thought, that of the possibility of a life beyond anything she had known heretofore, a life whose every breath was trust, and whose joy was unalloyed because there was no care in it to break the deep, sweet peace. The longing for some change of this sort in her own heart did not take her interest from the work she had just begun around her. Instead it seemed to deepen her interest in all in the house, and to make her heart throb anew with love to her Saviour.

With the little book in her hand which Mr. Stafford had loaned her she passed through the hall that afternoon on some errand for her aunt, and returning saw Harry Knowles hovering restlessly about the parlor. It came to her that perhaps she might say something to help him, but what could it be? She felt hardly ready yet without more thought and preparation. She might do more harm than good. Following an impulse she offered him the book to read awhile, and then went back to her room, half sorry that she had deprived herself of the pleasure of finishing it. However, she had read enough to remember, and there lay her Bible. She took it up and read. Somehow the words seemed to fit all the other circumstances of the day, and to help her on to the one great desire that was growing deeper in her heart, that she might forget to fret and worry and learn to trust Jesus entirely for all that was to come. She read a chapter and part of another. The words seemed especially fresh and new to her. She began to wonder if she had been giving her whole mind to her Bible reading of late. Then suddenly from out the printed page there came a command. It was not so very marked, not more than other verses she had read, and yet it

158

seemed to her to have a special significance for her, and to remind her that there was a young girl of nearly her own age upstairs, over whom she had been shown her own influence, who was perhaps needing help from her at this very moment. She felt that she must go, though she could scarcely tell why, and she laid aside her Bible and knelt to ask God's help before she went.

As she knocked at Mamie Williams' door she wondered at herself for coming, and how she was to explain her visit. She decided that if any one answered she would say she had come to ask them to go out to church with her that evening, though she had hardly made up her mind before that to go herself. She felt much embarrassed at herself in that one minute after she had knocked, and heartily wished herself back to her own room. But she had not long to wait. The door was thrown open after a moment of what sounded like scuffling inside, by Mamie herself, this time without gum in her mouth, but with rather red cheeks and her hair floating in wet strings down her back over a towel. Her face and hands were a brilliant, tender pink, giving strong evidence of a severe scrubbing Celia had recommended the night before. She instantly recognized what it meant, and her heart sank that at her advice this girl was spending her Sunday afternoon in such a way. Perhaps the angels knew that by making herself sweet and clean, she was coming nearer to the kingdom of God than she had ever yet been.

The other roommate occupied a comfortable lounging spot on the bed. Her hair was tumbled and her dress loosened, and in her hand was a paper covered book. Celia had opportunity afterward to observe that it was the same one that Miss Williams had been reading the day before.

Miss Simmons did not rise from the bed, but she greeted the intruder with a languid surprise, and withal a show of pleasure that made Celia feel she was not unwelcome, and told her to sit down. She was munching cheap candy from a box which lay beside her on the bed, and she held it out at once to the guest saying:

"Sit down. Have some candy, do. I had it give to me last night." This with a significant giggle interpolated into her natural drawl. Then looking at her roommate, she said, apologetically,

"You must excuse Mame. She's took an awful fit of cleanin' up. I don't know what she's getting ready for, but she's made herself a sight. Her nose's as red's a beet. Did you want something or did you just come in to kill time?"

Celia accepted the chair, declining the candy as graciously as possible, saying she seldom ate it, and made known her request that they would go with her that evening to meeting. She bethought herself of the service she had attended that morning, and that possibly it might interest these two to go and hear the minister who lived under the same roof with them, and urged that as an incentive, describing the pleasant room, the good singing, and perfect friendliness she had met, with an enthusiasm that surprised herself.

"I can't go," said Miss Simmons, promptly, "I'm expecting company." There was the same conscious drawing in of the breath when she said this, evidently meant to express a certain and especial kind of company, that Celia had noticed in Mamie's talk the night before. It made her heart sink with the utter uselessness of trying to work against such odds, till she remembered her new half-formed resolves, not to look ahead for results, but to do the work trusting the rest to God.

Mamie's cheeks had grown redder, if that was possible. She was sitting on the edge of a chair with the hair brush in her hand. She seemed a trifle shy.

"It's awful nice of you to ask us," she said, "but I don't know but perhaps I'm going to have company, too. It wouldn't do to be away, though I ain't just positive, you know."

"Couldn't you bring them along?" said Celia, promptly, as if it would be the most natural thing in the world to do, though her heart misgave her at the idea of taking the oily youth she had seen in the parlor waiting for Miss Simmons not long before.

"Oh, no indeed!" snickered Miss Simmons, "he wouldn't go a step. He ain't that kind. And besides he'd be mad, for he said he might be going to bring another fellow along he wants me specially to meet. He wants to see me very perticular to-night anyway, so I couldn't think of going out," and Miss Simmons retired behind her book.

Mamie had meantime been puzzling over the problem of how to please herself and her new object of adoration at the same time, and seemed to have arrived at a solution.

"I don't know but I *might* go after all," she said, slowly, looking down at the toe of her shoe. "Say, Carrie, if he should come would you be sure and tell him I had gone out with someody *else?*—you could tell him it was a *very special* friend who had invited me, you know, and he would think it was another fellah. That might have a good effect on him, you know. I believe I'll try it this time anyway. I'll go, Miss Murray, if you want it so much. It's a good thing to get people jealous once in a while, don't you think? Say, was that you down in the parlor singing this morning early? It was awful sweet! Who else was there? It didn't sound quite like Mr. Yates, but I didn't know any of the others sang. It wasn't Harry Knowles, was it? He's too young for you anyway. You don't say it was the minister! My! He's awful talented, ain't he? Wouldn't it be romantic if it should turn out you was to marry him some time? Did you ever know him before? I've heard of stories like that lots of times."

Celia's cheeks rivaled Mamie's in hue, and her anger had risen rapidly. She did not dare trust herself to rebuke this girl, for her desire to do her good was still strong. She quickly looked about for a turn to the conversation.

"Are you fond of singing? Then come downstairs and let us sing now. I think some of the others are down there. We can have a very pleasant time, I'm sure. I have some Gospel song books. Put up your hair and come." She walked to the door trying to steady her fluttered nerves, and still that queer beating of her heart, half indignation, half something else which she did not understand, and which she did not wish to countenance.

"My land!" said Mamie, beaming, "I'd come in a minute, only what'll I do with my hair? It's about dry, but it'll take me an hour to do it all up after washing, it's so tangled and slippery. Perhaps you will fix it for me. Do, that'll be nice. Then you can show me how to do it like yours."

Celia was dismayed. She would scarcely have chosen Sunday afternoon for a lesson in hair-dressing, but how could she refuse on that score, as the request had been put in answer to one of her own? To handle another person's hair at any time was to her a sore trial. She shrank from contact with any one except her nearest and dearest. But how was she to refuse? How was she to get an influence over Mamie if she let her see she was unwilling to do what she asked of her? For a minute her repugnance of the coarse girl, with her coarse hair, red face and loud, grating words was so intense that she almost yielded to her desire to turn and flee from the room and shake the dust from her feet, and tell her aunt Hannah to take her away from the horrible boarders and never let her see any of them again. Then she gained control of herself, and though her cheeks were still red at memory of the careless words of the girl, she consented to undertake the hair; and even the deeply absorbed Carrie on the bed, who had been furtively watching the stranger during all, never suspected what a trial she had quietly taken upon herself.

Having undertaken the task, she did it well. She had a naturally artistic eye and hand and there was some pleasure, after the dislike had been overcome, in making Mamie's hair look as she had often thought it ought to look. Quickly and deftly she twisted it, smoothed it here and there, and fastened it firmly, and after it was accomplished Mamie stood and surveyed herself.

"It looks awful plain," she said, hesitatingly, "and it makes me seem queer, 'cause I ain't used to it, but I guess I like it. Don't you, Carrie?"

"It looks real stylish," answered that young woman, enviously, mentally resolving to try her own that way as soon as the others had left the room.

Celia went to wash her hands, with a heavy heart. She must certainly have mistaken that voice which she thought called her to go to that room. What had she accomplished but teaching the fashions this afternoon? How was she ever to know whether a thing was a duty or not? She went down to the parlor with her singing books, and found Mamie there before her looking pretty and a trifle shy in consciousness of her new coiffure. She was talking to the tenor brakeman who was evidently lost in admiration of her charms. She went at once to the organ and started the singing, but she found that the brakeman's tenor was not quite so pleasant as that which had blended with her own voice earlier in the day. The other boarders heard the music, and one by one dropped in, all joining in the words when they were familiar until even Miss Burns was there. Mr. Stafford had come in also. The minister joined in the singing, though he sat in a shaded corner of the room for the most part and sang softly, as if he were weary. Celia found that her thoughts kept wandering to him and wondering what was the matter, and she grew exceedingly annoyed over this fact, as she remembered Mamie Williams' careless words a little while before. She was glad when the tea bell rang and called them from the organ.

The church party was larger than she had expected. Mamie had wheedled Mr. Yates into being one of the number. She was the kind of girl who always wants a young man along when she goes anywhere. The other three young men joined the group also, perhaps at Harry's solicitation, or it might be out of interest in the minister who had been singing with them.

They were starting out of the door. Aunt Hannah was behind with Harry Knowles. Miss Burns had volunteered to stay with Mrs. Belden during the evening. Celia stepped down to the pavement beside Mamie and walked on.

"Say, he's awful nice. I like him. I wish he *would* marry you, 'cause I like you both," said romantic Mamie, in a confidential whisper.

"What do you mean? Who?" said Celia, startled, and having a vague idea of the tenor brakeman.

"Why, Mr. Stafford, the minister!" said the other girl.

"You must never say anything like that again," she said, in a suddenly chilling tone which almost froze Mamie's eager enthusiasm for a minute. "It is utterly absurd and ridiculous."

She wished afterward that she could have turned it off with a laugh, and let the girl see that she had no notion of any such thing, without making such a tragic thing of it, but indeed she had felt so annoyed at the second bold intimacy of the girl, which seemed to her like the handling and mixing up of sacred things by clumsy hands untaught and unknowing what they did, that she had almost stopped in her walk and gone back to the house. However, she managed to steady her voice and her steps and keep on.

"Why?" asked Mamie, half timidly, "don't you like him?"

"Certainly, I don't dislike him. But neither of us have any idea of any such thing. It is very annoying to have it suggested. He is simply a boarder." She said it freezingly.

"Oh," said Mamie, in a frightened tone, "I didn't mean any harm. I just thought it would be nice, that was all." After that she dropped behind with Bob Yates who had come up, and Celia walked with aunt Hannah and Harry Knowles.

"She's an awful queer girl in some ways," confided Mamie to her escort a few minutes later. "I just said she and the minister would make a nice match, and she got just as mad as a hornet. My! She scared me so I didn't know but I'd cry!" and then she giggled in a way Bob Yates much admired.

Celia sat in the meeting too much annoyed to rally her spirits and enjoy what was going on. She scarcely heard the hymns or realized the sermon. The voice of the minister, cultured, earnest, tender, loving toward his people, awakened in her the knowledge that she was more interested in this man than she wanted to be. She did not wish to hear his voice and like it, and his sermon she knew she would enjoy and therefore tormented herself with her annoyance, so that she did not hear it, and saw between the lines in her hymn book, ever and anon, a sweet pictured face in a velvet frame. She called herself a fool, and wondered that there was anything about a man whom she had so short a time ago not even heard of, to make her feel so uncomfortable. Then she turned to watch Mamie's face and her heart sank again as she reflected how useless it had been to try to do anything for her. True, her hair was becoming and neatly arranged, and the black eyes of the young man beside her were admiringly turned toward her occasionally, but perhaps that was only another source of harm to the poor girl. After all Celia's resolves, her day seemed to be ending most miserably.

How could she know that at that very moment the young girl beside her was listening to the minister with undisguised amaze, as he read the words of his text, "And to her was granted that she should be arrayed in fine linen, clean and white: for the fine linen is the righteousness of saints." She did not know about the hurried getting out of bed to read the promised verse the night before, nor how the verse itself had impressed itself upon the young girl's mind, perhaps the more because it was about dress, and one great theme of all themes of interest to her mind;—unless perhaps one might except those of love, courtship and marriage. If Celia had been told all this, it might only have discouraged her the more that the Bible itself meant no more to Mamie than a fashion book might have done, and so it was a wise thing that Celia could not see and know until all God's plan was worked out to the finish, and she was given eyes perfected through his teaching to understand the whys and wherefores.

The sermon which followed was simplicity itself. If Celia had not been so taken up with her own uneasy heart, she would have recognized the skill of the preacher, as he plainly and simply drew the meaning from what might have otherwise been to many minds before him an empty and meaningless passage. Even the feather-brained Mamie was able to understand and to carry away with her the few facts she had wished to know when she first read the words, together with their deep spiritual meaning. She had felt a pang of disappointment when she heard that this incomparable person, this child of luxury had spoken of, was the church, Christ's bride, and she told herself, half enviously that she had nothing to do with the verse at all, of course. But, immediately, the preacher made it plain to every one in the house that he and she individually did belong, ought to belong, by right were, members of that church for whom Christ died, and that it was only through their own wills that they deliberately put themselves outside its pale, that really, to every one present, it had been granted as a privilege, and it was their own fault that they did not accept and wear it. He spoke at length of the difficulty of keeping such garments white and pure in the midst of a world of work and constant contact with that which would soil, how only the children of the rich could afford to dress in a color which would so easily soil, and how only those who could go and have such garments washed in the blood of the Lamb could keep them pure and white. Then he talked about that righteousness of the saints until even Bob Yates dropped his eyes from the earnest, eloquent face of the speaker, and began to look into his own heart and wish that he might some way be different, and Mamie's cheeks glowed and her heart beat fast. She had forgotten, for the time, Mr. Harold Adams, and even the admiring glances of her escort to church that night. She even forgot the new arrangement of her hair, and ceased to feel the back of her head, to discover how perchance it might be affecting those who looked upon her from the rear. She resolved, in some way, to discover for herself how she might wear this fine linen, and when the closing hymn was announced, she stood up with the others, and sang in a loud voice the words, meaning them in her heart more than any words she had ever sung before. She felt a strange, sweet thrill of longing, new and faint, but real, as the hymn went on.

> "O Jesus Christ the righteous! live in me,
> That, when in glory I thy face shall see,
> Within the Father's house, my glorious dress
> May be the garment of thy righteousness."

Mamie felt for the first time in her life that night, that she had really a strong determination to go to heaven when she died. The white linen could be worn then, if not before. The minister had said it might be worn now also. Well, perhaps—

Her heart was softened, and on the way home she confided the coincidence of her verse the night before and the minister's text to Mr. Yates, who was deeply interested and impressed. Celia would have been surprised, perhaps, if she could have heard the brakeman telling Mamie at the door that she had helped him, that he wanted to be better than he had been and he was glad she was that kind of a girl.

As for Celia, the minister himself had walked home with her. She hoped that Mamie had not seen, and her cheeks burned red and her embarrassment did not lessen during the entire walk. He asked her to help him in his Sunday-school work, and she accepted the class he offered her, after much hesitation, but she was stiff and unlike herself, and aunt Hannah wondered greatly why Celia seemed so cold and uninterested in things. She sighed as she went about preparing for the night, and wished that Celia's mother had lived; nobody could understand a girl like her own mother, she thought. Then she knelt as she always did, and laid her care at her Master's feet, and rested with an unburdened heart for the next day's work.

Chapter 22

One morning, about eleven o'clock, Molly Poppleton was up in the third-story hall attending to the rooms on that floor. The chambermaid was not well, and Molly had been put back in her work a good deal, so that it was late and she was in a hurry. She thumped the water pitchers down hard, slammed the doors, and punched the pillows into shape with extra vigor on this account, but, suddenly, in the midst of making up the University student's bed, she came to a sharp halt and straightened up to listen. She was not mistaken. She certainly had heard sounds of distress. They grew clearer now as she went to the hall door, and she quickly located them. They were low, half-suppressed sobs, following quickly upon one another, as though the weeper were in deep distress. After listening, she marched down the hall, and without more ceremony threw open the door of a room. There lay Mamie Williams across the foot of her unmade bed crying bitterly and shaking with sobs. Molly Poppleton was at all times a straightforward maiden, and she believed in coming to the point at once; it was the way she had been brought up. So, without apology for intruding into the young girl's trouble, she demanded what was the matter.

Mamie raised her head long enough to show a red nose and blurred eyes, and to see who had come in without knocking. Then she went on crying harder than ever.

Molly shut the door with a slam and said:

"For mercy's sake, do tell me what's the matter? Are you hurt? Do you want a doctor? Or are some of your friends dead?"

Mamie shook her head and finally controlled herself sufficiently to sob out:

"No, M-m-molly. It's my heart! It's broke!"

"Oh, well, if that's all, you'll get over it! They always do! I've been there myself, and I know that state don't last long. You better get up and wash your face while I make the bed." And Molly proceeded energetically to throw open the window and shake up the pillows.

"Oh Molly! You don't know. You never was crossed in love!" wailed the miserable girl, without stirring, and then she sobbed the harder.

Molly turned irately from the bureau where she had begun to dust.

"Crossed in fiddlesticks!" she said, sharply. "You'll find you ain't near so hard hurt as you think for. And as for me, I've had my chances in my time like other girls, and plenty of 'em at that, an' I perferred to live single. It's much more independent. It's my opinion you ain't old enough to be away from home anyway. You better go back to your ma if you've got one."

But as this only set Miss Mamie to crying the harder, the perplexed Molly marched down to find Miss Grant and report the case.

"Miss Grant, you're needed up there in that three-center room. That silly thing is actin' like a fool over some poor sickly fellow, that couldn't support her ef she got him, I s'pose. She says she's been crossed in love an' her heart's broke, an' she's cryin' fer dear life. It's my opinion she better be crossed with a good spankin', an' I wouldn't feel sorry to be the one to give it to her neither."

But the latter part of this sentiment was lost upon her hearer who had already started with swift steps for the third story.

A moment later Mamie felt a cool hand on her hot forehead, and Miss Grant stooped down and took her in her arms and kissed her. She was so surprised to be kissed, that she stopped crying for a minute. Then the sympathy of the eyes that met hers started her tears afresh, and she buried her head in the motherly arms held out to her and cried like a hurt child who had found a comforter. After she had cried a few minutes and been soothed by the woman who seemed to have the gift of soothing from above, as others have a gift for music or painting, she was able to tell her poor little sad, commonplace story.

"It was Mr. Harold Adams at the store. And he was awful handsome. The girls all thought so. I fell in love with him the first time I saw him. Yes ma'am, he was the head clerk there, all this winter he had charge. The owner went to New York and left him here to run the business. He was awful smart, they said. He used to pay me lots of attention at first, and he's told me many a time he loved me better than any one else"—here she broke into fresh sobs—"and it was only when that ugly girl with bleached hair and a pretty face came, he got to going with her, and now I'd planned a way to look nicer than her and get him back, and he's been real nice to me for a whole week—she was away—they all said she was sick, but now it turns out she was getting ready to be married, and he's to be sent to have full charge of a three-cent store up in Ohio, and they say she's going along. The girls had it all ready to tell me this morning when I went in to the store, and they just couldn't laugh enough at me, till I nearly sank through the floor. They was always jealous of me. First one twitted me an' then another, till I got so mad and felt so bad I just come home. He's a goin' to marry her, they say, an' it's all been no use after all, an' oh, my heart's just broke!"

It is commonly supposed that women who do not marry and have no children cannot enter into the feelings of young people, and are not able to sympathize with them. But God had somehow given this woman a sweet insight into natures in distress, which helped her to be able to give comfort wherever she went, to say the right word and do the right action. She bent down now and kissed the tear-wet face.

"You're awful kind," moaned poor Mamie. "But you don't know how it is yourself. You ain't never been crossed in love."

A shadow of the passing of a great dark cloud, tipped with brilliant light, went across Miss Grant's face, leaving the reflection of the light there, ere she spoke again.

"Listen! Mamie," she said, and her voice was very sweet and tender, and her eyes looked soft and dewy, as though she saw things beyond the range of human vision, "I want to tell you a story all about myself."

Yes, she actually went back to those dear, bright days so long ago, when she had found a kindred spirit and had lived in a sweet elysium of hope, and dreamed those rose-colored visions of youth. Some women would have counted it a desecration to the memory of her dead hopes and sacred love before the eyes of a vulgar girl who wept over a man a hundredfold more vulgar; would have thought it an evidence of lack of good taste and delicacy to do so. Not so this woman. Had she not sent swift petitions to the throne as she came up the stairs asking for guidance? She felt in her heart that this story of hers, which had never before passed her lips to mortal ear, told here, might help this poor, friendless, untaught girl: might, perhaps, lead her to see life in a different way, and to begin to try to live it for the God above, instead of for her own selfish pleasure. And she knew the man she had loved, who had been in heaven these years, well enough to be certain he would be glad also to have her tell the story, if it could in any wise help a soul to find comfort. And so she told it, simply and eloquently. She even let herself dwell on the tender passages, the little things that make such a story beautiful in the eyes of a girl. She spoke about the flowers he had sent her, the pretty, simple gowns she had worn that he admired, and the ribbon he stooped and kissed, as it floated from her throat, that last time he parted from her, saying she would soon be with him now to stay; and how she treasured it yet.

Before she was half way through the story, Mamie had dried her eyes and sat up on the bed, her face expressing intense interest. She had forgotten her own troubles in the trouble of another. Her tears, which were dried on her own sorrows soon flowed silently for Miss Grant. She wondered at that peaceful face, which shone bright even through the mist that would gather in her eyes, as she told of the dark days when her hopes were taken from her, and of the time when she wandered about forlorn, until the Lord spoke to her and comforted her. When the story was finished, Mamie found she could look up and talk. She seemed to have risen above her recent grief. There was a longing for something in her heart, she scarcely knew what.

"I always thought it would be an awful thing to be an old maid," she said bluntly, "but if I could look like you, and be like you, I wouldn't mind it—not much!" There was a look of admiration on her face. It was not much encouragement, but Miss Grant was not one who let her work depend upon results. She went steadily on talking, cheering, advising, drawing out the girl, until she had a pretty thorough understanding of what her life had been hitherto. She did not wonder that the heart seemed broken, nor that what seemed to the poor girl to be the life love had been freely given to an unworthy object. What better had been set before the girl? She had been untaught and unguided. Before she left her, Mamie had confided to her the story of her Bible reading and of all her thoughts about the garments of fine linen, and this missionary of the Most High had sifted out from the chaff of foolish talk and worldly longings the grain of earnest desire after better things and found joy, the joy of encouragement in it. She even knelt beside the girl with her arm about her waist, and prayed for her as Mamie had never heard herself prayed for before, and then, instead of sending her back to the atmosphere of selfish strivings and silly thoughts of what should be noble things, she advised her to stay away from the three-cent store, at least for that day, and come down in the kitchen, as she had some work for her there which might take her mind off her trouble for a little while.

It is true that Molly sniffed when she saw her come into the kitchen with her red eyes washed and a white apron on, but Miss Grant wisely sent Molly to work in another part of the house, and herself carefully inducted the awkward novice into the mysteries of making some most delectable cake, to be used in the celebration of Miss Burns' birthday that evening. It spoke well for Miss Grant's ability to read human nature, that she chose cake to teach Mamie. If it had been a lesson in bread-making or how to cook potatoes, it is doubtful if the girl would have been interested. Cake, now, somehow, seemed "sort of stylish," and belonged to the festive side of eating; therefore she enjoyed learning how to make it nicely, and she came to the dinner-table that evening beaming with satisfaction over the cake which she had iced and decorated with smilax and candles herself. She told them all that she made the cake, and it received much praise, especially from Bob Yates, who asked for a second piece and said some low words of commendation that brought a smile and a bright flush into the girl's face, just as Molly passed the ice cream which was also a part of the evening's celebration.

"H'm!" said that worthy woman coming out into the kitchen the better to converse with herself, "I thought so! She's got over it sooner than most of 'em. It generally takes over night at least just to let the glue dry, but she must have used some lightnin' stuff. Her heart ain't more'n skin deep anyway."

Chapter 23

The days that followed were filled with new things for Mamie Williams. However shallow her hurt had been it was deep enough to make her shrink decidedly from returning to the store. The young man whose charms had fascinated her was not yet gone, and Miss Simmons brought word from day to day that there had been delay in sending him away. The yellow haired girl seemed to have returned to her place behind the candy counter. After this report had gone on for about a week, Mamie suddenly manifested a desire to return to her position, with the expressed hope that she might still win her lover back, but Miss Hannah, feeling that this might be the turning point in her life, had a long talk with her, the result of which was that she appeared in the kitchen an hour after, with red eyes, a meek air and a clean gingham apron and made herself generally useful. Molly, who had kept herself informed of the state of the case nodded approval and announced to Miss Grant at the first opportunity that she didn't know but that girl had some chance of growing a little sense after all.

It is doubtful whether Mamie's resolution would have outlasted the next day, however, had not several things occurred to strengthen what Miss Grant had said to her during that long earnest talk. The first was the announcement that the charming Mr. Harold Adams had departed from the city to parts unknown, taking with him a goodly portion of the profits of the three-cent business, which he had, by a careful system of bookkeeping, been laying up for himself against this day. Neither had the yellow-haired girl shared in his booty. She seemed to be as happy as ever, and as the days went by was reported to be "making up" to the new head of the business, who had come to straighten out affairs.

Mamie, on the announcement of this news, betook herself to her room for a whole morning, where she cried and was angry alternately, and from whence she came out a wiser and a meeker maiden, quite ready to do what Miss Grant should ask of her, and to look for another position. But that lady was in no haste to urge the girl to apply for another position. Life in such a store, as Mamie would be likely in her present stage of development to get into, was too dangerous and risky a thing for the unformed girl, who seemed to be hesitating on the brink of better things. After careful thought, and much discussion with Celia, Miss Grant told Mamie that she would like it very much, if she would be willing to help her for two or three weeks, with upstairs work, sweeping and table setting, until she could find another second girl who suited her. She told her she would give her what she had been paying to the second girl who had just left, and that she would of course have her board, so that she might be able to look about her leisurely for the right place, and still lose nothing by being out of work. Mamie, after a struggle with her pride, and reiterating many times to her roommate that she only did this for a few days as a favor to Miss Grant, finally accepted, and was somewhat surprised that she was not scoffed at by Miss Simmons for "doing housework," which to the minds of both girls had always been menial service quite beneath them.

But it turned out that Miss Simmons had other things to think of than Mamie Williams' affairs. It was scarcely three weeks after Mamie had left the three-cent store, when it was discovered that the said Miss Simmons had "eloped" with the friend of the oily youth who had been visiting her. Just what she had eloped from, as she had no friends or kindred in the city who seemed in the least interested in her welfare, it was perhaps hard to make out, but she left a note in Mamie's Sunday dress pocket stating that she had eloped, and bidding an affectionate farewell. It was no more than was to have been expected, Miss Grant thought afterward, as she turned over pile after pile of romantic, third-class, sensational novels in the closet, after the departure of the young girl, but she sighed and brushed away a tear, that she had not been permitted to help this girl also. She had by this time some hopes of Mamie. The affair of Miss Simmons, she feared, might perhaps upset her, and excite her desire for some romance herself, but happily it worked the other way, rather frightening her, and making her cling close to Miss Grant, asking her advice daily and almost hourly. This effect became still more salutary when it was learned some days after that the young man with whom Miss Simmons had eloped had already a wife in another state. During the passage of these events Mamie cried a good deal, but there was growing in her face the shadow of a sweet womanliness which gave promise of what might be in the future if all things went well. She had not even the brakeman to brighten this hard time for her, for he had been sent out West on some special work by one of the heads of the road, and would not return for a month. Mamie learned to efface herself somewhat, and gradually seemed to be cultivating some of Celia's quietness and repose of manner. Celia, on her part, was much interested in the girl. She kept her in mind daily, and was always trying to help her, and praying for her.

"I'm not sure, auntie, after all, but she may develop enough to become a ribbon girl some time," she said one night, when Mamie had left them.

Aunt Hannah smiled dreamily. She was beginning to have much hope of her young protégée herself.

"Yes," she said, with her far-away look in her eyes, "she may be fit for the white linen dress some day. Who knows?"

"You mean the tailor-made one?" asked Celia, mischievously.

"The heavenly-made one, anyway, dear. She told me to-night that she was beginning to feel as if she really prayed like other people now."

There were other influences at work also. Mr. Stafford was holding meetings every night in the new chapel, and the boarders had as a family adopted that church as their own. It was becoming a regular thing now for every one who was able, to attend service morning and evening on Sunday, and several of them had dropped in to the special meetings. Miss Hannah, Celia, and Mamie Williams had been there

every night. Harry Knowles had joined the choir, and his friends rejoiced that at last all his evenings were securely filled for him. His face
was bright and interested. He was enthusiastic in sounding the praises
of Mr. Stafford, and ready to do anything to help in the church work,
though as yet he did not seem to have made any move to number
himself among the Christians. Celia was deeply interested in a class of
big boys who were most of them beginning to attend the services. She
kept herself in the background with them as much as possible. No one
could say of her that she was trying to get the attention of the minister.
She tried with all her might to keep away from him, insomuch, sometimes, that he noticed it and was puzzled and troubled. He sometimes
sat with his eyes shaded by his hand up in his room when he was weary
with his work, and thought about it. Did she dislike him? Or was there
some one else who so filled her life that she had no desire to have other
friends? More and more her sweet, womanly face, and her pleasant
ways were making their impression upon his mind. He began to confess it to himself by and by, and he thought of what his friend Roger
Houston had said about finding a wife that night he had met him in
search of a boarding-place. His heart told him that there was more
possibility of such a thing happening than he would care to confess to
his friend just yet. In fact, Mr. Houston had visited Mr. Stafford several times, and once had remained to dinner with him, since which
time he had unreservedly gone over in favor of the new boarding-
house, declaring that the cooking was as good as they had at his own
home, though perhaps not quite so stylishly served. He had laughed, it
is true, at Bob Yates, who that evening favored the house with one of
his high-keyed solos, while Roger and Mr. Stafford tried to talk in the
latter's room directly over the organ; and he had mimicked Miss
Burns' laugh—for he was a born mimic—and had denominated
Mamie Williams and Carrie Simmons as "giggling kids," but he admired Miss Grant, and declared Celia to be artistic in the extreme. He
kept talking about her after they came upstairs. He was an artist by
profession, and he begged his friend to ask her to sit as a model for
him, and was surprised at the prompt way the suggestion was
squelched. He asked if Celia's character was as fine as her face, and

pondered much afterward over the slow thoughtful answer of his host, "Yes, I think it is." He was so possessed of the idea of catching Celia's expression on canvas for a picture he had it in mind to paint, that he asked again as he was leaving, "And you don't think you can ask that girl to sit for me, Horace? I like that style of face awfully, and I don't know just where else to turn for it."

"I don't think there *is* another face anywhere just like hers," answered the minister slowly again.

"Now look here, Horace, you talk as if you were personally interested in her. Don't go so far as that, I beg of you. You ought to marry a rich girl, for you never will allow yourself to get money any other way, unless you fall dead in love with it. Well, I suppose I may ask her myself. It won't hurt my feelings, if she does refuse, you know. Where can I find her?"

A firm line came around the minister's mouth, as he said, decidedly.

"I would rather you would not do that, Roger. She is not that kind of a girl."

Afterward, the young artist remembered his friend's face, and whistled on his way home as he thought it over.

But though Mr. Stafford had watched Celia for several months now, had seen her under varying and trying circumstances sometimes; had shown her little attentions, which were the outcome of a frank talk he had within himself, wherein he confessed a deep interest in her, she still held aloof from him. Miss Grant had given up trying to make it out. Celia was too deep for her.

Meantime Bob Yates came home from the West. He had been working hard and was glad to get back again. He had been promoted to an engineer's position, and was off duty every evening now. He seemed much struck with the change in Mamie Williams. Miss Grant noticed it the first evening at dinner. There was a deference about his manner when he addressed her that was new. She noticed also its reflex influence on Mamie. Had she taken a lesson from Celia's reserve, or were the influences of prayer and daily life about her, and her new hopes and resolves making the change? Miss Grant wondered. Mamie flushed a little, but she drooped her eyes modestly, and was quite unobtrusive during the entire meal, a thing so unlike the old Mamie Williams that the contrast was marked. Bob Yates admired it evidently, for he cast many glances across the table at her, and his own loud, jolly voice seemed somewhat toned down, in harmony.

Celia passed through the hall behind them after dinner and heard Mamie shyly decline an invitation to the theatre. "I'd like awful well to go, but we all go to meetin' every night now," she was saying. "I promised in the meeting last night I'd bring somebody along to-night and I don't just like to break my promise. Mebbe you'd just as soon go to meetin' as the theatre to-night, then I'd have somebody to take to keep my promise with. The minister's awful good, and the singin' is fine. They'd like your voice in the choir, I know."

And so Bob Yates willingly gave up the theatre to go to meeting. He was not greatly concerned where he took his amusement. The theatre had no especial attraction for him, but he had thought of it because Mamie had once told him she would rather go to the theatre than anywhere else in the world. In fact, the prospect of a "good sing" was rather more enticing in itself than sitting still and listening to the singing of other people.

That night the minister was very much in earnest. He preached a soul searching sermon. Some of Celia's boys arose, when at the close of the sermon the invitation was given for all who would like to belong to Christ to stand with those who were Christians during the singing of a hymn. Mamie sat quite still, her cheeks pink and her eyes downcast during the singing of the first verse and part of the second. She held one side of the hymn book with Bob Yates and her hand trembled a little. He was singing with his usual fervor the deep, heart-stirring words, but Mamie did not sing. Just as the second verse was nearly finished, she suddenly rose with a jerk and an embarrassed countenance, leaving the singing book in the hands of the man by her side. He looked up astonished, and went on singing, but not quite so loud as before, and his words seemed to be getting mixed up. He fidgeted on his chair, and when they began to sing the next verse, he arose also and stood beside Mamie, offering her again the book. She took it, looking down, her heart fluttering gladly that he had arisen too, and kept her company, and so they stood until the benediction was pronounced.

"Say," said Mamie, softly, when they had walked half of the way home in an embarrassed silence, "what did you mean by that? Did you mean what the minister said? What made you do it?"

"Mean it? 'Course I did!" answered Bob, heartily. "My mother used to be a good woman, an' I've always meant to turn that way some time myself. The first time I ever heard Mr. Stafford, I made out he was more'n half-way right, an' to-night I thought so again. I don't know as I should 'a' said so out'n out fer folks to see, ef you hadn't, but I calculated I wanted to be on that side ef you was, so I stood up. Why?"

"Well, I didn't know," said Mamie, embarrassedly, "I was afraid mebbe you just did it out o' politeness. But I'm real glad you meant it."

"Are you? Sure?" He looked at her searchingly by the light of the next street lamp, and then added, "Well, I don't mind tellin' you 'twas you that did it. That what you said about wearin' a white dress got me to thinkin'. You seem most's if you was wearin' it yourself since I come home. I didn't know but 'twas my 'magination, but when I see you get up in meetin', I knew it was that there white dress in the Bible you was wearin'. I mostly made up my mind while I was out to Ohio, I wanted to be fit to walk along side o' you."

Mamie's heart fairly stood still with a joy she had not known before and only half understood. It was the joy of having helped another immortal soul to find the Light.

"I'm only just startin' myself," she murmured low. "I ain't half fit for that white dress yet, but I'm goin' to try, an' I'm awful glad you think I helped you."

"Well, then, let's start out together, and mebbe we can help each other," he said, and she murmured with downcast eyes, "All right," as he grasped her hand in a hearty clasp, and then helped her up the steps into the house.

Other young men had, on occasion, clasped Mamie's hand in more or less hearty grasp on the way home from places of amusement, but no hand ever touched in her the chord of such true, healthful, honest friendship, and purpose to do right. She felt as though she had been uplifted in some way and yet she knew not how nor why.

A little later Harry Knowles sat in Miss Grant's little private sitting-room, his head leaning on his hand, his whole attitude indicative of deep thoughts.

"I tell you, Miss Grant," he had been saying, "it was that three-cent girl. When I saw her stand up there all by herself, right in the middle of a hymn, too, when no one else was rising, it made me ashamed. Here was I who had been brought up to pray and read the Bible and know how to be good, and had a good mother, sitting still; and that girl, who never had any bringing up to amount to much I guess, *coming,* right away as soon as she was asked. I can't stand it any longer, and I wanted to talk to somebody about it, so I came to you. I knew you would help me, and it would seem some like having mother to tell it to. I've made up my mind to be a Christian. Yes, I'll tell the minister by and by, but I wanted to talk to you first, and he was busy anyway. But I don't know as I'd ever have done it, if it hadn't been for Mamie Williams to-night."

Verily the mysteries of influence in this world are great, and past understanding, and we cannot tell if our actions may not affect the eternal welfare of some one whom we have never seen.

Certainly, Mamie Williams, as she sat reading her Bible that night, did not dream that she had helped to bring Harry Knowles to Christ.

> "Hast thou not garnered many fruits
> Of other's sowing, whom then knowest not?
> Canst tell how many struggles, sufferings, tears,
> All unrecorded, unremembered all,
> Have gone to build up what thou hast of good?"

Chapter 24

Celia Murray had gone to her room and locked the door. It was just after church, and aunt Hannah was busy in the kitchen. It was the only time during the day when she might hope to have entire possession undisturbed, of the room which she shared with her aunt. She could not remember a time in her life before, when she would have cared whether her aunt came in upon her, or came to the door and found it locked, or not, but this time she did. She wanted to be entirely alone and face her own heart.

The winter had passed by on rapid feet, and they were well on into the spring. The meetings which had been held in the little chapel had continued for several weeks, and during that time Harry Knowles and Mamie Williams and Bob Yates had professed publicly their faith in Jesus Christ. The University student had taken his church letter out of its hiding-place in his trunk and put it into Mr. Stafford's church, and the school-teacher had sent to his far-away home for his and both were working hard for the salvation of others. Family worship had been established daily in the boarding-house, not in the morning, because the coming and going of the boarders was at such different hours that it would scarcely have been possible to get them all together, but in the early evening, just after the six o'clock dinner, while they still sat about the table. No one was obliged to stay, but all chose to, unless called away by something urgent. Mr. Stafford conducted it, and read a very few verses and prayed. Once or twice, when he had been absent for a day, Miss Grant had read part of a chapter, and asked Harry Knowles once, and once the brakeman to pray, and they had each done so; stumblingly and with few words, it is true, but Miss Hannah had been glad and gone about her daily work feeling joy at the place in which the Lord had set her.

They had grown to be a very pleasant family, in spite of the various elements of character and up-bringing which they represented. They talked about their abiding-place as HOME, and each one felt it to be that in the true sense of the word. Miss Grant had taken care to observe each birthday with some little unusual festivity in the way of eatables, and at Christmas and other holidays they made merry enough to forget, most of them, that they were away from their own kindred.

Mr. Stafford had grown to be a part of the household so fully that it would have brought dismay to each one if there had been a thought of his leaving. Even Celia had unbent, and he and she had become good comrades in a way, though there was always a dignified barrier which Celia kept up, which prevented his showing her any of the ordinary attentions which young men like to show to the young women whom they admire. Having quieted her conscience by keeping up this wall of conventionality and excusing herself from anything of a social nature which he offered her, she shut her eyes to consequences and enjoyed his presence in the house. How could she do otherwise? She read the books he loaned her, and conversed about them with him afterward, and she visited the poor and sick for him sometimes and took them little delicacies. There had been times, it is true, when it troubled her that she let herself enjoy his society as much as she did, but she had been learning during the winter months to put this aside and think no more about it. Occasionally she prayed to be delivered from a trouble which she sometimes saw hovering like a shadowy cloud over her own life, and looking at aunt Hannah resolved to trust the Lord to make her what he would have her to be, even if it must be in spite of sorrow, as he had done with her aunt. But now a time had come when Celia must face her heart and understand herself. If it was to be that she must come out of the ordeal bowed in spirit, then she must face it and accept it, but she must understand herself now.

It had come to a sudden crisis in this way.

Mr. Stafford had been away for nearly two weeks. A telegram had

come to him, when Miss Grant was out. Molly had taken it up to him
and a little while afterward had been surprised to see him standing in
the kitchen door; his grip and umbrella in hand, and a drawn, anxious
look upon his face. He told Molly to tell Miss Grant he had been called
away by tidings of sudden illness and did not know how long he would
be gone. They had heard nothing from him until Saturday evening of
that week, when his friend Roger Houston had called to get some
church notices from Mr. Stafford's room to hand to the minister who
was to supply the pulpit the next day.

It was Celia who opened the door for him and showed him to the
second story front room. With a possible view to prosecuting his petition that she would give him a sitting some time, he lingered a moment.

"It is very sad indeed," he remarked to Celia, as though she knew all
about the matter. "You knew there was no hope of her life? Oh,
haven't you heard? Well, I suppose Stafford has had his hands too full
of other things to think of writing. He gave me no particulars, only said
all hope was gone and she could linger but a few days longer at most.
He asked me to get this man to preach, and arrange everything for
him. It will be very hard for him, he depended upon her so much.
There was a peculiarly close relationship between them. He never
missed writing to her regularly and some of her letters were wonderful.
He read bits of them to me once or twice. She was a wonderful character. He will miss her immeasurably."

Then Mr. Houston looked up from the papers he had selected from
the minister's table, to the face of the girl who stood silent in the doorway. He was wondering whether he dared venture to ask her to let him
sketch her face some time, but when he looked at her he remembered
his friend's words, "She is not that kind of a girl," and concluded that
his friend had been right, and it would be better not to ask her this
time. He wondered what it was about her that made it seem impossible
for him to speak to her about it, as he would to many another pretty
girl just as nice and refined as she was. He fancied as he looked again
that she was white about the mouth, but, of course, that must have
been all his fancy.

It was not until late the next Saturday night, after all the house had retired, that Horace Stafford returned to Philadelphia, and letting himself quietly in with his latchkey, went to his room. They did not know he had returned the next morning at breakfast time, for one and another were wondering who would preach, and saying they wished their own minister was back, that they did not know whether they cared to go to church or not, and all those other things people will say when they love a minister, just as if he was their God, that they went to church to worship him, and when he was absent they had no object for worship. He had called to Molly, as she passed through the hall early in the morning, and asked her for a cup of coffee, and told her not to mind if he did not come to breakfast, as he needed all his time for preparation, having been away so long. He had gone to church early, while those who were going out were dressing, so that it was not until she was seated in church and saw the little study door open, and the minister walk out and into the pulpit, that Celia knew that Horace Stafford was back with them again.

She had gone through many changes of feeling since the night when Roger Houston had spoken those few commonplace words to her. She had not asked him then what he meant, nor who it was who was lying so low, who was so dear to Mr. Stafford. Instinctively she knew. It was the young woman of the pictured face, so sweet and lovely, within that velvet frame. Something had arisen in her throat while she listened, that froze the words she would have spoken, an expression of sympathy for him, and her heart was filled with conflicting emotions. She had dreaded Mr. Stafford's return. It was as if she had had her convictions verified now, and knowing his heart was engaged she wished to put him entirely from her thoughts. It seemed impossible though, for constantly the surmises would come up among the boarders, why Mr. Stafford was away, when he would return, etc. She obliged herself to repeat a few of Mr. Houston's sentences, a very few it is true, so few that the boarders were left in doubt as to whether the one who was lying so low and keeping the minister away was man, woman or child, and when Miss Burns asked if she knew whether it was one of the family, his mother, perhaps, Celia answered briefly, "He did not say," and then wondered if she had done wrong in not telling what she was so certain of, though she silenced her conscience by saying that Mr. Stafford might not care to have them know he was engaged at all. Then Celia had tried to fill the week with earnest hard work. She had succeeded in persuading Dobson & Co. to let her induct Mamie Williams into the ribbon business, with a view to possibly succeeding her sometime in the future, and she found that she was able to keep busy. Mamie was a tractable enough pupil, and growing quick to appreciate the fine distinctions in manner and actions which Celia strove to inculcate. But there was still room for improvement, and Celia worked early and late at her chosen task, moulding the young woman's character as carefully and eagerly as though she had been an artist making a model for some marvelous statue.

"When you get her done, Celia dear, I'm afraid she will be too good for the engineer, and I can see he wants her," said Miss Hannah, with a quiet smile.

"Well, that's all right, auntie dear," said Celia, with a thoughtful sigh. "He'll make her a good husband, and I don't believe she'll be too good for him. It seems to me her influence on him has been wonderful. He seems to change as fast as she does. I never would have dreamed it last fall."

"I thought so, dear. Do you remember the talk we had about him some time ago? There is more good in most people than we suspect. You have to live with them awhile to find it out," said Miss Grant.

"You mean *you* have to live with them, auntie, and *I* have to live with *you* to find out about them. I never would have found all these boarders out in the world, if you hadn't been here with your 'saint's eyes' to read them."

Miss Hannah smiled, but she watched Celia furtively and wished that she could read *her,* and understand what made the little cloud which seemed to settle down upon her usually bright girl and make her heavy hearted these days.

But to go back to church. Celia's heart throbbed painfully when she saw the minister walk into the pulpit. She knew by his face that his dear one was dead. It was not that his face wore a look of bitter grief, it was rather one of chastened exaltation. He preached a sermon about heaven that morning that seemed as though it had been written by one who had recently been very near to the portals, seen them open and caught glimpses of friends, and of Jesus within. Celia forgot her heart throbs and listened, forgetting, too, for the time who was preaching, in the absorption of the words he spoke. She had had a struggle to keep back the tears during the closing hymn, when they sang;

> "And with the morn those angels' faces smile,
> Which I have loved long since, and lost awhile."

She knew why Mr. Stafford had selected it. He sat during the singing with shaded brow and bowed head. Celia could not sing. She felt as if she were choking. She turned as soon as the benediction was pronounced and the solemn hush following it broken, to hide her tears by searching for her umbrella which had rolled beneath the seat. When she rose again and turned around, the minister was standing in the aisle beside her. He put out his hand and clasped hers, and a light of joy lit up his face which looked pale and worn, as he said, "I am so glad to see you again."

They were commonplace words. He might have used them to any member of his congregation; yes, and with the same tone and look too, perhaps, she told herself as she hurried excitedly homeward, but they sent a thrill of mingled joy and sorrow through the young girl which she did not understand and could not control. One minute she was fiercely glad, and the next minute she was plunged in a whirl of shame and despair that it had affected her so. And now she was locked into her room. She took off her hat and coat and sat down, but she could not think. She could only feel the joy, and the certainty that it was not hers. She tried to face herself and shame herself with saying plainly to her heart, "Celia Murray, you have fallen in love with Mr. Stafford. Yes, and you did it when you knew he belonged to another woman. Yes, you knew it well enough, though you wanted to pretend that maybe it was not so, because no one had told you so. But now you love him and he *does not love you!* He has just buried his heart, and you know you would not consider him the noble gentleman you think he is, if he should forget that love was 'so peculiarly close in its relationship.' And you love him in the face of that! Aren't you ashamed! He does not love you, and he never will, and you must not *let* him, and oh—*what* shall I do?"——

The poor girl threw herself upon her knees and begged for forgiveness and help. She felt she had done wrong to let her heart grow interested so easily. She tried to remember some of God's gracious promises for help, and to remember that he would bear her trouble for her, but her head seemed in a whirl of excitement and she could not think connectedly. She heard the dinner bell ring, and she rose and bathed her face, but decided she would not go down. She wanted to be by herself. Molly came up pretty soon and asked what was the matter. She told Molly to tell aunt Hannah she had a headache, and would not come down now, and then she bathed her throbbing temples and lay down to try and grow calm before aunt Hannah should come as she felt sure she would.

Wise aunt Hannah! She knew something was amiss! She had not watched her girl in vain. She had seen the start and the change of color when the minister came into the pulpit and again when he took her hand; she had seen other things during the months which had passed. Just what the trouble was she did not understand, and she would not ask Celia yet. If Celia needed counsel, she felt certain she would confide in her sooner or later. In the meantime she could pray.

Miss Hannah did not go up to her room for some time. Instead, she arranged a dainty tray with a tempting little lunch and a fragrant cup of tea. Under the corner of the napkin she had slipped a little note which was merely a scrap of poetry with the penciled words above it, "Dear child;" written hastily. It read:

> "Dear child:
> " 'God's plans for thee are graciously unfolding,
>   And leaf by leaf they blossom perfectly,
> As yon fair rose from its soft enfolding,
>   In marvelous beauty opens fragrantly.
> Oh, wait in patience for thy dear Lord's coming,
>   For sure deliverance he'll bring to thee;
> Then, how thou shalt rejoice at the fair dawning
>   Of that sweet morn which ends thy long captivity.' "

Then she laid beside it a lovely rosebud which Harry Knowles had brought her the night before, and sent the tray up by Molly. She herself went to the third story, and read to Mrs. Belden nearly all the afternoon.

Chapter 25

Celia aroused herself from her unhappiness in time to hurry to her Sunday-school class. She purposely went late that she might not be obliged to walk with any one, and she intended to hurry home before any of the others from their house had left the chapel, but it so happened that one of her scholars had a sad tale to tell her of trouble and need, and she was obliged to linger and get the particulars. There was an address to be taken down and several items of information she would need in helping him to find work. When this was done and she glanced hurriedly round to see if the others were gone, she saw that one of her boys was lingering with an embarrassed expression, half smiling, half doubtful, as though he might wish to speak a word with her. Something told her that this heart was ready for a quiet personal word and here was the time. The other boarders were gone, the minister with hat in hand was standing by the front door talking with a man. He was evidently about to go also. There were one or two groups in earnest conversation, a teacher with two of her class, three women in a corner, and a young man and a young girl talking. "Ben," she said, "can you sit down and talk with me a few minutes?"

The hunger for souls was awakened within the young teacher. Her own heart's unrest and sadness made her long to plunge into some other interest. She put her whole soul into the words she spoke, and the young man listened intently. There was no doubt but that she had reached his heart and that he was on the point of yielding to the Holy Spirit. Celia prayed as she talked and forgot herself, forgot everything but her desire for this soul's salvation. She listened to his hesitating, low words in answer to her earnestly put questions with bated breath.

She could almost hear her own heart beat while she waited for his final decision, as he sat minute after minute thoughtfully looking down at the toe of his rough, unblackened shoe and trying to fit it between two nails in the floor, where the boards were somewhat worn away by the many feet that tramped over them.

The decision was made at last, and the boy, with a furtive glance around him, drew his coat sleeve hurriedly across his eyes as he strode out of the room after having murmured an incoherent good-bye.

Celia stooped to pick up her rubbers which lay under the seat, and then looked about the deserted room. The sexton was doing something to a refractory window, which refused to go up and down right. He was used to busying himself while lingerers kept the church open. Celia thought everybody else was gone, till, as she neared the door, the minister arose from one of the back seats and came toward her.

"Would you mind sitting down a few minutes longer?" he said. "I want to tell you something, and it seems to me that I can tell it better here than anywhere else."

Celia felt her heart throbbing and her knees suddenly grew weak, so that she sat down more because she felt she could not stand without tottering than because Mr. Stafford had asked her to do so. The day had been an exciting one for her, and her emotions had been stirred to their depths by the wonderful talk she had just had with the boy Ben. What could be coming now? She could not understand, and yet she felt in some way that it would have to do with the things which had been hurting her so all day, and would probably hurt her more. She passed her hand across her forehead wearily, and tried to brace herself to bear whatever might be said. Perhaps he would ask for sympathy in his sorrow, and how could she give it? She sent up a swift prayer for help.

Mr. Stafford must have seen the weary expression and the piteous baffled look in her face, for a troubled one came over his own, as he took a seat in a chair near her, and asked, anxiously,

"Are you too tired just now? Perhaps I ought to wait. I know you have been working hard, and your work is telling, too, I could see by that boy's face as he went out, that he will be a different fellow from this time forth. Now, if you would rather go right home, please say so."

But there was a note in his voice of longing to be heard now, that made Celia push aside her desire to slip out of it on the plea of weariness and assert, a little coolly perhaps, that she could hear him now just as well as to wait.

Her manner made his heart sink, but he began what he had to say with a frank, "Well, then I'll try not to keep you long.

"Miss Celia," it was the first time he had ever called her that, though several of the other boarders had adopted it from hearing Molly Poppleton address her in that way, "I do not know whether or not you know that I have been passing through deep waters during the past week; I have been by the deathbed and then by the grave of one who was very dear to me. I felt as though I wanted to tell you about her, not only because I need the sympathy which I know you can give, but because she knew all about you and your work, and was deeply interested in you."

If Mr. Stafford had not been looking down and struggling to control his voice, so that it would be steady and without the deep emotion he felt, he would have noticed that Celia's face grew swiftly white. It was worse then than she had feared. Not only was she asked to give sympathy, but this other woman had known all about her. They had talked her over together. Why this should seem so dreadful to the girl she could not quite understand, but at the time it seemed more than she could bear. It was well Mr. Stafford did not pause for a reply, for Celia would have been incapable of giving any just then.

"She had been ill for a long time," he went on, his voice breaking a little, "we knew she could not stay with us much longer, and yet, you will understand that it was hard to part with her."

He told in a few words of her beautiful life of sweet patience and cheerfulness in the face of pain that had endured for years, till Celia felt ashamed of her selfish jealousy, and longed to shut herself away from sight that she might cry in quiet. The great tears filled her eyes and fell unheeded on her hands. She felt herself the meanest and smallest of mortals, and this other one beautiful and good and bright enough to be, as she was, with the angels. And yet her heart was very miserable.

She longed to speak a word of sympathy, but knew that she could not, and blamed herself for it.

"I want to show you her face," he said, putting his hand in his breast pocket and bringing out a little velvet case, which Celia knew even through her blinding tears. He opened and placed it in her hands, the lovely face with its velvet-blue eyes looking into hers, as he said, "She was my only sister, you know, and she was *so good* to me." Then the strong man bowed his head on his hand and covered his eyes.

He did not see Celia start, as he said this, but he heard the difference in her startled exclamation,

"Your sister? Why! I thought!"—and then she stopped, and when he looked up, as he did at once, her face had changed from white to rosy red.

He looked at her face, lovely behind its tears and blushes, and read the dawning sympathy, and was glad, even in his sorrow.

"You thought what,—may I know?"

"Why, I—" said Celia, embarrassed and hesitating, blushing deeply, "I—I did not know you had only one sister!" she finished, desperately.

"But what was it you thought? May I not know?" he asked again, with a searching look at her face.

"No," said Celia, dropping her eyes to the picture, and trying to hide her embarrassment by wiping away the tears with her handkerchief.

"Then may I tell you and you will say whether I am right?" asked the minister, a daring light coming into his eyes. "You thought that she was some one even nearer, and dearer than a sister?"

He looked at her long and earnestly and seemed to be satisfied with the answer of her mute, drooped face.

"Oh, Celia, did you not know that you were the only one who ever had or would occupy that place in my heart? Have you not seen that I love you? Don't you know it? and don't you care, just a little, Celia?"

The front chapel door stood open, and the afternoon spring sunshine was flickering fitfully across the floor. They could see the people on the street passing, loitering and talking, some looking curiously in as they passed, but none seeming to notice them. Celia felt it all as she sat dumb in the midst of a whirl of joy and sorrow and shame, and she knew not what else. She could not answer. She could not look up. The minister's eyes were upon her, and she felt what the look in them would be, and knew she could not bear the joy of seeing it. The silence was long and could fairly be heard. The sexton who was growing hungry, came back from the little alcove where the primary class was held and where he had been straightening the chairs for the evening service and distributing hymn books. He drew quite near to them now, and slammed books and put down windows significantly. Celia, feeling that she must say something, murmured low, still with downcast eyes, "How should I know it?"

The minister laughed and then grew grave. "That is true," he said, "I never could tell you, because you would not let me. But *she* knew it, and she was glad of it, and loved you, and left her blessing for you." Then he turned suddenly to the sexton, a new tone in his voice. There was something about Celia that no longer discouraged him.

"Thomas," he said, "I am going now. Will you kindly see if I left my Bible in the primary room?"

Thomas went with alacrity to search the primary room.

The minister watched the sexton until he had disappeared, and then he stooped swiftly and picked up Celia's gloves which had fallen unheeded to the floor. As he handed them to her he reverently touched his lips to one of her little, cold, ungloved hands. She lifted her face for a moment, and in that moment he got his answer from her eyes.

The sexton was coming back without the Bible, which the minister suddenly discovered to have been lying on the floor under his chair all the time, and the two stood decorously apart, Celia trying to keep her cheeks from growing redder, as she walked to the open door and looked out into the glad spring sunshine, gladder than any sunshine her eyes had ever looked upon before.

Some little child, perhaps, had dropped a flower upon the steps, and as she stood waiting for the minister, she saw it. It was then she remembered the rose on her lunch tray and its sweet message of hope

"God's plans for thee are graciously unfolding,
And leaf by leaf they blossom perfectly."

Her heart thrilled over the joy that this had come true, while she realized that her happiness was yet only in the bud, and she could see the promise of the day-by-day opening of it for her. Oh, why had she been doubting? Why could she not trust him perfectly? She lifted her heart in one swift breath of penitence and thanksgiving. She felt in that first gush of joy that she would never doubt her Lord again.

Then she turned to walk down the glorified street and gaze on the familiar surroundings under a halo of joy.

Chapter 26

It was noon and it was June, and there was to be a wedding in Mrs. Morris' boarding-house that was. It was not *the* wedding, that is the wedding nearest and dearest to aunt Hannah's heart; *that* was to be later, and in the new chapel, and about it most of the boarders had not even heard, as yet. Later, when they knew, the bridegroom of the first wedding said it was a pity they had not fixed things up sooner, so they could have had a double wedding; that would have been "real nice," and Celia and Horace Stafford had looked meaningly at one another, and never hinted that such an arrangement would have been other than entirely satisfactory to them, provided "things had been fixed up" in time. They had their little quiet laugh over it, of course, and kept their secret.

Meantime, the present wedding was a source of deep interest to every member of the household. Each one contributed something to the general plans. The parlor, that used to be so dismal was itself in bridal array. The organ at the further end was literally smothered in palms. The palms and flowers were Mr. Roger Houston's contribution. He was not a boarder, but he had become a frequent visitor at the house, and seemed to be as much interested as any one in the event. But the arrangement of the palms was Celia's, and Celia was to sit behind them and play the wedding march in the softest, sweetest tones she could coax from the old organ. They made a lovely background for the bride and groom, and they completely hid the organ and the player. Under the mantelpiece and above it, where used to hang the crayoned visage of the deceased Mr. Morris, were more palms; and the imitation-marble mantelpiece, which Celia always said looked as mottled as though it were made of slices of Bologna sausage, was covered with a bank of lovely roses, white and pink and yellow and crimson. If the wedding had been Celia's, she would have preferred to have the roses all white, but the bride in this case was extravagantly fond of color, and had declared herself in favor of "lots of roses all colors" so longingly, that Roger Houston said "Let's please her for once if she wants *green* roses, even if the white would be better taste, Miss Murray. It's her first wedding, you know, and after all a rose is a rose." But the colors were arranged with Celia's own skill, and no two colors dared but harmonize.

Out in the dining-room the long white table was dressed in trailing vines of smilax, and roses; and the largest and most orthodox wedding cake that could be procured occupied the place of honor. All about it were evidences of Molly Poppleton's art, and everything spoke of readiness for the ceremony to begin.

Up in her room the bride was being arrayed. The dress was a simple white muslin plainly made, but she was to wear a veil. It would perhaps have been more sensible to have worn a traveling dress, as she was to go away at once, but Mamie (for of course you know the bride was Mamie Williams, and the groom Bob Yates) had always cried and said she shouldn't feel that she was really married if she didn't wear white, when Miss Grant counseled economy and good sense. Seeing her heart so set they did not try to persuade her, but managed to change her purpose of purchasing a flimsy white silk which would never be of any use to her afterward, and persuaded her to take instead this simple white lawn. She had demurred, but finally consented. She was never wholly reconciled to the change, however, but was somewhat consoled by the fact that it was white and she was to have a veil.

Celia herself dressed her hair and arranged the soft folds of the veil, and kissed her, and told aunt Hannah afterward that Mamie Williams was really lovely in her pretty array. Miss Hannah thought so too as she came up to give the girl a few last words, as her mother might have done, perhaps, had she been there. She found Mamie standing by her bureau with her open Bible before her. Miss Grant did not know that the white vision of herself in the glass had prompted her to turn to that first Bible verse of hers and read it over again, "And to her was granted that she should be arrayed in fine linen, clean and white; for the fine linen is the righteousness of the saints." Nor could she know that the softened, glorified look on her face came from the thought in her heart that now, perhaps, even she might one day wear that pure heavenly dress of clean white linen, the garment of Christ's own righteousness.

Bob Yates had saved up a nice little sum, and now there was waiting for them, not many blocks away, a new, neat house of four or five rooms, as daintily furnished as a bird's nest. There Mamie was to put in practice the culinary arts she had learned from Miss Grant and Molly Poppleton, and to entertain her friends, and some of the young girls with whom she had grown intimate during her time of selling ribbons with Dobson and Co., for she had attained to that and taken Celia's place, and now in turn was to give it up to a young girl from the minister's Sunday-school class.

And they were to take a real wedding trip, too, like all the girls in the stories Mamie had read, in the days when she used to fancy Mr. Harold Adams held the key for her of all such delights. They were going to Atlantic City to a hotel for a whole delightful week, and then they were going to see Mamie's mother, and all her little brothers and sisters, and her gruff, hard-working father. After that Bob Yates would take his bride to visit his married brother and sister out in Indiana—the far West, Mamie called it—and then they would come back to their little house and their new furniture, and their dear church and their respective Sunday-school classes. It was all very beautiful, and Mamie felt very happy and all the boaders felt happy for her. She went back in memory to the time when Mrs. Morris was there, and felt, rather than thought, how different her life was now, and in fact how different everything was, and thanked God for the change. She thought of Carrie Simmons with a pang, and wished that she could have done something for her. Perhaps, if Miss Grant had come sooner Carrie might have been saved. Mamie had so far forgotten her old pride that she actually felt a little glad that Carrie could not look in from all her own sorrow and misfortune and shame and misery, in which she had heard she dwelt, and see her own joy and happy sur-roundings.

Miss Grant had gone down to the kitchen to watch things while Molly Poppleton got on her best gown for the ceremony, and every-thing was progressing toward the last exciting minute, when the door-bell rang. The second girl who was setting chairs in the dining-room in the best possible way to economize room, went quietly to the door, her neat blue and white striped gingham and white waitress-apron and cap making a decided contrast to the slatternly Maggie who used to answer the door in Mrs. Morris' time.

The large oldish-looking woman, and the tall, grizzled man, unmis-takably a farmer, who stood together on the step stared at the girl when the door was opened, in undisguised amazement.

"Why!" said the woman at last, looking up at the number over the door as if mistaken in her whereabouts, "isn't this,—at least—isn't this a boarding-house?"

"Yes, it is," responded the maid, "won't you walk in? Miss Grant is busy just now, that is she will be in a minute, but I guess she can see you first. Did you want to get board?"

She had ushered them into the bedecked parlor, which happened at the moment to be entirely uninhabited, as the boarders were all in their rooms donning their gala attire.

But she saw that they had evidently not heard her question, so tell-ing them to be seated, she went for Miss Grant.

The strangers, however, did not sit down. Instead, they stood staring around.

"For the land sake!" ejaculated the woman at last, looking around her more and more bewildered.

"Wal, it's pretty nice, 'pon honor, M'ria, I wonder now you ever give it up fer an ole fellow like me," and he looked at her quizzically.

But the look was lost this time. She was taking in the familiar pat-tern of the carpet, which somehow looked strangely bright, and noting all things new and old about the room.

Then came Miss Grant with her soft grey cashmere, made more

lovely by the cloud of white tulle she wore about her neck, which seemed to blend so tenderly with the creamy white of her hair.

She stood a moment looking doubtfully at the visitors, seeing something familiar about the woman's face, but for an instant not recognizing her.

"Miss Grant, don't you know me? I'm Mrs. Morris—leastways that used to be me name. I'm Mrs. Sparks now. I married out there in Ohio, and I'm real comfortably fixed. He"—nodding her head toward the man—"has a farm and a nice house, and owns several houses in the town besides. But I couldn't rest comfortably noways, a-thinkin' of you an' the hole I left you in, an' at last me husband found out what was the matter, an' he just brought me on to see how you was gettin' along, and to say he'd help you out of it, if you got badly stuck and pay some of the bills I left behind me, but when we got here everything looked so kind of different, somehow I couldn't think 'twas me own house. You don't look as if you was hard up. What's the meanin' of it all ennyway, an' what's goin' on? Are you expectin' company?"

Miss Grant's face shone with welcome and her greeting was cordial, even in the midst of this busy time.

"We're going to have a wedding in half an hour," she said, "and you're just in time. They will both be delighted to have you here for they are two of your old boarders. And you can relieve your mind about me, for I'm not in any hole at all, and coming here was the best thing that ever happened to me in some ways. I'm grateful to you for giving me a full fledged boarding-house. I find every month that I am getting on a little more financially. It isn't great riches, but it is sure."

"A wedding! For the land sake!" said Mrs. Morris-Sparks, sententiously.

After Miss Grant had excused herself in haste, to answer a call from Molly, the guest called after her.

"It must be that nice niece of yours, Miss Murray, but I didn't never think she'd take Bob Yates, she used to be so awful stiff with him, but land alive, you never can tell!"

Miss Grant smiled to herself as she hurried down the hall. She would not explain now, as the visitor would soon see for herself.

That evening, after all the guests were gone, and the bridal pair had departed, Miss Grant took Mrs. Morris-Sparks, and slipping out the front door, let her in by a latchkey to the adjoining house which had for months been closed, with a "For Rent" sign in the window. This however had disappeared. She carefully locked the door behind her, and turning up the gas, pointed out the place where wide double doors had been roughly drafted on the wall between the two houses. She also enlarged upon some other improvements, among them a wide bay window to be added in both first and second stories of the front of the house. Then she took her upstairs, and showed a suite of rooms beautifully furnished, and told the story of how the minister had bought this house and furnished these rooms for himself and Celia, and that the houses were to be connected, and the remainder of the room used to enlarge the boarding-house, in which scheme their hearts were deeply interested. She told her, too, how with careful looking to the little details she had been enabled not only to make both ends meet, but to have a trifle over, and how she hoped in the coming year with the enlargements and her present experience actually to make it a paying business.

And Mrs. Morris-Sparks looked and listened, and shook her head, but all she could say was, "For the land sake! Who would 'a' thought it!"

Chapter 27

Hiram and Nettie Bartlett had been talking a good deal lately about running down to Philadelphia to see aunt Hannah and Celia. Hiram was feeling that a little ready money in his business would enable him to get through a hard time which he saw ahead. Nettie was missing aunt Hannah dreadfully, as the hot days grew longer. They had decided that it would be a good thing to forget and forgive, and open their home and as much of their hearts as was necessary to their relatives. Aunt Hannah would manage the kitchen, and Celia would manage the children, and Hiram would manage Celia's money. Having decided matters thus, and made some changes in the arrangements of the rooms, to suit the new order of things, they began to feel very sure that it was to be. Of course aunt Hannah and Celia were thoroughly tired of living in a boarding-house by this time, and would welcome the change, and they had but to speak the word and they would fly back to Cloverdale. But before they came, it would be a pleasant change to take the children to Philadelphia for a visit.

No sooner had they decided this than Nettie wrote to aunt Hannah.

The letter reached Philadelphia in the midst of plans for Celia's wedding. They read it together, Celia and aunt Hannah, and looked at one another in dismay. Somehow, in the joy of the life they were living, they had forgotten to write Nettie anything about Celia's proposed marriage. Perhaps it was but natural, as Nettie very seldom answered aunt Hannah's long letters, which had been written at regular intervals at first, until she began to feel that they were not desired. But now they both felt that Nettie must be invited.

Celia summoned all the cousinly feeling she had ever possessed for

Nettie, and wrote her a nice letter, putting into it a little touch of her sweet girlish joy over the happiness that had come to her. She finished with a cordial invitation to them all to come on, though the addition to the family at this time would be extremely inconvenient.

Celia did fret a little over their coming. Hiram would be disagreeable and Nettie would want to manage everything, and the children would be always about when they were not wanted.

She was sitting one evening thinking about it, with brow knit in troubled thought, when Mr. Stafford came in. He watched her a moment, and then taking both his hands he placed them over her ruffled brow and smoothed the wrinkles out. Then he bent and kissed her forehead fondly.

"What is the matter dearest?" he said. "I mean to make it my business always to keep that troubled look away from your dear face."

"Oh, Horace! How can I help it? I have tried and tried, but I do not seem to be able to conquer the habit. Indeed, I am ashamed of it. Can you not tell me how I can conquer it?"

"Only by casting all your care upon him, who careth for you. Listen, Celia, have you ever heard this?

> " 'Wherefore should we do ourselves this wrong,
>   Or others, that we are not always strong;
>   That we are ever overborne with care,
>   That we should ever weak or heartless be,
>   Anxious or troubled, when with us is prayer,
>   And joy and strength and courage are with thee?' "

Then Celia opened her heart to him and told him the story of her winter, beginning with her birthday and the little bookmark aunt Hannah had sent.

"And I thought then, Horace," she went on, "after that money came to me, my 'daily rate' for 'all the days of my life' that I would never doubt any more because I had money, and with that I would be able to relieve most of the other anxieties. But I found it wasn't so. I began to fret about other things, and then after I got money, I wanted love, and now I have that, I find I'm still fretting."

"It's because you don't remember that it's 'for every day,' dear, and that means for every need of every day. You trust for one set of things, but you think you have to worry along and look out for another set. Here is a quaint old poem I came across the other day that I cut out and put in my pocketbook to read to you some time. It fits in right here, let me read it.

> " 'I have a never-failing bank,
>   My more than golden store;
> No earthly bank is half so rich,
>   How, then, can I be poor?
>
> " ''Tis when my stock is spent and gone,
>   And I not worth a groat;
> I'm glad to hasten to my bank,
>   And beg a little note.
>
> " 'Sometimes my banker smiling says,
>   Why don't you oftener come?
> And when you draw a little note,
>   Why not a larger sum?
>
> " 'Why live so niggardly and poor,
>   My bank contains a plenty;
> Why come and take a one-pound note,
>   When you can have a twenty?
>
> " 'Nay, twenty thousand ten times told
>   Is but a trifling sum,
> To what my Father has laid up
>   For me in God the Son
>
> " 'Since, then, my banker is so rich,
>   I have no need to borrow,
> But live upon my notes to-day,
>   And draw again to-morrow.' "

Nettie Bartlett settled herself for the homeward trip from Philadelphia with a discontented look. She slapped Johnnie when he went to get a drink—which he did the first fifteen minutes of the journey—because he stepped on her toes. She jerked the baby up who was endeavoring to pick a piece of orange peel out of a pool of tobacco juice on the floor, and then settled into her discontented silence again. She was thinking about the fall sewing and house cleaning, and the endless darning and baking and cleaning, with no aunt Hannah to fall back upon. Occasionally, she reflected upon the bride's pretty dress, or had visions of Celia in her cloud-like veil looking up with happy eyes into her husband's face, and a half jealous feeling shot through her heart. She knew how Celia felt, or thought she did. She had felt so herself, but of course all such nonsense was passed. She looked gloomily across at Hiram, who was staring stolidly out of the window, with his inevitable newspaper lying across his knees. Then she curled her lip and told herself that Celia would soon have the sentiment taken out of her by the prose of everyday life.

"You made a great mistake by not cultivating that minister-cousin-in-law, Nettie," remarked Hiram, snappily. "I talked to him every chance I got, but it takes women and compliments and that sort of thing to work on men, and especially ministers, I guess. You ought to have invited them to our house for part of their wedding trip. I'm dead certain he's rich. Did you see all that furniture he's fixed out for Celia? He'll spoil her the first thing off."

"You made a great mistake yourself, when you let aunt Hannah, and Celia, too, go away from our house, and you can't ever undo it. Yes, I saw the furniture, but his mother sent it, for Celia said so. We might have had a few blessings, and our children would have been brought up right, if aunt Hannah had been with us. She always brings a blessing wherever she goes, and we've had nothing but ill-luck since she left us," and Nettie put her handkerchief to her eyes and wept while the train sped rapidly through the darkness.

Some weeks later, Celia seated in the pleasant study of the suite of rooms which were her new home, and yet her old home, engaged in the delightful task of classifying and placing in a cabinet the various clippings which her minister husband had gathered about him during his bachelor years, came upon this poem. She paused to read it and smiled with a little echo of the peace it spoke in her heart, and bent her head to thank her Father it was true.

> "The child leans on its parent's breast,
> Leaves there its cares and is at rest;

The bird sits singing by his nest,
   And tells aloud
His trust in God, and so is blest
   'Neath every cloud.
He has no store, he sows no seed;
Yet sings aloud, and doth not heed;
By flowing stream or grassy mead,
   He sings to shame
Men, who forget, in fear of need,
   A Father's name.
The heart that trusts, forever sings,
And feels as light as it had wings;
A well of peace within its springs;
   Come good or ill,
Whate'er to-day, to-morrow brings,
   It is his will."

CHRISTIAN HERALD ASSOCIATION AND ITS MINISTRIES

CHRISTIAN HERALD ASSOCIATION, founded in 1878, publishes The Christian Herald Magazine, one of the leading interdenominational religious monthlies in America. Through its wide circulation, it brings inspiring articles and the latest news of religious developments to many families. From the magazine's pages came the initiative for CHRISTIAN HERALD CHILDREN and THE BOWERY MISSION, two individually supported not-for-profit corporations.

CHRISTIAN HERALD CHILDREN, established in 1894, is the name for a unique and dynamic ministry to disadvantaged children, offering hope and opportunities which would not otherwise be available for reasons of poverty and neglect. The goal is to develop each child's potential and to demonstrate Christian compassion and understanding to children in need.

Mont Lawn is a permanent camp located in Bushkill, Pennsylvania. It is the focal point of a ministry which provides a healthful "vacation with a purpose" to children who without it would be confined to the streets of the city. Up to 1000 children between the age of 7 and 11 come to Mont Lawn each year.

Christian Herald Children maintains year-round contact with children by means of a *City Youth Ministry.* Central to its philosophy is the belief that only through sustained relationships and demonstrated concern can individual lives be truly enriched. Special emphasis is on individual guidance, spiritual and family counseling and tutoring. This follow-up ministry to inner-city children culminates for many in financial assistance toward higher education and career counseling.

THE BOWERY MISSION, located at 227 Bowery, New York City, has since 1879 been reaching out to the lost men on the Bowery, offering them what could be their last chance to rebuild their lives. Every man is fed, clothed and ministered to. Countless numbers have entered the 90-day residential rehabilitation program at the Bowery Mission. A concentrated ministry of counseling, medical care, nutrition therapy, Bible study and Gospel services awakens a man to spiritual renewal within himself.

These ministries are supported solely by the voluntary contributions of individuals and by legacies and bequests. Contributions are tax deductible. Checks should be made out either to CHRISTIAN HERALD CHILDREN or to THE BOWERY MISSION.

Administrative Office: 40 Overlook Drive, Chappaqua, New York 10514
Telephone: (914) 769-9000